WHAT READERS ARE SAYING*

"Readers are entertained and inspired."
> —Elinor Griffith, *Reader's Digest*

"An incredibly moving story."
> —Michael Fischler, Hollywood Producer

"Riveting from its intriguing start to its explosive climax."
> —James Miller, author of THE CONVERGENCE

"I was truly blown away."
> —Carol J. Stair, Attorney

"Last Chance is difficult to put aside for the night."
> —Russ L. Russell, Police Commander,
> Sanger, California

"A terrific novel."
> —Thomas E. Baer, High School Principal

---

*Titles are for identification purposes only. Comments are those of individual readers and do not necessarily reflect the opinions their employers.

D1363375

LAST CHANCE

FACT-BASED FICTION

IRA HARRIS SPECTOR

ARIUS PUBLICATIONS

AUTHOR'S NOTE

During the last two decades, millions of Americans have been downsized. A great number of these people did not find other employment and became homeless, living out of public view in cars, hidden encampments, and emergency shelters.

Contrary to popular belief, these "hidden" Americans greatly outnumber their tragic counterparts—the panhandlers and street people who society normally equates with homelessness. Many of the hidden homeless can be successfully re-employed. But without an address and a telephone number no one will give them a chance.

This is a story about someone who did.

The companies, organizations, and characters in LAST CHANCE are fictitious, and any resemblance to real companies, organizations, or persons, living or dead, is purely coincidental. However, the information regarding homelessness in America is based on fact.

LAST CHANCE is published by Arius Publications, a division of
Arius Incorporated
121 Edelen Avenue, Los Gatos, CA 95030
(408) 357-4852

E-mail: ariuspub@hotmail.com

See back of book for ordering information

Library of Congress Catalog Card Number: 97-94337
ISBN: 0-96603-690-5

Arius second edition 1999

Cover: "Jason's Dream" by Andrew Pennick, DuArte Design, www.duarte.com

This book is dedicated to

Barbara Spector—my wife, soul mate, best friend

And to those among America's homeless who, against all
odds, are fighting to return to the mainstream

"Paint him yellow and use him as a speed bump."

—*The vice-mayor of a Northern California town telling merchants what to do with a homeless man. (From a story in the San Jose Mercury News.)*

Part I

THE MONDAY NIGHT CLUB

ONE
Monday, January 9

1

"FIRING YOUR EMPLOYEES can be one of the most rewarding aspects of your job," Jason Howell said, his voice resonating over the PA system. He was addressing a lunch meeting of the San Francisco Chapter of the Young Turks' Organization, an elite group of CEO's who, like Howell, were under forty years of age.

"You'll reap rewards almost immediately," Howell continued. "Unlike the disposal of surplus capital equipment and furniture, no buyers have to be found; nothing has to be crated and shipped. All it takes is a modicum of effort and a huge drain on the bottom line will exit under its own power."

To illustrate his point, Howell told the story of Cytex, his current turnaround project. It began three years ago when a venture capital group asked him to take over a struggling electronics company. His first act was to assemble all personnel in the cafeteria.

* * *

"By the authority of the board of directors of Cytex," Howell announced to the one hundred employees gathered before him, "I am your new president. I have been invited to take the helm because this company has been drifting aimlessly, wasting time and money inventing high-tech solutions for which there are no problems. Therefore, drastic measures are in order."

An uneasy murmuring arose in the cafeteria.

"I will now interview each of you. When I am finished, the payroll will be slashed by two-thirds."

The murmuring ceased and a pall fell over the room.

Howell abruptly turned from the crowd and disappeared behind a partition. A burly security guard took up a wide stance in front of the partition, lifted a clipboard, and called out the first name in a booming voice. A fifty-year-old engineering manager, one of the company's founders, hesitantly stepped forward. In an effort to look younger he removed his glasses and stuffed them into his plastic pocket protector.

Howell was seated at a desk reading the manager's personnel file. He did not bother to look up. Since there was no chair, the man stood nervously before his new boss and waited.

After a long moment Howell closed the file and reached into the manager's eyes with a look so cold that the man began to shiver. Howell continued to watch as the man fidgeted. Finally he asked, "Why should you be allowed to remain at Cytex?"

The manager began a rambling response. After two minutes, Howell cut him off, shook his head no, and dismissed him with a wave of his hand.

The first group of employees fired this way were stunned as they maneuvered slowly through the crowd and toward the exit.

The faces of the next group were ashen, and they departed more quickly.

By the midpoint of this exercise, the remaining employees had plenty of time to consider the havoc that joblessness would wreak on their lives. Those subsequently fired rushed out tearfully, leaving behind a sense of doom for those still waiting their turn.

But not everyone felt the same way. The survivors congregated in a far corner of the cafeteria as if the others had been infected with a deadly disease.

After Howell had hand-picked thirty-three employees, he gathered them around him. "Cytex now has a promising future. But for any of you to participate, all of you must agree to a 25 percent pay cut, with another 25 percent of your salary to be used to buy worthless Cytex stock options through a payroll deduction plan."

The Chosen Ones listened carefully.

"Although there are no guarantees," Howell continued, "the employees of my previous companies have done well. Even the janitors bought homes and had money left over to send their children to college."

Thirty-three pairs of eyebrows arched in unison.

"If you agree to these terms, our venture capital investors will give Cytex one last chance. They will commit additional funds for a blockbuster product that builds on the technology the company currently possesses. If Cytex develops this product, I guarantee it will send shock waves throughout the computer industry. I will then merge the company, and your stock options will be worth a fortune."

Howell paused to let this sink in. "Now, do *all* of you agree to these terms?"

The Chosen Ones nodded eagerly and signed up.

* * *

At this point in Howell's lecture, the Young Turks were nodding eagerly as well, anxious to return to their companies and implement what they had learned. "In conclusion," Howell told his audience, "this restructuring exercise yielded a talented team dedicated to the success of Cytex. The example illustrates how to turn downsizing from a crude cost-saving measure into the most effective motivational weapon in your arsenal."

The question and answer period was next, and a Young Turk in the back stood. "Mr. Howell, it was fascinating how you turned the ax into a whip. But has this tactic withstood the test of time?"

Howell's steel-blue eyes fell upon the questioner. "It has indeed. Cytex remains staffed with that same core of team players. For the last three years they have worked eighteen-hour days, seven days a week towards the success of the company."

"Let's cut to the chase," said another Young Turk. "How has Cytex performed? What's the bottom line?"

Howell smiled to himself. At these meetings, regardless of the subject, someone invariably asked that question. "The bottom line is excellent. We have developed that blockbuster product I mentioned, and it will be unveiled tomorrow to a merger partner. I expect to close the deal within six months. My employees sense it, too, and the air is so thick with anticipation you can cut it with a knife. In every cubicle, at every workstation, even in the bathrooms, people are planning how they will spend their stock proceeds. Suffice it to say that starting with a judicious dose of downsizing, I have pulled a company from the brink of bankruptcy, grown it to twice its former size, and turned it into my biggest deal yet."

With that, Howell turned and walked out of the room to a standing ovation.

2

HOWELL STOPPED by his office just long enough to meet with his senior staff, and to check his e-mail and phone messages. Then he changed into his sweat suit and drove to San Carlos, a small reliever airport south of San Francisco International. He had an appointment to meet Bill Henderson, a real estate executive and Howell's racquetball partner. Before their regular match this evening they would visit some prime investment property in the hills above Petaluma, a Victorian riverfront town north of San Francisco. To avoid the rush hour traffic the plan was to fly to Petaluma in Henderson's Beechcraft Bonanza.

"Wait until you see this property," Henderson said as the Bonanza taxied to the runway. "It's a real gem—ten acres of virgin meadow on a ridge line. Great subdivision potential. Someone will make a huge killing planting luxury homes all over that hillside; it might as well be you."

Howell nodded. His net worth would swell when Cytex was sold, and he wanted his investments lined up.

Twenty minutes later the small plane landed at Petaluma Airport. A jeep rental was waiting, and by late afternoon the two men were standing at the crest of a tall hill east of the town.

Henderson's cell phone rang, and while he took the call Howell walked through a stand of tall trees marking the northern boundary of the property. On the other side he found a three-acre meadow bathed in golden sunlight. An unusually warm January breeze, carrying the fragrances of eucalyptus and evergreen trees, gently rustled the leaves. Howell removed his jacket and carried it over his shoulder as he strolled along the meadow's perimeter, studying the topography and estimating the maximum number of luxury homes that could be built on the land.

At the property's western edge he sat on a rocky out-cropping and gazed at the ponds and orchards dotting the valley below. *Bill is right,* he thought. *This place is special.* He had a vision of aging executives falling all over themselves to cash in their stock options so they could retire up here. Howell began to toy with the notion of keeping one of the better locations for himself when his companion tapped him on the shoulder and said it was time to go.

3

THE RETURN FLIGHT was along an offshore airway running parallel to the coastline. The setting sun left a chill in the cockpit and Henderson turned on the cabin heat. But Howell wasn't aware of the cold; he was still thinking about the killing he would make by developing the meadow.

An air pocket jerked Howell back to the plane. He looked over the left wing across ten miles of ocean, watching the fog pour through the Golden Gate. It gave the illusion of a great white comforter moving into position, protecting The City from the cold January night. Here and there amber lights blinked through. Over the cabin speaker, an air traffic controller was broadcasting a SIGMET, warning pilots of a major winter storm bearing down from the Gulf of Alaska. Howell looked beyond the aircraft's nose, assessing the low overcast now spreading over the coastline. "How's the weather at San Carlos?" he asked.

Henderson smiled confidently. "It's good. That storm they're talking about won't hit for a while. As soon as we're clear of San Francisco's Bravo airspace, I'll head inland. We'll be on the ground in about fifteen minutes, and at the racquetball club in plenty of time for tonight's match."

Another air pocket—stronger—rocked the plane.

Howell cinched his seat belt. Directly below, the fog seemed to swirl, and the few holes remaining closed ominously as he watched. To his right, a dark wall of clouds had mushroomed over the Pacific, their tops dusted pearly orange in the deepening twilight.

The next air pocket struck with a vengeance. The bottom fell out and the small plane plunged fifty feet before hitting a brick wall. Henderson's navigation kneeboard leaped into the air and floated for a moment before crashing to the floor. The engine sputtered and stopped momentarily before resuming its deep-throated roar.

Howell grasped for a hand strap. "What the . . . ?"

Henderson righted the plane and scanned the engine gauges. Deep lines had furrowed in his brow.

Howell held his breath.

The engine droned on.

After a long moment, the pilot turned to Howell. "The gauges all look norm—"

"Wait a second," Howell interrupted, "I smell fuel."

Henderson sniffed at the air, his body visibly tensing. Suddenly the engine sputtered again, more forcefully this time. The fuel odor increased and the engine surged and missed, continually shaking the plane. Acrid white smoke entered the cabin through the heater vents and mingled with the smell of raw fuel. Henderson closed the vents, switched wing tanks, turned on the auxiliary fuel pump, and adjusted the mixture control.

Nothing seemed to help.

Howell felt powerless and he cursed himself for being in a situation in which he lacked control. "What's wrong?" he asked, taking a deep breath, trying to stem the adrenaline surging into his bloodstream.

"Damn! That last air pocket must have caused a fuel line to loosen. I just had the fuel filter changed, and it looks like the line wasn't secured properly. Raw gasoline is squirting all over the engine. I have to shut the fuel off to avoid a fire." Henderson seemed to be breaking this news to himself as much as to his passenger.

Howell, still clutching the hand strap, felt his heart skip from the adrenaline rush. He pressed his free hand against his chest. "W-what does that mean?"

Henderson rotated the fuel selector to the OFF position and looked at Howell. "It means we're going down."

The engine shuddered for several seconds, coughed, and then was still, its deep-throated, irregular pulsation now replaced by the high-pitched hiss of air rushing by the cockpit. Howell watched in disbelief as the propeller began windmilling, a taunting reminder of the once-powerful engine. He swallowed hard as Henderson eased the airplane into a glide.

"Bay Approach, MAYDAY! MAYDAY! MAYDAY!" the pilot shouted into the microphone. "Bonanza Four-Nine-Whiskey-Hotel is ten miles west of the Golden Gate. We're descending through five thousand feet. Engine out!"

The radio came alive. "This is Bay Approach. Confirm that Bonanza Four-Nine-Whiskey-Hotel is declaring an emergency."

"Affirmative! I need a vector to the nearest airport!"

"Bonanza Nine-Whiskey-Hotel, San Francisco International is at eleven o'clock and sixteen miles. They're reporting two hundred overcast, visibility one mile in fog and light drizzle. The wind is two-one-zero at six. Suggest heading one-one-zero."

Although the temperature in the cockpit was dropping rapidly, Henderson was sweating. "No! SFO's too far to glide! Is there anything closer?"

"Negative, Nine-Whiskey-Hotel.   Report number of souls onboard and say your intentions."

Without the roar of the engine, the volume of the radio was too loud, and the controller seemed to be shouting at the men.

Henderson reached for the radio and turned down the volume. "Jason, there's no way we can glide sixteen miles to SFO. We can make the coast but the clouds are obscuring everything, and I can't tell where the water ends and the cliffs begin. We have to land in the ocean. There's no other choice."

Howell watched the altimeter unwind below forty-five hundred feet. "But can we survive a water landing? How will they find us in the fog?"

Henderson shrugged.

The clouds loomed closer.   Howell's eyes darted around in desperation. Then he spotted something over the land. "Bill, to your left! Isn't that Golden Gate Park? I remember reading about someone who landed a plane in there."

The pilot looked out of his window.   Through the overcast, a long dark rectangle was dimly outlined by streetlights. "I got it," he said, immediately banking to the left. "We'll break out a couple of hundred feet over the park, and help will be real close—"

The radio interrupted Henderson. "Bonanza Four-Nine-Whiskey-Hotel, radar contact lost. I repeat, say intentions."

"To get out alive," the pilot said to himself.

"What should I do?" Howell asked, trying to keep his heart from jumping into his throat.

"Roll our warm-up jackets into a ball. Use them to cushion your head."

Three thousand feet.

Howell reached behind him, took the jackets off the rear seat and began to roll them up.

No, no, he thought, dropping the jackets at his feet, *I've always been a player and I'm not going to stop now.* "Bill, I want to help. I'll look for the ground."

"Okay, we'll be on instruments shortly and I've got to keep my attention inside the cockpit. When we break out we'll only have a few seconds to pick a landing spot; I could really use your help."

Howell looked at the cloud tops, now blood red and coming up fast. At fifteen hundred feet the small plane shuddered as it dipped inside, engulfing the men in a ruddy light that quickly turned to gray and then to inky black. Bright white flashes interrupted the emptiness. Henderson leaned forward and switched the wing strobes off. Howell rubbed his eyes, blinking to dissipate the white spots.

One thousand feet.

"How much time?" Howell asked.

"About sixty seconds."

Howell turned his attention outside and stared intently at the black void in front of them. Suddenly the curtain lifted and Howell blinked. Ragged gray wisps sped by. Lights flickered dimly. "The ground!" he shouted.

Henderson glanced down. He quickly turned on the landing light and lowered the gear. The hissing sound in the cockpit deepened as the wheels locked in place and the airplane decelerated. Next the flaps came down. They were settling fast and Howell's mind went into overdrive, desperately trying to make sense out of the jumbled image it was receiving. To his left, at ten o'clock, a string of streetlights appeared. "I see the main park road! Can you make it?"

Henderson had no time to answer. He rolled the small plane left to line up with the roadway. The steep turn caused the Bonanza to descend more quickly. The pilot yanked the control wheel back as the ground rushed up.

Too fast!

They landed hard on the left main gear and catapulted back into the air at an awkward angle.

"N-O-O-O!" Howell screamed, his voice all but lost in the wail of the stall horn. He squeezed his eyes shut and held his breath. Suddenly there was a shriek of tortured metal as the aircraft hit the stanchion of a streetlight, shearing off the left wing and violently whipping the aircraft counterclockwise. Howell's head wrenched the opposite way and his chest pressed against his shoulder harness with such force it squeezed all of the air from his lungs and cut his scream short.

For several seconds it was unearthly quiet.

Howell's mind raced. He knew it was time to pray, but he didn't know what to say. He knew it was time to regret the things he had left undone, but all that came to mind was not having a will. Now his estranged brother, Anton, the person he despised most in the world, would inherit his estate. That idea distressed him even more than the prospect of dying.

Howell's eyes jerked open to branches rushing by in a blurring arc. Then the right wing hit a tree trunk, roughly straightening the Bonanza's path. Now, coming up fast, illuminated by the landing light, was a large tree grove.

Dead ahead.

Jason Howell squeezed his eyes shut and tensed his body. He now knew that as bad as things were, they were about to get worse.

Much worse.

4

" . . . *stop it, Anton, I wanna get off!" the little boy
pleaded. His older brother ignored him and pushed
harder on the swing. "P-p-please stop!" the child begged,
his little hands gripping the chains as tightly as he could.*

*Anton added a twisting motion, trying to break his
brother's tenuous hold. "Stop crying, Jason. You're such
a baby."*

*The swing was now moving so fast that the weight of
the child's tiny body could no longer keep the seat from
snapping downward at the top of the arc.*

*"Make him STOP!" the six-year-old yelled at his par-
ents, who were sitting nearby on a park bench. "H-HELP
ME-E-E!" The boy screamed at the top of his lungs, but
his parents, engrossed in conversation, were oblivious to
the older brother's mischief.*

*The little boy knew he had to get off. And he had to do
it without giving his brother the satisfaction of seeing him
fall from the top of the arc. He would leap when the swing
was near the ground. He steeled himself. Ready . . . now,
JUMP!*

*The little boy's forward momentum carried him
through the air, and he landed hard and tumbled head-
over-heels. He wanted to cry, but the wind was knocked
out of him.*

*He turned toward his parents' bench and his heart
sank. They were gone! Looking around in desperation, he
spotted them walking down a path, hand-in-hand. They
were fading rapidly. The little boy tried to stand but his
legs wouldn't hold him. All he could do was sob and crawl
after his parents with no hope of catching up. Behind him,
over the clanging of the swing, Anton was laughing . . . .*

5

IN THE DRIZZLY GLOW of a streetlight, the park people stood like bizarre sentries around the wreckage, strangely attracted to it, yet afraid to get closer. The Bonanza had come to rest at the foot of a large eucalyptus tree near the northeast perimeter of the park. Its left wing was clipped, its right wing angled back, its tail bent upward. Blue smoke rose from the crushed metal that was once the engine. Live wires crackled and the smell of aviation fuel hung in the air.

After a long moment a man in a dirty windbreaker tentatively approached the right side of the wreck and peered into the cockpit. In the flickering glow of the panel lights he saw two bodies.

"Poor bastards."

The right-side door had cracked open, and the man pulled it wider for a better look. The passenger was slumped against his shoulder harness, his head canted to the right. Blood ran from a gash on his left temple. The pilot's upper torso had slipped under his seat belt, propping up his arms in a grotesque gesture of surrender.

The man picked up a warm-up jacket from the floor of the cockpit and went through it, pulling out a wallet.

"Hey, what the fuck are you doing!" shouted another man as he broke from the line and headed toward the wreckage. He wore Army fatigues, its khaki colors all but obliterated by the grime of the street.

"Just checking for ID," the first man said defensively.

"Like hell—leave that shit alone!"

The first man jumped off the wing and darted into the woods. The second man started running after him, but then thought better of it. Instead, he went over to the smoking wreckage and cautiously climbed on the mangled right wing. His heart was beating rapidly, and he kept his body tensed, ready to leap at any sign of fire. He kneeled and looked inside.

Suddenly the victim nearest him flailed his arms and screamed "JUMP!"

The man in khakis jerked backwards, flew through the air, and ended up sprawled on the muddy ground.

The park people laughed nervously.

"Fucking wet brains," he cursed as he stood up. Then he softened his tone. "Look, friends, I need some help. We got a chance to save a couple of souls. Let's pull 'em out before she blows."

Nobody moved.

"GODDAMN ASSHOLES!" the man shouted. He stared at the wreckage as his mind flashed back to a time when he was a sergeant in Vietnam. And in spite of years of hard drugs and rotgut wine, he still remembered how good it felt to pull wounded men out of downed aircraft. In an odd way he was grateful for the accident and the opportunity to be a hero once again.

With greater determination he climbed back on the wing. The victim nearest him was now motionless except for fitful breathes, as if he were crying. The sergeant unbuckled the man's seat belt and gently eased him onto the wing.

Since several minutes had passed without a fire, another man summoned the courage to offer assistance. He and the sergeant carried the victim twenty yards from the wreck and stretched him out in a protected area behind a clump of trees.

"Now here's the plan," the sergeant said to his helper, "I'll see about the pilot while you go out to Fulton Street, find a phone booth, and call 911. Tell 'em a plane crashed in Golden Gate Park, near Sixth, between Fulton and JFK Drive. We got two casualties. Hurry your ass back!"

The helper trotted off while the sergeant returned to the cockpit, climbed into the passenger seat, and felt the pilot's neck for a pulse. It was weak. He carefully released the man's seat belt so his arms could come down. "Sir," the sergeant said, tapping the man's cheek with two leathery fingers, "can you hear me?"

The pilot's eyes fluttered. His breathing was short and shallow. His body quivered. "I-I can't . . . f-feel . . . my legs. I-I'm . . . cold."

"What's your name, buddy?"

"B-Bill."

"You married, Bill?"

"Y-yes."

"Kids?"

The pilot grimaced. "Y-yes," he answered, in a barely audible whisper.

"Okay, Bill, hang in there for me. For your family, okay? Just think about your family, okay? Help's on the way."

"The m-master switch . . . turn it off . . . f-fire."

"Which one is it?" the sergeant asked, trying to make sense of the array of switches on the instrument panel.

The pilot attempted to point, but his body convulsed and he coughed blood.

The sergeant's eyes were tearing from the smoke. It was impossible to read the labels on the panel. He chewed on a fingernail and tried a switch in front of the pilot.

The panel lights remained on.

"H-hurry . . . f-fire," the pilot gurgled.

"What the fuck," the sergeant said, reaching for the next switch. He couldn't see that it was labeled WING STROBES.

6

THE EXPLOSION and shock wave didn't stir the man lying on the ground behind the trees. Nor did the glowing and twisted pieces of aluminum spiraling through the air and landing around him. Nor did the shouting, the sound of people running, the wail of sirens.

By the time he came around, the noise had settled down to the clatter of fire equipment and the squawk of police radios. He opened his eyes and grimaced. His head seemed clamped in a vice, the vision in his right eye tunneled. His chest was sore and it was hard to breathe. The smell of oily smoke lingered in his nostrils.

He had no idea who he was, where he was, or even *why* he was. For a time he watched flashing red and white lights reflect off the wet leaves above him.

Eventually he sat up. There was something sticky on the left side of his head, and it stung when he touched it. He tried to stand but his right leg was a mass of pins and needles and he immediately collapsed.

After a long moment, he struggled back to his feet, using a tree branch to steady himself. He tried walking and managed a few steps without falling. In the dim light a path appeared.

Follow the path, urged a voice within.

Hugging himself, he trudged forward, dragging his right leg behind him. The path ended at a broad street that was funneling the wind. He stood shivering, waiting for the voice to tell him which way to go. But there was only silence. Confused, he sat on a bench and curled himself into a ball.

7

THE MAN ON THE BENCH didn't notice the figure approach. The newcomer wore a stained navy pea coat and a blue knit cap.

"Name's Chuck," the stranger said, easing into conversation. "Did'ya hear all them sirens earlier? Whaddya think happened?" He casually dropped his duffel bag on the ground.

The man on the bench held his head in his hands and rocked back and forth. He heard the words but they had no meaning. The stranger might as well have been speaking Martian.

"Hey, buddy, can ya help me out?" Chuck persisted, irritation creeping into his voice. He walked around to appeal to the man's other side. "Look, friend, this big storm's coming, and I couldn't get my sorry ass into a shelter. I need a few bucks for a place to flop."

The man on the bench shivered and rocked back and forth.

Chuck lifted the man's head and looked into a pair of empty eyes. He sighed and was about to leave when a glint of something yellow on the man's wrist caught his attention. He tugged at the man's sleeve.

A gold watch!

Chuck stared at it for a moment and then made a decision. "Say, you look real cold, friend. Tellya what . . . why don't we trade that watch for my coat? I'll even throw in my hat." Chuck checked the street for witnesses. Finding none he unclasped the watch and it quickly disappeared. Keeping his side of the bargain, he took off his coat and hat and put it on the shivering man. Patting him on the back, Chuck said softly, "Well, friend, you didn't do too bad in this deal. It don't look like you'll be needing that watch no more, and my clothes just might save your life." Now shivering himself, Chuck grabbed his duffel bag and hurried east along Fulton Street, toward the Western Addition.

The touch and the gentle words ignited a tiny spark in the man on the bench, and he got up and followed. But Chuck was disappearing rapidly.

Countless blocks later the man stood on a street of boarded-up shops. In the doorways, men in drab clothing huddled, watching him warily.

The wind was whipping now, and the drizzle had grown into the large, cold drops of an angry winter storm. The spark that set the man into motion was now extinguished. Only the instinct to survive remained, and that drove him into the shelter of the last empty doorway.

TWO
Monday, January 9
Late Evening

1

THE RAIN FELL in wind-driven sheets, forcing torsos to compress in doorways and legs to retract. Rags, food wrappers, and other debris floated in the rivulets running along the gutters. For a time, human activity ceased on the street until two men wearing backpacks turned the corner. The smaller man clutched the hood of his parka; the bigger man held a hand up, trying to shield his face from the stinging rain. In the other hand he carried a small brown paper bag that he pressed against his side like a running back protecting a football.

Partway down the block the big man turned to his companion. "Pete, you're one crazy son-of-a-bitch for giving up our shelter on a night like this."

The smaller man shrugged. "I missed the weather report. Anyways, we couldn't pass up our one night on the town. Hey, we might get lucky . . . you never know." His voice carried a light Texas drawl.

Pete's unflagging optimism never ceased to amaze Marty. His companion always looked on the bright side, regardless of the circumstances. It was a good thing, too. Without Pete, Marty knew he never would have made it on the street this long.

Suddenly the big man paused. "Christ! It looks like all the damn doorways are taken."

"Well, then, I reckon we gotta kick some ass."

Marty edged into the nearest doorway. At his feet was a man wearing a pea coat and a knit cap. He was curled in a ball and held his head in his hands. "Hey fella, move along," Marty said. His huge frame usually made a lot of conversation unnecessary.

The man slowly raised his head.

"Move on bud!" Marty ordered.

Empty eyes blinked.

Pete stepped closer and cocked his boot.

Marty held up his hand. "Wait a minute . . . look at his face." Even in the dim light, it was obvious the man was hurting.

Pete backed off. "Shucks, it looks like another nut case got dumped on the street. Like we don't got enough around here already."

Marty dropped his backpack in the corner of the doorway and carefully placed his parcel on top of it. He pushed back the hood of his parka, shook out his long brown hair and brushed droplets from his beard.

"See if he's got ID," Pete suggested.

Marty knelt and went through the man's pockets. "Nothing."

"What do you reckon we ought to do with him?" Pete asked, eyeing the brown bag. "Man, I could sure use some first aid right about now."

Marty reflected for a moment. "I think this guy needs some too. But if we call the cops, they'll roust us and the other poor folks around here just for grins. Hell, why don't we share the doorway with him? Later we'll go to The Club like we planned. And if the poor bastard is still here tomorrow, the cops will get him during their morning sweep."

"Okay," Pete said, sitting on the man's right. "At least his body's warm . . . for now."

Marty reached for the brown bag and squeezed in on the man's left. He took out a small bottle of brandy and unscrewed the cap.

The man's head moved back and forth as the bottle was passed in front of him.

"Did you bring the Tylenol?" Marty asked.

Pete looked puzzled. "You want some now? We just got started."

"No, I think this guy could use it. See his face? It's all screwed up."

Pete reached into his pocket. "Here, pal," he said, prying the man's mouth open and tossing three capsules into it.

"Give him some brandy to wash it down," Marty suggested.

Pete held the bottle up and the man suddenly reached for it. "Hey, he's showing some life. Should I let him hold it?"

"Why not?" Marty said absently.

The man grabbed the bottle and swallowed the Tylenol with several gulps.

"How's that, buddy?" Pete asked, taking the bottle back and wiping the neck with the sleeve of his parka. "You know what's funny, Marty?" he asked, taking a swig.

"No."

"We were asshole-to-asshole in the shelter so we started The Monday Night Club. Then everyone found out. Now it's asshole-to-asshole there, too. So here we are, squeezed into this crummy doorway and—"

"—I know, more assholes," Marty finished. "It's our fate."

"We just *gotta* get our own place."

Marty smiled to himself. A little brandy and Pete always brought the conversation around to his favorite subject. "I'll drink to that," Marty said, taking the bottle and lifting it in a toast.

Pete picked up the empty brown bag and blew his nose into it. "Yeah," he said dreamily, "we could party whenever we wanted. I can't wait to get back in the saddle."

Marty passed the bottle back. "With hookers?"

Pete shook his head. "No, no, with *real* ladies. You didn't know me when I was working, but I was a regular stud-o-la. Get paid, get laid, I always say."

"Hey, why wait for our own place?" Marty asked. "A good-looking fellow like you could meet lots of women."

"Yeah, like where?"

"At the library."

"Sure, and then what? Invite 'em over to our men's shelter for a cup o' tea?"

"I see your point."

"But with our own place," Pete went on, "we could sleep in once in a while instead of hauling our asses out of bed at goddamn five-thirty every goddamn morning. And we wouldn't have to lug our stuff around."

"Uh-huh," Marty said, checking on their companion. "I think he's feeling better." The left side of the man's mouth had curved upward in a twisted smile.

Pete eyed their companion while tipping the brandy bottle to finish it off.

The big man glanced around and stood. "Okay, it looks like the storm's eased. We better get our asses over to The Club." He tossed his backpack over his shoulder while Pete casually dropped the empty bottle into the man's lap. The two men walked into the rain.

Crash!

Marty and Pete turned at the sound of breaking glass. The man was in trail, sliding his foot along the pavement.

"Let's make a run for it, Igor," Pete said, limping and holding his arms out. "The monster will never catch us!"

Marty thought for a moment. "No, we can't let him wander around in this weather. He might die. What the hell, let's take him with us. Tomorrow I'll figure something out."

2

THE MONDAY NIGHT CLUB evolved by accident. One day, while looking for a spot out of public view, Marty and Pete climbed a rubble-strewn slope and discovered a cement alcove. Although it wasn't a large space, it could comfortably accommodate a dozen or so people and there was plenty of air circulation for a fire. Initially, it was a weekly sanctuary for Marty, Pete, and a few friends, offering a one-night break from the strict rules and close quarters of their men's shelter. But word of The Monday Night Club spread quickly, and now the fire was going every night of the week.

Because the only access to The Club was away from the street, the fire was out of view of the special police units that targeted the homeless under a program called Project Vector. In order to distinguish these units from regular street patrols, officers wore lightening bolt insignias. Mayor Walter Babcock instituted the program in response to complaints from the business community about San Francisco's burgeoning homeless problem.

Under Project Vector, street people caught loitering were heavily fined and stripped of their possessions. During the previous calendar year, twenty thousand $79 tickets were issued, but only thirteen were paid, resulting in thousands of bench warrants and arrests.

This harsh handling of the homeless alarmed San Francisco's liberals. In placation, Mayor Babcock added social workers to Project Vector's police patrols. "We must ensure humane treatment of the homeless and provide direct referrals to emergency shelters and inexpensive housing," he announced at the time.

Unfortunately, the city's limited budget meant that there were neither enough social workers nor enough shelters to support this aspect of Project Vector. As a result, Chief of Police Rudolf Conti designated several unofficial "safe zones," where the homeless were allowed to congregate without fear of being ticketed.

But gang members, drug dealers, and other unsavory characters were attracted to these unpoliced areas, making them too dangerous for the homeless who invariably drifted back into the neighborhoods, parks, and commercial areas, where the police would ticket them and return them to the safe zones. The result was that the homeless were in perpetual motion, on a forced march to nowhere.

Since the Monday Night Club was not in one of the so-called safe zones, Marty kept an eye peeled for Project Vector patrol cars as he and Pete helped their guest negotiate the muddy and uneven embankment leading to the alcove's opening.

As Marty entered the cement pocket he noticed that the storm had doubled The Club's normal attendance. Some people were drying out near the fire; others, further back, were under buried under blankets or tucked inside of sleeping bags. Marty was certain if aliens landed here, say, a million years after their first visit to earth, they would think the humans in this cave hadn't evolved at all.

Stan, a regular at Marty and Pete's homeless shelter, was tending the fire. His ponytailed black hair contrasted sharply with his surplus marine fatigues and army boots.

His face carried a permanent smirk as if he were the sole recipient of an inside joke.

Marty knew Stan's tough appearance was a façade that helped the man survive. Unlike many of the homeless who used the buddy system for mutual protection, Stan was alone. He had difficulty making friends, and was openly jealous of Pete's relationship with Marty. When Marty and Pete first started The Monday Night Club, they hoped that Stan wouldn't learn of it. But the man had his nose in everything, and he made it his business to be at The Club with Marty and Pete every Monday night.

Stan looked up as the three men approached. Marty had his arm around the waist of their limping guest. "Who's your girlfriend, Marty?" he asked loudly as he casually tossed a scrap of damp lumber into a blazing fifty-gallon drum. The fire hissed and sparks rose briskly toward the concrete roof.

"He's *your* date, Stan," Pete answered. "Marty got him just for you. See his face? He's happy."

"Sit, Happy," Marty said, picking up on the nickname. He guided their half-smiling charge onto a crate next to Annie, a tired-looking woman who appeared considerably older than her real age of thirty-five. Annie gazed at the flames and dragged on a cigarette, lost in another time and place. Next to her, two men, a white-haired Caucasian in his sixties and a younger Hispanic, were playing poker on a large cardboard box.

With his hands locked behind him, Stan strutted over to inspect the newcomer. "Gee, what a good doggy. What other tricks does he do?"

"He begs—just like you do, Stan," Pete said.

Stan's smirk evaporated and he threw Pete a daggered look. Then he turned to the older of the two card players. "Hey, Doc, you used to be a vet'narian. Why don't you check this guy for rabies? You can shine a light up his asshole and see if his brains are rotted." Stan's smirk returned. "I'm talking about Pete, of course."

Doc rearranged his cards. "Sorry, Stan, I've been out of the veterinary business a long, long, time."

Sanchez, Doc's card partner, spoke up. "Hey, Stan, I'll loan you a flashlight."

"Okay, let's cut the crap," Marty said impatiently. "Stan, what's the work situation for tomorrow?" Stan always knew where the odd jobs were. In spite of his obnoxious attitude, Marty figured him for someone who might eventually pull himself out of homelessness. Marty didn't care for the man, but he respected his ambition.

"Tomorrow? Just shit work," Stan answered. "The hot dog distributor near the Civic Center needs a cleanup crew in the morning. Pays ten bucks and all the stale dogs and soggy pretzels you can eat."

"God, I hate that job," Pete groaned. "Piss on those stinking carts."

"That's what you usually do, Pete," Stan said.

"I said cut the crap!" Marty glared. "Can't you two spend a few peaceful minutes together? JE-SUS!"

Annie came out of her trance. "You tell 'em, Marty," she said. "I listen to those bitches at my shelter argue every night. The only reason I come here is for some peace and quiet."

"Me too," Marty said. "So how've you been, Annie?" he asked gently. "You working?"

Annie nodded. "I got this part-time job with a house-cleaning service on the Peninsula. The pay sucks, and there's not much left after bus fare and lunch. But at least I'm off the streets while I'm waiting for the shelter to open. Mostly, the job keeps me from sitting around and thinking about my kids—the bastards took them from me just before Christmas . . . ."

Annie's voice trailed off and she turned back to the fire.

Marty nodded in sympathy and walked over to Stan. "Any refreshments left?"

"Nope. All gone. On account of the storm, there was a lot of people in need tonight. You should've been here earlier."

"We got caught in a downpour and ducked into a doorway in the Western Addition," Marty explained. "That's where we came across Happy."

Stan looked as though a light bulb went off in his head. "Wait a second," he said, gingerly stepping over bodies. He made his way to a corner of the alcove and returned with a gallon jug. With a mock bow he handed it to Marty. A dark purplish liquid sloshed inside.

Pete rolled his eyes. "Oh, no, he's trying to serve up that *Chateau de Crud* again."

Marty unscrewed the cap and winced. "You got that right," he said, pushing the bottle at Pete. "Have some."

Pete waved it off. He knew better.

Stan took the jug from Marty. "Now, now, girls, we have a guest. Where *are* your manners?" He went over to Happy and held the jug to his lips. Their guest took a sip and was in the process of taking a second when suddenly, in a double take, his face turned bright crimson.

Doc and Sanchez stopped playing cards and broke out laughing.

Happy gagged and coughed, upchucking the purple liquid all over the front of his clothing.

THREE
Tuesday, January 10

1

A FEW CAULIFLOWER CLOUDS drifted lazily across an azure sky. The bright sunshine made San Francisco's commuters squint as they drove to work. But the employees of Cytex Corporation were not among them. They were at their stations well before sunrise, preparing for the 11:00 a.m. arrival of the executive committee from I-Cubed, S.A., a Swiss-based electronics conglomerate. The Swiss were seriously considering buying Cytex.

Greg Thompson, vice president of engineering, sat by the phone in the conference room. He was worried. It was unthinkable that his boss would be late for the most important meeting in the history of the company.

Greg pushed a button on the intercom. "Sally, any word yet?"

"No. I just tried Mr. Howell's car phone. It's not in service. And still no answer at his condo."

"Check all the hospitals; God help us if something happened to him." Greg knew he could handle the technical part of the dog and pony show, but he was ill-equipped to field questions from the Swiss about the company's strategic plan. Where could his boss be?

Greg glanced at his watch: it was 10:30 a.m. Not knowing what else to do, he decided to go through a final check of the equipment. He walked over to a control console, typed a command into the keyboard, and a computer screen came alive. While the demo program loaded, he settled into a contoured chair and fitted an opaque wraparound visor over his eyes and ears.

He remained in darkness for a moment, with his finger poised on a button on the armrest. He took a deep breath, pressed the button, and suddenly was surrounded by the moist, reddish world of a human stomach. He felt like a fly that had been swallowed.

This was virtual reality at its best, made possible by the company's prototype *Reality Engine,* an advanced high-speed processor that projected stereoscopic color images onto a pair of wide-angle TV screens inside the visor. Cytex called their invention C-REAL.

As many times as Greg had visited the virtual stomach he still wasn't used to it. He had been holding his breath and now exhaled slowly. Moving his head he could view the glistening cavern from different angles. Looking down, he saw the churning of partially digested food as the stomach rippled, emptying its contents into the small intestine. Out of the visor's headphones the grumbles and squeaks of the digestive process echoed in stereo. Greg's own stomach began to spasm. He quickly turned toward the target. There it was, to his left, a grayish gastric tumor protruding from a vein-filled wall.

Greg gripped the *forceball*, a spherical control device that sensed pressure. Pushing on the ball, he moved toward the tumor until it was the size of a boulder. He squeezed a trigger at the base of the forceball and a green laser target light encircled the mass.

Greg was about to fire the red laser ablative scalpel when he became aware of a persistent buzzing in the distance. He removed the visor and returned to reality.

He would soon be sorry he did.

"Mr. Thompson, are you there?" Sally said over the intercom. "There's a homicide inspector on the phone. He insists on talking to 'the man in charge.'"

Greg sat at the conference table and picked up the phone. "This is Greg Thompson."

The caller cleared his throat. "Mr. Thompson, my name is Inspector James Brodsky, San Francisco Police Department. I need to ask you a few questions."

"Y-yes?"

"As you may have heard, a small plane went down last night in Golden Gate Park. The pilot and a passenger were blown up in the subsequent explosion and fire. *I* have been assigned to the case." The inspector's voice resonated with self-importance.

"Yes?"

"Does Mr. Jason Howell work there?"

"Yes . . . he's our president."

"Is he missing?"

"I-I guess . . . but he's only a couple of hours late," Greg replied, in denial.

"From the plane's tail number and other physical evidence at the scene, we've identified the pilot as Mr. William Henderson, a real estate executive who flew to Petaluma yesterday. The control tower's records indicate the plane took off from San Carlos about 3:00 p.m. The pilot's wife wasn't certain but she believes her husband was accompanied by your Mr. Howell."

"God no!"

"Now I wouldn't draw any conclusions yet, sir. There may be another explanation as to Mr. Howell's whereabouts. We haven't identified the second victim as we're still collecting body parts. But we do know it was an adult male," Brodsky said, pausing to clear his throat again, "if you get my drift. When was the last time you saw Mr. Howell?"

"Yesterday, after lunch."

"Did he say where he was going?"

"No."

"Describe him for me."

"He's . . . ah, in his late thirties, six feet tall, medium build, sandy-brown hair, blue eyes. We should have a photo in personnel."

"What kind of car does he drive?"

"A four-door Mercedes sedan."

"All right. As you can imagine, this accident has caused quite a stir. The media is jumping all over us to identify the second victim, but we can't release any information until the coroner says so. Under the circumstances, a positive ID could take some time. And then there's the matter of notifying the next of kin."

Greg dropped his forehead into his hand.

"Now, I'm going to need that file photo as well as Mr. Howell's dental and medical records—ASAP."

"I'll transfer you to Sally . . . his secretary," Greg said, stabbing at a button on the intercom.

For a time, Greg sat numbly with the receiver pressed against his ear. The possibility of losing Jason Howell at this critical juncture was incomprehensible. "Please, please, not now," he prayed into the dead phone.

The intercom buzzed and Greg jumped.

"Mr. Thompson," said the receptionist, "the Swiss gentlemen from I-Cubed are here."

2

FOR A REASON no one could explain, the Civic Center Plaza, the large square in front of City Hall and the mayor's office, was a safe zone—except when a newspaper criticized the appalling and unsanitary conditions in the area. The next day the police would swoop down and chase the homeless away, but they were always allowed to return.

Marty and Pete sat on their backpacks on a street bordering the area, resting after spending the last few hours cleaning hot dog carts. The late morning sun was warming the air and drying out the deepest layers of their clothing.

Happy, wearing his purple-stained pea coat and blue knit hat, was sitting between his caretakers. He was holding his head in his hands again. A day-old hot dog hung limply from his mouth like a Groucho Marx cigar.

An elderly African American woman wearing a pastiche of sweaters abruptly stopped in front of the threesome. Her bright yellow hat was tilted smartly. She set her shopping bags on the pavement and considered the men for a moment. "What you fools lookin' at?" she asked angrily. "Jus' cause I ain't got no home, it don't mean I ain't. human. Didn't your momma teach you nothin' about America? We's equal no matter what!" She was shouting now.

"Hello, Kate," Pete said. "Want something to eat? We've got a couple of extra dogs."

"I don't eat no damn dogs. No cats neither, you fools! JEE-ZUS!" With that she gathered her bags and moved on.

They watched her shuffle toward the Civic Center Plaza, her socks sagging around the tops of her tennis shoes. The sides of her legs were black and blue, the dead giveaway of a bag lady.

"Ol' Kate's whacked out again," Marty said.

"Don't be too hard on her," Pete replied. "I reckon she gets agitated after spending a rough night outside."

"She's not the only one," Marty said, nodding at Happy who was moving his head from side to side, the hot dog in his mouth marking time like a metronome.

Pete studied Happy. "Yeah, he's hurting again; he ain't eating. But can't say as I blame him. A breakfast of cold franks and warm sodas ain't all that appetizing."

Marty drained a can of soda and belched. "It's funny how everything gets turned around on the street. The housed people get to eat *hot* franks and *cold* sodas. But for us, everything's backwards, like we're seeing the world through a broken mirror."

"Maybe, but once in a while things work out."

"How's that?"

Pete squinted into the sun. "Like now for instance. We're outside enjoying this glorious day, instead of sitting behind some crummy desk watching the clock, hoping that Friday's envelope holds a paycheck and not a pink slip, afraid that the damn bank will repossess the house and car. I reckon that's one worry we don't have."

"Yeah, but I'm afraid we're going to wind up like ol' Kate," Marty said, holding up his hand and making a tiny gap with his thumb and forefinger. "We're only a *skosh* away from walking in her shoes—"

Suddenly Happy moaned.

Pete looked at Happy's face. "You need some more Tylenol, fella. You partied hard last night." He plucked the hot dog out of Happy's mouth and gave him three capsules and some orange soda.

Marty scratched his beard and stared at Happy. "There's something strange about this guy."

"What?" Pete said, eating Happy's hot dog. "He's just a little more whacked out than ol' Kate. You know, I'm beginning to like the fella. At least he don't bullshit like Stan, that ass—"

"I have an idea," Marty interrupted, not wanting Pete to get started on Stan. "I'm going to take him to City General Hospital. His color's good, but he's acting like his head's hurting real bad. I'll catch up with you at the library."

"Okay, but watch out for the mayor's Nazis."

"They won't bother us if we keep moving."

3

PUBLIC TRANSPORTATION was out of the question. Happy looked awful: His sweatpants were mud-caked, and his purple-stained pea coat emitted a foul odor. So they walked. Marty held his charge's arm as they headed south toward the hospital, their pace hampered by Happy's limping gait. But Marty didn't mind. The air was warm, and the Tylenol was working. Happy's twisted smile had returned.

By the time they reached City General, it was early afternoon. Indigent patients filled all of the chairs and every available space on the floor. Having missed the news last night, Marty wondered if World War III had broken out.

He guided Happy gingerly around the bodies and joined a long line snaking toward the registration window. Above the window, a large sign said TRIAGE. After an inordinate wait, it was finally Marty's turn. "I'd like to have my friend here examined," he announced. With one arm he kept Happy behind him.

"Patient's name?" the receptionist asked, not bothering to look up from her computer screen.

Marty figured he would have to give the hospital some kind of name for their paperwork. He didn't think he should say he found the man in a doorway. "Happy Rappaport," he replied.

"Address?"

"Western Addition . . . I forget where."

"Insurance?"

"Beats me."

The woman finally looked up. "Are you a relative?" she asked impatiently.

"No."

The woman's fingers flew over the keyboard for the longest time. For the life of him, Marty couldn't figure out what was so complicated about the word "no."

"And *your* name?"

"Woody Wilson." At the library, Marty was reading about World War I, the Treaty of Versailles, and President Woodrow Wilson.

"The nature of Mr. Rappaport's illness?"

"Ah . . . bad headaches. He's in terrible pain."

The woman glanced at Happy who was now standing on his toes and peering at her over Marty's shoulder. He had his thumb in his mouth. She sighed and typed something into the computer. "Please have a seat; we'll get to him as soon as—"

"But his face gets all twisted," Marty insisted. "And there aren't any damn seats."

"We'll get to him as soon as we can. Now take a seat. NEXT!"

Marty's mood blackened. He turned abruptly and guided Happy into the waiting area. An old man wearing several layers of clothing was sleeping across three chairs. He was snoring. A hospital tag hung from his wrist, and a beat-up wooden crutch lay on the floor. Marty shook him. "Hey, pops, wake up!" he growled. "You've got company."

The old man opened a wary eye. He sat up quickly when he saw a six-foot-six-inch bearded hulk looming over him. "Okay, take it easy, brother," he said. "Didn't get much sleep last night with all these folks coming and going during that storm."

Marty had Happy sit. "I'm going upstairs to the cafeteria," he told the old man. "If you watch my friend and save me a seat, I'll get you something to eat. What do you want?"

"Hmmm, let's see . . . coffee with skim milk and a turkey sandwich on wheat toast with lettuce and tomato and lots of mustard. Hold the mayo."

Marty rolled his eyes. "Just *make sure* you watch this guy. Don't leave him alone for a damn second."

Marty went upstairs and waited in another long line. It seemed like forever before he placed his order. He was nervous about leaving Happy with the old man, but he figured he and his charge better eat something if they were going to hang around all day.

When he finally returned to the waiting room carrying a tray of sandwiches and coffee, neither Happy nor the old man was in sight. Instead, three slouching young men wearing do-rags and gang colors had commandeered the old man's seats.

Behind him, Marty heard laughter. He turned. Two other gang members were playing monkey-in-the-middle with Happy, shoving him back and forth. The man's knit cap was skewed, he was mumbling, and his face was twisted again.

Marty's blood boiled. He shoved the food tray into the hands of a bystander and rushed over. Grabbing the nearest punk by his leather jacket, he slammed the young man into the wall with such force his do-rag flew off his head. The youngster crumpled to the ground, moaning. The other gang member took off.

Someone yelled, "SECURITY!"

An alarm sounded.

Using a body tackle, Marty hoisted Happy over his shoulder and rushed out of the hospital.

It was early evening by the time the two men caught up with Pete at the library. On the way Marty had stopped to give Happy more Tylenol. But his charge remained agitated, and Marty was having trouble managing him.

Pete was sitting at their regular table and looked over his newspaper as Marty and Happy joined him. Across the front page the headline said:

MONDAY'S PLANE CRASH CLOSES PARK

"How'd it go?" Pete asked, putting the paper down.

"Terrible," Marty said sullenly. "Seeing a doctor was like trying to shit sideways. Happy got us into a gang fight, I nailed a punk, and we had to make a run for it."

Pete laughed. "It figures. So what's Plan B?"

Marty glanced at the clock on the wall. "I guess we take him to the shelter."

4

GREG THOMPSON SAT in his office, struggling with conflicting emotions. On the one hand he was elated by the success of his demonstration of C-REAL; on the other hand he fretted about the company's future.

The dog and pony show had begun with an apology and a half-truth. Greg told the Swiss that Jason Howell had been detained while on a business trip. Greg quickly started the demonstration and, as he had hoped, the execs forgot about Howell when they experienced the virtual stomach. Although this tactic had bought some time, Greg knew that a merger with I-Cubed would be unlikely if his boss wasn't part of the deal.   Three years ago, when he took over, Howell directed Greg and his staff to cease designing crude virtual reality systems. He ordered the engineering department to focus all of its resources on the design of the reality engine, the critical link between the computer and its input/output devices.

At the time Greg questioned the wisdom of this strategy since a reality engine, by itself, was nothing more than an expensive boat anchor. But Howell told Greg that when C-REAL was ready, powerful visors and sensors would be inexpensively mass-produced by the Japanese game makers, and advanced multimedia computers would be available from nearby Silicon Valley.

Howell had been right on the money. With a minimum investment, his vision had positioned Cytex as the technical leader in virtual reality systems, giving Greg and his co-workers the opportunity for unimaginable wealth.

Until yesterday, that is.

Sally entered the conference room and interrupted Greg's musing. "I called Inspector Brodsky for an update. They have Mr. Howell's dental and medical records, but no results yet. However, I did learn something new," she said, "and I'm afraid it's not good."

"W-what?" Greg asked, not sure he wanted to know.

"They found Mr. Howell's Mercedes in the parking lot at San Carlos Airport."

Greg's body sagged. "I guess I'd better inform Chairman Simpson." Albert Simpson III headed the board of directors and was the lead venture capital investor. Greg knew the Chairman abhorred bad news.

"I'll get him on the line for you," Sally said.

5

MAYOR WALTER J. BABCOCK was having a dinner meeting at Les Moules. The Louis XV decor, the classical music, and the soft lights were designed to soothe. Seated at the mayor's regular booth were Rudolf Conti, the Chief of Police, and Homicide Inspector James Brodsky, who had been invited by the chief to update the mayor on yesterday's plane crash.

Mayor Babcock took a delicate sip of fifteen-year-old *Chateau Margaux* and turned to the chief. "The first order of business, Rudy, is a status report on Project Vector."

Chief Conti put his wine glass down. His tall frame, angular features, and full head of black hair were in stark contrast with the mayor's squat body, rotund face, and balding pate. "Vector is doing well," the chief replied. "We've been able to reduce the panhandler population in the downtown shopping area by 70 percent. And the numbers from the Chamber of Commerce indicate this year's Christmas sales were up 8 percent. That's the good news. The bad news is that the homeless are roosting in other parts of the city, especially the Civic Center and the parks, where their numbers have mushroomed."

Inspector Brodsky cleared his throat. "If *I* may say so, sir, we're being too soft. We shouldn't arrest the beggars when they don't pay their loitering tickets. Of course they won't pay. They *want* to be jailed to get deloused, a hot meal, and a warm place to sleep. Then we let them go."

"What are you suggesting, Inspector?" the mayor asked, slicing a succulent piece of *Cervelle de Mouton.*

"*I* would order the Project Vector patrols to increase their hostility. Deliberately provoke the vermin by kicking them. When they react, give them a taste of the baton. A whack in the knee works wonders." Brodsky paused to lick his lips. "And for those we arrest, shackle them in a work crew and force them to clean up the mess they've made of our streets and parks. Work them long and hard, and if they slack off, whack them again." Brodsky's eyes grew wide.

"No, I don't think so, Inspector," the mayor said between bites. "Although Project Vector has the support of the business community, we're walking a fine line with my liberal constituents. Then there's the damn ACLU who's always challenging Vector's constitutionality. With the mayoral election in November, we don't want to give them any more ammunition."

"The mayor's right," Chief Conti said. "Besides, we don't have the manpower to intensify Vector. All we can do is herd the homeless when they wander from the safe zones. Keep them in motion and hope that eventually they'll tire and leave The City."

The mayor looked at his watch. He still had to attend the opening of an art gallery before joining Mrs. Babcock at the symphony. It was time to move the meeting along. "What's the latest on last night's critical incident, Inspector? Have you identified the second plane crash victim?"

Brodsky took a huge gulp of the *Margaux*. The mayor winced, making a mental note to exclude the inspector from future dinner meetings.

"Everything points to Jason Howell," Brodsky replied, placing his hand over his mouth too late to cover a belch. "I'm just waiting for forensics to confirm it from the physical evidence."

"You're not giving me anything new, Inspector," the mayor said, holding up his wine glass as if to inspect the clarity of his *Margaux,* while in truth he was avoiding Brodsky's beady eyes. "Jason Howell was a good friend, a highly-respected member of our business community, a man of extraordinary vision and refined taste, and most importantly, a generous contributor to my campaign. We dined here often. I'll need to schedule a news conference shortly."

"The lab is working on it, sir," Brodsky replied.

"Inspector," the chief interjected, "why don't you find a phone and get an update from the coroner?"

Brodsky took another gulp of wine and stood, allowing his linen napkin to slide from his lap and onto the floor.

6

THE SANDSTONE BUILDING that housed the St. Andrew's Shelter for Men was an annex of a church and had originally functioned as a religious school. The central hall, once an auditorium, now served the eating, sleeping, and recreational needs of the men. The floor was tiled in gray asphalt and the walls were painted pale green. Beyond the picnic tables, all the way to the stage, was the sleeping area. When the building was converted into an emergency shelter in 1982, eighteen cots lined the walls. Now, nearly every inch of floor space was used to accommodate the seventy-two men who were packed into the shelter each night.

During the day, the stage was used to stack the cots so that the floors could be washed and polished. To one side of the dining area, a dozen folding chairs formed a semicircle around an old television set. Across the central hall was a library area stocked with worn paperbacks. Other rooms housed the kitchen, the laundry, offices for the staff, and community toilets and showers.

Although the building was no longer officially associated with the church, the shelter's staff still encouraged religious studies. After dinner, about twenty of the men attended a Bible class in the library area. Those uninterested in religion watched television, talked, or played cards; those not feeling sociable went directly to their cots to read or stare at the ceiling until the lights went out at ten o'clock.

It wasn't easy to get Happy in for the night. While waiting in line for the shelter to open at 7:00 p.m., Marty persuaded Stan to give up his cot and spend another evening at The Club. Stan grumbled until Marty handed him most of the money remaining from this morning's hot dog detail. Pete sighed as he watched their dream of private housing drift further away.

Next, Marty persuaded the staff to skip the screening process normally applied to new clients. Marty promised that he and Pete would be responsible for Happy, and the staff wouldn't have to concern themselves with his care and feeding. Tomorrow, he assured them, their guest would be history.

Marty had a good relationship with the staff. On occasion, when someone violated the rules prohibiting drinking, drug use, or vulgar behavior, Marty acted as the shelter's bouncer. The staff preferred not to call the police since patrol cars fostered complaints by the neighbors, and the shelter's existence was tenuous as it was. Things ran smoothly with Marty around.

Before dinner, Pete removed Happy's clothing for cleaning. It was then he noticed the injury on the left side of his head, at the hairline.

Now, at the dinner table, Happy was seated between his caretakers. He was wearing borrowed striped pajamas and a gray flannel bathrobe. Pete was feeding him beans and rice, the shelter's usual fare for Tuesday. The warm surroundings and a hot meal seemed to have a calming affect, and he was half-smiling again.

"What do you reckon happened to Happy's head?" Pete asked as he spooned beans into a twisted, gaping mouth.

Marty inspected the injury. "Beats me. There's no telling if he got injured because of his mental state or if his mental state resulted from the injury. In any case, he definitely needs to go back to the hospital."

"Why don't you let the staff arrange it?" Pete asked, eating some of Happy's beans.

"I don't think so. I told them he wouldn't be their problem. Besides, I think a decent meal and some rest will do him more good than spending tonight in that horrendous waiting room, which is probably still jammed. His injury isn't fresh, and I don't think a few more hours will make any difference. Tomorrow he goes back to the hospital—but this time I'll be better prepared."

7

INSPECTOR BRODSKY'S FACE was smug when he returned to the mayor's table.

"The victim wasn't Howell," he said out of the side of his mouth.

"That's great news!" the mayor effused.

"I'm not so sure, sir," Brodsky whispered, as he sat down.

"What do you mean?" the chief asked, using his normal voice.

Brodsky glanced around to see if anyone was listening. "Before Howell's medical records arrived," he said, continuing to whisper, forcing the mayor and the chief to lean closer like schoolboys sharing a secret, "forensics identified a piece of melted plastic they found in the wreckage. It came from a Cytex ID badge. At that point we all thought it was a matter of getting confirmation from Howell's medical records. But when the records arrived, the coroner determined the second victim wasn't Howell."

"Are they certain?" the chief asked.

"Absolutely. When they got into it, the torso was smaller and the teeth were all rotted. Wait until you hear what they found in the stomach."

Mayor Babcock had been savoring a mouthful of crème brûlée. He abruptly put his spoon down. "I can assure you I don't want to know."

"Who's the second victim?" Conti asked impatiently.

Brodsky shrugged. "All we have to go on," he replied, measuring his words as he watched the mayor swallow, "was a fingerprint taken from a dismembered hand found impaled on a tree branch. The print was faxed to the FBI for priority processing. In the meantime, we're examining fragments from the victim's clothing—he was wearing some kind of military uniform."

The mayor pushed his dessert away. "This is bizarre; what the hell's going on?"

"*I* think I know, sir," Brodsky said, keeping his voice low.

Mayor Babcock pressed on his sinuses. "Go ahead."

"The FAA said the plane went off the radar screen at 5:25 p.m. About twenty minutes later we received an anonymous 911 reporting the accident. Residents on Fulton then heard an explosion."

"That's fascinating, Inspector," the mayor said, "but what happened to Howell? Are you saying he was thrown from the plane before it blew and he's in the trees somewhere?"

Brodsky took an easy sip of water. He was clearly enjoying himself. "Not at all. I believe Howell and the pilot were alive at the time of the crash. I believe Howell was pulled out by the scum who live in the park. The victim in the uniform was one of them. He was trying to get the pilot out when the plane blew."

"If Howell was rescued," Chief Conti said, "then where the hell is he?"

"I'm not saying he was rescued," Brodsky replied matter-of-factly.

"Look, man, what *are* you saying?" the chief demanded.

Brodsky leaned forward. "He was kidnapped."

"My God!" the mayor spurted, his face turning rosy red. "Why the hell would the homeless do that?"

"In retaliation for Project Vector. They got into his wallet, realized he was a VIP, and decided to hold him hostage." Brodsky paused to let this sink in. "Gentlemen," he continued, "we've got a band of homeless terrorists on our hands."

FOUR
Wednesday, January 11

1

THE LIGHTS OF ST. ANDREWS flooded on at precisely 5:30 a.m., and moans and groans filled the central hall. Marty awoke in a mood as black as the predawn night. He had slept little. His dreams were short, troubled vignettes, interrupted frequently by the sneezing and coughing of the men around him. In the shelter's tight living quarters, when one man got sick, it seemed as though everyone got sick. Except for Pete. Pete never *got* sick because he continually suffered from a cold or an allergy.

While standing in line for the showers, Marty heard the weather report on the radio. The forecast was fog and drizzle well into the evening. It was going to be another long day until the shelter reopened at 7:00 p.m.

At breakfast Happy fidgeted and mumbled as Pete tried to feed him oatmeal. It was hopeless. Pete was coughing badly, and he kept missing Happy's gaping mouth. Even when Happy captured some of the mush, it drooled down his chin.

"You look like shit," Marty remarked, as he took his seat at the picnic table.

Pete dabbed around Happy's mouth with a paper napkin. "Yeah, I reckon he does."

"No, Pete, I mean YOU."

"What? Am I having a bad hair day?"

Marty sighed. "C'mon, why don't you come with us to the hospital and have that cough checked out? As a bonus you can watch me execute my plan to get rid of this guy." Marty reached into his pocket and held up an elastic bandage he had taken out of the shelter's first aid kit.

"I'd love to see your plan," Pete said. "But I ain't going to that damn hospital so I can be ignored on a first come, first serve basis. Do you think I want to hang around all day with a bunch of sick assholes and gang members? Remember what happened the last time I was there?"

"No."

"After I told the doctor that I was homeless, he tells me to remain in bed for full week and use a vaporizer every two hours. Give me a break!"

"So what are you planning to do?"

"Go to work and replace the money you keep giving away."

"You got anything lined up?"

"Not yet. But before Stan left for The Club last night, I heard him talking about a construction company that needs some laborers for a few hours. Maybe they'll let me sweep up or something."

"Will you be at the library later?"

Pete nodded as he dressed Happy in his coat and hat. But it wasn't easy because the man continued to fidget, and his head bobbed from side to side. "He's sure getting harder to manage."

"Yeah," Marty agreed. "But now that his clothes don't stink I can take him on the Muni bus and get rid of him that much quicker. Got five bucks?"

Pete reluctantly dug into his pocket. "Okay, but you'd better be successful this time. He's killing us financially."

2

"WE MUST ASSUME Jason Howell is gone," Greg Thompson said, ignoring his breakfast of fresh fruit, baked bread, and French roast coffee. He was dining at the fashionable Poppanono's in the financial district, addressing Cytex's silver-haired chairman of the board.

Albert Simpson III picked up his knife and fork, and extended his elbows in a smooth motion that exposed just the right amount of cuff. Then he divided a pineapple slice into equal, bite-sized pieces. "What have you heard from the police?"

"Not a thing. I keep telephoning, but the cop in charge, this Inspector Brodsky, won't return my calls. And no one else at the SFPD seems to know anything. I guess we should hold a company-wide meeting. Rumors are flying."

"That's proper," the chairman said, moving a mint leaf to the side of his plate. "Even if Howell's demise is not official, you must tell the employees what you know. Make your announcement short, and as late in the day as possible so that the employees can use their own time to get over the shock, thereby minimizing losses to productivity."

Greg nodded. "What about Howell's replacement?"

"I'm meeting with the Board of Directors this afternoon," Chairman Simpson said. He set his fork on the side of his plate and looked squarely at Greg. "I'm going to recommend you as interim president."

"Uh, thanks for the vote of confidence."

"Indeed. I didn't make this decision lightly. Last night I dined with I-Cubed's executive management, and I must say the Swiss were quite impressed with you and your demonstration of C-REAL. As Jason anticipated, they're excited by the prospect of merging Cytex into I-Cubed. Of course we will have to convince them that the merger will work without Howell. That will be my job. Then we must convince them that the reality engines can be cost-effectively mass-produced. That will be your job.

"What selling price are they talking about?"

"Their marketing model requires a price of one thousand dollars per engine."

Greg was stunned. One thousand dollars was much lower than his most optimistic projections.

"I assured our Swiss friends that Cytex can accomplish this," Simpson continued. "But time is short. The competition will soon be nipping at our heels. To maintain our strategic advantage, shipments to customers and distributors must begin by May 1."

Greg was worried. The company had a long way to go from an engineering prototype to tens of thousands of inexpensive engines. And because Cytex didn't have its own production facilities, success depended on finding a manufacturer to mass produce the devices for them. It gnawed at Greg, so he threw it out. "Mr. Simpson, as you know, C-REAL is highly complex and has a large labor content. I just don't see how we can get assembly bids low enough to meet the price target."

Simpson dabbed at his mouth with a linen napkin and eyed Greg. "And as *you* know, there's a lot at stake here—for all of us. We're very close. Until we find a permanent replacement for Jason Howell, we must not lose momentum. I'm counting on you to step up to the plate and hit a home run."

Greg bit his upper lip. "Then we have no choice but to go overseas for our manufacturing. But there'll be enormous logistical and quality control problems with a product of this complexity. There's no margin for error. I guess I'll have to go abroad to support the contractor for the duration. Only my wife just gave birth and—"

Simpson set his napkin down and motioned for the check. "Just make certain your passport is current."

3

IN THE MORNING rush hour traffic, the packed Muni bus moved in fits and starts like a squirrel scurrying along a power line. Marty managed to find a seat in front for Happy and stood beside him. But boarding passengers and the vehicle's jerking motion worked him rearwards. Now, near the back of the bus, all he could see of Happy was his blue knit cap bobbing back and forth.

Suddenly a woman screamed.

The bus braked hard, throwing all standing passengers forward. The driver, a big African American man, got up and rushed toward Happy.

People in the front of the bus were yelling.

A scuffle ensued, the door opened, and the driver, holding Happy by his scruff, summarily ejected him.

Marty was caught off-guard. By the time he started for the rear exit, the driver was back in his seat, lurching his passengers backward in a frenzied attempt to close the gap in traffic. Marty watched helplessly as Happy, looking like a lost puppy, fell behind in the drizzle.

When Marty found his footing, he shoved bodies aside and forced his way toward the rear exit. "STOP THE BUS!" he yelled.

The bus accelerated.

Marty yanked the emergency cord. "STOP THIS FUCKING BUS!"

The bus screeched to a halt, and Marty and the other standing passengers flew forward with a vengeance. As the exit pole flashed by, Marty tackled it, rotating his large frame and using his momentum to separate the rear doors. As soon as Marty was outside, the bus roared off, surrounding him in a cloud of diesel exhaust.

When the smoke cleared, Happy was nowhere in sight. Marty was worried. Finally he spotted his charge across the street, sitting on a bench in a small neighborhood park, holding his head in his hands and rocking back and forth.

A patrol car with a lightening bolt on the door pulled up in front of Happy, and two police officers in rain slickers got out. Marty hurried over. One of the cops started questioning Happy, while the other took out a ticket book.

"I said what's your name, pal?" Happy's interrogator demanded, poking him in the chest with a baton.

"Sad-lup quazil lemro," Happy said.

The cop's partner began writing the ticket.

Marty shook his head and started to walk away. Then he stopped. *Damn it, we're only a few blocks from the hospital. God knows what these cops will do to him.*

Marty approached cautiously.

"What do *you* want?" the lead cop asked, removing his baton from Happy's chest and pointing it at Marty.

"I'm taking care of him," Marty said.

"Fine," said the cop with the ticket book. He held his pen ready. "You can start by telling us how to spell your pal's name. He's incoherent."

"Actually, I don't know his name. He's injured. I'm taking him to City General."

"Look, fella," the cop with the baton said impatiently, "we found this guy loitering. Then you come out of nowhere, telling us you're his buddy, but you don't even know his name." He waved the baton menacingly.

Marty took a step back. "Excuse me, Officers," he said, keeping his hands clasped together and in full view. "I'm Martin Dubichek. I live at St. Andrews. Give *me* the ticket. I'm just trying to help this guy out. Honest." Marty slowly pulled out his ID.

The two cops looked at each other.

The lead cop relented and took the ID. "All right, here's the deal: You take the ticket and you and your buddy hustle your sorry asses out of here. This neighborhood is off-limits. Do I make myself clear?"

"Yes, sir, thank you, Officers."

4

IN HIS LARGE wood-paneled office on the fifth floor of the Hall of Justice, Chief Conti was on the phone. He was stalling the press as Inspector Brodsky sat in a side chair, drumming his fingers on the chief's polished oak desk, leaving oily smudges. The chief's lack of clutter amazed Brodsky. Sharpened pencils of equal length were lined up on the right side of the desk. On the left, a picture of Conti's blue-blooded wife with their Norman Rockwell kids was angled so both the chief and his visitors could admire his family. Even the trash in the chief's wastepaper basket was arranged according to size.

By contrast, Brodsky's office was a tiny cubicle on the fourth floor. He had a rusty and dented steel desk laden with papers and files. Brodsky hated Conti for his fancy desk, his fancy family, his fancy figurehead job, and his fancy fucking dinners with the mayor.

The chief put the phone down. "I don't know how much longer I can keep the media at bay. Do you have any news on the second victim?"

"Yes, sir. I wanted to report it to you personally because of the sensitivity of the matter," Brodsky replied, pulling out a small pad. "The fingerprint report just came back from the Feds. They identified the victim as Louis A. Sykes. He was a Staff Sergeant in Vietnam. Got the Silver Star. But as a civilian he was a total screw-up, a vagrant who lived in the park. His rap sheet is full of the usual petty crimes—shoplifting, public intoxication, et cetera, et cetera. There was a warrant for his arrest for fifteen loitering tickets."

"But do you have anything more on Howell?"

"As a matter-of-fact I do," Brodsky answered smugly. "The victim's wallet was turned in last night, empty, of course, except for a key card to a racquetball club."

"Where was it found?"

"In the Richmond District, six blocks north of the accident site. An elderly woman found it lying in the gutter while she was walking her dog. *I* had placed the Richmond Substation on alert for any evidence on Howell that might turn up, so the information was forwarded directly to me."

The chief was looking with disdain at the smudges Brodsky had spread on his desk. "Quite frankly, Inspector, I'm having trouble with the idea that Howell was kidnapped by a homeless gang. In all of my years on the force, we could always count on the homeless as being passive. But finding his wallet so far from the scene, and the fact that Howell hasn't surfaced, gives your theory some credence."

"We need to rescue him quickly," Brodsky said.

"What are you recommending?"

Brodsky jutted his jaw. "Give *me* the resources to sweep the park, the soup kitchens, the homeless hangouts. *I'll* find witnesses and make them talk. There aren't many places they can hide Howell. If we can get him out swiftly and bring the scum to justice, then we look good. But if they kill him or if he remains captive and the FBI takes over, the story will stay on the front page and—"

"—we're in deep shit," Conti finished. "Okay, Inspector. Just make sure your activities remain *peaceful* and *discreet*. The mayor will have my ass, and I'll have yours, if this thing escalates into a war with the homeless."

"You can count on *me*," Brodsky said disingenuously.

5

MARTY GUIDED his charge to the rear of the parking lot of City General and propped him against a car. Happy was transforming rapidly, and Marty was worried. The man now mumbled continually, his limp was less severe, and he was more preoccupied with his surroundings. Marty tried talking to him in soothing tones and that seemed to help. But Marty knew that the success of his scheme depended on keeping Happy passive a while longer. After that close call with the police, Marty was more determined than ever to leave Happy at the hospital. The man was trouble. If Marty had been arrested, it would have cost him his cot at the shelter, and he would be sharing a bench in the Civic Center with ol' Kate.

He removed Happy's knit cap and secured the elastic bandage from the shelter onto his charge's forehead. Marty pulled out the edge of the bandage and emptied two packets of ketchup into the gap. A red circle appeared and started spreading.

Marty replaced Happy's knit cap, pulling it down to cover the stain. Taking a deep breath, he guided his charge into the emergency waiting room. Happy appeared to forget his surroundings and was now preoccupied with the moisture on his forehead. His left eye angled upwards as if he thought he could see what was there. *"Slabot kawoosh whattoo?"* he asked.

Marty looked around the room. Although it was not as crowded as yesterday, there were still no empty seats. In the corner by the vending machines, the old man from the day before leaned casually on his crutch. Spotting Marty he limped over. "Hey, friend, I never got that sandwich."

"You were supposed to watch this guy," Marty said.

"I did. You were gone a long time. I had to go."

"To see the doctor?" Marty asked suspiciously.

"Nah, to the crapper," the old man said in a raspy whisper. "This waiting room's my squat. Every once in a while a nice fella like you trades me my seat for a sandwich." He gave Marty an exaggerated wink.

Marty dug into his pocket. "Look, here are a couple of bucks. Can you watch him without going to the crapper?"

"Sure, I'll do anything for two bucks."

"Now listen carefully. I'm going over to the TRIAGE line. Stay nearby where I can keep my eye on the two of you. Talk to him softly, or else he won't remain still."

"Killip sarcor buttu," Happy remarked.

The old man looked Happy over. "If I gotta make conversation, it'll cost three bucks."

"All I got left is fifty cents."

"Deal."

Marty removed Happy's knit cap and stuffed it into his pea coat. Then Marty stood in line and watched the two men limp over to an Asian woman who was sitting with a child. The old man started to say something, but the woman took one look at Happy's bandage and the widening red circle, and grabbed her child and left.

So far, so good, Marty thought.

Twenty minutes passed.

"NEXT!" the receptionist shouted.

Marty stepped up. It was the woman from yesterday. "Ah, yes," Marty began, "my friend and I have been waiting here for twenty-four hours and I was just wondering how much longer it'll be?"

"Patient's name?" the woman asked impassively.

"Happy Rappaport. And I'm Woody Wilson," Marty added, rubbing his hands together.

She typed something into her computer and examined the display. "Oh yes, 'headaches.' We'll call—"

"—I'm afraid he's much worse now," Marty interrupted, his voice rising. "You see, we stepped out for a breath of fresh air and two Project Vector cops attacked us in the parking lot!" Marty had originally planned to blame yesterday's gang members for Happy's head injury, but this morning's encounter with the police added extra spice to his plan. "One of them struck Mr. Rappaport with his baton and opened his head," Marty said, pointing to Happy who was using his index and middle finger to taste the red liquid oozing from his bandage.

The receptionist's mouth dropped.

It was time for Marty to ask for the order: "Look, lady, if you don't get this man medical attention immediately, he's going to hire one of those TV lawyers and sue YOU, THE HOSPITAL, AND THE POLICE FOR MILLIONS!"

At the sound of familiar words, Happy looked in Marty's direction, blinking rapidly as the dormant neurons in his brain began to fire. Suddenly Jason Howell crossed the threshold into self-awareness. But he had no sense of place, day, or time. Instinctively he checked his watch.

His Rolex was gone!

Confused and frightened, Howell tried to absorb his strange clothes, his strange surroundings, and the crowd of strange-looking people around him.

He panicked.

Howell seized the old man's shoulders and began shaking him. The old man dropped his crutch, broke Howell's grip, and sprinted, limp-free, out the door. Howell picked up the crutch, and wielding it like a club, began swinging it widely at the people around him.

Someone yelled, "SECURITY!"

An alarm sounded.

Three security guards appeared and it took all of them to subdue Howell.

Although things hadn't turned out exactly as he had planned, Marty was satisfied his charge would finally receive proper medical attention, and he quickly exited the building.

He took side streets in case the police were looking for him after he had caused yet another commotion at the hospital. He couldn't take public transportation because he had given the last of his money to the old man. So he hiked over to the Civic Center Plaza where he spent the day lost among the other homeless.

It was late afternoon when Marty arrived at the library. He was starving and anxious to get to the shelter. It was Wednesday and that meant St. Andrews would be serving spaghetti, his favorite.

Pete, sitting at their usual table, was coughing into the afternoon edition of the newspaper.

"What's new, Pete?"

Pete looked up. His eyes were red and watery. His nose was running. Without saying a word he shoved the front page at Marty.

PLANE CRASH VICTIM SURFACES

San Francisco - Cytex president, Jason Howell, battled his way free from his captors this morning. Howell, 39, a highly-regarded businessman, was a passenger on the small plane that crashed in Golden Gate Park Monday evening.

A police source close to the investigation said Howell was removed from the wreck and kidnapped by a band of homeless guerrillas. One of the alleged kidnappers, Louis Sykes, a Vietnam veteran, was killed when the plane exploded.

The source added that the rebels appear to be retaliating for Project Vector, Mayor Babcock's controversial solution to the homeless problem. Jason Howell is known for his support of the mayor.

The victim was constantly moved in an effort to thwart authorities who began searching for him when they determined that the businessman was not on the plane when it burned.

This morning, police interrogated the homeless in Golden Gate Park, while Recreation and Park Department bulldozers leveled illegal encampments.

"Because of intense police pressure," said the source, "the renegades hid Howell in the crowded waiting room of City General. They forced him to wear homeless clothing and a bandage around his head.

"After one of the kidnappers—a big, bearded man in a green parka—stepped away for a moment, Howell grabbed a crutch and attacked a second kidnapper, who fled from the hospital."

Howell is said to be in fair condition, and has been transferred uptown to the University Medical Center for treatment.

Meanwhile, a set of fingerprints taken from the bogus bandage is being analyzed by the FBI. Citizens are asked to report all suspicious homeless to the police.

Marty's eyes grew wide as he read. He dropped the paper and leaned on the table. The color had drained from his face.

"Good work, Marty," Pete sniffled.

Part II

THE GOLDEN FLEECE

FIVE
Wednesday, January 11
Early Evening

1

REPORTERS AND PHOTOGRAPHERS scurried around the University Medical Center, obstructing operations, trying to scoop each other over the Howell kidnapping story. The hospital's director considered fumigating the building, but the extra security guards he was forced to hire had already decimated his budget.

At 5:00 p.m. Greg Thompson emerged from the elevator on the fourth floor and was immediately intercepted by a beefy guard. "I have an appointment with Dr. Sorensen," Greg announced as he held up his driver's license. Although he tried to sound authoritative, he hadn't slept much and his voice squeaked.

The guard eyed the license suspiciously and ran a thick yellow fingernail down a clipboard. Then he escorted Greg to a small conference room, unlocked the door, and stood outside with his arms folded. Greg felt like he was being held captive.

By pulling strings with the hospital's director, Cytex Chairman Albert Simpson III had arranged for Greg to meet with Howell's neurologist. Greg's assignment was to get a detailed prognosis and call Simpson later.

Greg looked around the windowless room. A bookcase of medical texts occupied one wall, a blackboard another. Hanging on other walls were brightly-colored charts showing human organs in various degrees of dissection. He took a chair at a conference table. The centerpiece was a human brain floating in a bell jar.

Greg averted his eyes to a clock above the door. He watched the second hand sweep around, unable to fathom that only two days had passed since Jason Howell's plane had crashed.

Suddenly the door flew open and a tall, broadshouldered man in an Armani suit brushed past the guard. He carried himself with an air of supreme self-confidence. "I don't give a damn if I'm not on your list," he said.

The guard started to object, but backed off.

"And who are you?" the visitor demanded of Greg as he abruptly closed the door on the guard.

"Greg Thompson. I work with Jason . . . uh, Mr. Howell."

"I'm Anton Howell, Jason's brother. What do you know about his condition?"

"Nothing yet, but the doctor should be here shortly."

Anton took a seat across the table and stared at Greg. His eyes, instead of blue like his brother's, matched the opalescent gray of his suit. He was taller, too, and broader at the shoulders. But in every other way he was unmistakably a Howell.

He can see inside me, Greg thought, shuddering.

"Tell me what my brother has been doing these days," Anton finally said. It was more of an order than a request.

Greg had unconsciously melted into his seat. He now sat up, relieved to have the silence broken. "Under your brother's leadership, our company, Cytex, has developed a way to create incredibly realistic 3-D simulations."

Anton's eyes watched Greg.

"And if we meet our price goal," Greg volunteered, "anyone could afford our product. It's called C-REAL. It's essentially a box that turns a personal computer into a powerful virtual reality system."

"For what purpose?"

Greg pointed at the pickled brain. "For example, one of our virtual reality systems could replace this crude teaching tool with life-like images that are projected inside a wrap-around visor. Brain surgeons could practice the latest procedures as if they were operating on a live patient. We can even shrink a cybersurgeon and insert him into the brain."

Anton's face showed no reaction.

"It really does work," Greg said, trying to assure himself as much as Anton. "C-REAL could raise the standard of medical care to a much higher level. And its applications aren't limited to medicine. The same imaging techniques can be employed in other disciplines. But we need the financial resources and marketing clout of a large parent company to take advantage of the opportunities. Cytex is too small."

"Who does my brother have lined up?"

"A Swiss company called I-Cubed . . . ." As soon as the words left his mouth, Greg realized he had gone too far. This was highly confidential information. *But he's Jason's brother,* Greg rationalized.

Anton shifted the subject. "How would your invention fit into my business? I'm a commercial real estate syndicator."

Greg exhaled. "Virtual reality could be used during the project's design phase. With the appropriate applications software, you can take a prospective buyer on a walk-through as if the project already existed. It would make for a more informed purchase."

"Oh really? Now I'm not so sure your gadget is such a good idea. When it comes to real estate, there's nothing worse for the seller than an informed buyer."

The door opened and a gray-haired doctor walked in. "I didn't expect two gentlemen," he said.

Greg jumped up. "I'm Greg Thompson," he said, pumping the doctor's hand. "And this is Anton Howell, your patient's brother."

The doctor turned to Anton. "I'm Dr. John Sorensen, the chief neurologist here."

Anton remained seated. "Tell me about my brother," he said, getting right to the point.

"He's doing remarkably well considering all he's been through. We've given him a CAT scan and a battery of other neurological tests, and the results are encouraging."

"Good."

"But your brother received a trauma to the side of his head, just above his left temple, causing a hairline fracture and cerebral edema of the parietal and frontal lobes of the brain." Dr. Sorensen pulled out a pen and tapped on the jar. "He also had some hemorrhaging about here. But it was short-lived and surgical intervention is not required. The hairline fracture is healing nicely on its own."

"Good."

"Of greater concern to me is the edema, or swelling, which has been exerting pressure on the right side of his brain over here." Dr. Sorensen moved the pen around and tapped the other side of the jar. "I'm treating him with dexamethasone, an anti-inflammatory."

"What's his condition?" Anton asked.

"Because of the crossover effect of brain signals, the injury to his left temple has caused right-side weakness in his face, his arm, and his leg. He's aphasic, meaning he's having some communication difficulties, and he's suffering from post-traumatic amnesia, meaning he has no memory of his two days on the street."

"From what I've read, he didn't miss much," Anton remarked dryly.

"On the other hand," Dr. Sorensen continued, "his memory of events prior to the accident appears to be intact, and his speech has already improved since his transfer from City General this morning. But he's still somewhat disoriented."

"Is he going to be all right?" Greg asked anxiously.

The doctor turned to Greg. "If you're asking if he'll return to the man he was before his injury, I can't answer that; only time will tell. The effects of a head injury sometimes manifest themselves weeks or months after the trauma. For example, he may have periodic headaches or develop epilepsy. Then there are a host of psychological issues that are out of my area of expertise."

Anton wasn't buying. "Tell me your experience with other patients."

Sorensen returned to Anton. "Mr. Howell, your brother nearly died in a plane crash. Putting aside his severe head trauma, any individual who undergoes a near-death experience can develop personality disorders. I've seen some patients struggle with depression, some become zealots for one cause or another, and some who aren't affected at all. Again, only time will tell. At the moment, all that is medically certain—assuming there are no serious setbacks—is several weeks of physical therapy."

"When can I see him?" Anton asked.

"Perhaps on Friday. Because of his disorientation and communication difficulties, he's declining visitors at the moment. I must respect that. But I can assure you he's comfortable and looks remarkably fit. Whoever cared for him did a reasonably good job."

2

AT LES MOULES, the Pachelbel *Canon* played softly in the background. Mayor Babcock was in good spirits. His plan was to end the day with a fine meal of *Lievrè aux Choux*, complemented by a fine bottle of *St. Emillion*.

"Howell's kidnapping turned out to be a blessing," the mayor said to Chief Conti. "With the populace afraid that a militant group of homeless are roaming the streets of San Francisco, Project Vector has garnered tremendous popular support. My liberal critics have crawled back into their holes. Here's to my victory in November." Crystal clinked and a sip of ruby red *St. Emillion* flowed into the mayor's grinning mouth.

The chief shifted nervously. "Walt, the kidnapping is a crock."

Mayor Babcock's grin evaporated. "What?"

"It's bogus. I had a feeling that Brodsky was barking up the wrong tree, so I personally questioned the hospital's receptionist and she said that a large, bearded transient was trying to get medical attention for Howell. Although the transient used an alias for himself and Howell when he registered, his motives were well-intentioned."

Babcock set his wine glass down. "Damn it, Rudy, if the public learns our kidnapper was a Good Samaritan, I'll look foolish. Why is this Brodsky character on the case?"

"Although he swaggers around, the man has a reputation as a hardworking cop. He's put a lot of felons away. But his obnoxious personality has kept him from advancing beyond his present rank. And like a lot of cops stuck in a rut, he's looking for that one big break and the concomitant publicity to pull himself out. However, the homeless aspect of the case is throwing him. He hates beggars."

"Hmmm," the mayor said absently, sitting back and pressing his fingertips together. "Suppose we allow Brodsky to continue looking for his rebel band? But he never finds them because POOF!"—Babcock gestured widely with his hands—"they've disappeared into the faceless mass of homeless humanity. Meanwhile I'll continue to build popular support for Project Vector. Of course, we'll need Howell's cooperation."

"Not necessarily," the chief said. "I called his treating physician to set a time for an interview. The doctor said there was no rush since his patient can't recall what happened. His memory of those two days on the street is wiped out. It could be weeks before he remembers, if ever."

"Ah, amnesia . . . that's wonderful," the mayor said, his grin returning. "Things might work out after all. And even if Howell eventually remembers what happened, he probably won't talk to the press. He's only interested in doing deals and making money. Unlike that self-aggrandizing inspector of yours, Howell avoids media attention except when it suits his purposes. But just to be on the safe side, I'll call him to enlist his cooperation. Naturally, it'll cost me political capital, but it'll be worth it."

Conti looked worried. "Walt, even if you get Howell's cooperation, sooner or later the truth will surface."

Babcock's eyes twinkled. "That's precisely why you must give your man Brodsky free reign in the investigation. Let him talk to the media as much as he wants. Make him think he'll get all the credit when he breaks the case. That way when the story blows up—"

"—he'll get all the blame," the chief smiled, clinking glasses with the mayor.

3

COLD EVENING FOG swarmed around the rusty VW van. It was parked on a street of tents and frail plywood shacks. In the amber glow of the streetlights, the hodge-podge of crude shelters made this forgotten section of China Basin look like time had warped back to the Great Depression.

Inside the van, Marty and Pete were finishing a couple of deviled ham sandwiches, a meager dinner that con-sumed all the change Pete had in his pocket when they ducked out of the library.

William Randolf Jefferson, a sinewy African Ameri-can, was making coffee on a camping stove. He had rigged it with a metal hood that vented the fumes through a hole cut into the van's roof. An oversized orange tabby napped on the driver's seat.

"So you helped this rich dude and now the whole city is looking for you?" Willie asked, adjusting the flame un-der a red kettle.

"That's about the size of it," Marty said.

"It's a fucking disaster," Pete added.

"Well, it's kinda cramped in here, but you're welcome to stay with me and Shoo," Willie said, nodding at the cat. "The cops don't hassle us in the Basin because we're not in the open and we don't bother no one. And in the adjacent neighborhood there's the baseball stadium, the yacht har-bor, Multimedia Gulch, and new condos going up all the time. On a clear day we even got a view of the skyline."

"And there ain't no Stan," Pete added, blowing his nose into a paper napkin.

"Where did you get that monster cat, Willie?" Marty asked. "I've never seen one that big."

"Ol' Shoo? I didn't get him—he got *me*. One day, a couple of years ago, I was sitting here in the back of the van, reading. I hear this loud crash, like someone dropped a brick on the roof. So I go to the front and roll down the window and this big ball of orange fur jumps in and flies past my face. He acts like he owns the place. I say, 'Shoo! Shoo!' and he promptly climbs in my lap and starts purring." Willie looked at the cat and grinned. "We've been a team ever since."

"How do you feed yourselves?" Marty asked.

"I'm a Redeemer."

"You scrounge for empties?" Pete asked.

"Uh-huh. Without us Redeemers, the recycling system wouldn't work. In a good week, I can make a hundred bucks. There's an unlimited supply of beer cans and wine bottles in the trash bins around the yacht harbor."

"I'll bet," Pete said.

"For extra money, I fix cars on the street," Willie added, nodding at a tool box in the back of the van. "I'm pretty good at it, too."

The three men sat in silence, waiting for the coffee to brew. Then Marty said, "Willie, I really appreciate you taking us in. We're desperate."

"Don't mention it. After all, you guys welcomed me into The Club."

"I wish we could've gone there," Marty said. "But we can't risk it."

"What are the chances the cops will make you?" Willie asked, pouring coffee into three metal cups.

"I don't know. Since me and Pete don't have police records, any fingerprints they get won't do them any good unless they catch us. And they don't have Pete's description. He wisely refused to go to the hospital. As for me, all I can do is shave my beard, get a haircut, and change my clothes. There's not much I can do about my size."

Pete warmed his hands on his cup. "That's all fine and dandy, Marty, but I reckon we can't stay in this damn van forever. We got to get that money we was saving for our apartment. Right now we got less than them people in the plaza." Pete stared at his shoes.

"You're right," Marty said. "That money gets us out of town. Look, I have an idea—Willie, what time is it?"

Willie squinted at his watch. "About six."

"If you hurry, you might get into St. Andrews to-night—"

"—yeah," Pete interrupted, "suddenly there's a couple of vacancies."

"Pete will give you the combination to his locker," Marty continued. "There's about two hundred bucks in a sock. After breakfast tomorrow morning, bring the money and our clothes back here."

"How will I get into St. Andrews?" Willie asked.

"I'll give you a note for the staff. I've done it before. It'll say Pete and I have to work late for the next couple of days. Take Doc with you."

"We'll pay you for your time," Pete said.

"Okay, I'll do it, but I won't take any of your money. You guys are going to need all of it. Anyway, a night in a warm shelter is reward enough. What's for dinner?"

"Spaghetti," Marty said sullenly.

Pete hung his head and Marty put a hand on his friend's shoulder. "Okay, maybe I was dumb to try and help Happy—I mean Howell—but we didn't do anything wrong. Maybe he'll remember we didn't kidnap him and things will go back to the way they were." Marty tried to sound cheerful. "In the future I'll be more careful with money, and before you know it we'll have our own place. I promise."

"Ha!" Pete said without looking up.

4

THE LOUDSPEAKER STIRRED Jason Howell from a light sleep. He slowly raised himself on his elbows and looked around. He saw a window, a bathroom door, a closet, a television on the wall. Nothing registered at first, and having to associate each object with a name was a slow process. After a time, he remembered he was in a hospital.

He thought hard and recalled that a doctor had told him he had been in an airplane accident, and that unknown street people had pulled him out of the wreckage and hid him in a crude kidnapping attempt. The media wanted to interview him, but hospital security would ensure he got his rest.

He found the TV control on the side of his bed. On the Six O'clock News a reporter was standing in front of a cement alcove with a helicopter hovering overhead. The camera switched inside where a cop in full dress uniform was giving an interview. Other cops, in riot gear, were standing at attention, legs spread apart, holding riot batons.

The cop being interviewed boasted how he tricked a vagrant into leading him to the lair of the kidnappers of Jason Howell. At the bottom of the screen a label identified him as "Inspector James Brodsky, SFPD." As he talked, the inspector tossed a bedroll into a fire raging in a fifty-gallon drum.

That place seems familiar, Jason thought.

The camera panned to a dozen homeless people in handcuffs. It zoomed in on one of them, a ponytailed man in fatigues. He was smirking.

That man seems familiar, too.

Maybe I was kidnapped, Jason thought, but somehow it doesn't feel right. The program went to a commercial break and he clicked the TV off.

Jason lay back on his pillow. He placed his hands behind his head, closed his eyes, and tried to remember. But his last clear recollection was of a beautiful meadow, high on a hill. After that there were only fragmented images, some frightening, some pleasant.

The door to Jason's room opened and the nurse walked in. "Your wife is here," she announced smiling.

Jason snapped his eyes open. He suddenly experienced the same disoriented feeling he had when he found himself at a welfare hospital with no idea how he got there. *Wife? I don't remember being married. I must be worse off than I realized . . .*

The nurse stepped aside and a strikingly beautiful red-head in a smartly-tailored business suit walked toward him.

. . . or perhaps better, he thought, as the draft of the open door advanced her perfume. He raised himself on his elbows as she approached.

"Hello, darling, you're looking well," she said warmly, her green eyes sparkling. She turned to watch the nurse leave the room.

"Shame . . . to you," Jason said through the left side of his mouth. "How did you get pasht . . . shecurity?"

"Mostly with a wink and a smile. But it doesn't hurt that my driver's license says 'Howell' as in 'Elizabeth.' But please call me Liz."

Jason concentrated for a moment. "You're . . . ah, the shister-in-law I never met. Shorry I didn't attend your wedding."

"You weren't invited."

"That's true. But I wouldn't have gone anyway. The lasht time I shaw Anton was at Uncle Matt's funeral. Let's shee, if memory sherves me . . . actually, it's not working too well at the moment . . . that was fifteen years ago. You could shay my brother and I aren't close."

"Well, people change," Liz said, pulling a chair up to his bed. "Anton is very concerned about you. As we speak he's somewhere in the hospital getting word on your condition. I came directly from work. I couldn't locate him, so I decided to see for myself how you were doing."

"Ashide from ventilating my brain," Jason said, pointing to his bandaged head, "I'm doing okay . . . although I'm having shome trouble shaying the 'esh' shound."

"I think you're shaying the 'esh' shound jusht fine."

Jason smiled crookedly, holding Liz's eyes for a second. Then he said, "What have you heard about my . . . kidnapping?"

"Just what's on the radio. A commentator said this is the first time the homeless have organized and become militant. He said it's because they're tired of being pushed around. Residents are worried. The mayor made a speech promising to increase Project Vector patrols. But, frankly, the whole business sounds ridiculous—"

The door opened, held by a doctor saying something to a nurse.

"I'd better not press my luck," she whispered, abruptly standing. "I'll return with Anton. The two of you should take this opportunity to reconcile. I understand that he and I are the only family you have."

"You're right, Liz. I'm lucky to be here and I shuppose I should make the mosht of it."

SIX
Thursday, January 12

1

THE NEWSPAPER'S FORECAST of early clearing was grossly optimistic. It was late morning, and China Basin was still engulfed in a thick, gray shroud. The streets were quiet except for an occasional profanity emanating from Willie's VW van.

"O-OUCH!" Marty yelled. "GODDAMN-IT! Take it easy Pete! You don't have to pull my hairs out one-by-one!" Pete was sawing off Marty's hair with a dull knife he had found in Willie's toolbox.

"Serves you right!" Pete shot back. "Everything about you is thick—your hair, your neck, your brains. Anyways, cool your jets, I'm about finished. With the change of clothes Willie's bringing and this new doo, you won't be recognized. You look like the horse's patoot."

Shoo, curled like a giant caterpillar on the driver's seat, interrupted his perpetual nap and looked at Marty with a critical eye.

"Thanks a—" Marty began.

"Wait," Pete said, staring out the windshield. "There's a cop car headed this way."

"Oh, no," Marty said, slinking down. "Does this heap run? Did Willie leave us the keys?"

Pete shrugged.

The cruiser was only half a block away.

"Let's scram," Marty said. "We'll hide in one of the shacks." Staying low, he cracked the van's side door.

Pete didn't move. "You go, Marty. My tank's running on empty."

The big man stopped. "I'm not leaving without you." Marty tugged at his friend's arm while stealing a glance outside. The patrol car, now directly across the street, had a lightening bolt insignia on the door. The driver was talking on the radio while his partner was idly sipping coffee out of a paper cup.

"Okay, this one last time," Pete said wanly.

The men hustled out the side of the VW and ducked into a plywood shanty that was propped against the wall of an abandoned warehouse. Pete sat cross-legged on a stained mattress at the rear of shanty. Marty knelt and peered out of the plastic garbage bag that someone had draped over the opening.

The driver got out and walked around the VW.

Shoo jumped out of the van and scrambled into the shanty, rubbing against Marty's leg. "W-H-A-A-H!" he meowed loudly. Marty scooped up the huge tabby and held him to his chest. "M-r-r-r-r," Shoo purred.

The cop momentarily looked in the direction of the shanty, and then turned his attention back to the van. After inspecting it, he slid the door closed and spoke into his belt radio.

A few minutes later a yellow tow truck turned onto the street, its lights flashing as it backed up to the VW. Marty cursed under his breath as the van was hoisted. "They're towing it," he announced in a loud whisper.

"It figures," Pete said. "How much is it gonna cost to get it back?"

Marty released the makeshift curtain and sagged onto the cement floor. "All of our money," he said, hugging Shoo. "All of our money."

2

JASON WAS DOING slow hospital time, watching the evening news as reporters interviewed shoppers, the homeless, the police, and each other in a desperate attempt to keep the kidnapping story alive. Earlier, on a talk show, a psychologist profiled the typical homeless kidnapper, blaming childhood abuse, alcoholic parents, and the absence of family values. But without a victim to interview, additional crimes by homeless terrorists, or suspects in custody, Jason knew his story would eventually fade.

He felt markedly better today. Although his body was still sore, his speech had improved and he was thinking more clearly. He hadn't shaved since the accident, and he decided to let his stubble grow into a beard to make it more difficult for the media to recognize him after he went home from the hospital.

He even took a phone call from Mayor Babcock. The mayor began with gratuitous small talk and good wishes before getting to the point: "I understand you can't identify your kidnappers, so I've instructed the police not to pester you. But I assure you that Chief Conti and I are doing everything possible to bring these criminals to justice. In the meantime, if you remember anything—*anything at all*—please contact me or the chief directly."

"Sure, Walt," Jason said, waiting for the mayor to reveal his hidden agenda.

"And one more thing . . ."

Here it comes.

". . . this situation is politically sensitive for me, and I would consider it a personal favor if you refrain from talking to the media."

"Of course, Walt."

"Good, good," the mayor said, his voice smiling. "So Jason, when you're feeling up to it, let's have another one of our fabulous dinners at Les Moules. I'll treat this time."

"Sure, Walt."

After the mayor hung up, Jason's mood turned melancholy. Although he had returned to the same world of cross-purposes and political intrigue, he felt he was no longer the same Jason Howell. Something had changed him during his two lost days. But the only thing he knew for certain was that he hadn't been kidnapped: his conversation with Babcock convinced him of that.

He reclined and closed his eyes, attempting again to remember what had happened to him. He could see the meadow clearly, but beyond it was an impenetrable black curtain. Drained, he allowed himself to drift backward, toward familiar memories at the edge of dream-sleep . . .

. . . he was at Cytex, preparing for a trip into the virtual stomach. But when he activated C-REAL, he found himself in a treeless valley bordered by undulating foothills. He pushed on the forceball and glided above the valley floor until he reached the taller hills. He was about to turn and go the other way when music floated down. It was Jim Morrison and The Doors singing "Light My Fire." Curious, he pulled on the forceball and floated up. At the top of the highest hill he found himself over a meadow that sloped gently to a ridge line. It was the land Bill Hender-

son had shown him, except it had a magnificent Spanish-style house set among the trees below the ridge line. Between twin oaks, a hammock swayed gently in the breeze. Through the kitchen window, a woman was preparing a meal. On the meadow, a Dalmatian puppy chased butterflies. The scene mesmerized Jason: it didn't seem like a virtual world; it seemed real. Even more unsettling was his feeling that he belonged here with the woman, the hammock, and the puppy. He was about to descend toward the house, to see the woman's face, when the music became mixed with a cacophony of human voices, calling out and drawing him to the other side of the hill. He pushed on the forceball and glided over the ridge line. Stretching before him was a rocky plateau. The sound was emanating from a large circular pit in front of him. Smoke drifted from the opening. Cautiously, he approached the edge and looked down. Fifty feet below, surrounded by sheer walls, were dozens of people in shabby clothing. Some were tossing wood into a bonfire and singing, while others sat alone, crying out for help, their voices echoing against the walls. A few were attempting to claw their way up the impossibly steep sides of their prison. The stench of smoke nearly overwhelmed Jason, and he tugged on the forceball to retreat back to the meadow. But the control wouldn't respond! He was being drawn over the edge. Then he remembered the visor. Stay calm, he told himself, it's not real. Simply remove the visor and you'll be back at Cytex. He grabbed at the visor, but it was gone! Down he tumbled into the pit, faster and faster, catching glimpses of sky, walls, fire, people. He was going to hit the ground! He squeezed his eyes shut. But the impact never came; his fall had somehow been cushioned. Opening his eyes, he found himself in the outstretched arms of a big bearded man with long brown hair and hazel eyes. "Welcome back to our world," he said . . .

"Welcome back to our world," echoed a deep baritone.

Jason woke with a start.

Anton was standing over him, smiling.

"Oh . . . hello, Anton," Jason said, sitting up and holding his bandaged head. "I-I just had the strangest dream. I was operating my company's product, and I was drawn into a pit of homeless people."

"Your man, Greg Thompson, told me about C-REAL and its many uses. But I think the homeless pit is one application you ought to skip."

Jason rubbed his eyes. "I didn't expect any visitors until tomorrow. Doctor Sorensen said—"

"Never mind him. A reliable source told me that you have already been visited by a complete stranger so I didn't think you would object to seeing your own brother."

"Stranger no more," Liz Howell said, stepping up from behind Anton. "Hi, Jason," she smiled. "You're sounding much better today. Did they say when you'll be going home?"

"Sunday, although I'd like to stay another week to give the media more time to lose interest in me. But they need this room for the next high-profile kidnap victim."

Anton put his arm around his wife. "Liz and I would like you to stay with us. After hospital food, I'm sure you would appreciate some home cooking." Anton winked at his wife. "Of course Liz can't cook worth a damn, but she knows this restaurant where they'll box up a fine 'home-cooked' meal for us. Stay as long as you like. We have plenty of room, and it would give you and me an opportunity to get reacquainted. If you go directly home, you won't get any rest. The media will camp by your door."

Liz smiled encouragingly.

Jason briefly considered the offer. "It's a deal."

SEVEN
Friday, January 13

1

A DRIZZLY DAWN DESCENDED on the Civic Center Plaza. Marty watched City Hall develop slowly against the sky like a Polaroid photo. This was the first time he had studied the granite and marble masterpiece. The golden dome over the Great Rotunda was embellished with statuary and surrounded by a wrought-iron balcony. The ornate windows were framed by tall columns. They reminded Marty of the bars of a jail cell.

He gazed at the front entrance of the building. Above the door a large banner was draped. In large blue letters it proclaimed:

SAN FRANCISCO—World's #1 Best Destination

Marty sighed. He wanted to share the irony, but his friend was finally asleep, pressed against the big man's chest for warmth. This was Pete's first chance to catch some shut-eye since yesterday morning, when Willie's van

was towed.   Shortly afterwards, the shanty's owner returned and Marty and Pete had no other choice but to hide
in the Civic Center Plaza. The bench they now occupied
was a mere twenty yards from the mayor's office. Another
irony.

Although Marty was exhausted, sleep had been impossible. His muscles were cramped from sitting in one position all night, and his face and neck itched badly from a
nasty red rash he got from shaving his beard at a service
station.   Marty didn't dare scratch with Pete sleeping
soundly. Instead he gnashed his teeth and distracted himself by looking around. The plaza was strewn with litter
and sleeping bodies. The more fortunate were sheltered
under blue tarps secured to the limbs of gnarled, leafless
trees; others were curled in sleeping bags or sandwiched
between large pieces of cardboard. To his right he saw the
outline of a body under a soiled quilt. Next to the sleeper
were two shopping carts brimming with clothing, empty
bottles, and whatnot. A beat-up bicycle, its tires nearly
flat, leaned haphazardly against one of the carts.

Marty knew that the Civic Center was one of the most
dangerous places in San Francisco. He wondered how the
sleeper managed to keep his stuff from being stolen. Another glance and he knew: Under the quilt was a large dog,
with only its scarred white rump sticking out. The dog
seemed to be mocking Marty and the other humans in the
plaza.

Since no one was stirring at the moment, Marty decided it was probably safe to close his eyes for a few minutes. He immediately succumbed to sleep.

    . . . the blond cheerleader waved to him from the side-
line. He nodded confidently to her as he assumed his
stance behind the quarterback. The stadium was on its
feet. It was the fourth down, four yards to the goal line,

ten seconds remaining in the game. His team needed a touchdown to win, and it would all come down to him. In the huddle the quarterback had called a straight-ahead power play out of the 'I' formation. As fullback, he would plow through the hole created by his lead blocks and blow the defenders away. He took a deep breath and bit down on his mouthpiece. His massive body was a deadly machine. Adrenaline surged and muscles screamed. Nothing could stop him now. The center hiked, and the quarterback handed him the football. In a smooth and practiced motion he tucked it under his arm, squared his shoulders, and found the hole. Just then a thick cloud of yellow jackets swarmed around his helmet, buzzing with incredible ferocity, attacking his eyes, ripping at his nerve endings like a thousand chalks screeching on a blackboard. The ball slid out of his hands. He fumbled! The crowd groaned. His team members shook their heads in disgust. The cheerleader put her head down. He fell to his knees, swatting at the dark cloud and the buzzing, the relentless buzzing . . .

Marty jerked awake.

A squad of twelve leaf blowers was advancing behind a huge wall of dust and debris. Pete abruptly sat up, and he and Marty were forced to bury their faces in their hands. Even through the earsplitting noise, Marty could hear Pete's hacking cough.

After the blowers passed, Marty wiped dirt from his eyes and looked at Pete. A trickle of blood oozed from his friend's mouth. Marty looked at his chest where Pete had been resting his head. There was a large blood stain.

Pete stopped coughing and slouched on the bench, his head flopped back in exhaustion, his eyes lidded and glazed, his breathing labored. Even in the monochromatic light, even with his friend's face caked with dirt, Marty detected a bluish cast.

It was decision time.

"Pete, you've *got* to go to the hospital."

Pete made a gurgling sound.

"C'mon Pete, we need to get you mended," Marty said, putting a hand on his friend's shoulder.

"No, they'll arrest you—you're wearing the same clothes." Pete's voice was barely audible.

"They won't get me because I'm not going with you. While the hospital's fixing you up, I'll get fresh clothes and visit. Hey, I'll wear a goddamn dress if I have to." Marty forced a smile.

"Something in green would be nice," Pete said, chuckling at the image of the big man in drag. That started another fit of coughing, and more red spittle oozed from his mouth.

Marty dabbed at it with his sleeve. "I'm going to call an ambulance now."

"Don't leave me alone," Pete pleaded. "I'm scared." A tear squeezed out and rolled a track in his grimy face. His breathing was rapid and shallow.

"You'll be okay, buddy."

Pete grabbed the big man's parka. "Marty, I'm scared I'm gonna die . . . without ever being happy."

Marty patted his hand. "You're not going to die. And of course you've been happy. What about all the good times we had at The Club?"

"Before Stan?"

"Okay, yeah, before Stan."

Pete took a painful breath. "You wanna know a major truth?"

"Sure."

"Even before I lost my home I never had nobody."

"What about all those babes you said you dated?"

"I lied."

"Well, it doesn't really matter because we're still going to get our own place, and then you can have lots of babes. When you're better we'll head south and live in Hollywood."

"Where we gonna get that kind of money?"

"I'll visit Howell and tell him what really happened— how we saved his life. He'll be grateful and we'll get a fat reward."

"But what if he ain't grateful?" Pete said shivering.

"Then I'll *really* kidnap him. I've got nothing to lose."

Pete laughed and started coughing again. Then pain contorted his face, and he closed his eyes.

Marty quickly stood and looked around for someone to watch his friend while he called 911. Across a spotty patch of lawn, an elderly black woman was sitting on the ground with her back against a wall. Two shopping bags lay on the ground next to her, and a yellow hat rested on her lap.

Marty approached. "How are you doing, Kate?"

The old woman looked up. "Marty? That you? You shave or somethin'? You got a haircut?"

Thank God she's having a good day. Marty kneeled on one knee. "Listen, Kate, Pete's over there on that bench. He's not feeling well. Would you keep him company while I make a phone call?"

"Sure, I'll sit with him. Bring back some coffee, hon'—I take lots o' cream an' sugar."

"Sure." Marty stood and hurried back to the bench while Kate gathered her shopping bags. Pete's eyes were closed. "Kate's going to stay with you," Marty said softly.

His friend didn't respond.

Marty gently shook him. "Pete?"

Pete opened his eyes and blinked. "What's today's date?"

Marty scratched his neck. "Ah, Friday the thirteenth."

Pete managed a weak smile. "It figures. That would be the day I wind up with Kate." He was breathing a little easier now and a bit of color had returned to his face.

Marty squeezed Pete's shoulder. "I'll be back before you know it."

Pete reached for Marty's arm. "I love you."

"Hey, I love you too," Marty managed. He bit his lip and turned away, walking briskly toward City Hall. He went through security at the front door and found an empty phone booth. Clearing his throat, he dialed 911. In his most sophisticated voice he told the dispatcher his name was Bill Taft, president of the Chamber of Commerce of Cincinnati, Ohio. He was calling to report a seriously ill man on a bench across from the mayor's office at City Hall. The poor soul was having difficulty breathing. He was going to wait with the man until medical assistance arrived, and he expected such help would be immediately forthcoming. He didn't want to be delayed for his morning business meeting with the mayor.

The dispatcher assured Mr. Taft that the paramedics were on their way.

Next, Marty went downstairs to the men's room, used the toilet and washed up, gingerly patting the rash on his face with cold water. Afterward he stood in the hallway and panhandled spare change from a tall, middle-aged man in a finely-tailored suit. Although the man initially hesitated, he quickly changed his mind and dug deeply into his pockets. On his first try, Marty had coffee money for him and Kate.

Marty figured he had been inside for fifteen minutes. He paused at the main entrance holding two containers of coffee and scanned the plaza. The ambulance had arrived and had already loaded Pete. Bystanders were milling about. A police car, its lights flashing, was blocking the street. A cop was diverting traffic. Marty watched the paramedics close the rear doors and drive off.

Good, Pete was on his way.

After a few more minutes the police cleared out, and Marty went back to the bench where Kate was sitting. She was hugging herself, looking at the ground.

"Thanks for staying with Pete," Marty said. "Here's your coffee. Lot of cream and sugar."

"They took him away," Kate said, ignoring the coffee.

"Yeah, I saw. Is he going to City General?"

Kate looked up at Marty and shook her head. Her face was a mix of grief and pain. "He's goin' to the morgue. He jus' up an' died in my arms. He was callin' out for you—"

"NO!" Marty screamed.

Something cold and hard gripped Marty's heart, squeezing it mercilessly.

"NO!"

Both coffee cups crashed to the ground.

Marty shook his fists at the sky and turned toward City Hall, toward the mayor's office. He raced across the street, oblivious to the horns blaring and the cars screeching to a halt. In his mind he was back in college, running on an open football field. Nothing was going to stop him. He took the front steps two at a time. As he approached the security station, a guard hurriedly drew his gun and stepped in front of Marty. "YOU! STOP! STOP!"

Marty lowered his head and raged forward, knocking the deputy aside as if he were shrugging off a rookie lineman.

2

"THE MAYOR, he's tryin' to kill us, one-by-one," an agitated woman was telling a reporter on the noon news. Her bright yellow hat sat askew on her head. Jason propped himself up in bed and stared at the screen.

Damn, she looks familiar.

" . . . and when this fella died in my arms 'cause he ain't got no home, his friend went to complain to the mayor. We's citizens too;"—her voice was rising—"we got a right to see The Man. Then the goons shot him in the chest! You shoulda seen the blood! We ain't animals, you damn fools!" she shouted.

The scene abruptly shifted to a second reporter on the front steps of City Hall. "That was an eyewitness account of how a homeless man, upset over the death of his friend, tried to force his way through the security station at City Hall. Police say, however, he had no weapon, and although a deputy sheriff was knocked down, no one was injured. The homeless man was taken into cust—"

Jason clicked the TV off. He could no longer watch such news stories with dispassionate eyes; he could no longer think of these people simply as by-products of modern society, a nuisance like barnacles on a ship.

There was a knock on the door and Greg Thompson walked in. "How are you feeling?" he asked.

Jason welcomed the diversion. "Better. What's happening at Cytex?"

"The I-Cubed demo was an unqualified success." Greg went on to describe how Chairman Simpson believed the merger prospects with I-Cubed were excellent—especially now that Jason Howell was back at the helm. Then he told his boss that the Swiss had set a tough precondition.

"Yes?"

"We must price C-REAL at a thousand dollars."

"Did you agree?"

"Simpson did. Without you we were negotiating from a position of weakness. So the decision was made to send manufacturing bid packages to subs in Korea, Taiwan, and Singapore. We're in a holding pattern for the next two weeks while we wait for their replies. This may be a good time for you to get away."

"That's what I was thinking. Have Cytex issue a press release tomorrow."

"Where are you off to?"

Jason rubbed his stubble. "South America."

EIGHT
Saturday, January 14

1

MARTY LAY FLAT on his back, slowly stirring out of a drugged, deathlike sleep. His tongue felt heavy. His eyelids felt heavy. Even his chopped-up hair felt heavy.

His first thought was that he had been abducted by aliens and transported to a world where the pull of gravity was stronger than normal.

He didn't care.

And although he heard birds chirping in the distance and sensed bright sunlight around him, he had no desire to open his eyes.

Then he flashed on Pete.

The sadness was waiting, coiled in his gut. It exerted immense pressure against his insides, forcing him to turn on his side and curl into the fetal position. His mind ordered tears but his body, too dehydrated, disobeyed.

He opened his eyes and squinted against the shaft of light in his face. He moved his head out of the light and found himself in a small cubicle, barren except for the metal cot on which he was lying. The sunlight came from a barred window across the room.

Marty swung his feet over the side of the cot and stood shakily. His face still itched, and he idly scratched it while he considered his clothing. He was wearing blue-striped pajamas, at least one size too small.

Wincing from his stiff joints, Marty walked over to the window and looked through the bars. He saw a small yard enclosed by a high chain link fence crowned with barbed wire. In the distance, rolling hills were silhouetted against a deep blue sky. From the angle of the sun and the chirping of the birds, he figured it was early morning.

A sudden stomach cramp forced him back to the cot. As he waited for the pain to subside he wondered where he had been jailed. He was obviously in some sort of solitary confinement, but why in the country? That part didn't make sense.

At the door, keys jangled and a lock clicked. A big African American man in street clothes walked in. "How are you feeling?" he asked.

"Cramps," Marty grunted as he sat up.

"Hunger pains, most likely. My name is George. I'll get you over to the cafeteria for breakfast. But first you'll have to get cleaned up." George cocked his head at Marty's ill-fitting pajamas. "Hmmm, it looks like I'll need to find you more suitable clothing. Dr. Argus will be seeing you later this morning, and you'll want to make a good impression."

Dr. Argus? Good impression? Marty was confused. Clearly this wasn't a regular jail. "Ah, where am I?"

"Petaluma State Hospital."

"Is this a . . . mental institution?"

"Actually, we prefer the term 'mental health hospital.'"

"Are you an . . . orderly?"

George shook his head. "This is your first time, isn't it? Well, if you're expecting *One Flew Over the Cuckoo's Nest*, I'm afraid you're going to be disappointed. There are no orderlies, no forced medications. Patients are respected by the staff and have rights under the law. And, if you please, my title is 'Psychiatric Technician.' We consider the term 'orderly' an insult to our profession. If you want to be a permanent guest, all you have to do is call us orderlies. Otherwise, my job, with your cooperation, is to make your stay as beneficial and brief as possible."

George escorted Marty to the showers, after which he was issued extra-large jeans and a flannel shirt. He suspected they came from George's own wardrobe. A satisfying breakfast followed, and George showed him to his regular room. It was painted in a light blue pastel and had art posters on the walls. There was a bookcase filled with paperbacks. Laid out on the bed were a towel, extra underwear, and another flannel shirt.

During breakfast, Marty learned from George this was the Acute Care Unit, a co-ed facility designed to treat patients that were involuntarily admitted to state care under Section 5150 of the California Welfare and Institutions Code. Under the code, he could be held no longer than seventy-two hours. Since he had spent his first twenty-four hours sedated in what the hospital referred to as the "side room," it meant he would be released on Monday, the day after tomorrow.

Marty knew several people who had been "fifty-one-fiftied" after freaking out on the street. Invariably, they were sent to City General's Psycho Ward. But because of the facility's horrendously crowded conditions, the buzz on the street was to take all the meds the doctors prescribed in order to sleep through the ordeal. By contrast, Petaluma was The Ritz. He still wasn't sure why he had been sent here instead of jail. *Maybe they don't know it was me with Jason Howell.*

Marty was free to roam around the ward. He checked out the recreation room, also decorated in pastels. The room had a pool table and a television, which hung high on the wall. A small library was stocked with books and magazines. Near the door, a bulletin board featured a poster labeled "Patients' Bill of Rights." Tacked beside it was a menu from a local Chinese restaurant offering free delivery service to the patients and staff.

Marty picked up a *Newsweek* and wandered outside to a fenced-in yard. Male and female patients were sitting at picnic tables. He found an empty table and starting paging through the magazine. He had settled into an article on economics when a voice inquired, "Mr. Dubichek?"

Marty looked up at a man in a white coat. His gray hair, bifocals, and kind face gave him a fatherly look. "I'm Dr. Clifford Argus," he said smiling. "May I join you?"

"Sure, Doc," Marty answered, closing the magazine. He immediately liked the man. A full day of sleep, a decent breakfast, and the fact he wasn't in jail had worked wonders on his state of mind. "Call me Marty," he said, shaking hands.

Dr. Argus pulled up a chair and opened a file folder. "Okay, Marty, how are you feeling?"

"Better, thanks."

Dr. Argus studied the file. "It seems you had a problem at San Francisco City Hall yesterday morning," he began in an easy tone. "Would you care to tell me why?"

"Uh . . . sure," Marty replied, caught off guard. He planned to grieve about Pete privately and wasn't prepared to discuss it right out of the chute. Reluctantly, he explained about spending the night in the plaza and how his best friend Pete got sick and died before the ambulance arrived. He told the story quickly, matter-of-factly, skipping details. Still, he couldn't get through the telling without being flooded by images of him and Pete having dinner at the shelter or hanging around the fire at the Monday Night Club, joking, and talking about their own place. Marty paused as a wave of sadness welled up and choked off his voice. He put his face in his hands and wept.

Dr. Argus disappeared briefly and returned with a box of tissues. When Marty regained his composure, the doctor asked, "Why were you so anxious to get into City Hall?"

Marty blew his nose and shrugged.

"Before the incident, when was the last time you had a decent meal?"

Marty counted on his fingers. "Four days . . . last Tuesday night at my shelter," he said, wiping his eyes. "Sunday night before that."

"And the last time you had a good night's sleep?"

Marty thought for a moment. "I don't know, maybe a week ago."

The doctor made some notations. "And you're feeling better now?" he asked, peering over his glasses at Marty.

"Yes, doctor, definitely," Marty replied, managing a teary-eyed smile.

"Good, good," Dr. Argus said, standing. "That's all for now. Enjoy the beautiful weather, we'll chat again tomorrow."

NINE
Sunday, January 15

1

JASON SAT in an overstuffed chair in Anton's living room, toying with the expensive cane his brother had given him. It was made of polished hardwood and topped with a heavy ivory handle in the shape of a wolf. He would use it to buttress his weak right side.

At the hospital this morning, Jason's wrap-around head bandage was replaced with a small pad, and he was wheeled to his brother's car. The two men then drove to Anton's 1930's two-story house in the fashionable Marina District.

After Anton settled his brother on the living room couch and turned on the AFC Championship Game, he left to help his wife prepare a special Sunday dinner. Soon the aroma of roast turkey filled the room, and Jason knew he would be celebrating a belated Thanksgiving with his family.

The room was decorated with black and white lacquered furniture, a modern and masculine decor remarkably similar to the style Jason had chosen for his condo in Pacific Heights. Jason turned his attention to the view outside. He was idly watching the yachts bobbing in the marina across the street when Anton entered the room wearing an apron and holding a mixing spoon.

"Everything's under control," his brother announced. "We'll be feeding shortly." Then Anton lowered his voice. "I wasn't kidding about Liz's cooking disability. If you see her unsupervised in the kitchen, run like hell. If you wait until you smell smoke it'll be too late."

Liz came up behind Anton. "I heard that!" she said, feigning anger. "It's true, of course."

Jason smiled. "That aroma you're creating tells a far different story; I'm starting to drool. You two didn't have to go to all this trouble."

"It's no trouble, little brother," Anton said affectionately. "How about a drink? I have a twenty-year-old bottle of brandy I've been saving for a special occasion. I'll open it to commemorate our reunion."

"Great idea."

Jason sipped the brandy and half-watched the football game while Anton and Liz set the table. The drink warmed him, and he closed his eyes, allowing his mind to drift back to the meadow. He made a mental note to call Henderson's company and make an offer. He had no plans to develop the land, but after the vivid dream in the hospital he now felt compelled to own it.

On the TV, an excited announcer was describing a brilliant catch by a wide receiver. In the noise of the cheering crowd Jason thought he heard the howling wind, the rain whipping, the crackling of a fire.

A back lunged into the end zone. The stadium roared.

Someone whispered, "Happy."

He opened his eyes to Liz standing in front of him, smiling warmly.

"Dinner is served, " she said.

2

IT WAS IMPOSSIBLE for Marty to watch the AFC Champion Game while the other patients incessantly critiqued the action on TV. It seemed as if everyone in the Acute Care Unit thought of themselves as a football expert. It drove Marty nuts. No matter, he thought, I'll be out of here tomorrow.

I still can't believe they don't know who I am.

While in bed last night Marty formulated a plan. When he had told Pete he would contact Jason Howell for a reward, he was just jawing, trying to give his friend hope. But after some solid rest and decent food he could think more clearly, and now it seemed like a good idea.

He read in this morning's newspaper that Howell was going to South America on Tuesday for a two-week vacation. After Marty was released on Monday, he would immediately find a public phone and call Howell's company. In his professional voice he would ask for the man's secretary and simply say, "Please inform your boss that the gentleman who saved his life last week is calling." He was sure when Howell got that message he would make himself available, and Marty could explain what happened.

The more he thought about it, the more Marty convinced himself that Howell would not only clear him, but would reward him as well. He didn't want much—just the money he and Pete had saved, and maybe a little extra for his trouble. With a stake and the police off his back, he could start anew.

Marty now understood when he charged the security station at City Hall, he was trying to get a deputy sheriff to shoot him and end his miserable existence. But with Howell's help he could pull himself out of homelessness. Pete would want that for him.

3

"I'D LIKE TO catch up, Anton," Jason said, taking a helping of turkey and cranberry sauce. "Fifteen years ago at
Uncle Matt's funeral, you mentioned you had just received
your broker's license and were selling commercial real
estate. I bet you were good at it."

Anton nodded. "In those days I was handling property
for big-time developers. Life was simpler then. But I was
greedy and started putting my own limited partnerships
together. For a while it was impossible to do a bad deal. I
operated under the greater fool theory: I borrowed heavily
because there was always a doctor, a dentist, or a lawyer
willing to pay the ever higher rents I needed to service my
debt."

Liz caught Jason's eye. "It was during that 'greater
fool' period when your brother and I got married."

Anton ignored the remark. "In the early nineties the
recession hit and the floor dropped out of the market. My
empire began crumbling, and I've been scrambling ever
since."

"I'm sorry," Jason said. "But isn't commercial real
estate in reasonably good shape these days?"

"Yes. The only question is whether I can keep the
Howell Development Corporation afloat long enough to
take advantage of it."

"It *has* been a strain," Liz acknowledged. "Sometimes
my meager income is all we have to live on."

Anton's expression turned dour. He picked up his
glass and took a deep sip of Chardonnay.

Jason turned to Liz. "What do you do?"

"I'm the event manager for the Penniston Hotel on
Nob Hill. I organize corporate meetings and functions."

"And how is business for you?"

"Good at the moment, although it was tight for several years because San Francisco was considered an undesirable location for meetings."

"Why?"

"The Chamber of Commerce attributed it to our huge homeless population. Then Mayor Babcock got elected on his 'Safe Streets' platform, and instituted Project Vector. He claims to have reduced the homeless population, but my sense is that there are as many as before. All Babcock has done is keep them away from the business districts and tourist attractions."

"Speaking of the homeless," Jason said, turning to his brother, "when we were growing up there were never so many people living on the street."

"I remember," Anton said wistfully. "The few bums we had hung around the railroad yard, or camped out of public view. Now you can't go to a park without someone asking for a handout.

"If you ask me," he continued, "people who want to work can find jobs. They can be handymen or gardeners; they can flip burgers; they can be janitors for God's sake. I'll let you in on a secret little brother: all of my janitorial services hire illegal aliens. If there are jobs for illegals, then there are jobs for regular citizens." Anton refilled his glass with Chardonnay and turned to Liz. "As you know, I was eight years old and Jason was six when our parents died in an auto accident. We were not only homeless but *parent-less* as well. Sure, we lived with foster families. But they boarded us for money, and didn't give a damn about our well-being or whether or not we had a future. In spite of that negative environment, we overcame all of the obstacles, got ourselves educated, and became responsible members of society."

"True, Anton," Jason said. "But for those who can't lift themselves up by their bootstraps, don't you think the government should play a bigger role in helping people get back on their feet?"

"Absolutely not!" Anton retorted. "Not when they're inherently lazy. Not when you and I work hard and our reward is being taxed to death to support a system that only encourages people to be ne'er-do-wells—"

"All right, all right!" Liz interjected. "Enough about society's problems. I'm much more interested in learning what Jason has been doing . . . ."

4

MARTY SAT alone in Dr. Argus' office awaiting his next counseling session. He knew from other patients that this meeting would involve dredging up painful memories. It wouldn't be easy.

The doctor came in, greeted Marty, and settled at his desk. "Begin with high school," Dr. Argus said.

"I went to high school in a small Michigan town and graduated about twenty years ago. Then I attended college on a sports scholarship. I played fullback and we won a lot of games. I was a hero of sorts. The coach said I had pro potential. But during my senior year I didn't play much because of a knee injury, and I was passed over by the NFL scouts.

"About a year after college, I got a job coaching football at my old high school. I liked working with kids, and they seemed to like me."

"Did you marry?"

"Uh-huh," Marty answered, hesitating for a moment. "Her name's Suzanne; she was a cheerleader."

"Children?"

"One, Billy. He's a teenager now. I haven't seen either of them in years."

Dr. Argus scribbled in his file. "Where are they now?"

"In Michigan," Marty said, shifting uncomfortably. "When Suzanne was pregnant, I got surplused because of budget problems. The school turned my football program over to the Phys Ed teacher.

"In order to put food on the table, I worked for a building contractor for several years. But things turned sour in the trades as well. In those days the unemployment rate in Michigan was in the double digits, and people weren't buying cars or homes or much of anything else. A lot of my buddies went to California to find work."

Dr. Argus took more notes.

"I kept asking Suzanne to give the West Coast a try. But she didn't want to leave her family and friends, or take Billy out of school. Finally she agreed when a buddy got me a construction job in South San Francisco. For the next five or six years I made enough to get by. But with the cost of living so high in the Bay Area, we didn't save much."

"Please continue," Dr. Argus said.

Marty rubbed his cheek. He didn't like thinking about what happened next. He took a deep breath. "Then the recession hit California and there were many months when I didn't work. First we depleted our savings. Then we sold everything we could. I started drinking like there was no tomorrow. But tomorrow came, I took one look at it, and I drank some more.

"For a time Suzanne was patient with me. But eventually she tired of my broken promises and divorced me. She took Billy . . . I wasn't in any shape to fight it. Anyway, with her smarts and good looks, I figured she'd remarry and Billy would have a nice home. And that's exactly what happened. Suz returned to Michigan and married a pharmacist." Marty blinked back a tear.

"Then what did you do?"

"I moved into a tiny studio apartment and took odd jobs. But those dried up, too, and the next thing I knew I was out on the street.

"I should've returned to Michigan before things got out of hand. But during the rare times I had enough money for a bus ticket, I was too embarrassed. My sister, Abigail, and other relatives and friends still live there. Their memories of me as a star player and teacher differ quite a bit from reality.

"About three years ago, I woke up inside a refrigerator carton, hugging a bottle of rotgut whiskey. I crawled out and found myself in a doorway in the Mission District. The sun was shining, and I could see myself clearly in the store window. I hated what I saw.

"It was then I realized I'd be dead pretty soon, and I cried when I thought of Billy learning that his dad, the football hero, had died a drunk.

"So I sobered up, and that enabled me to participate in various shelter programs. My current shelter, St. Andrews, lets their clients stay longer than the usual one or two months. Unofficially I've been helping the staff enforce the rules. They called me 'Shelter Sheriff.'

"I've also been working now and then and saving for my own place. I've taken some computer classes, and on my own I've been studying history and economics in the library—two subjects I enjoy but glossed over in college."

Dr. Argus removed his glasses and looked at Marty. "Are you handling your drinking now?"

"Absolutely. But to be perfectly honest, Doc, me and my buddy, Pete—I told you about him yesterday—left the shelter every Monday night. We had this club in a cement alcove where we could visit with pals, play cards, and have a few drinks like regular people. The rest of the time we were sober as church mice."

Dr. Argus replaced his glasses and took copious notes. Marty watched him and wondered if the man was ever affected by the stories he heard.

When the doctor finished writing he looked up and said, "Okay, Marty, let's revisit the incident at the Civic Center last Friday. What were you doing out of your shelter on Thursday night?"

Marty was ready. He wanted to be as truthful as possible without revealing that the police were after him. Marty knew the critical parts of his story could be checked with the shelter staff. "Well, it started last Wednesday. Pete and I were working late as casual laborers, so we gave our cots at the shelter to Willie and Doc, two friends of ours. Willie was living in a VW van in China Basin, and that's where we slept Wednesday night.

"Thursday morning it got towed by the police. We felt responsible, so we told Willie to take the savings we had in Pete's locker at the shelter and use it to get the van released.

"Due to red tape, Willie couldn't get his van that day. So he and Doc stayed in the shelter another night, and me and Pete stayed at the Civic Center Plaza."

"What happened to Pete?" Dr. Argus inquired.

"Pete got real sick. On Friday morning, after spending the night in the cold and the drizzle, he took a turn for the worse. He woke up coughing blood. I was worried."

"What did you do?"

"I called 911. They sent an ambulance. But . . ."

"Okay," Dr. Argus said, studying Marty carefully. "But why did you rush into City Hall?"

"I don't know," Marty answered. He didn't think it was a good idea to admit to being suicidal.

"Did you feel that someone in City Hall was responsible for your problems and your friend's death?"

"Oh, no, Doc, *I* was responsible. I should've gotten Pete medical care sooner. I tried, but he refused to go to the hospital. He was a stubborn S.O.B.

"After he died, I felt guilty and I didn't know what to do. I panicked. I couldn't think straight. I guess I was seeking help." Marty looked sincerely at Dr. Argus. "And I guess that's what I'm getting now."

Dr. Argus seemed pleased. He closed Marty's file. "That's all for today. By the way, you're free to use the telephone at the nurse's station. Is there anyone you would like to call?"

"Uh, no thanks." Marty knew he couldn't phone Howell's secretary and leave the telephone number of a mental hospital.

"Okay, Marty," Dr. Argus said standing, "enjoy the rest of the day; we'll have our final chat tomorrow."

5

"I'M A TURNAROUND SPECIALIST," Jason told his family. "Over the years I've bailed out companies involved in graphics, multimedia, and now virtual reality."

"What exactly is virtual reality?" Liz asked.

"It's a system that allows you to step through 'the looking glass' into a software-generated world."

"Any reality would be better than the present one," Anton said, sipping Chardonnay.

"How does it work?" Liz asked.

"Although the technology is sophisticated, the concept is fairly straightforward. You wear a wraparound visor that completely blocks out the real world. Inside are two miniature color television screens that display a computer-generated 3-D image in front of the viewer. Sensors on the visor detect your movements, and the computer instantly changes your view and perspective accordingly. As you turn, you can see to your right, to your left, or behind you, just like in the real world. Stereo headphones provide computer-generated sounds, and integrated microphones allow you to talk to other cybernauts who might be sharing your world."

"The ultimate Nintendo," Anton said.

"You're right. Games were among the first commercial applications. But until recently, the lack of processing power in the machine's front end—the reality engine—limited the experience to a cartoon world. But my company, Cytex, has developed an incredibly powerful engine called C-REAL. It allows the display of 3-D images that are virtually indistinguishable from real life."

Anton's eyes glazed over.

"I'm not just talking about a fancy way to watch 3-D movies," Jason explained. "If you're wearing a wired glove with pressure feedback, you can actually touch objects in the virtual world. For practical purposes, when you're immersed, the virtual world *is* the real world."

"What *are* the practical purposes?" Liz inquired.

"Simulations, primarily. For years, companies have designed their products on a two-dimensional computer screen. If they wanted to try a new product before tooling up for production, they had to build a full-scale mockup. With VR, that's no longer necessary. Now you can 'step' through the computer screen and test drive that new car or fly that new airplane or—"

"—walk around a real estate project," Anton finished.

"Exactly. There's also a multitude of training applications. Doctors can try new surgical techniques without risk to patients; police and soldiers can practice tactical procedures; athletes can hone their skills—all without leaving the comfort and safety of a computer station.

"At the VR Center at Stanford University," Jason went on, "they have a virtual racquetball setup. You don a head-mounted display and find yourself standing on a racquetball court. The computer provides you with a cyber-partner according your skill level. You hold a racquet rigged with pressure feedback so you actually feel the 'hit' of the ball. My racquetball partners weren't aware of it, but I often used the setup to polish my game."

Anton laughed. "I can just picture you running around in a Buck Rogers helmet, swinging at imaginary balls."

"You're right, Anton. Watching someone totally immersed in virtual reality is a lot stranger than the experience itself, which is surprisingly natural."

"It sounds exciting," Liz said.

Anton downed the remainder of his Chardonnay. "I'll get excited when you find a way to squeeze more money out of my bankers."

TEN
Monday, January 16

1

MAYOR BABCOCK FROWNED at his newspaper. Although his approval rating had inched up after the Howell kidnapping story, it still had a long, long, way to go.

Shaking his head, he dropped the paper onto his desk, lifted a Wedgwood cup, and took a satisfying sip of Kona coffee. Getting re-elected in November was going to be a bitch. Sometimes he wondered why he coveted a job with so many problems.

Of course there were a few perks—like being chauffeured around in a limo. But the perk he appreciated most was Jeanette Garcia, his petite and always cheerful receptionist. Besides her good looks, the woman could brew a magnificent cup of coffee in spite of her limited office allowance. By contrast, his wife, Margaret, managed to turn even the most expensive Jamaican Blue into a pale brown purgative.

Mayor Babcock was puzzling over this paradox when his intercom buzzed and Jeanette's melodic voice announced the arrival of Chief Conti.

The door opened and the chief entered briskly.

"Sit down, Rudy," the mayor said, gesturing at a red leather side chair. "Coffee?"

"Please."

As if by magic, Jeanette glided into the office holding a polished carafe and another Wedgwood cup. She poured coffee for the chief and freshened the mayor's cup.

Babcock winked as Jeanette backed out of the office and closed the door. He stared at the door for a moment and then turned to the chief. "What brings you here, Rudy?"

"I need to brief you on the homeless man who stormed into City Hall on Friday morning."

"I was hoping the incident would inject some sympathy points into this poll," the mayor said, picking up the newspaper and waving it. "Unfortunately the reporters didn't buy it as an attempt on my life by another homeless rebel. What about him?"

"At the time of the incident, I was on the way to my monthly meeting with the county sheriff when this homeless man in a parka hit me up for spare change. His face was red and splotchy, and he had the haircut from hell. But his clothes and his large size made me suspicious, so I gave him some coins and tailed him. He bought two coffees and then stood at the front entrance, watching an ambulance drive off. Afterwards, he crossed the street and walked over to a bag lady in the plaza. After a brief conversation, he suddenly dropped the coffee and raced into the building. I was standing on the steps as he charged right past me.

"It took five deputies to restrain him. But he wouldn't calm down, so paramedics were called and they sedated

him. As a precautionary measure I had him psyched upstate. Now here's the best part: Yesterday I cross-checked
his fingerprints with those we lifted from Howell's phony
bandage."

The mayor put his cup down and stared wide-eyed at
the chief. "Wait a goddamn minute . . . are you saying he
was the Good Samaritan?"

"That's *exactly* what I'm saying. His name's Martin
Dubichek."

"What set him off?"

"I wondered about that, too. So I kept digging, and
learned that the ambulance was taking away a vagrant who
had expired in the plaza, a man by the name of Sherwood
Petersen. His fingerprints matched another set found on
Howell's clothing. Petersen and Dubichek were friends
who lived at the St. Andrews Shelter for Men."

"Hmmm," the mayor said, digesting the news. "Who
else knows?"

"No one. And to keep it that way I made sure both
fingerprint records were purged from our computer."

"Can you do that?"

"Certainly. There's no requirement to maintain fingerprint files on individuals who aren't criminals or suspects."

The mayor was excited. "Will they hold him upstate
until the election's over? I don't want him talking to the
press."

"I'm afraid not. In order to extend a commitment beyond seventy-two hours the evaluating psychiatrist would
have to find that the patient is a danger to himself or to
others."

"What are the chances he'll fail his evaluation?"

"Virtually zero. Because of the demand for beds, the
patient would probably have to strangle his evaluating

psychiatrist to be recommitted. Even then it's not for certain."

"When is he being discharged?"

"Later this morning."

"Can we stop it?"

"Perhaps. I could tell the hospital's director we need to investigate the man's background. After all, he did storm City Hall. I'll say we need time to assure ourselves that he doesn't have a vendetta against you."

Babcock pursed his lips. "How much time can we buy?"

Conti shrugged. "It's not in our control. By law, fourteen days is the next level of involuntary treatment. That's not much, but the longer he's institutionalized, the less credibility he'll have with the media. And it'll give us a chance to think of something else. Shall I call the hospital's director?"

Babcock took another sip of Kona coffee. "Do it."

2

MARTY WAS REMINDED of last Monday, which had started with the same crisp and clear weather but ended in a ferocious storm that dumped Jason Howell into his lap. Little did Marty know the price Pete would pay for agreeing to save the life of a stranger.

Today, however, there were no storms in the forecast and no gloom in Marty's outlook. He would contact Howell and get another chance. Change was in the air.

He whistled as he gathered the toiletry kit and the items of clothing George had given him. Shortly, he would have his final evaluation with Dr. Argus, and then be released. A patient had told him to expect a short session this time, one designed to help Marty cope with any future problems. It would end with a pamphlet describing where Marty could seek professional assistance before his problems got out-of-hand. The patient affectionately referred to the exit interview as the "kiss-off meeting."

Marty strolled into Dr. Argus' office and took his seat by the doctor's desk.

"What are your immediate plans?" Dr. Argus asked, pouring tea from a thermos into two Styrofoam cups.

"I expect to get assistance from this rich fellow I know," Marty said, accepting a cup. "I did him a big favor and he owes me. I'll call him later."

"And if for some reason he doesn't help you?"

"Then I'll go back to my shelter." *Like hell*, Marty thought.

Dr. Argus smiled. "I've talked with the staff at St. Andrews and they have the highest regard for you. They'll take you back as soon as space becomes available."

Marty nodded and forced a smile.

"This morning you'll take a bus to San Francisco, and what you do afterward is entirely up to you. But I want your assurance that you'll eat and sleep properly from now on."

"Yes, Doc," Marty said.

"And when you feel your problems are mounting and life is getting too hard, you'll seek assistance at a crisis center, won't you?"

"Certainly, Doc," Marty said, nodding enthusiastically. "You can count on me."

The two men sipped tea and chatted comfortably for a few minutes. Dr. Argus made a final notation, closed his file, and looked at his watch. "That's it, Marty. Are you packed and ready to go?"

"Yes, Doc. I just want to say thanks and—"

The phone rang and Dr. Argus held up his hand.

Marty knew he still had to get a pamphlet.

The doctor was listening intently. Deep creases had furrowed in his brow. He removed his glasses and slipped them into a jacket pocket. Argus' actions made Marty nervous.

The doctor cradled the handset and pushed a button on his desk. Almost instantly, George and two other psychiatric techs appeared.

"Is there a problem, Doc?" Marty asked worriedly, setting his cup down.

"I'm afraid so. There has been a change of plans. You're going to be with us a little longer."

Marty's mouth dropped. "W-why?"

"That was the hospital's director. You've been certified under Section 5250 of the California Welfare and Institutions Code, which means you will receive two weeks of additional treatment. I must inform you that if you don't cooperate, it can be extended."

Marty was stunned. Before he could react he was surrounded by the techs. They grabbed his arms but he shook them off and leaned menacingly toward Dr. Argus. "I don't understand," Marty said, clenching his teeth, trying to control his anger. His temples were pounding.

Dr. Argus quickly stood and moved backward. "I'm sorry Marty, truly I am. But the San Francisco Police Department needs to make certain that you don't have a vendetta against Mayor Babcock. I personally think they're making a mistake. Give me time; perhaps I can get the matter resolved and—"

"YOU CAN'T DO THIS TO ME, YOU BASTARD!" Marty shouted, beating on the desk. His cup tumbled and tea spilled. "YOU HAVE TO LET ME GO. THE ONLY PERSON WHO CAN HELP ME IS LEAVING THE COUNTRY TOMORROW! HE'S MY LAST CHANCE!"

Marty felt his feet fly out from under him, and he fell forward and heavily onto the floor. With practiced speed, the techs used large Velcro restraints to secure his arms and legs behind him. Strong hands lifted his head and gauze was taped over his mouth. He struggled, flexing powerful muscles against the restraints, but it was hopeless. Marty was lifted off the floor, turned over, and strapped into a gurney.

Dr. Argus walked around his desk. "I'm sorry, Marty, I truly am. I'll prescribe medication to relax you." The doctor motioned to the techs.

Marty sank into a deep depression as he watched the hallway lights pass overhead. The gurney stopped abruptly, a door opened, and Marty found himself back in the side room.

3

JASON WAS STRETCHED flat on the couch holding a magazine in front of his face. He must have read the same sentence ten times. God, he was bored. His physical therapy session had killed a few hours this morning, but spending the remainder of the day in his brother's house with nothing to do was getting him down.

He put the magazine aside and stood to shake out a cramp in his right leg. He walked around the living room for a few minutes and then decided to explore the rest of the house. He climbed the stairs slowly, leaning on his wolf-cane for support. The door to the master bedroom was ajar. He opened it wider and looked inside. The room was decorated in the same stark, masculine style as the rest of the house. The only feminine touch was a colorful jewelry box atop a black laminated dresser. He limped inside the room and picked it up. The cover had a Renaissance painting of two kissing cherubs surrounded by flowers. He lifted the lid, and in clear crystalline notes it played "Let Me Call You Sweetheart."

"May I help you find something?" inquired a woman's voice behind him.

Jason clunked the lid and turned. "Oh, Liz . . . I was admiring your music box. I hope you don't mind me poking around. I was going stir crazy."

"That doesn't surprise me," she said evenly. "Your brother would have been climbing the walls by now."

Jason set the box down. "I didn't expect you. Are you finished for the day? I could use some company."

"Unfortunately, no. There's an event at the Penniston this evening, and my assistant manager is out with the flu. I have to change and go back. I'll be working late."

"Do you have a minute to chat?"

Liz looked at her watch. "Yes."

Jason followed her downstairs. He sat on the living room couch while she settled across from him in a white love seat. She kicked off her heels, tugged at her dress, and placed her feet on an ottoman.

Jason traced the curve of her legs and caught a whiff of her perfume. He unconsciously leaned towards her. "I want you to know that I appreciate your hospitality," he began, "but I'll be moving back to my condo in the morning."

"What about the press?"

"They think I'm going to South America."

"I hope you're not leaving us because of Anton; he's not his usual self."

"No, it's not Anton."

"Is it C-REAL?"

Jason shook his head no. "The project's on hold for a couple of weeks. But before I explain why I must leave, may I share something with you?"

"Of course."

Jason clasped his hands over his right knee. "I'm no longer interested in turning around companies and grooming them for sale. After Cytex there'll be no more deals."

Liz looked surprised. "What are going to do?"

"I don't know. Other than racquetball, my career has been all-consuming. I've never developed outside interests."

"Just high-tech and racquetball?"

"Well, that's not quite true. Just before my accident I was planning to diversify my holdings. I had flown to Petaluma with my racquetball partner, Bill Henderson, a real estate agent who wanted to show me this beautiful hilltop meadow. The idea was to fill it with luxury homes and make a killing."

"You're definitely your brother's brother."

"I'm not so sure; I have no desire to go forward with that project, either."

"Really?"

"Just before you and Anton visited me in the hospital I was dreaming about the land. It had a one-story Spanish-style house that blended nicely into the hillside. There was a woman, a pool—even a puppy. The dream was vivid, as if I were getting a glimpse into the future. This morning I called Henderson's company and made an offer on the meadow."

"What are you going to do with it?"

"I don't know, and that's strange, too. This is the first time I've done anything without a clear purpose." Jason released his knee and stretched his leg. "It's unsettling."

Liz watched Jason.

"It's this unsettled feeling that brings me to why I must leave. I know I wasn't kidnapped. And now I'm thinking that learning what happened on the street might help me understand why I'm changing—why I no longer feel like my life needs to be measured by the size of my bank account. Maybe it's as simple as being helpless for the first time in my life, and having total strangers care for me."

"But don't you remember *anything?*"

"I've had a few flashbacks. Some were even quite pleasant. Unfortunately, the people who know what happened are hiding from the police."

Liz absently tapped her chin. "I know this attorney, Samantha Paxton. She has helped me locate fly-by-night promoters who hold 'Get-Rich-Quick' seminars at the Penniston, and then skip town without paying their bills. Sam is efficient, discrete, and has excellent contacts inside the SFPD. If your homeless heroes are on the planet, she'll locate them."

Jason stood. "Okay, let's give her a call."

ELEVEN
Tuesday, January 17

1

THE SIGN IN FRONT of the Victorian house in Pacific Heights simply said "Law Offices." Jason walked up the front steps, leaning on his cane for support. At the front door were several brass nameplates. One of them read "Samantha Paxton, Attorney at Law— Third Floor."

Jason slowly climbed the three flights and found himself in a small reception area. The room was paneled to chair-rail height in zebrawood. Above the wainscot the walls were covered in a lustrous green velvet. Objets d'art were grouped on end tables in softly-illuminated and appealing vignettes.

Jason announced his arrival to the receptionist and sank into a George III library chair. He picked up an African fertility statue and was turning it over when a confident woman's voice said, "The statute is androgynous; it helps people regardless of status or gender."

Jason righted the statue and set it down. "Like the ideal attorney?"

"Exactly," she said.

Using his cane, Jason pulled himself to his feet and found himself returning a firm handshake with a stylish brunette in her forties.

"Hello, Mr. Howell," Samantha Paxton said.

"Please call me Jason."

"All right, and you may call me Sam."

"I hope you'll pardon my appearance," he said, gesturing at his pea coat and knit cap.

Sam cocked her head. "It looks like your standard-issue, press-avoidance uniform."

"I'm supposed to be in South America."

Sam nodded and directed Jason into her office. She offered him a client's chair in front of her desk. "So what can I do for you?" she asked, picking up a yellow pad.

Jason summarized the official version of what had happened to him on the street, and told her he didn't believe a word of it. "I'm here because I need to find the people who helped me; I need to know what really occurred."

"Why?"

"A new me has been emerging ever since I awoke, and filling in the blanks might explain why. Additionally, there's still a lot of the old Jason Howell remaining, and he doesn't appreciate being manipulated for political purposes by a certain high-ranking city official."

"And that would be Mayor Babcock?"

"Yes."

Sam scribbled in her yellow pad. "How much time do I have to find your homeless heroes?"

"Two weeks; afterwards I must focus my full attention on the merger of my company."

Sam shook her head. "Only two weeks? You do realize this isn't your typical missing person's assignment."

Jason started to say something but Sam raised her hand. "Wait a second—let me think."

Jason waited.

Sam leaned back in her chair and looked out the window. A long moment passed. Then she turned to Jason. "My missing person matters usually go to a private investigator. But in this case, I believe you need an attorney as an intermediary."

"Why?"

"To get the protection afforded by the attorney-client privilege. The phony kidnapping story has placed the mayor's political future at risk. If he learns that a private investigator is digging around and asking questions on your behalf, it'll set off bells and whistles. He might strike preemptively and attempt to discredit you by spreading additional falsehoods, undermining your merger in the process. But if all communications are channeled through me, no one will know for whom the investigator is working."

"You're hired."

"Fine. But we still must be careful with our communications. The attorney-client privilege won't do you any good if a conversation is overheard, or if our correspondence falls into the wrong hands. You should be especially careful about what you say on the phone or commit to writing when we're talking about the fugitives."

"Are you suggesting a code name?"

"Yes."

Jason thought for a moment. "How about 'Golden Fleece?'"

Sam smiled. "And so begins our quest."

2

SPEWING BLUE-BLACK SMOKE, the old Pontiac Trans Am roared north along Highway 101. Inspector James Brodsky was hunched over the steering wheel, re-playing this morning's telephone conversation with How-ell's secretary. She reported a strange call from a man named Martin Dubichek. In a raspy voice he asked for Mr. Howell. She told him her boss had left the country. The man abruptly hung up. Brodsky then ran the name through CAL-NET, the police computer system. Sure enough, a vagrant named Dubichek had been psychoed at Petaluma State Hospital after storming City Hall last Fri-day.

Although he doubted it, there was a chance this Dubi-chek knew something. Brodsky's week-long hunt had gone nowhere, and he needed some fresh leads. If nothing else, this high-speed drive in the country might clear his mind and give him a new perspective.

At the main entrance of the hospital, Brodsky down-shifted and laid a thick layer of rubber as he expertly exe-cuted a squealing right turn into a quiet, tree-lined drive-way. He was surprised—no, shocked—by the manicured grounds and the Victorian homes and fine cottages that flashed by. He even caught a glimpse of an athletic field with a volleyball court and a barbeque area. This place looks more like a country club than a goddamn mental in-stitution, he thought. No wonder the vagrants in the plaza periodically storm City Hall.

Brodsky strutted into the Administration Building, held up his badge, and demanded to see Martin Dubichek. A clerk issued a visitor's pass and gave him directions to Ward J-4, several blocks south of the Administration building. But Brodsky fumed when the clerk told him to turn over his revolver. Although forcefully arguing he was a veteran homicide inspector with the SFPD, Brodsky was firmly informed he had no jurisdiction at the hospital and therefore he would be treated like any other visitor. Under state law, weapons were forbidden. This was for his protection as well as for the safety of the patients.

It insulted Brodsky that a lowly clerk thought that any of the nuts in this fairy farm could disarm *him*.

When he found Ward J-4, Brodsky felt a little better. The building was surrounded by prison-quality fencing topped with barbed wire. At the main door, he leaned on the intercom and announced with bravado, "*I'm* Inspector James Brodsky, SFPD. I'm here to interrogate one of your inmates, Martin Dubichek." He waved his pass at a security camera and was buzzed inside. A psychiatric tech escorted him to the visitor's room.

Brodsky expected thick glass booths with telephones on each side. Instead, the room had tables, chairs, and pastel walls. Soothing music played on a stereo. He couldn't believe it.

Brodsky sat at a table, drumming his fingers. Presently, a white man in jeans and a flannel shirt, accompanied by a black man in matching clothes, entered the room. Both men were huge. Brodsky wondered how one distinguished the inmates from the orderlies. If he were in charge, the inmates would be forced to wear striped pajamas with matching hats.

The white man was led to a seat across from his visitor. The black man then joined the man who had escorted Brodsky into the building, and the two techs stood nearby with their arms folded, watching warily.

"Martin Dubichek?" Brodsky opened.

"Who are you?" the big man asked in a monotone. His shoulders were slumped and his eyes were flat.

"*I'm* Inspector James Brodsky from the San Francisco Police Department, and *I'll* ask the questions." Brodsky knew how to take control. He threw the inmate a look of disdain as he plucked a printout from his pocket and snapped it open. "It says here you attempted to break through security at City Hall last week. Is that true?"

The big man gazed at the ceiling and nodded.

"And you're being held on suspicion of being a threat to the mayor. Is *that* true?"

The big man thought for moment and nodded again.

Brodsky was on a roll. He had this big dumb Dubichek character wrapped around his finger. "Now, this morning, you telephoned a company called Cytex and asked to be put in touch with their president, did you not?"

The big man thought again and then nodded.

"What did you want to tell him?"

The big man remained silent.

Brodsky sighed heavily. "Now, I want you to listen carefully," he said, using a tone as if he were speaking to a child. "WHY-DID-YOU-CALL-HIM?"

The big man motioned for Brodsky to lean forward, as though he had a secret he didn't want the two techs to hear. When he had the inspector's ear he whispered, "I was going to tell him he's a big PUSSY, just like you are." The word "pussy" was accompanied by a puff of air and a large wet tongue in the inspector's ear.

Brodsky's blood boiled, his face bloomed, and the veins in his neck bulged. He threw the table aside and leaped onto the patient with his hands around the big man's neck. The patient's chair collapsed under the weight, and the two men crashed in a heap onto the floor.

The two large techs rushed over and untangled Brodsky from the patient. The inspector was kicking and screaming as he was dragged out of the room and unceremoniously ejected from the building.

3

ON THE SECOND FLOOR of City Hall, Chief Conti spotted the mayor's stocky frame down the hallway. His Honor had his staff in tow, with high-ranking officials trailing the mayor by a few steps and lower-echelon staff following further back. With the mayor at the point, the entourage looked like ducks in a "V" formation.

When the group reached the large double doors of the mayor's office, the chief waited for His Honor to glad-hand and back-slap everyone, telling them their loyalty and hard work would be the key to his re-election.

And we all get to keep our jobs, Conti thought.

When the mayor finished schmoozing, he turned to the chief. "Can't whatever it is wait until tomorrow, Rudy?"

"I'm afraid not."

Babcock grimaced as he led the chief into his office. He pointed at a side alcove used for one-on-one meetings and went over to the bar. "Want some sherry, Rudy? The day may be old but the evening is young. Let me rejoice in the glow of optimism and goodwill I just experienced from my staff before you shoot me between the eyes with your inevitable bad news."

"Nothing for me, Walt."

"All right," the mayor sighed, pouring himself two fingers of sherry in a crystal glass. Then he shrugged and filled the glass to the top. "What is it?" he sighed, sinking heavily into a wing chair.

"I just received a call from the Director of Petaluma State Hospital. He's steamed. This afternoon, one of our homicide inspectors tried to strangle the Good Samaritan."

"Oh, no, don't tell me it was . . ."

"I'm afraid so."

"BRODSKY!" Mayor Babcock screamed as he brought his glass down hard on a coffee table, splashing sherry onto his hand. He sagged further into the chair and licked at the sherry as if he were cleaning a wound.

"I don't know what set him off," Chief Conti continued, "and I don't give a damn. Brodsky's out of control. We've got to get him off the case. *Now.* But I wanted to talk to you first since I have no one else to take the heat if the media gets wind of his bogus investigation."

The mayor looked wanly at the chief. "Do you think he knows whom he attacked?"

Conti shook his head. "I doubt it. He told his lieutenant he was following a lead from a nutcase who called Howell's company. He says he didn't get any useful information.

"With your permission I'd like to use this incident to justify an administrative transfer. Brodsky can pass his remaining years impounding cars or cleaning the horse stables. No—I have a better idea: I'll assign him to the front desk at the Hall of Justice and give him a daily dose of the public."

The mayor closed his eyes and pressed his sinuses between a thumb and a forefinger.

"With Howell out of the country the media is quickly losing interest," Conti said. "I should be able to quietly suspend the kidnapping investigation without serious consequences. Shall I transfer Brodsky?"

"Yeah," the mayor growled, "nail the son-of-a-bitch."

TWELVE
Friday, January 20

1

"JASON, ARE YOU THERE?" the voice insisted. Wrapped in a towel and still dripping from the shower, Jason limped down the hallway to his answering machine.

"Pick up, Jason, it's Sam. I've got good news."

Jason quickly lifted the receiver. "You've located the Golden Fleece?"

"We got lucky—but let's not push it by discussing it on the phone. Can you come over?"

"Thirty minutes."

Sam intercepted Jason at the top of the stairs, took his arm, and steered him into her office. "After our meeting last Tuesday," she began, "I called my private investigator, Tim Riley, an ex-cop with the SFPD. I told Riley you didn't buy the kidnapping, and were looking for the street people who helped you.

"Last Tuesday evening, Riley asked a friend at the Hall of Justice to access CAL-NET, the state's computerized law enforcement network. Starting with the morning you surfaced, Riley's contact searched for incidents that might relate to your case. He found two: One involved a homeless man who was ticketed for loitering near City General shortly before you turned up; the other occurred last Friday when the *same man* was sent to Petaluma State Hospital for psychiatric evaluation. He had a breakdown when his friend died in front of City Hall."

Jason rubbed his temple. "There was something about that on the news,"

"Riley thought it was highly unusual that the man was sent upstate since San Francisco generally places its short-term cases in the psychiatric unit at City General."

"What's the man's name?"

Sam glanced at her notes. "Martin Dubichek."

Jason thought for a moment then shook his head. "It doesn't ring a bell."

"Dubichek's three-day evaluation period was over last Monday, and Riley called Petaluma to see if he could learn where the man had gone. But the patient was still there. An assistant administrator said Dubichek had been recommitted for another fourteen days. Riley asked for permission to visit him, but it was denied because the hospital had restricted visitors to his immediate family. Riley pressed and learned that an SFPD cop named Brodsky had visited the patient, and tried to strangle him."

"You're kidding."

"Unfortunately, I'm not. Riley then asked for the treating psychiatrist. He told the doctor he was working for a wealthy client who was trying to locate a certain homeless man in order to help him. Riley said he needed to interview Mr. Dubichek to determine if he's that man.

"At first the doctor refused. But the story about the wealthy benefactor corroborated something Dubichek has been claiming, so the doctor said he would try to get Riley's visit cleared."

"And?"

Sam took a deep breath. "Yesterday, Riley's visit was approved. He immediately went to Petaluma and met with Dubichek. Security was tight, so he had to watch what he said. He showed the patient a glossy photo of you."

"What did the man say?"

"Something about you being 'happy.' Riley suggested Dubichek might be getting things backwards since you had a serious look on your face."

"And?"

"Then the patient added: 'That's what happens when you're forced to see the world through a broken mirror.'"

"Weird," Jason said, rubbing his temple again.

"Yes, it is."

"No, I mean Dubichek's 'broken mirror' remark . . . I think I heard that on the street; tell me more."

"Sorry, that's it. Dubichek ended the visit. Anyway, Riley wasn't really interested in making conversation; he was after Dubichek's fingerprints on your photo."

"Go on," Jason urged.

"Next, Riley drove back to San Francisco and ran the prints through the criminal computer system. But someone had purged that portion of Dubichek's file. So he faxed a copy to a friend who works in the Latent Fingerprint Unit at the Department of Justice in Sacramento, where they keep the master files. Early this morning his friend verified the prints against those lifted from your head bandage: Martin Dubichek is definitely your man."

"Great work, Sam!"

"Thanks, but we're not done. Riley believes Dubichek is suicidal. He doesn't think the man will last much longer if he's kept in the hospital. The irony is that they could hold him indefinitely if they think he'll harm himself."

Jason felt his excitement ebb. "What can we do?"

Sam held up a law book. "A few years ago there was an amendment to this Welfare and Institutions Code. The amendment entitles patients to a hearing within four days of recommitment. It's an informal affair conducted by a certification review hearing officer."

"Can I appear on his behalf? As soon as he knows I'm in his corner, I'm sure it'll buy us time to get him out."

"Yes, the hearing is open to the public. But you'll risk blowing your story about being out of the country."

"I don't care; let's get the ball rolling."

"We can't just yet. While you were on your way over, I called the hospital to inquire about the hearing. It was scheduled for this afternoon, but Dubichek has requested a postponement. The hearing is now set for Monday."

"Why would he postpone it until after the weekend?"

Sam slowly shook her head. "I'm not sure. Maybe Mr. Dubichek has other plans."

"Sam, with his friend gone, he's probably the only one who can help me. We've got to get him out—now!"

Sam thought for a moment. "We'll need the cooperation of Dubichek's psychiatrist, the director of the hospital and, most importantly, Dubichek himself. The hospital might release him early if they believe he won't do anything rash, *and* if a leading citizen—like you—were willing to sponsor him. But you'll have to guarantee close supervision, including housing and employment."

"Easy. I'll give him a job at my company. And he can use my spare bedroom until he gets his own place."

Sam stared at Jason. "Are you willing to give a total stranger the run of your home—especially a man with a record of violence and mental instability? You'll have to trust him with your possessions."

"I've already trusted him with my life," Jason said.

"I see your point. But we're getting ahead of our-selves. First we have to persuade Dubichek to play along. That'll buy us time to lean on the hospital to release him, or, if necessary, have you appear at his hearing."

"Can we call him?" Jason asked.

"No, I tried. We'll have to find a way to visit him."

"Do we know anything about his relatives? Maybe we can get one of them to drive up and I'll tag along."

"Wait a minute," Sam said, opening a file. "Riley faxed his report. Yes, here it is: Dubichek has a sister, Abigail, in Michigan. Even if we could secure her coop-eration, I doubt we could get her out here in time."

Jason had a twinkle in his eye. "Why don't you pose as Dubichek's sister and I'll be your husband?"

"I'm flattered," Sam said. "However, I'm afraid I can't involve myself in the defrauding of a state institution. I won't be of any use to you if I get disbarred. I don't even want to know what you're planning."

Jason stood. "You're right, of course. Oh, by the way, may I have a copy of Riley's report? It so happens I'm taking a trip, and I'd like something to read on my way."

2

MARTY WAS SITTING on his bed finishing a letter. He was feeling pretty good, all things considered. During the past few days he had plenty of time to adjust to the facts of life, and he could think clearly now. He understood that the mayor was behind his commitment. With Pete gone, Marty was one of the two remaining people who could discredit the phony kidnapping story. The other was Jason Howell, and Marty figured the man didn't remember and had simply accepted the official story.

Marty knew he wasn't going to be released.

Ever.

And he knew what he must do. In his letter to Suzanne he told her what had happened and asked her to relay the information to Jason Howell. Maybe the man would send her some money. Then he apologized for screwing up her life and Billy's.

Marty stood, folded the letter, and stuffed it into the pocket of his shirt. Then he lifted his mattress, removed a rope made from lengths of sheet, and hid it in a bath towel. With the towel tucked under his arm, he walked down the hallway to the bathroom and locked the door.

3

SEVERAL PATIENTS and their guests were having lunch in the visiting room of the Petaluma State Hospital. Jason, dressed in slacks and a sports jacket, was pacing back and forth, using his wolf-cane for support. Because of his meeting with Sam he had missed this morning's physical therapy session. But that wasn't the reason he was pacing. "Liz, I'm nervous," he admitted when his path took him by her table.

"It's *Abby*," Liz whispered. She wore light makeup, a nondescript skirt and blouse, and had her hair pulled back. "And why be nervous? They'll be bringing him out any minute."

"Because . . . ah, Abby, I have a feeling that my life is about to change."

"You did say Petaluma has that affect on you."

"This isn't the part of Petaluma I meant. By the way, my offer for the meadow was accepted without a counter, which means I paid too much. My Scottish ancestors must be turning over in their graves. But I don't care. Escrow should close by the end of this month."

"Why don't you show it to me after we're finished here?" Liz said. "After all, I *am* your wife."

"Let's see," Jason said, "that makes it twice in two weeks."

4

MARTY HOPED the pipe running along the ceiling was as strong as it looked. He tied one end of the makeshift rope around a section emerging from a load-bearing wall, then looped the free end into a noose and pulled on it. Good, it held.

Marty stood on the toilet seat and fitted the noose around his neck. He felt drained, distant, as if he had been partying all night and now it was time to go home. He took a deep breath and exhaled slowly. He lifted a leg to take a step. In a few seconds he would be free—

Someone banged on the door. "Dubichek? You in there?"

Damn that George! "Hey, can't a guy take a crap without being hassled!" Marty yelled, planting both legs on the toilet seat. He knew George would break in if he heard strange noises.

"Hurry up. You've got visitors. Your sister Abby and her husband are here!"

Marty was taken aback. *His sister?* "Who . . . ?" he said, buying time. He was hesitant to remove the noose; he was *so* close.

"Your family, Marty!" George said in an exasperated tone. "Mr. and Mrs. Rappaport."

5

JASON LEANED toward Liz. "Calling ourselves the Rappaports was brilliant," he whispered. "What gave you the idea?"

"We needed a last name, and the investigator's report said that Mr. Dubichek registered you at City General as 'Happy Rappaport.' I was pretty sure that name would get his attention."

"Good thinking."

The main door opened and two burly psychiatric technicians entered, escorting a large man. Jason didn't recognize him.

Liz jumped up and moved toward the trio. They stopped as she approached. She stood on her toes and threw her arms around the patient's neck.

Jason prayed it was the right man.

"Oh, Martin," she cooed, "it's s-o-o-o nice to see you."

The patient looked startled. "Uh . . . hi," he said. "It's nice to see you too." He inhaled her fragrance. "Real nice."

Liz released him and stepped back. "Is that a new hairstyle?"

"Yeah, it's the grunge look," Marty said, recovering a bit. "It makes a certain statement, don't you think?" Marty showed her the side of his head. "A friend of mine gave it to me, but he's no longer with us I'm sorry to say."

Jason, now standing next to Liz, cleared his throat.

She took his arm. "And of course you remember my husband Happy."

The two techs watched intently.

Jason moved forward. Marty's face showed immediate recognition. "Yes, we've met," he said, shaking hands enthusiastically and leaning toward Jason's face. "I used to have long hair and a beard. Remember?"

Jason stared into Marty's eyes. Suddenly he felt dizzy as if the room were spinning and he were falling. He began to sway when the big man reached out with his free hand and steadied him. "Y-yes, I *do* remember," Jason said. "Ah, why don't we sit down?"

The techs watched, arms folded, while the patient and his visitors sat around a table. The big man opened. "So, Happy, I thought you were out of the country."

"I changed my plans. When I learned you were here, I decided to accompany Abby. How are you doing?"

"Okay . . . at the moment. I was trying on a new necktie when you arrived."

"Are you ready to be released?" Liz asked gently.

"Yes, yes, definitely. Can you help me?"

"We believe so," Liz answered. "We have an attorney, Samantha Paxton, who's familiar with your case. She has a wealthy client who'll give you a good job. You did him a big favor, and he's grateful."

Marty glanced at Jason. "Yeah, that's right," the big man said, his eyes welling up.

Liz paused while Marty wiped his eyes on his sleeve. "With your permission," she said, "Sam will talk to the hospital's officials about securing your release."

Tears streamed down Marty's cheeks. "That's great, sis," he sniffled, glancing over at Jason, who was looking at the floor and dabbing at his own tears.

"Okay," Liz said evenly, "Sam will inform the officials that you have a sponsor, and she'll try to get you released over the weekend. If that doesn't work we'll all appear at your hearing on Monday." Liz took the big man's hand. "Can you wait?"

"Uh-huh," Marty said, managing a smile. Then he turned to a teary-eyed Jason. "Thanks, Happy," he said.

Part III

THE CROSSFIRE

THIRTEEN
Saturday, January 21

1

RAY GORNEY LOVED to watch. In the Christmas of his fifteenth year his parents bought him a telescope, hoping their reclusive son would develop an interest in astronomy. Young Ray took the instrument up to his roof, pointed it at the heavens, and verified the moon was cratered and Saturn was ringed. That done, he promptly trained it on the windows of the houses around him. He found his neighbors much more interesting, even if they were only eating dinner or talking on the phone. He took copious notes, creating intricate stories about their lives.

One day he realized if you watched people long enough, you would learn their secrets. At that moment young Gorney knew he would be a private investigator when he grew up.

Four decades later, at age fifty-five, Ray Gorney had refined his tastes. He now favored watching the wealthy, the fortunate few who considered the world their private playground, where the main attractions were money and power, and the rules of normal human behavior were sus-pended.

Gorney retrieved a Snapper Bar from the glove box of his aging Ford Fairlane. Using his teeth, he liberated the candy and tossed the wrapper behind him. Since he never carried passengers, he used the rear of his car for his trash, and over time the Fairlane developed a pungent aroma as if a rodent had crawled into a crevice and expired.

By contrast, Gorney kept the front of his car—his business end—clean and well-organized. On the passen-ger seat was an expensive leather attaché case, trimmed in 18-karat gold. Inside, arranged neatly in compartments, were a cellular phone, two microcassette recorders, and an assortment of state-of-the-art surveillance equipment, in-cluding powerful binoculars and a night vision camera. A hidden compartment concealed his prized handgun, a 9-mm Walther P-38.

When it came to surveillance, Ray Gorney had no equal. Fueled by junk food and caffeine, he watched with the intensity of a dog in a car, alert for the return of its owner. His peers called him "The Watching Machine" and "The Famous Shamus," two nicknames Gorney re-ceived with great pride.

On this cold and clear winter afternoon, Gorney was stationed in Pacific Heights, an exclusive San Francisco neighborhood of Victorian mansions and luxury apartment buildings. Approximately two hours ago he was hired over the phone by Newman, Branlov & Conklin, a power-ful law firm with offices on both Coasts. Gorney accepted the assignment and within minutes a courier arrived at his office with a detailed file on a prominent businessman, Jason Howell, a passenger on the small plane that crashed in Golden Gate Park last January 9.

The file contained Howell's address and his unlisted telephone number. It also included recent newspaper clippings and photographs. A handwritten note stated that the subject was supposed to be recuperating in South America from his head injury, but had, in fact, remained in San Francisco.

It was Gorney's practice never to store files or any other case materials in his car. Everything was committed to memory. Four times each day, Sid, his faithful assistant, dropped off junk food and picked up his boss' exposed film rolls, microcassette tapes, and any other items that might compromise the assignment.

Gorney ingested the Snapper Bar in two crunchy bites, leaned back, and allowed his massive frame to settle into the wide cavity that time and pressure had molded into the driver's seat. He spent the next twenty minutes contentedly watching Howell's building, sipping coffee, and listening to classical music on the radio.

When he noticed the electric gate to the underground garage ascend, Gorney placed his coffee in a plastic holder and readied his binoculars. A Mercedes sedan nosed into the driveway, the door opened, and the building's doorman got out and stood at attention on the driver's side.

Gorney watched.

A man with a cane emerged from the building and limped down the front steps. Gorney focused on the man's face. In spite of his odd clothing and scruffy beard, Gorney easily identified him as Jason Howell.

As the subject climbed into the car and started the engine, Gorney snapped a wide-angle shot and several close-ups. He allowed the Mercedes to travel a full city block before cranking up the Fairlane and pulling away.

2

JASON PARKED his car in front of Sam's building and limped up the stairs. He noticed the climb to the third floor was easier today. Sam greeted him in jeans and a heavy sweater, explaining that the heating system was off for the weekend. She invited him into the conference room where a small electric heater was making ticking sounds.

Jason sat near the heater. His injured temple was throbbing, and he gratefully accepted the offer of tea. "Your investigator was right about Dubichek being suicidal," he began. "We arrived just in time. But after Liz and I finished talking to the man, his outlook had turned hopeful. However, I'm concerned what he might do if we fail to spring him. And I don't think we should roll the dice at some bureaucratic review hearing. Let's get him out *now*."

Sam reached for a file and opened it. "All right, I'll start with Dubichek's doctor."

Jason stood and paced while Sam dialed. His headache had escalated, and he massaged his temple as he listened. Sam was telling Dr. Argus she was calling on behalf of her client, the prominent citizen who had sent an investigator to interview Martin Dubichek. The client would now like to sponsor Mr. Dubichek, and give him a job and a place to stay. Would the doctor recommend releasing the patient under those circumstances?

Jason stopped pacing and turned toward Sam.

Sam gave him the thumbs up sign.

So far so good.

Sam quit advocating and listened. After a period of silence she finally said, "I understand, Doctor." Then she hung up and looked at Jason. "I'm afraid we're only partway there. The doctor has agreed in principle to a sponsorship, but unfortunately that isn't enough. By law, Dubichek's release must be authorized by the hospital's director, which won't be easy. The director has been asked by the chief of police to hold Dubichek pending their investigation. The police suspect the patient is seeking retribution for his friend's death and might pose a threat to the mayor."

"BULLSHIT!" Jason exploded, slamming his fist on the conference table. His cup became airborne and tea spilled onto the conference table.

"Jason, are you okay?" Sam asked.

He rubbed the pink scar on his temple and stared at the spreading puddle. "Sorry. It's these headaches . . . they're pretty bad sometimes."

"What can I get you?"

"Tylenol helps."

"I'll be right back." Sam disappeared, returning with a bottle of Tylenol and a glass of water. While Jason swallowed the capsules, she blotted the tea.

"Sorry," Jason apologized again.

Sam gave him a long, worried look. Then she said, "We're going to need help, Jason. We're going to need someone who can grab that director by his jug handles and shake him. Do you have any ideas?"

Jason thought for a moment. "Yes, I do."

3

THE MAÎTRE D' CUT a fine figure in his tuxedo. "Was everything to your liking?" he inquired of his two distinguished guests. His French accent glided easily beneath a mellifluous voice.

"Oh, yes, Jacques, it was a truly memorable meal," Margaret Babcock replied, fluttering her eyelashes.

"Yes indeed, Jacques," the mayor chimed in, neatly folding his white linen napkin into a triangle and placing it on the table.

Margaret smiled coquettishly at Jacques. "Don't you think my husband should bring me to Les Moules more often?" she asked, fingering a diamond and gold necklace. "I do so enjoy it." Her jewelry sparkled in the candlelight.

The mayor rolled his eyes. "Margaret, you wouldn't enjoy being here so much if you had to listen to the problems I endure at this table, especially from Chief Conti."

Margaret pouted.

Jacques pressed his fingertips together, his face conveying just the right amount of sympathy.

Mayor Babcock glanced at his watch. "It's time to go to the opera," he said brusquely.

As the couple stood, another waiter arrived with a coat over each arm. The maître d' took the ermine and held it for Madame Babcock while she climbed in. Then he held the cashmere for the mayor.

"Thank you, Jacques," the mayor said, buttoning his coat. "Now, will you please see about our car?"

Jacques bowed. "Your Honor and Madame, it has been done." Then he lowered his voice and leaned toward the mayor's ear. "But, Monsieur Mayor, I must apologize in advance. There is . . . how you say? . . . a vagabond standing just outside. He appeared when I sent for your limo. We tried to shoo him, but he stubbornly refuses to leave. I hope his presence does not ruin your evening."

"Don't worry, Jacques," the mayor said, squeezing Margaret's hand. "My driver is a highly-trained police officer, and he'll see to it that there's no trouble. Remember, keeping beggars away from our fine dining establishments is one of my highest priorities as your mayor."

Jacques nodded agreeably and held the door, again bowing. He watched the mayor's wife take her husband's arm as they strolled toward the Lincoln Town Car. The driver stood at attention by the rear door. Jacques was greatly relieved to see that the vagabond had disappeared.

Just as the couple reached the limo, the beggar suddenly emerged from the shadows of a doorway and moved toward the mayor. He was wielding a cane. The mayor motioned for his wife to get inside. The driver opened his overcoat, exposing a holstered gun. In the blink of eye his right hand was on the pistol.

Jacques' heart skipped and he went down on one knee.

The vagabond said something to the mayor and then removed his hat. After a brief exchange, the mayor shook his hand and gestured for him to climb into the limo and join Madame.

Jacques' mouth dropped to his chest.

The mayor got in, the driver closed the door, and they were off.

Jacques, who in reality was Lyle Coons from Raleigh, North Carolina, exhaled slowly. "Well, I'll be darned," he said in a momentary lapse of maître d' decorum.

4

MARGARET HUDDLED against the left side of the limo, trembling and clutching her Gucci purse. Jason, sitting in the middle, toyed with his cane.

"Margaret, I believe you've met my good friend, Jason Howell," the mayor said casually as the limo motored across town toward the opera house. His wife's discomfort seemed to amuse him.

Margaret studied the scruffy face. After a moment, recognition filled her eyes. "A-aren't you recuperating in South America?" she managed.

"That's my cover story, Mrs. Babcock. But I have business in town, and I promised your husband I would avoid the media."

"That getup ought to do it," the mayor chuckled.

"It's amazing how people avoid looking at me, Walt. You ought to try it when you want to walk around as though you didn't exist."

"I'll certainly keep that in mind," the mayor said, opening the limo's mahogany-paneled bar. "Would you care for some cognac to celebrate your discharge from the hospital? I have a nice bottle of *Remy Martin XO* in here."

"Sure."

"Me, too," Margaret said. Although she normally didn't indulge after dinner, she was taking now.

The limo stopped at a light and the mayor poured three cognacs.

"To health, happiness, and prosperity," Jason toasted, clinking snifters.

"Thank you, Jason," Margaret replied, cautiously sipping as the limo began moving.

"Yes, indeed," the mayor said, swirling and sniffing the cognac. "So, Jason, to what do we owe the pleasure of your company?"

"I need a favor so I can return a favor."

The mayor took a sip, eyeing Jason over the top of his glass.

"It involves a man by the name of Martin Dubichek."

Mayor Babcock stopped sipping.

"During the past week he's been a patient at Petaluma State Hospital. His doctor says he's ready to be released if someone sponsors him. I would like to be that someone, if it can be arranged confidentially."

The mayor stared at Jason. "That's very charitable of you. But what does any of this have to do with me?"

"The hospital's director won't release him because he's been misinformed that the patient is a threat to you."

"I see. So what would you like me to do?"

"Straighten the director out, for starters."

"What else?"

"Halt the investigation of my alleged kidnapping, if you haven't already done so."

"Now why would I do these things?"

Jason detected a stiffening in the mayor's body. It was time for the bottom line. "Because as Mr. Dubichek's sponsor, I'll counsel him to stay away from the media. You know how much they like homeless hero stories."

The mayor sipped thoughtfully. "Well, well, dear friend, you've gone to extraordinary lengths to have this meeting. Might there be another reason for your strong interest in Mr. Dubichek?"

Jason anticipated the question. "You're right, Walt," he replied, changing his tone just enough to emphasize what he was about to say. "I'm doing another deal. My biggest yet. And it could be costly to have our merger partner read a sensationalized account of my time on the street. As you know, I'm not in a position to contravene malicious rumors and innuendoes from my competitors. If Mr. Dubichek remains unsupervised, I'll have no control over who he talks to and what he might say."

"Yes, of course," the mayor acknowledged, his lips broadening into a smile.

Jason smiled back. He knew the deal was done. Holding the mayor's eyes, Jason said, "I would like to propose another toast: To your victory in November."

Margaret raised her empty glass and hiccupped.

5

AFTER LOSING Howell on Restaurant Row, Ray Gorney resumed his stakeout in Pacific Heights, waiting for his subject to return home. Thirty minutes ago, when the man Howell parked his car on a side street and ducked into an alleyway, the investigator had to let him go; at three hundred pounds Gorney could no longer gumshoe after his subjects.

It didn't matter. As the consummate professional, he would turn this minor setback into a major opportunity. As soon as Gorney verified Howell's sixth-floor apartment was still dark, he retrieved his cell phone from his attaché case and made a call. Ten minutes later Sid arrived in an unmarked white van and pulled up next to the Fairlane. Through the driver's window, Gorney passed an envelope containing an exposed film canister and a microcassette tape, and received a large white bag packed with Maxi-Burgers, Snapper Bars, and several containers of black coffee.

Sid parked the van and went into the building's basement through a side door. He wore a maintenance uniform and carried a small toolbox. Five minutes later he emerged and drove away.

Gorney devoured two MaxiBurgers as he listened to the overture to Rossini's "The Thieving Magpie" on San Francisco's classical music station. He was finishing his second cup of coffee when the subject's Mercedes pulled into the building's garage. He tossed the empty container behind him and dabbed at his mouth with a paper napkin.

After a few minutes, Howell's lights came on. Gorney inserted a tape into the in-dash cassette, pushed an unlabeled button next to the radio, and waited. Out of the Fairlane's speakers came the squawk of an answering machine rewinding.

"Jason, please call me at the Penniston," the woman's voice said.

A moment passed and Gorney heard the sound of dialing.

"You're working late," Howell said.

"I'm not really working, but that's another story." Her voice sounded tired. "What's happening with the . . . Golden Fleece?"

Gorney jotted down GOLDEN FLEECE in a notepad. He picked up a fresh container of coffee, removed the lid, and tossed it behind him.

"He's out tomorrow morning."

"That's wonderful," she said, her voice perking up.

"I'll tell you more in person."

"Are you going to pick him up?"

"No, I've made other arrangements."

"And I assume he'll be staying with . . . ah, Mr. Rappaport?"

"Yes."

Gorney wrote RAPPAPORT in his pad.

"Does the Golden Fleece know?"

"Yes."

"May I stop by at lunch time and say hello?"

"Yes, that should work."

The conversation ended and Gorney pushed the stop button on the cassette. He took another sip of coffee, and pondered the situation. He had no idea what the two were talking about, but their carefully coded conversation excited him. He replayed the day's events in his head: Howell in a homeless outfit; Howell meeting with a lawyer; Howell ducking into an alley on restaurant row; and finally, the woman caller. None of it added up. Not yet. But in time it would.

It always did.

FOURTEEN
Sunday, January 22

1

THE SUN MARCHED over the playing field, melting the morning frost and drawing the chill from the air. Marty grabbed an easel from the recreation room and led a group of rapacious Forty-Niner fans into the sunshine. Since it was the Bye Week before the Super Bowl, there were no games on television, and Marty was tired of watching people mope around.

As he had done so often in his coaching days, Marty gathered his team around him and used X's and O's to outline his football strategy. For a touch of realism, each patient pinned the number of a favorite player to the back of his shirt. Other patients, men and women, stood along the sidelines, chatting and making wisecracks.

Marty played quarterback. He huddled with his offense and then positioned them on the line of scrimmage. The call was a slant pass to the receiver on the left. Because the team didn't have a football, they used a roll of toilet paper.

The center hiked and Marty faked a hand-off to the running back, took a three-step drop, and hurled the toilet paper over the heads of the pass rushers. One end came loose and the roll streamed like a comet before falling into the outstretched hands of the receiver. Stunned by his catch, the receiver almost forgot to run. A lineman tackled him, but not before he gained twelve yards.

The people on the sideline cheered and applauded.

Next, Marty called a running play. The center hiked and Marty underhanded the roll to the running back, who managed to twist out of a tackle before being dropped near the line of scrimmage. In frustration, he pounded his fists on the ground while several defensive linemen jumped on top of him for good measure. Then the rest of the players, including Marty, added their bodies to the pile.

Shaking his head, George tapped Marty on the shoulder. "Hey, Dubichek, what are you trying to do, kill everybody before you leave? I'll be out of a job."

"I was just showing them a few plays," Marty said sheepishly, untangling himself from the pile. "I guess we got a little carried away."

"Well, we better get you out of here before people *do* get carried away. Are you ready to go?"

"You bet. Is my ride here?"

George nodded in the direction of the driveway on the other side of the chain link fence. "Look over there."

Marty couldn't believe his eyes. Waiting at the entrance was a burgundy limo. The driver, wearing sunglasses and dressed in a dark suit, was standing at attention by the open trunk. "You're shitting me," Marty whistled.

"No, sir, Mr. Dubichek, that's your ride; you're leaving in style."

While Marty rushed off to get his things, George and the patients stood at the fence staring at the Lincoln Town Car. In surprisingly short order, Marty appeared at the front entrance. He had his green parka tucked under one arm and a small parcel under the other. The package was neatly wrapped in brown paper and tied with twine. Inside were toiletries, pajamas, and a flannel shirt—all presents from George. The driver placed the small parcel in the center of a large, empty trunk. He held the rear door for Marty, who entered with a flourish.

The buzzing on the patient's side of the fence increased.

Marty retracted the power window and waved.

Someone yelled, "Way to go, Marty!"

The crowd roared its approval.

Marty, grinning widely, reached both arms out of the window and held up his fingers in the twin victory sign.

2

"LET ME TAKE your coat," Jason said to Liz. "And may I get you something?"

"Perhaps later . . ." Liz was looking beyond Jason, at her brother-in-law's living room. "Déjà vu," she exhaled.

"You're referring to my decor?"

"If I didn't know better, I would accuse you of stealing our furniture. You are definitely your brother's brother."

"Yes, our tastes are remarkably similar," Jason said, holding her eyes before turning to put the coat away.

Liz settled into an overstuffed armchair and placed her purse on a black lacquered coffee table. When Jason returned she said, "I came early to talk to you before you get involved with Mr. Dubichek. Do you mind?"

Jason took the couch opposite her. "Not at all."

"I hate to involve you in this . . . but after we returned from Petaluma I fought with Anton. It was pretty bad."

"Are you okay?"

Liz nodded. "I wanted you to know since your relationship with him will undoubtedly be affected."

"Go on."

"Anton was coming off a bad day of meetings with bankers and attorneys, all of whom pressed him to place the Howell Development Corporation in bankruptcy. Afterwards he went drinking. When he came home, I went on and on about our trip to Petaluma. In retrospect, I should have been more sensitive, but I was excited about helping Mr. Dubichek and seeing your hilltop property."

Jason stared at Liz.

"He got very angry. He said if his brother wanted to help deranged vagrants, fine. But he didn't want me involved with your obsession."

"What did you say?"

"I told him that if you asked me to help you again, that's damn well what I would do. Then he raged. The music box you admired is history." Liz wiped a tear out of the corner of her eye. "Before he stormed out, he paused and gave me this . . . hateful look. It terrified me, so I packed a bag and went to the Penniston. I haven't seen him since."

"I'm really sorry, Liz. *I'm* the one who should have been more sensitive. In my rush to find Mr. Dubichek I didn't stop to consider my brother and how he might feel."

"No, no, it's not your fault. Anton and I have been having problems for some time. The truth is I've stayed at the Penniston on more than one occasion."

Jason had never seen his brother angry. He was trying to imagine what it would be like. All that came to mind was a cornered lion, frenzied, filled with hate, ready to pounce and destroy.

Liz read Jason's eyes. "Don't worry, I've notified the hotel's security."

3

SITTING ALONE in a criminal interview room at the Hall of Justice, Inspector James Brodsky nibbled indifferently on the tuna sandwich he had brought from home. Okay, maybe he got a little carried away during his interrogation of the Dubichek derelict. But clearly he had been provoked. He didn't understand why his superiors refused to listen to his side of the story. He now suspected he had been set up, and the mayor and the chief were probably laughing at his expense.

The front-desk job was the worst assignment in the police department. He would rather clean the toilets than deal with the riffraff who wandered in complaining about *this* kited check or *that* neighbor's music being too loud. He despised them. With a hateful scowl, he took their statements and gave them a little pink card with their case number stamped on it. His only satisfaction was knowing that the pink card would be all they would get. The SFPD didn't have time for petty nonsense when violent criminals and homeless scum ran rampant on the streets. The front desk was bullshit busywork, a royal waste of time.

It gnawed at Brodsky that he had been disciplined so severely. During his fifteen years on the force, there were times when an interrogation in this very room turned ugly. Sure, if a perp screamed too loudly or showed visible bruises, the lieutenant might chew Brodsky's ass a little. But the Dubichek derelict hadn't been harmed, so Brodsky knew this punishment was completely unjustified.

No, something doesn't smell right, he thought, absently pushing his tuna sandwich away. Each day he had checked with Records Management to see who had been assigned the Howell kidnapping investigation, and each day the answer came back the same: no one.

And just today, when he asked his lieutenant about the case, he was astounded to learn the investigation had been shelved due to lack of evidence and a shortage of manpower. He couldn't believe it!

Brodsky replayed his visit with Dubichek. What was the man's connection to Howell? What did he really know? Reflecting on it, Brodsky couldn't shake the feeling that Dubichek fit the profile of one of the kidnappers. But the vagrant's computer file indicated nothing unusual. That was throwing him. Maybe there was some kind of foul-up. If Dubichek really was one of the kidnappers, and if Brodsky nailed him with some brilliant investigative work, he would have to be exonerated.

With renewed optimism, Brodsky checked his watch. He had just enough time to access CAL-NET before his shift resumed. But he had to be careful. Although rarely enforced, it was illegal for anyone not assigned to a case to use the computer network unless a need-to-know existed. Certainly, Brodsky reasoned, if anyone had a need-to-know, he did.

Brodsky took the elevator to the fourth floor and hurried past the Homicide Section, praying he wouldn't run into any of his former colleagues. Further down the hallway, he stopped at the Bureau of Criminal Investigations, opened the door and peeked inside. On the far side of the room there were a few clerks and a couple of uniforms congregating in the coffee area, but the rest of BCI were on their lunch break. Just inside the door he spotted an unused terminal behind a partition.

Brodsky strolled over, logged in, and entered "Martin Dubichek" in the search menu. While waiting, he peeked over the partition and verified that no one was paying attention to him.

A summary page appeared, listing the case as nonworkable.

He scrolled down and saw the same information he had seen last Tuesday, before he went to Petaluma.

Wait! Here's an incident he had glossed over earlier: Dubichek was ticketed for loitering a few blocks from City General, an hour before Howell turned up! Brodsky's heart began racing. He selected FINGERPRINTS from the menu bar. The screen displayed:

* PURGED *

He couldn't believe it! Brodsky chewed on a nail. Only someone very high up had the authority to wash the file.

Chief Conti.

But why?

Why? Why? Why?

Brodsky was nearly beside himself, his thoughts flowing furiously. Something was going on, some cover up involving Dubichek and the chief. But what could it be? His instincts told him it must have something to do with the mayor's re-election campaign.

He leaned on an elbow and drummed his fingers on the desk. What if the mayor and the chief knew the Dubichek character was one of Howell's kidnappers? And what if the mayor didn't want to bring the vagrant to justice in order to keep the public behind Project Vector? Yes, that must be it! He wouldn't be surprised if just before the election, the chief personally broke the case and took all of the credit.

Now Brodsky's demotion made perfect sense. Those scheming bastards couldn't take the chance he would quickly nail Dubichek and undermine their plan. Okay, he had to admit the mayor and the chief were pretty shrewd, but he was smarter. Now that he knew their scheme, it was going to cost them plenty to buy his silence.

Brodsky stared at the terminal, allowing his mind to fast-forward. First, he would get Dubichek to confess on tape. Next, he would stop by Conti's fancy office with an armful of incriminating evidence. He would casually drop it on the polished oak desk. "Rudy," he would say, "we must make certain the media doesn't learn any of this. Surely they would demand a full investigation." Brodsky shook with excitement as he pictured the chief's face. He would have the bastard by the short and curlies.

Suddenly Brodsky became aware that the conversation level in the room had risen. He peered over the partition and saw clerks filing in. He glanced at his watch: it was one o'clock. He cleared the terminal and returned to his station at the front desk.

Feeling a warm glow, he doodled guns and daggers on a yellow pad and continued to daydream. "No, chief," he mumbled to himself, "mere reinstatement isn't going to be sufficient; a promotion to lieutenant and a commendation in my file is more—"

"Excuse me," a woman said, clearing her throat.

Brodsky looked up. "Yes?"

The woman blurted, "My-husband-started-drinking-after-church-and-then-the-bastard-locked-me-out-of-our-apartment-and-I-don't-want-one-of-your-goddamn-pink-cards."

"Ma'am, please try and remain calm. Give me your phone number and I'll speak with your husband. I'll be happy to straighten him out for you."

"Well . . . thank you, Officer," the woman said surprised.

"You're very welcome," Brodsky replied, smiling.

4

"CAN I TAKE your things to your room?" Jason asked the big man at his door.

"Sure," Marty said, handing over his small parcel.

Jason took the package and looked behind Marty. "Is this it?"

"Yup. Every year it seems like I've got a little less."

Liz stepped up. "Hello, Mr. Dubichek," she said, taking Marty's hand. "I'm Liz Howell. It's nice to see you again. Won't you please come in?"

Jason had been blocking the doorway. He stood aside. "Oh, I'm sorry, Mr. Dubichek, please come in. I'll hang your coat."

Marty handed his parka to Jason. "Call me Marty. I still think of 'Mr. Dubichek' as my old man."

"Okay, Marty, shall we go into the living room and . . . ah, get reacquainted."

"Sure."

Marty sat on the couch next to Liz. He inhaled her perfume deeply a couple of times and then settled in. Jason took the overstuffed chair opposite the couch.

"Nice digs, Mr. and Mrs. Howell," Marty said, gazing around. "It's . . . very dramatic."

"Thanks, Marty. Please call me Jason."

"And please call me Liz. But I should explain that Jason and I aren't married."

"We met about ten days ago," Jason offered.

"I understand," Marty said, nodding.

"Liz is really my brother's wife," Jason added.

"Uh-huh," Marty said.

"How about lunch?" Liz asked, changing the subject.

"Sure."

Liz got up and both men stood.

"There are cold cuts in the refrigerator, and bread in the pantry," Jason said. "Can I give you a hand?"

Liz shook her head and smiled. "Don't worry, I have no intention of going near the stove or anything sharp. But if I need help, I'll scream."

The men took their seats. "So how was your trip?" Jason asked.

"Great. First time I ever rode in a limo. Thanks. By the way, why did the driver leave me at the corner?"

"The driver is an undercover cop. Since the police department leaks like a sieve, I would prefer to keep our arrangement confidential."

"Undercover cop? Whose limo was that?"

"The mayor's."

Marty eyes grew large. He mouthed the word "mayor" as if he hadn't heard it correctly. "You had me picked up in the *mayor's* limo?"

"Yes."

"I'll be damned; how'd you swing it?"

"It was part of the deal to get you released. It was the least Babcock could do."

"What's the rest of the deal? Who do I have to kill?"

Jason smiled. "It's not like that. First let me share with you something Mayor Babcock told me. As he explained, the only reason they thought I was kidnapped was because of this overzealous police officer, Inspector Brodsky."

"Oh, yeah, I had a visit from him last week . . . fella's kind of jumpy."

"I heard he attacked you. Why did he do that?"

"I called him a 'big pussy.' I figured he was putting on an obnoxious act to provoke me and give them a reason to extend my commitment. So I acted first. That Prozac is great stuff."

"He assaulted me, too," Jason commented, "and I've only seen him on the Six O'clock News."

"I'll never forget the man. It was like touching excrement—no matter how much you wash your hands, the awful feeling of it remains."

"The mayor shares your sentiment. He said Brodsky took circumstantial evidence, concocted the kidnapping story, and spread it around. Although the mayor and the chief were upset, they were committed to the story for political reasons." Jason paused and softened his tone. "Babcock also told me about your friend. I'm sorry."

Marty bit his lip and looked at the ceiling.

Jason quickly added: "The good news is that the kidnapping investigation has been terminated, and Brodsky has been severely disciplined."

"Good," Marty said. Then he thought for a moment. "So the rest of the deal is that I don't talk to the press?"

"Right."

"Why should I play along?"

"As I'm sure you know, the mayor is under tremendous pressure from his supporters in the business community to reduce San Francisco's homeless population. His re-election hangs in the balance. If you tell your story, he'll reopen the investigation and characterize you as raving homeless lunatic with a vendetta against him. You'll be arrested or institutionalized again, and I won't be able to intervene unless I can testify about what really happened to me on the street.

"On top of that, I need your help. I'm uncomfortable with having such a large gap in my memory."

"But couldn't I just make stuff up?"

Jason shook his head. "No. First of all, I don't want you to tell me what happened; I want you to take me back to the street and *show* me. I remember fragments, and I want to see how much more I can recall on my own. If I hit a wall, then I'll ask you to fill in the blanks. Hopefully, that won't happen. I'm convinced the memories are all in there; I just need the associative experiences to release them."

"What do you mean?"

"Take last night for example. After meeting with Babcock I stopped at a phone booth in the Civic Center Plaza to call you about your release."

Marty was aghast. "You were in the plaza at night? Don't you know how dangerous that is?"

Jason nodded. "Fortunately I was in the homeless getup I was wearing when you found me. I was ignored by everyone, including the taxis I tried to hail. So I decided to take the Muni. But when the bus arrived, it scared me, and it took an enormous amount of self-control to board it. Something bad happened to me on a bus, didn't it?"

Marty nodded knowingly. "Yup."

Jason leaned toward Marty. "Here's the deal: help me retrace my steps and then we'll talk about employment."

"Do you have a job in mind?"

"Not yet. But after we spend time together, I'll have a good idea. Think of it as an extended job interview."

"When do we go?"

"Tomorrow night, which happens to be the two-week anniversary of my accident."

Liz came in showing her hands. "The cold cuts are on the table and all fingers are present and accounted for."

Jason waited for an answer from Marty.

"Okay, I'll do it."

"Do what?" Liz asked. "Who are you two characters planning to knock off?"

"Me, most likely," Jason said. "I'm going back on the street."

5

WITH A BOUNCE in his step, Inspector James Brodsky exited the Hall of Justice and turned onto Bryant. It was a lovely day to take a stroll. He was using his midafternoon break to initiate the first link in a chain of events designed to reverse his fortune.

He allowed his mind to explore his bright future. After his promotion to lieutenant he would move into a one-bedroom condo in a San Francisco high-rise. No more tedious commute. Longer range—say in three years—he would put in for captain and move into a larger apartment with a study and a view of the Bay.

When he retired it would be with a hefty pension. He would spend his golden years as a security consultant for a large corporation, leaving plenty of time for the illegal big-game hunting expeditions that could easily be arranged with the right connections.

Of course, for the chief to be around to promote Brodsky to captain, the mayor would have to remain in office. Brodsky made a mental note to volunteer for Babcock's re-election campaign.

Although strolling slowly, Brodsky's heart was pounding. He had fantasized himself into a frenzy. The only thing in his way was the minor matter of getting the Dubichek derelict to confess. Tomorrow was Brodsky's day off, and he would pay the degenerate another visit. This time, however, he would have a wire under his Father McCallister disguise. He fondly remembered how he wore his priest outfit the day Howell had surfaced. He visited a soup kitchen with the intention of getting one of the waste cases to confess to their knowledge of the kidnapping. But the winos were too incoherent to tell him anything useful. After the kitchen closed, he left with a smirking vagrant in fatigues, making small talk until the derelict led him to the kidnappers' lair. It was a brilliant piece of police work.

Brodsky stepped inside a phone booth and took several calming breaths as he dialed the Petaluma State Hospital.

A woman answered.

He cleared his throat. "Good after-r-r-noon, ma'am, this is Father McCallister from San Francisco calling, and I'm inquirin' about one of my par-r-rishioners, a Mister-r-r Mar-r-rtin Dubichek.

"You see," he continued, "the man missed church today, and I just learned he was stayin' with you fine people. I'd like to make an appointment to pay him a sur-r-r-prise visit." Brodsky took a deep breath and suppressed a giggle with his hand, knowing he had rolled his "r's" perfectly.

"Don't worry, Father," the woman said. "I'm sure you'll be seeing him soon. He was released earlier today."

Brodsky, still holding his breath, stiffened.

"In fact," she went on excitedly, "he's quite a celebrity around here. A car picked him up before noon. When the driver registered we learned that Mr. Dubichek was returning to San Francisco in Mayor Babcock's very own limousine! Everyone here is—"

Brodsky gasped, and the phone slipped from his hand.

"Father McCallister?" the handset said as it banged against the phone booth. "Are you there . . . ?"

6

AFTER EATING LUNCH, Jason, Liz, and Marty remained at the table. "Before my accident," Jason said, "I thought I had everything. But financial success and material possessions no longer satisfy me; I'm ready for a change."

"Well, I've got nothing," Marty responded, "and I'm ready for a change, too."

"My situation is a hybrid," Liz said. "My husband and I had everything, and we're currently in the process of losing it all. But at least we've had a roof over our heads." Then turning to Marty she asked, "What is it really like being homeless? I've seen TV programs and read articles, but I don't feel I truly understand it."

"It's worse than I can describe, Liz—worse than anyone can describe. It's a lonely existence, full of fear. The homeless are afraid of the police, gangs, drug dealers, and each other. Mostly, though, they're afraid they'll never get out of homelessness. They feel subhuman, partly because that's the way society treats them and partly because of their own guilt. Caseworkers refer to the homeless as 'marginal people.' They're talking economics, of course, but the term has a certain Darwinian ring to it, don't you think?"

"But aren't there some individuals who choose homelessness as a lifestyle?" Jason asked.

Marty rolled his eyes. "Like 'King of the Road' by Roger Miller? It kills me that people still have this romantic notion of carefree vagabonds, their possessions tied to a stick, making hobo coffee around a fire, crisscrossing the country on freight trains, laughing at the poor slobs spending nine to five at their jobs. There may be some free spirits like that floating around, but *I* sure as hell haven't met any.

"More realistically, the homeless can be placed in three categories," Marty continued. "We've got the discarded workers, the substance abusers, and the mentally ill. Many of the discards can be salvaged. But you don't have a lot of time to screw around before they sink into the two other categories.

"Imagine spending years in a manufacturing plant. Then one Friday you get a pink slip. Although you're skilled, there's no market for someone who's good at making widgets. Maybe they think you're too old to learn something new. Maybe they think you were getting paid too much. Eventually the unemployment checks stop coming, and you find yourself sitting on your couch on the sidewalk.

"Even if you're one of the lucky few who gets into a shelter, every day's the same. There's no point in making plans since you're powerless to implement them. Over time, your brain suffers from disuse, and it becomes tough to concentrate. Your mind wanders and reality slips away. It's like there's this unseen force tugging at you, spiraling you down until one day you find yourself standing on a street corner pushing a cup at the people passing by.

"How long were you homeless?" Liz asked.

"About three years."

"My God, how did you manage to survive that long?"

"I was luckier than most. I quit drinking and that enabled me to stay in the better shelters. But even so, life was no picnic. There's an old Woody Allen joke about a hotel guest who complained that the food was not only awful, but the portions were too small. Well, shelter conditions can be horrendous, and then they don't let you stay. It doesn't matter if you have no place to go. It doesn't matter if it's storming outside. Every day of the week at 7:00 a.m., you're out on your butt.

"Sunday mornings were the worst. The streets are empty. Regular people are tucked away in nice, warm beds. Public buildings are locked, so you can't go inside to get out of the weather, sip some water, or use the toilet. If you sit on a park bench, you risk getting arrested. No one gives a damn what happens to you. No one cares where you go. No one is expecting you. More than any other day of week, Sundays made me feel terribly lonely and reminded me how different I was from the rest of the human race."

"How long could you stay in an emergency shelter?" Jason asked.

"It could be as short as a day or as long as a month, so I had to keep rotating. But it didn't matter since the shelters are all pretty much the same. You sleep with one eye open and keep your shoes pinned under the legs of your cot, otherwise someone will sneak up and steal them. Lots of folks refuse to sleep in Armories or other emergency shelters no matter how cold it is outside because of the danger. I got by because of my size.

"I met my friend Pete a couple of years ago. He was sleeping in an adjacent cot when a pair of shelter queens jumped him. I bounced them pretty good. Pete was grateful and we became buddies. He didn't have a college education like I do, but he was streetwise and funny. Mostly he was optimistic: He never gave up on the idea that someday he'd get out of homelessness—only he didn't figure on it being inside a pine box.

"We heard that the St. Andrews Shelter for Men screened out anyone with a police record, and that they let clients stay up to two years if they participated in a formal job training program. St. Andrews is considered a 'transitional facility' because it helps folks get back into the world, not just survive. Me and Pete applied for the program and eventually were accepted.

"We were at St. Andrews for the last eighteen months. Pete was learning cable TV installation; I took computer classes. I got pretty good at clicking my way around Windows.

"The stability of being in one place allowed us to develop friendships, work occasionally, and save some money. We felt more like human beings. We even had a weekly social club outside the shelter. I was just beginning to share Pete's optimism that we'd get back into the real world when you came into our lives, Jason."

"I'm sorry."

Marty looked at his hands. "I guess it's not your fault. With so much stacked against us, sooner or later me and Pete would've taken the fall anyway. That's the problem with a system that propagates human misery. They should gas all the homeless like the radio shock jocks have been suggesting."

A pall settled over the table.

"It sounds like hell," Liz said finally.

"It was, especially when Pete died. To me, hell is losing everything you have, bit by bit, until all hope is gone and there's nothing left to live for."

"I can relate a little," Liz said. "To me, hell is standing by helplessly, watching a failing business destroy your husband and your marriage."

"And for me," Jason added, "hell is achieving all of your goals and realizing you're still not happy."

"That about covers it," Marty said. "Shall it be razor blades or rat poison?"

"Rat poison for me," Liz said, raising her hand.

The three fell silent again. Then Liz spoke. "Well, if we're going to stick around, then we're back to the idea of making changes."

Jason stood to stretch his right leg. He face was grim. "Listening to Marty has had a chilling effect on me. I never gave any thought to what might happen to the people I've downsized after they walked out the door. Maybe it's payback time."

"What do you mean?" Liz asked.

"I have no idea. But I'd like to know much more about homelessness. Maybe something can be done. There must be social scientists working on the problem."

Liz's face brightened. "Last month I caught part of *Crossfire* program on CNN. Experts were debating their solutions to homelessness."

"I'd like to see that show. Hearing opposing views might allow me to get a handle on the problem."

"I'll call the station for a copy."

"Thanks, Liz." Then Jason turned to Marty. "You've suddenly become quiet. Don't you think something can be done to reduce the homeless population?"

Marty stared at Jason. "I think that when all of this is over you're going to wish you had really gone to South America."

FIFTEEN
Monday, January 23

1

JASON LOOKED UP from the morning newspaper as
Marty entered the kitchen. "How was your room?"

"G-r-reat," Marty purred, stretching.   He was
wearing the extra-large pajamas George had given him. "I
can't remember the last time I slept so soundly. Maybe
never. My room is quiet, the temperature perfect, and the
bed like a womb. I'm permanently ruined for cots." He
went over to the refrigerator and looked inside. "Are you
sure we have to go back to the street?"

"It's just for a couple of days."

"Too bad," Marty sighed, pouring himself a glass of
orange juice.

"Would you like part of the newspaper?"

Marty took a seat at the kitchen table. "Sure."

"Let me guess . . . the sports section."

"You got it."

The two men read and ate in silence. After a while
Marty put the paper down. "So what's on the agenda for
today, Boss?"

Jason looked up. "I'm going to physical therapy this morning. When I return I'll take you to my barber to get that haircut touched up."

Marty ran his fingers through his chopped-up hair. "No thanks. I think I'll keep this a little longer . . . it's all I got left from Pete."

Jason nodded. "Okay, what should I buy in preparation for the street?"

"Some things you can't buy."

"Maybe so, but don't we need bedrolls or sleeping bags? I feel like we're going camping in the buff."

"I'll tell you what, get a couple of sleeping bags and pick up a pint of brandy, the cheapest rotgut you can find."

"Why do we need rotgut?"

"You'll see."

"Anything else?"

"Cash . . . a couple of thousand in tens, twenties, hundreds."

"Why?"

"We might need to buy our way out of trouble."

"I guess that's right. Money talks—"

"—and bullshit walks," Marty finished.

"That's my cue," Jason said, reaching for his cane. "Will you be okay for a couple of hours?"

"Are you kidding? I'm just wondering when I'm going to realize I died and went to heaven."

After Jason left, Marty took a long hot shower and dressed in his jeans and flannel shirt. He had another cup of coffee and finished the newspaper. Then he wandered around the apartment. In Jason's office he checked out the customized computer system built into a black laminated wall unit. And in the home theater there was a big-screen TV and a rack of audio and video equipment. A control panel routed music to various rooms. Marty was perplexed how someone could have so much and not be happy. It would be a long time before he unraveled that one.

Yesterday when Liz and Jason were talking about changing their lives, Marty didn't say much because he had already gone through some heavy changes of his own. In Petaluma it became clear that one way or another he was not going to remain homeless. He couldn't do it anymore. Yet, ironically, he would soon be leaving the lap of luxury to go right back into the street.

It wasn't going to be easy.

Especially without Pete.

He went into the living room and looked out of the window. In the distance, between two tall buildings, he saw a slice of the bay. He opened the window and leaned out. Mixed with the smells of the neighborhood, fresh ocean air rode on a breeze out of the west. The morning fog was breaking up, giving way to a patchwork of blue. According to the newspaper there would be full sunshine with unseasonably warm temperatures in the afternoon. As far as Marty was concerned, the mild weather was the only good thing about going back to the street.

Lining Jason's block were late-model Benzes, Beamers, and Sport Utility Vehicles. There was only one clunker, a black Ford Fairlane, parked across the street. Marty first noticed it yesterday when the limo dropped him off. Its windows were heavily-tinted and the car sagged on the driver's side.

This morning its windows were fogged. Marty was about to dismiss it as just another heap with a homeless person living inside when it occurred to him that San Francisco's law against the "vehicularly housed" would be strictly enforced in this neighborhood. He made a mental note to mention the Fairlane to Jason.

2

EXCEPT FOR the winter rainy season, the cities along the San Francisco Peninsula are blessed with a pleasant and sunny climate. To the east, the bay waters cushion the air temperature; to the west, the coastal hills block the ocean fog. The one exception is Daly City, a bedroom community south of San Francisco. Due to a quirk in the local geography, the town is generally enshrouded in fog even when the sun is shining everywhere else. For this reason it was more out of irony than reason for the owners of Brodsky's apartment complex to name it *Casa del Sol.*

But in truth, during the fifteen years Brodsky had lived in his one-bedroom garden apartment, he hadn't paid much attention to the weather. The rent was right and the complex was quiet. And until recently, he stayed home just long enough to sleep and to fuss over his prized gun collection. The rest of his time, including most evenings and weekends, had been consumed by his job.

Over the years, perhaps two or three times a week, he remained late in The City to use the police gym. There he grunted and sweated with the mangy cops from the narcotics division, reveling in their stories of breaking into dope dens, drawing addicts into a cross fire and blowing them away. Although Brodsky's position as a homicide inspector carried more status, he secretly envied the narcs. By the time he was called to a murder scene it was too late; the deed had already been done.

Today was his first day off in recent memory, and he now despised his dark and dingy apartment. Everything about it depressed him. He briefly considered escaping to the police gym, but he was too embarrassed to face the narcs. So he sat at his kitchen table, drumming his fingers, his emotions alternating between rage and despair. All he could think about were his enemies, how they had foiled him at every turn and how he would love to torture those bastards—the mayor, the chief, and especially the Dubichek derelict.

Brodsky shook himself, afraid if he dwelled on such thoughts they would take control. He took several deep breaths, telling himself to focus and *calmly* think things through.

Okay, it was clear when he located the derelict in Petaluma, Brodsky forced his enemies' hand. They moved Dubichek quickly, using the mayor's limo so no one would suspect that the vagrant was a hunted criminal. But where would they take him? It had to be a secret hideout where he could be kept sedated and guarded until they were ready to unveil him.

Setting his jaw, Brodsky swore an oath: He would find the derelict, torture him, and make him confess. Then he would have the goods on all of those bastards. No more Mr. Nice Guy; the stakes had been raised.

Feeling a tad better, he padded into the living room, following a well-worn path in his green shag rug to the gun cabinet. He gazed lovingly at an impressive array of shotguns, pistols, and semiautomatic weapons. For a special emotional lift he removed his favorite gun, a Colt Python .357 Magnum, a blockbuster weapon that never failed to send a thrill through his loins. When he fired it at the police range, it bucked like a stallion, exploded like a bomb, and everyone around knew something extraordinary had happened.

He picked up his cleaning kit and returned to the kitchen table. He applied a small amount of gun oil to the cleaning rod and carefully inserted it into the eight-inch barrel. The rhythmic movement of the rod—in and out, in and out—soothed Brodsky, helping him to focus.

His first task was to determine where the mayor's limo had taken the derelict. How could he find out? He certainly couldn't ask the mayor. But what about the driver? The mayor used two drivers who were undercover cops. Perhaps he could learn which of the two picked up the derelict, and befriend the man over a few drinks.

Brodsky stopped stroking while he considered the idea. No good. It was too risky. Besides, the thought of socializing with an inferior was distasteful. There had to be a better way. Maybe with the right cover story, he could peek at the limo's travel log.

He thought hard as he placed the buffing rag in the palm of his hand and gently polished the barrel of the Python in long flowing movements. His mind drifted to an article he had read in this morning's paper about the hit-and-run death of a little black child. The incident occurred about the time the mayor's limo was transporting Dubichek. Yes, that would make a fine cover story.

"I think I'll drop by City Hall tomorrow," he said to himself, placing the long barrel of the pistol under his nose, savoring the smell of cold steel and gun oil.

3

"WHEW, IT SMELLS like piss!" Jason grimaced as he sat cross-legged on his sleeping bag. He leaned his wolf-cane against a corner of the filthy doorway, removed his knit cap, and held it over his mouth and nose.

Marty shook his head. "Jeez, Jason, you've been on the street all of five minutes and already you're whining."

"But this is *awful*," Jason said, breathing through his mouth. "Even with a brain injury I would have remembered an odor *this* bad."

"You're forgetting about the huge storm we had the evening of your accident. Storms tend to cleanse everything. Otherwise, more or less, this is how things are.

When a drifter comes to town, he can tell from the smell that it's okay to hang around in a particular doorway or under a stairwell. Think of it as a marking procedure like cats use to identify their turf. Problem is, if you spend a lot of time in these doorways, everything begins to smell and taste like piss. Once that happens, you've arrived."

"Is that what the rotgut is for?" Jason asked from behind his hat.

"Yup, it tempers a lot of nasty things," Marty said, pulling the brandy out of a brown paper bag, unscrewing the cap, and passing it to his companion.

Jason put his hat back on, took a sip, and gagged. "Speaking of that storm," he said hoarsely, "how do you suppose I got here from the accident site? I was wearing sweats, and somewhere along the line I acquired this coat and hat."

"I've been wondering about that, too. Me and Pete found you about three hours after the accident. You were muddy and soaking wet. We figured you were one of the mentally ill who roam the streets."

Jason took another sip, coughed, and loosened the top button of his pea coat. "I may never uncover that part of the story," he said, shoving the bottle at Marty, "but maybe we can piece something together. Let's start with the time of the accident. The mayor told me that a homeless Vietnam veteran pulled me out of the plane before it exploded. He died trying to save the pilot."

"I hadn't heard that," Marty said, taking a swig. "But it restores one's faith in homeless vets. It's a good thing, too, since there are so many on the streets. Did you know that more vets are homeless than all of the soldiers killed during the Vietnam War?"

Jason looked at Marty. "Is that a fact?"

"I'm afraid so," Marty said, passing the bottle to Jason. "Anyway, you didn't have any ID when we found you. Was your wallet in the plane?"

"No. Babcock told me that it was found empty, several blocks from the park."

"What about jewelry?"

"I had a Rolex watch; it was never found."

Marty thought for a moment. "Suppose someone traded you their hat and coat for your watch."

"Is that possible?"

"Sure. A street person might swap the most valuable thing he had for the most valuable thing you had. Street people barter all the time, though gold watches generally aren't involved. Considering the storm that night, I'd say you got the better part of the bargain."

"I guess that's right."

The bottle was passed back and forth for a while without conversation. Across the street darkly-clothed men were planted in littered doorways, passing bottles of their own.

Marty was beginning to think his companion was drawing a blank, and that they were wasting their time. Perhaps the smell of urine and the absence of Pete made things too different. Impatiently he asked, "Is anything coming back?"

"No, not yet."

Marty drew his knees up. "Jason, don't get me wrong. I understand what you're trying to do. But being here . . . especially without Pete . . . is getting me down."

"Let's give it a little more time. If it's not too painful, tell me what you and Pete talked about."

"Well, after some brandy Pete got all dreamy-eyed about having our own place. That generally led to a discussion about women. He was a typical bachelor in that respect," Marty said, winking. "You know what I mean."

"Not any more."

Marty nervously edged away. "Uh . . . why's that?"

Jason laughed. "Don't get me wrong. Over the years I dated women quite a bit. And there was a time when I was on San Francisco's 'Most Eligible Bachelor List.' The problem was that women invariably wanted a lasting commitment from me. But as long as I remained wedded to my job, it was out of the question. And as I got older, my relationships degenerated more quickly. A couple of years ago, rather than endure the hassle, I dated only when I needed a female companion to accompany me to a social event or a political function.

"But recently, the idea of settling down seems to be rattling around in my brain. Maybe it was there all along, and it got knocked loose when I hit my head."

Marty took the bottle. "Mind if I ask you a question?"

"Go ahead."

"Liz, she's married to . . . ?"

"Anton, my older brother."

"But you said you first met her a couple of weeks ago."

"Yes. I haven't been in contact with Anton for many years. Our parents died in an automobile accident when we were youngsters. My Uncle Matt, a bricklayer who emigrated from Scotland, was our only relative in this country. Unfortunately, he was barely able to provide for himself, so we were sent to foster homes. Anton was overly protective—I guess he was just trying to take the place of our parents. I found the situation intolerable and rebelled. Because we didn't get along, the State separated us, and then I discouraged his subsequent efforts to stay in touch. About fifteen years ago he gave up on me, but my accident reunited us."

Marty passed the bottle. "So you've reconciled?"

"I'm not sure," Jason said, taking a swig. "After leaving the hospital, I stayed at Anton and Liz's home. But things got off to a rocky start. My brother didn't approve of Liz helping me to locate you. And to make matters worse, his financial problems are affecting his marriage."

"Been there, didn't like that," Marty said. "Anyway, I think Liz is special."

"Yes," Jason said. A distant look drifted into his eyes and he began sipping brandy as if Marty didn't exist.

Marty laughed and grabbed the bottle.

"What's so funny?" Jason asked.

"You! You're soaking up this rotgut like a sponge."

Jason grinned. "I guess I was. It's not so bad once your taste buds are completely destroyed."

Marty swallowed the last of the brandy. "If Pete were here he'd say: 'I reckon there's nothing like cheap brandy and a pissy doorway to stimulate conversation about women.' Pretty good imitation of him, don't you think?"

Suddenly Jason closed his eyes.

Marty waited.

After a minute, Jason blinked. An odd look was on his face. "Get paid . . . get laid?" he said hesitantly.

"YES!" Marty whooped, high-fiving with Jason. "That's Pete, tell me more."

Jason closed his eyes again. "You and Pete wanted your own place because of all the . . . assholes?"

"Bingo!"

Marty and Jason continued high-fiving as a black Ford Fairlane drove down the street. They stopped their celebration and watched it turn the corner.

"Is that the old car you told me about?" Jason asked.

"Yeah. Who do you suppose is so interested in us?"

"I don't know. Maybe the mayor's paranoid; maybe he thinks we're planning to be guests on *Meet the Press*. I would be sorely disappointed if old Walt thought it necessary to have us tailed. But I rather it be Babcock than a competitor. The last thing I need is a picture of us in the tabloids."

"Want to move on in case he circles back?"

Jason picked up his things. "Yes, let's lose him."

4

THANKS TO HIS Russian-made night vision camera, Gorney was certain he had taken excellent close-ups of the two men. He was grateful to the Kremlin for deciding to dismantle the Red Army and sell it through the mail.

He looped around the block and parked fifty yards from the doorway. But his binoculars told him that Howell and the big man were gone. He suspected they had cut through the empty lot across the street.

Gorney was frustrated. His client would be expecting a detailed report. Two days on the case and by now he should at least have a theory. Instead, all he knew was that his subject, in homeless clothing, had taken to the streets in the company of a vagrant called the "Golden Fleece."

He exposed the end of a Snapper Bar, took a liberal bite, and contemplated the situation. Initially, he thought Howell's bizarre behavior was simply the result of his head injury. But the involvement of other people—the woman caller and the lawyer—tended to undermine that theory. Gorney shook his head. Over the years he had seen the rich behave in strange ways, but deliberately crossing into homelessness wasn't one of them.

He finished the Snapper Bar and tossed the wrapper behind him. But instead of disappearing it stayed in his peripheral vision atop of an immense pile of trash. Gorney angled the rearview mirror down and assessed the situation. It was time to clean out the back of his car.

With the Fairlane's tired springs complaining, Gorney jumped the curb and drove into the empty lot. Lumbering out, he opened the rear door and scooped and shoved his trash onto the ground. When he finished, he squeezed his massive frame behind the steering wheel and wheezed heavily. He was forced to rest for a long time before he could drive away.

5

THE TWO MEN STOOD at the entrance to the Monday Night Club. Marty was surprised to see the fire in the fifty-gallon drum going strong, considering the heightened police activity during the last two weeks.

"Well, well, if it ain't Dubichek and his girlfriend Happy," Stan announced loudly. He was at his usual station by the fire. "I almost didn't recognize you two, the way you switched beards. And that haircut, Marty, HOO-HA! It looks like you got one of them vacuum cuts, and someone plugged the machine into extra high voltage." Stan held his stomach and laughed.

"Actually, Pete gave me this haircut," Marty said somberly.

Stan softened his tone. "Yeah, I heard about Pete. I'm sorry . . . really."

"Me too."

The newcomers dropped their sleeping bags onto the ground and sat on crates near the fire. Jason stared into the flames. On the way over, Marty told him not to say anything even though he looked much different than news photos of a well-turned-out Jason Howell. His role at the Monday Night Club was to simply observe, and try to remember as much as possible. Hopefully, he wouldn't be recognized in the process.

"I heard you freaked out in the plaza," Stan said to Marty.

"Yeah, they put me in the psycho ward. What's been going on around here?"

"Let's see . . . the week before last this cretin with beady eyes and a phony Irish accent was hanging around the day shelter dressed like a priest. I saw through his act right away. I figured he was a pervert looking to buy himself some cheap homeless ass, so I let him follow me here. I was planning to stomp the living shit out of him. But he took off before I could get my hands on him.   Then, wouldn't you know it? The cocksucker turned out to be a cop. A short time later he shows up with the riot squad and a slew of TV reporters, and busted us. Burned our stuff. Took me and Doc and some of the others into custody, trying to get us to confess to belonging to a gang of militant homeless."

"Really?" Marty said. "Then what happened?"

"He took me into this interview room at the Hall of Justice, swaggering around and asking a lot of stupid questions. He kept shoving me and pinching my arm. I told him to fuck off. I said no amount of torture is gonna make a United States Marine talk."

Marty knew Stan was never in the marines—although he did serve in the soup kitchen.

"Anyways," Stan continued, "after a few hours he let me go. By then, it was too late for the shelter, so I spent the night at the Civic Center."

"What happened to Doc?"

"Oh, he confessed to everything. He needed a place to stay. He knew The Club wasn't gonna be any good for a while, and he's afraid of the plaza people. But they only held him overnight 'cause they didn't have nothing on him neither.

"The next day, Doc caught up with Willie, and the two of 'em got into the shelter, thanks to your note. At dinner, Doc told us how the cretin cop got all excited when he learned the old coot was a vet. Of course, Doc meant vet'narian. But the asshole was thinking Nam. That gave Doc an idea. He remembered this old science fiction movie about Commies parachuting down and taking over America. So he confessed to being the head of the Cabal, this secret group of homeless vets plotting to overthrow the government. The cop's mouth dropped to his feet. We all had a pretty good laugh over that one."

Marty grinned. "I'm sure the vets would do a better job at running things."

"Damn right," Stan agreed, tossing a piece of scrap wood into the fire.

A white-haired man appeared at the entrance to the alcove.

"Hey, speaking of the devil," Stan announced, "there's the King of the Cabal now."

"Evening, gents," Doc said as he approached.

Stan bowed. "Hail to the king."

"What king?" Doc asked suspiciously.

"Fuck-*king*!" Stan hooted, bending over laughing.

Doc shook his head and took a crate next to Marty. "How're you doing?" he asked gently.

"Okay," Marty replied.

"Sorry about Pete. By the way, thanks for that spot at the shelter. You're a lifesaver." Doc squinted at Marty. "Say, you're not wanting it back, are you?"

"No, no, Doc. Don't worry. Happy and I have a place to stay."

Doc eyed Jason in the firelight. "That fellow . . . he sure seems familiar," Doc said, rubbing his cheek. "But I can't quite place him. Must've killed too many brain cells."

"Speaking of killing brain cells," Stan said reaching down, "I still got my jug. I'm surprised the dumb-ass cop didn't toss it into the fire."

"You got that right," Doc remarked. "It would've blown us all to kingdom come, right on the Six O'clock News."

Everyone laughed.

Suddenly out of the shadows, a large animal with yellow eyes and sharp claws leaped through the air and landed in Jason's lap, causing him to yelp and fall backwards off the crate.

The men laughed again.

"Hey, it's Shoo," Marty said, grinning. "Willie must be around."

"Yeah," Stan agreed. "That's the only reason the damn cat gets to hang around here."

"What's wrong with ol' Shoo?" Marty inquired, unsticking one paw at a time from Jason's lap.

"W-H-A-H," Shoo said, as Marty held and stroked him.

"Yeah, Stan, what's wrong with the cat?" Doc asked. "He keeps the rat population down."

"*That's* what's wrong with him. He's diseased from eating all them vermin. It's the only thing keeping me from putting a pot on the fire and fixing us some *Shoo Stew.*"

A voice boomed behind Stan. "If you ever lay as much as a finger on my cat then we'll all be having *Stan-Wiches* for dinner." Daggers flickered in Willie's eyes.

More laughter.

Stan fell silent and tossed another scrap of lumber into the blaze.

Marty handed the giant tabby to Willie and said, "Let's go for a walk outside. We need to talk."

When the two men were alone, Shoo leaped from Willie's arms and crouched in the rubble, sniffing around like a lion stalking his prey. ·

"Hey, man, isn't that the rich dude?" Willie asked. "You kidnap him again?"

Marty shook his head. "So far, you're the only one who knows about Happy being Howell."

"What's shaking?"

"He got the cops off my back and now I'm working for him, kind of secretly. I'm staying at his place. Can you keep all of this to yourself?"

"Sure, I owe you for getting me into St. Andrews."

"No, I owe *you*. Do you know about your van?"

"Yeah. I was coming down my street with your money and clothing when I saw the tow truck and the patrol car. So I hightailed out of there. Figured you did the same. I spent the day at the library and ran into Doc. I took him with me to St. Andrews, thinking you might return to the Basin on Friday. When I went back to my street, this neighbor of mine told me you and Pete had spent the day in his shanty and the night in the Civic Center. I went there to look for you on Friday morning, and Ol' Kate told me about Pete. I'm very, very sorry."

Marty nodded. "But what about your van?"

"There's no way to get it back. Besides the fine and the towing and storage charges, they wanted me to pay the registration and show proof of insurance. It was hopeless, so I told them to keep the pile of junk. But I couldn't get out of paying the fine, and that's where your money went. I hope you don't mind."

"Not at all. Look, tell me what you need. Now that I'm working for Howell, I can help you get your van back." Marty pulled out the roll of bills Jason had given him.

Willie's eyes grew large. He stared at the money for a second and pushed Marty's hand away. "Thanks, but that heap of junk isn't worth what they're asking for it. For that kind of money, I could live for a year at a flop house. But to tell you the truth I like it at St. Andrews. Nice folks. They got me into a mechanic's training program. They said if you wasn't coming back, I can have your cot."

"It's yours."

"Great."

"But I need a favor."

"Name it."

"I need to show Happy the shelter. Can you and Doc let us have your spots for one night?" Marty peeled five crisp hundred dollar bills from the roll and handed it to Willie. "Use this to get nice hotel rooms."

Willie pushed Marty's hand away again. "With that kind of money me and Doc could get a suite on Nob Hill. No, we can stay here."

Marty held the money out. "It's not just for a room," he insisted. "It's thanks for helping me and Pete when we were desperate. You had your ass on the line for us."

"Okay, if you put it that way," Willie said, making the money disappear.

"And keep our sleeping bags; we won't be needing them after tonight."

"Sure, thanks."

The two men walked back into the alcove with Shoo purring loudly and rubbing against Marty's legs.

Inside, Marty found Jason hugging the jug. Even in the dim light, he could tell the man's eyes were watery and defocused, his mouth set firmly in a twisted grin.

Jason motioned for Marty's ear. *"Chateau de Crud,"* he slurred, "shee, I do remember."

SIXTEEN
Tuesday, January 24

1

JEANETTE GARCIA FANNED the door of the utility room to coax the exquisite bouquet of her coffee into the reception area. Although Mayor Babcock had a private entrance to his office, he often detoured through the main lobby to say a special good morning to her. And it wasn't lost on her that the aroma of her Kona coffee always brought a smile to his face.

Jeanette had fifteen minutes until the office opened. She walked over to the portico and looked outside. The steady drizzle meant another difficult day. In addition to the usual collection of citizens, media, lobbyists, and screwballs who sought appointments with the mayor, she would now have to placate wet and angry plaza people who would demand an audience with His Honor.

Although her job was stressful she wasn't complaining. As a single head of household with three small children and no savings, she knew how little it would take for her to join the people in the plaza. Jeanette prayed daily that the mayor would be re-elected so she could continue to work for him.

Someone rapped sharply at the door. Jeanette turned from the window. "The office isn't open yet. Please come back at eight o'clock."

A muffled voice said, "Ma'am, I'm an inspector with the SFPD, Homicide Division. I need to talk to you right away. I'm afraid it can't wait."

Jeanette cracked the door. A man in a beige raincoat and matching hat flashed a badge. "I'm investigating a hit-and-run death of a black child last Sunday, in the Mission District," he said, pushing his way in and closing the door in a single motion. "You see, a white man was the driver and the nig . . . I mean, the blacks are up in arms. The neighborhood leaders are holding an emergency meeting at a local church. Witnesses say a burgundy Lincoln Town Car, like the mayor's limo, rushed from the scene."

He took a couple of steps toward Jeanette and switched to a hushed voice even though they were alone. "This is a high-profile case and very sensitive. The poor child was only five years old."

"What a shame," Jeanette said sincerely. "But I can't help you, Inspector. Mayor Babcock walked to church on Sunday, and then he had a massage appoint—"

"That's good news," the inspector interrupted, "considering the negative publicity this situation could generate."

"Yes . . ."

"I'm on my way to the neighborhood meeting, and I need to assure the black leaders that His Honor's limo was not in the area. Otherwise these people will take their case to the press and we could have rioting. I don't have to tell you how badly the resulting publicity could hurt the mayor, this being an election year."

"It's not fair . . ."

"Of course not. But with your help, *I* can put this matter to rest. I just need to see the driver's log for Sunday afternoon."

"All right," Jeanette said, backing away from the inspector. She went over to her desk and began typing into a computer terminal. He followed her and leaned over her shoulder. She could feel his hot breath on her neck, forcing her to bend unnaturally over the keyboard. After what seemed to Jeanette like an eternity, the screen showed that the limo picked up a Mr. Martin Dubichek at Petaluma State Hospital on Sunday at 11:33 a.m. and dropped him off at a Pacific Heights intersection at 12:27 p.m.

Jeanette squeezed out of her seat and backed away while the inspector copied the information into his notepad.

"Good news," he said, flipping the notepad closed and putting it away. He was smiling satanically as he moved toward her. "The limo's route was nowhere near the accident scene."

Jeanette kept moving back until she ran into the edge of another desk.

"Between you and me," he said softly, moving closer, "*I* really didn't think the mayor was involved, but we have to check all leads."

"I-I understand."

He was in her face now, invading her personal space. She could feel his hot breath again, and now his thighs were pressing against hers. Jeanette was trapped against the desk and all she could do was bend further backwards, inadvertently arching her pelvis into his.

"There's one more thing . . ." he hissed, staring hungrily at her.

For the first time, she noticed that his eyes were blackish orbs with yellow flecks, more animal than human. She shuddered, tensing her body against his.

". . . it's vitally important you say nothing about my inquiry. You *must* completely forget it. If the media learns a homicide inspector has been investigating the mayor's limo in conjunction with the killing of a little black girl, they might print a story full of innuendoes. In that event, you will be fired. Do *I* make myself clear?"

"Y-yes," Jeanette replied, trembling.

2

MARTY AND JASON were on the same street near the Civic Center where two weeks earlier, Jason, as Happy, had watched passively while his caretakers cleaned hot dog carts. But this time Marty was doing the watching. He was standing in the drizzle with his hands in his pockets as his companion, on all fours, puked his brains out in the gutter. A group of Japanese tourists walked by, cutting a wide swath. One of them had his camcorder rolling.

"All finished?" Marty asked.

"A-r-r-g-h," Jason groaned as he slowly looked up at Marty. His eyes were bloodshot, his face a mirror of the ashen-gray sky.

Marty grabbed Jason by the back of his coat, dragged him across the sidewalk, and propped him against a red-brick wall. He placed Jason's wolf-cane beside him. Jason moaned as he put his hands on top of his knit cap. A fresh set of pink and purple stains covered the front of his pea coat.

"You . . . got . . . any . . . Tylenol?" Jason croaked in a frog-voice.

"Nope, toting the Tylenol was Pete's job. Look—you weren't supposed to drink out of that jug. Stan only *pretends* to drink. He uses the jug as an initiation rite for new members of The Club. It's a joke. No one knows what's in it."

"Now you tell me. I remembered drinking from it last time, so I thought it was okay." Jason gagged at the thought of the purple liquid. He pulled his hat over his face to shield his eyes from the light.

"Stay put," Marty ordered, towering over Jason. "I'll get the Tylenol."

"A-r-r-g-h," Jason groaned.

Marty left Jason slumped against the wall with his hat over his eyes and his mouth open, his white-coated tongue sticking out to catch the drizzle and soothe his burning throat.

Time passed with agonizing slowness. Suddenly he felt something drop into his lap. He lifted the edge of his hat and looked down at a bright, gleaming quarter. He retracted his tongue and shifted his eyes upward to the weathered and kindly face of an old woman. She was wearing a scarf on her head and holding an umbrella. "Bless you, young man. Now use that money to buy food; alcohol is the Devil's brew," she admonished with her finger.

"Yes, ma'am," Jason said in a grated voice, sitting up and retrieving the quarter.

She nodded and walked on.

He closed his eyes and leaned back, listening to someone playing a wild drum solo on the other side of the brick wall. Then he realized it was just the pounding in his head, and he wondered how long it would be before his brains exploded. Suddenly, above the din of the drums, he heard loud cursing. Reluctantly he opened one eye and saw a man in a beige raincoat rapidly approaching. The man began kicking wildly at Jason's legs. But his head hurt so badly that there was a delay before the pain registered.

"O-O-O-W!" Jason finally yelled, retracting his legs to his chest. "Why the hell did you do that?"

"Because you're in *my* way," the attacker screamed, "you-good-for-nothing-fucking-derelict-bastard!"

Jason watched the man climb into a silver muscle car and squeal away in a cloud of black smoke. He closed his eyes. *What next?*

He didn't have to wait long.

Someone was poking him in the chest with a stick.

"Go away and let me die in peace," Jason said, this time not opening his eyes.

"Not on *my* beat. Let's see some ID."

Jason looked up. There were twin cops glaring down at him. They both wore lightening bolt insignias on their shoulders. He shook his head and the two images merged into one. "Uh, I don't have it. My wallet was stolen, and I'm in the process of getting my ID and credit cards replaced."

"Oh, what a shame," the cop remarked. "And I suppose you lost your American Express Card as well?"

"As a matter of fact. And my Rolex, too."

"Wise-ass! Can you show me any means of support?" The cop was pounding his palm with the baton.

Jason reached into his pocket and pulled out a coin. "I only have this quarter at the moment but my friend is holding a lot of money for me."

"Okay, fella, it's off to the psycho ward with you!"

"Excuse me, Officer," Marty said as he approached slowly. "What seems to be the problem here?"

"Who the hell are you?"

"His friend; I can vouch for him."

The cop looked Marty over. Compared to Jason, Marty looked liked a respectable citizen. "This loony says you're holding his money. Is that true?"

Marty pulled out Jason's wad of bills and waved it.

The cop bit his lip. "All right, I want you two to get the hell outta here. If I catch you loitering on my beat again, I'm hauling you both in."

The cop left, and Marty pulled his friend to his feet. "You won't believe what happened," Jason said, rubbing his legs.

"Yeah, I would," Marty replied, removing a bottle of Tylenol and a cup of hot coffee from a paper bag. After Jason took the pills and sipped some coffee, Marty asked, "Did you remember being here with me and Pete?"

"Yes, there was something about cold hot dogs and warm soda," Jason said, swallowing hard. "But let's not talk about it now. *I beg you.*"

"Okay, do you feel well enough to walk?"

"No, but it's probably a good idea. Where to?"

"You'll see."

3

ONCE AGAIN, Marty took Jason to the emergency room of City General. And once again, because of his charge's odor and appearance, riding the Muni was out of the question. But this time, the trip to the hospital set a new slowness record because Jason inched along, holding his cane in one hand and his head in the other.

It was nearly noon when Marty guided Jason into the emergency room and maneuvered him through the mass of patients awaiting medical attention. Marty hoped he could avoid setting off the alarm during this visit. Maybe the third time's a charm.

Not surprisingly, there weren't any empty seats so Marty guided his charge over to the vending area and eased him into a gap between two machines. Then he walked to the front of the TRIAGE line and peeked at the receptionist: it wasn't the same woman from last time. Marty figured she took disability leave after her last dose of him and Happy. He found the back of the line and waited.

Twenty minutes later he felt a tug at his sleeve.

"Marty, how much is a crutch worth?" Jason asked weakly.

The old man was standing next to Jason. "You owe me," he said to Marty. "This guy attacked me with my lucky crutch and I never got it back."

"Oh, no—not *you*," Marty groaned.

"Yep, it's me. Pay up. That crutch was worth at least ten bucks. You owe me," he insisted.

Marty sighed and took out a hundred dollar bill. "I don't suppose you've got change?"

The old man's eyes bulged.

"Tell you what," Marty said, "go to the cafeteria and get us some sandwiches and coffee. You can keep the change."

The old man snatched at the bill, but Marty yanked it away. "There's one more thing."

"What's that?"

"You never saw us, *capeesh?*"

"My memory's kinda cloudy these days," the old man said, screwing a bony finger into his temple. He grabbed the bill and jogged up the stairs to the cafeteria.

"I remember him," Jason said feebly. "But why does he need a crutch?"

"It's a prop. He needs it because he lives here," Marty said flatly. He was almost at the front of the line and the lack of air circulation in the room was magnifying Jason's vomit odor. He had to get the man away from the area if his latest plan was going to work. Marty scanned the waiting room and spotted an empty seat nearby. "Behind you," he said pointing. "Grab that seat. I'll be there shortly."

Jason slogged over, plopped in the chair, put his head in his hands and closed his eyes. The patients on both sides of him wrinkled their noses and cleared out. Marty turned his attention back to the line. It was his turn.

A short time later, Marty took one of the empty seats next to Jason. "They should be calling you any minute," he said.

Jason slowly raised his head. "How did you swing it? Lots of people are ahead of me."

Marty held up a receipt. "I've already paid for your treatment. Cash on the barrel. I told them you were a wealthy eccentric and if they didn't see you immediately, there were plenty of other medical facilities that would take your money. I have a feeling they don't get too many cash customers here."

"MR. PETE PETERSEN," announced the loud-speaker.

Marty stood and aimed Jason in the direction of the treatment area and gave him a push. As soon as his charge limped off, several patients made a beeline for the empty seats. "They're reserved," Marty glared. The patients backed away. What a difference money in your pocket can make, he thought as he sat down and leaned back. If he had gotten Pete to the hospital under this circumstance, Marty had no doubt his friend would still be alive. But he knew he was trying to rewrite history by registering Jason in Pete's name, and it depressed him.

"Lunch is served," the old man said, holding a tray.

Marty sat up.

"Name's Edgar Chapman, but everyone calls me Crazy Eddie."

"I'm Marty. Pleased to meet you."

"Thanks for the money," Crazy Eddie said as he handed a sandwich and a cup of coffee to the big man.

"Now you can buy a crutch *and* get a room," Marty said.

"Yeah, I hate those shelters . . . way too dangerous for an old man. That's why I hang here. If something should happen, help's nearby."

"Theoretically," Marty said, through a bite of sandwich.

"So where do you hail from?" Crazy Eddie asked.

"Around here, Michigan before that.   How about you?"

"Originally? Wichita, Kansas. I was a foreman at a general aviation plant. The industry took a nosedive, and I lost my job and my health insurance. Then my wife got sick." He cupped his hand by his mouth and whispered, "The big C."

Marty nodded sympathetically.

"In order to pay for her treatment I had to sell my house and everything else we accumulated during thirty-five years of marriage. By the time I was poor enough to qualify for assistance, she was gone."

"I'm sorry," Marty said, sipping coffee. "When did you come to California?"

Crazy Eddie began counting on his fingers and then shrugged. "Some years ago," he said. "At first I lived with my son and his wife up in Oakland. They're good kids who were happily married until I showed up. Then they got to fighting. I was desperately looking for a job so I could get my own place. But there aren't any jobs around here for an old coot who spent his life in a small plane factory. So one morning, I left them a note: 'Thanks for everything, I'm moving out. I'll let you know when I'm settled. Love, Dad.'"

"When was that?" Marty asked.

Crazy Eddie shrugged again. "A couple, three years ago. I forget."

Marty stopped chewing and looked at Crazy Eddie. After a moment he said, "You've certainly kept fit."

"Yep. I've been reading the health magazines and pamphlets they leave around here. I jog every day and watch my diet, and I've lost thirty pounds as near as I can tell." He patted his flat stomach. "Those kids wouldn't recognize me."

"They haven't seen you since you left?"

"Nope, but I've seen *them*. Sometimes I take the BART train to Oakland in the evening. I stand behind the bushes outside their house and look through the windows to make sure they're okay. Last month my daughter-in-law gave birth." Crazy Eddie's face beamed. "I'm a grandpa."

Marty put his sandwich down. He was no longer hungry. He wondered why the old man's story was getting him down. He had heard similar hard luck tales during his years of homelessness, and he always shrugged them off. Maybe he now had room to feel sorry for someone else because he no longer felt sorry for himself.

Marty was pondering this when Jason returned. Much of the color had returned to his face. "Well, well," Marty observed, "it looks like you had a transfusion."

"Practically. They rehydrated me intravenously. I don't know what was in the IV bottle, but in short order I was feeling better."

"Meet Crazy Eddie," Marty said.

Jason shook hands. "Hello, again."

"What are you in for?" Crazy Eddie asked.

"Imbibing some purple liquid from a jug."

"Was it kinda oily and did it burn going down?"

"Yes."

Crazy Eddie grinned knowingly. "A fella came through here one time and told me about that jug. Rumor has it that a soldier brought it back as a souvenir of the Persian Gulf War."

Jason's mouth dropped. "What did he say was in it?"

"SCUD missile fuel."

4

MAYOR BABCOCK STUDIED Les Moules' menu while he used his forefinger to conduct Vivaldi's *Four Seasons,* playing softly in the background. For his main course, he was deciding between the rabbit special, *Lapin aux Framboise,* or the succulent and always satisfying, *Cervelle de Mouton.* It was a close call. The mayor set the menu down as a smiling Jacques arrived with Chief Conti in tow. The chief was wearing his five o'clock frazzle.

"I'm glad you could join me on such short notice, Rudy," the mayor said, standing and shaking hands. "Would you like an apéritif before dinner?"

"You should only know," Chief Conti replied. "I'll have the same thing, Jacques," he said, referring to the red drink in front of the mayor.

The maître d' cupped his hands. "Campari? *Tout de suite, Monsieur.*"

"Rough day?" the mayor inquired as the two men pulled chairs up to the table.

"I'm juggling a lot of balls right now," he said. "I wish I could make a few of them disappear."

"I'm glad you brought that up, Rudy. Don't you think a degree from magic school should be a prerequisite for political office?"

Conti's drink appeared in front of him. He swirled the ice and took a gulp. "I don't know what you mean."

"Politicians are like magicians: Their job is to create illusions."

"Like the illusion we've reduced San Francisco's homeless population?"

"Precisely. And that's why I asked to meet with you. The media has learned the Howell kidnapping investigation has been suspended. Did Brodsky leak it?"

"Possibly," the chief shrugged. "This morning I received a call from a reporter. I told him we're at a point in our investigation where we need to talk to Jason Howell, and we're waiting for him to return from South America. The reporter bought it."

"What will appear in the paper?"

"Nothing for the time being," Conti replied, taking an ice cube out of his mouth and pressing it against his forehead. "Since the homeless are remaining passive, the media thinks the kidnapping might have been an isolated incident. Interest is waning fast."

"Good, good—but it's clear we need something else to keep the public solidly behind Project Vector."

The chief shifted nervously. "What do you have in mind?"

"My instincts tell me the time is right for a symbolic gesture, one that will raise my standing in the polls while defining my opponents as soft on homelessness."

"I hope your plans don't require additional police resources. We're stretched pretty thin right now. Prostitution is unchecked, and drug use is exploding. We've completely given up on white collar theft."

It was the mayor's turn to shrug. "Now, now, Rudy, you know election year is no time to worry about nonviolent crimes—other than vagrancy, of course."

Conti sighed.

"It's time to herd the homeless out of the plaza," Babcock announced.

Conti looked incredulously at his boss. "Walt, you know that doesn't work; they're back the minute my men leave."

The mayor flashed angry eyes. "This time you'll make it stick. Everyone's calling the place 'Camp Babcock.' I won't have it!" The mayor slammed a fist on the table, rattling dishes and attracting stares of disapproval from other patrons.

Conti lowered his voice. "But it'll take 'round-the-clock patrols."

"I don't care," Mayor Babcock said, folding his arms across his chest.

"They'll move downtown."

"Now, now, Rudy, you know the downtown business district is off-limits. It's the heart and soul of my support. You'll beef up Project Vector patrols there as well. But you won't have to do it all alone. I have a commitment from the Recreation and Park Department to loan you the leaf blowing brigade." The mayor's tone was adamant.

Chief Conti took a big gulp of Campari. "I don't mean to question your instincts, Walt, but you know these actions will only drive the homeless into the better neighborhoods. They'll be sleeping on your constituent's front steps."

Mayor Babcock unfolded his arms and smiled. "Let me put it to you this way: My opposition has been scoring points with liberal voters by claiming that Project Vector is cruel and unusual punishment. But I believe those sentiments will evaporate when voters have to step over bodies, puddles of urine, or piles of feces to get into their homes." Mayor Babcock sipped his Campari to let the point sink in.

"That's where cleaning up the Civic Center Plaza comes in," he continued. "It'll show what my administration can do while making the voters think twice about turning The City over to the liberals."

"The devil they know," Chief Conti remarked.

Mayor Babcock had a faraway look in his face. "I want a sparkling Civic Center to be my crown jewel, a symbol of my ability to clean up The City." Then his eyes narrowed. "Send in the TAC squad so the homeless, my opponents, and the voters, all get the message that I'm dead serious this time."

Conti lowered his glass. "The 'Mean Team?' You're kidding."

"No, I'm not. Once the homeless are out, I want a lawn and flowers planted. I want the fountain turned on. When visiting dignitaries gaze from my portico, I want them to see children playing. Don't you get it? We'll be giving the public the illusion that what happens in the plaza will also happen to the rest of San Francisco during my next term."

"Okay," Conti relented, "as long as you realize that after the election, it's back to business as usual."

"Certainly, Rudy. After I win in November, you'll get your patrols back."

"And the day after the election the homeless will reappear in the plaza?"

"Like rabbits out of a hat," Mayor Babcock said, looking beyond Conti and motioning for the waiter. He was definitely going to order the *Lapin* special for dinner.

5

AFTER JASON'S REJUVENATION, Marty took him to the library. It was a huge mistake. Jason became glued to an Internet terminal, furiously downloading articles on homelessness. Because of the late hour, Marty was about to pick him up and carry him out the door when the librarian closed the lights and literally pulled the plug on Jason's terminal.

Now, at the rear of a long line for St. Andrews, Marty was concerned that the two men might not get into the shelter. Jason seemed to be recalling things remarkably well, and Marty felt that if they had to return to St. Andrews at a later date it would break the flow. Besides, Marty was determined to leave street life behind, once and for all.

Jason pulled his knit cap down around his ears and pulled up his coat collar to ward off the cold evening air. "Marty," he said, his breath visible, "I have a question."

"Uh-huh."

"I found a HUD report on the Net that said seven million Americans have experienced episodes of homelessness in recent years. A Columbia University study placed the number closer to thirteen and a half million."

"Uh-huh."

"If those numbers are correct, we should be seeing the homeless everywhere. Where are they?"

"Standing in this line," Marty said, staring straight ahead.

"Be serious."

"Okay, about 10 percent of the homeless live on the street. The rest are more or less invisible. These people don't panhandle. In fact, they avoid the dangers of the street as much as possible. Some stay in emergency shelters or hang around the library; some live in abandoned buildings; some stay in cars; and others camp in parks or under freeways. And even when a homeless person is walking down the street, or taking a bus, or sitting in a coffee shop, regular people might not notice them because unlike you," Marty said, gesturing at Jason's vomit-stained clothes, "they look pretty normal."

"How do they manage that?"

"Easy. If a person becomes homeless, it doesn't mean they're *property-less*. For as long as they can they'll store stuff in a car trunk or some other safe place. If they have decent clothes, they can put up a good front and try to get back into the mainstream. Some use general assistance money for lockers, and they cram everything they can in there—including themselves."

"You mean people *live* in lockers?"

"Until they're caught and evicted."

Jason scratched his beard. "How long does this go on?"

"Months, sometimes years. But if they don't find jobs before their stuff wears out or gets stolen, they're finished."

"How many stay in emergency shelters?" Jason asked.

"Citywide, around two thousand, about 15 percent of San Francisco's total homeless population."

"That's all?"

"Uh-huh."

The line started moving and Marty breathed a sigh of relief when he and Jason made it inside.

After cleaning up for dinner, they entered the main hall and walked over to the stage where a group had gathered. Marty told Jason to wear his hat pulled low over his head and to keep quiet.

Stan was on the stage addressing the group. "They're starting another big project in China Basin," he announced. "They need loads of casual labor. Sign-up is on Berry Street first thing tomorrow."

"C'mon Stan, big jobs like that are always union," Sanchez said.

"There's a nonunion gate," Stan countered. "It's in the contract. They're gonna use casual labor for the demolition phase."

"What, are they gonna send us in with the dynamite?" Sanchez retorted.

"Yeah, at minimum wage?" somebody else shouted.

"I guess," Stan said.

"But they pay by check and take out taxes," another man said. "And after I pay the cashing fees there's nothing left. If I gotta do slave labor, I like them small employers who pay off the books—cash on the barrel."

"Give me a break," Stan said. "Don't you remember when one of them 'small employers' hired us a few months ago? We spent the day cleaning up an empty lot in the Western Addition. It was a regular garbage dump. Full of maggots. The man said he'd pay us cash at the end of the day and take us back to the shelter. A truck came and picked up the Dumpster, but the bastard never showed. That job was off *my* books, too."

"Okay," Sanchez relented, "count me in." A few others raised their hands. Stan looked around for more workers and spotted Marty and Jason. "Hey Marty, you want in? They might even have something for Happy to do. Hell, we'll stick a broom up his ass and he can be the shop steward. I bet he's smarter than most of them union dodos that stand around doing nothing." Stan crossed his eyes and flapped his arms.

The men looked at Jason and laughed.

Jason crossed his eyes and flapped his arms.

They laughed harder.

When everyone quieted down, Marty said, "Thanks for the offer, Stan, but me and Happy are set."

"Doing what?" Stan wanted to know.

"Yeah, Marty, give," Sanchez said.

Marty didn't have an answer; Jason hadn't told him what kind of job he had in mind. The big man glanced at Jason who was staring at his shoes. "I-I don't know," Marty replied.

Several of the men crossed their eyes and flapped their arms. That started another round of laughter.

The dinner bell rang and everyone took their places at the picnic tables. Since it was Tuesday, they would be eating rice and beans. Jason sat between Marty and Stan, who made it a point to take Pete's former seat.

Stan grabbed a hunk of brown bread and leaned forward to catch Marty's eye. "Hey, how's about you and me buddying up now?"

"Thanks, Stan, but like I said, me and Happy are set."

Stan stiffened. "I can't believe you're gonna hang with a goddamn retard!"

Jason quietly forked baked beans into his mouth.

"Actually, Happy is part of this deal I made," Marty explained.

"C'mon, what deal?"

"Look, I *really* don't know. When I was psychoed I got a sponsor who's giving me a job. I just don't have the details." Marty, in frustration, kicked at Jason's leg under the table, unintentionally hitting a welt from this morning's attack. Jason yelped and jolted his fork sideways, propelling baked beans all over Stan's face and fatigues.

Someone yelled, "Food fight!"

"God-damn retard!" Stan snarled as beans ran in brown streaks down his face. He jumped up and cocked a fist.

Marty hurriedly stood and positioned himself in front of Jason, and Stan backed off.

Several staff members rushed over. Marty and Stan eased into their seats. "It's okay," Marty said to the staff, suppressing a grin. "Happy here didn't mean it. Poor guy hit his head and gets these spasms." Marty then turned to Stan who was wiping his face and brushing himself with a paper napkin. "Sorry about that. I was about to say Happy is part of my sponsor's package. At the moment, he's in my care. That's all I know about the deal. I swear it."

"Where are you guys staying now?"

"Believe it or not, Happy has his own place, and I'll be rooming with him for a while. We're just here for to-night."

Stan ate silently. Finally, he looked over at Marty and said, "Well, if things don't work out with the spasoid, you know where to find me."

SEVENTEEN
Wednesday, January 25

1

"**D**ROP YOUR COCKS and grab your socks!" someone chanted when the lights flooded on at 5:30 a.m. A communal groan rumbled through the shelter. Marty sat up slowly. It took him a moment to realize the old Army wake-up call was coming from Stan.

"C'mon guys, up and at 'em!" Stan commanded, walking down a row of cots and kicking at the legs. "I promised the Labor Supe I'd get all you lazy a-holes signed up early."

Marty stretched as he glanced at Jason in the cot next to him. His companion had deep circles under his eyes. "It looks like you didn't sleep much," Marty said.

Jason sat up and shook his head no.

"Well, it takes some getting used to with folks snoring, coughing, and banging into your cot when they get up to pee. Everything echoes in here. I should've had you buy earplugs when you went shopping for the brandy."

"That wouldn't have helped the farting."

Marty remembered the beans for dinner. A light bulb went off. "You could've gotten an extra pair for your nose."

Jason was watching Stan march his platoon toward the showers. "That guy is something," he said. "He must have made an impression on me. Last night, lying awake, I had time to think and I remember him arguing with Pete."

"Yeah, Stan and Pete were rivals—Stan felt he and I were a much better match. He could never understand why I hung around with such a 'weenie.'"

"Why did you choose Pete?"

"Stan doesn't need anyone. But without me keeping the street predators away, Pete wouldn't have survived as long as he did. As for me, his jokes and optimism made life a little more tolerable."

"How did Pete wind up homeless?"

"He grew up in a small town in Texas. Like me, he came to California seeking work in the building trades. Eventually Pete moved up from an apprentice to journeyman electrician.

"A few years ago he went into heavy debt to start his own shop. But he couldn't compete with the bigger operations and dug himself into a hole. Reluctantly he called his father for help, but the old man refused. Pete once told me, 'My dad's angry because I dared to leave our small town.' But Pete still cared about his old man. He kept this diary in his locker, and instead of writing 'Dear Diary' he wrote 'Dear Dad,' putting down all the stuff he wanted to tell his old man but couldn't. Pete never gave up on his father."

"Did his father give up on him?"

"I don't think so. I figured his old man was playing a waiting game, betting that sooner or later Pete would give up and come home. But the son was as stubborn as the dad." Suddenly Marty's eyes lit up. "The stuff from Pete's locker must be around somewhere. If I can find that diary, I'll send it home. His old man might want to read it."

"Good idea."

Marty ran a hand through his hair. "Do you think it's possible for Pete to go home, too?"

"Sure, I'll arrange it."

2

THE CONSUMMATE PROFESSIONAL, Ray Gorney had diligently remained on his subject's street ever since he had lost Howell and the big man early Monday evening. Using an old trick of his profession, he urinated in Baggies to minimize the need for bathroom breaks. But it was now Wednesday morning, and Howell hadn't returned. Gorney was worried. By the end of the day, he would have to report to his client, and he had no clue as to what Howell was doing.

To pass the long hours, Gorney watched Howell's neighbors. He knew the couple on the second floor wouldn't be together much longer. For the last two evenings the woman sat at the kitchen table, sipping wine, staring out the window. When the man finally came home they avoided conversation, but their body language spoke volumes.

Then there was the young man with binoculars on the fourth floor. Gorney noticed him on Monday evening. He was at his window eating ice cream and watching the Victorian mansion on the Fairlane's side of the street. The fellow was back at his post last night. This evening, Gorney would reposition his car and find out what was so interesting.

Gorney yawned as he retrieved a sausage and egg muffin from a white bag and took several big bites. He was dog-tired, and he hoped a hardy breakfast would restore his energy. He was about to reach into the bag for his coffee when the sound of a phone ringing came out of the Fairlane's speaker. Howell's answering machine picked up, and Gorney quickly pushed the record button on his dashboard.

"Jason, the *Crossfire* is coming," was all the caller said. It was the voice of the woman who called Howell last time.

Gorney carefully placed the muffin on a napkin, took out his yellow pad, and wrote CROSSFIRE below the words GOLDEN FLEECE and RAPPAPORT.

He stared at the list, shaking his head. In spite of the nourishment he was still too tired to think clearly. Perhaps when Howell returned the woman's phone call, things would fall into place. In the meantime, the woman's message was fortuitous. Gorney could now chance a nap since the sound of the answering machine rewinding would be his wakeup call, telling him his subject had come home.

Gorney tossed the unfinished muffin behind him, carefully wiped his fingers on the napkin, and closed his attaché case. Then he settled back, stretched his arms, and clasped his hands over his belly. But a burning sensation in his chest and the sour taste of the breakfast muffin rising into his throat were making it difficult to doze. He put an antacid in his mouth and allowed it to melt on his tongue. Soon he was sound asleep.

3

AFTER LEAVING St. Andrews, Jason told Marty he wanted to spend some time in the plaza. There were a few loose ends he needed to tie up, and afterwards, he assured the big man, they both would get on with their lives.

Marty deliberately steered Jason away from the bench where Pete had died. They walked around the people in sleeping bags, the bodies lying under blankets and cardboard, and past the blue tents fastened to barren trees. Seeing it again gave Marty the willies. They found an empty bench and talked as the plaza woke up. People stood and stretched, and began their morning ritual of folding tents and rolling up sleeping bags. Some of them stepped into the shrubs and relieved themselves.

Jason paused in the middle of a sentence. "I've been through this place many times on my way to City Hall," he said, "but I didn't pay attention to what was going on. I guess I never really looked."

"I've spent a lot of time here, too, and I still have trouble watching," Marty remarked.

"I can't believe people live this way."

"Believe it."

"Was it always this bad?"

"No. More homeless are squatting here now that Project Vector patrols are keeping them out of Union Square and the downtown business district. The newspapers call the plaza 'Camp Babcock.'"

Jason frowned. "Okay, we were talking about my bus ride to City General two weeks ago. It's the one memory that remains blocked. All I can recall is something about the police, and that I was very frightened. Help me out."

"Sure. I was taking you to the hospital on the Muni, trying for the second time to get them to treat you. Pete didn't want to come. The bus was full and we got sepa-

rated. A woman screamed and the driver ejected you.
Apparently you molested her."

"You're kidding," Jason said, his mouth agape.

"Nope. The bus took off before I could do anything.
When I got the bus to stop, you weren't in sight. I finally
found you on a park bench in the company of two Project
Vector cops who were writing you a ticket."

"You took the ticket for me."

"See, you do remember."

Jason shook his head. "Not really. I learned later that
the incident was used by my investigator to place you near
City General about an hour before I surfaced. Without
that ticket I wouldn't have located you in Petaluma."

Marty shivered. "I never thought I'd be glad to get one
of those damn tickets. Thanks for reminding me. I better
pay it."

"No, it was *my* ticket," Jason countered, "*I'll* pay it."

"Sure, okay," Marty said. He was being distracted by
something going on behind Jason.

Jason turned. "What is it?"

"Speaking of cops . . ." Marty nodded at a couple of
police vans and a large Department of Public Works trash
truck parked on the street. "I don't like it."

"What's happening?"

"I'm not sure, but it's probably no coincidence this is
the time of day when the plaza empties." Sure enough,
dozens of men and women were filtering into the surrounding neighborhood.

"Where are they going?"

"To get breakfast at nearby churches and soup kitchens."

When the plaza was almost empty, the back of the
vans flew open, and thirty cops in full riot gear deployed.
Bringing up the rear, DPW crews wheeled large trash bins.

The remaining homeless grabbed what they could and fled.

"It's time to go," Jason said.

"I don't think so," Marty said stiffly.

"What are you going to do?"

"Talk to the man in charge. I'm a respectable citizen, right? I've got a place to stay, right? I got money in my pocket, right? I want some answers."

"Marty, don't cause trouble. Let's get out of—"

The big man stood and marched over to a police captain who was barking orders, mostly instructing DPW employees to throw everything but the shopping carts into the trash bins. The TAC squad took positions around the perimeter of the plaza. Jason grabbed his cane and followed Marty.

"Excuse me, Captain," the big man said in his solid citizen voice. "May I inquire as to what you are doing here?"

The captain turned. "Who are you?"

"A taxpayer who pays your salary. I happen to be visiting this public plaza, and I don't appreciate seeing storm troopers confiscating people's possessions." Marty folded his arms across his chest. "This isn't Nazi Germany."

The captain softened his tone a bit. "Look, sir, maybe I don't like this any more than you do, but I'm under strict orders. The mayor wants the plaza cleaned up. Now back off and let me do my job."

Marty stood firm. "You're trashing what little these people have. You might as well shoot them."

"Back off, sir; otherwise I'll have to arrest you for obstructing a police operation."

At that moment the leaf blower brigade entered the plaza and made normal conversation impossible. It was gut wrenching for Marty to remember how the blowers had engulfed him and Pete in a huge cloud of dust. Marty glared at the captain, the buzzing sound grating on his nerves, turning his neck beet red. The urge to strike out, to punish, was overwhelming. He clenched his fists and tensed his body.

Jason grabbed Marty's arms. "LET'S GO," he shouted over the din. "NOTHING CAN BE SETTLED HERE. LOOK, I'LL MAKE A LARGE DONATION TO THE CHURCH SO THESE PEOPLE CAN GET THEIR THINGS REPLACED. I DON'T CARE WHAT IT COSTS!"

The captain looked incredulously at the scruffy man in the stained coat. Shaking his head, he turned and walked off.

Jason pulled Marty out of the plaza. "I'm glad you didn't nail that captain," he said. "Even with my connections I don't think I could've helped you."

Marty was silent. Finally he said, "It felt good."

"Confronting that cop?"

"No, not considering myself homeless anymore."

4

A SQUAWKING SOUND jerked Gorney awake, causing his heart to pound with such force he had trouble catching his breath. It was Howell's answering machine rewinding. With one hand he turned the volume down on the radio, and with the other he held his chest. The woman's message was followed by the sound of dialing.

"Hi, it's Jason."

"Welcome back. Did you accomplish your mission?"

"Yes. It was quite an experience. I'll tell you about it when I see you—and thanks for the *Crossfire*. When will it arrive?"

Gorney tweaked up the volume.

"Tomorrow. But if it's okay with you I'd like to stop by after work and hear all about your life on the street. It must have been an eye-opener."

Gorney cocked an ear.

"It was. The Golden Fleece gave me a crash course. Only this time I didn't sleep through class. Still, I need to learn more, much more. I'm looking forward to watching CNN's experts debate the issue on your videotape."

After the conversation ended, Gorney leaned back in his seat and patted his chest, encouraging his heart rate and breathing to return to normal. Finally, things were beginning to make sense. Jason Howell is simply an eccentric do-gooder who went undercover to experience homelessness. Although it wasn't terribly exciting, at least Gorney would have something to report to his client.

He was reaching for his attaché case to get his microcassette recorder when he a felt a tightness rising behind his breastbone. Dismissing it as another pang of indigestion, he popped an antacid. But this time it didn't help. The tightness was mounting and he began to sweat. Now he was feeling nauseous, and the interior of the car was spiraling. Damn, he thought, that last sausage muffin must have been tainted.

Determined not to mess up the business end of his car, Gorney shoved his attaché case aside, and it tipped into the passenger foot well. Then he maneuvered his massive body over the driver's seat so he could disgorge his breakfast on the pile of garbage in the rear of the car. When he finished, he expected to feel better.

But he was dead wrong.

The pain in his chest now radiated to his jaw, and his breastbone was in the grip of a giant vise that squeezed him so tightly he could only gulp air like a fish out of water. Sweat ran in streams from his forehead and stung his eyes.

Raymond Gorney was forced to admit that his problem went beyond simple indigestion. Struggling to breathe, sensing reality slipping away, he mustered his last ounce of energy and turned his huge frame back around. He desperately needed to get to his cell phone in his attaché, but the case was now wedged in the passenger foot well and impossibly out of reach.

The horn, unused in years, was his last chance. With great effort he lifted his arm and began pressing the button.

It worked, thank God!

To Gorney it seemed as if he were honking for an eternity. But in reality less than a minute had passed before someone opened the driver's door and pulled Gorney's hand away from the button. "Don't worry, sir, I'm a police officer. I'll call for help."

"My attaché case . . . a cell phone," Gorney gasped, pointing to the foot well.

The cop hurried to the passenger side, opened the attaché case and retrieved the cell phone.

The last words Raymond Gorney heard were: "This is Inspector James Brodsky; I've got a Ten-Fifty-Two in Pacific Heights . . . ."

5

JASON WAS BUTTONING his shirt, his hair still damp from the shower. "I heard sirens in front of the building," he said, walking into the living room.

Marty was looking out of the window. "You know that Fairlane that followed us to the Western Addition?"

"Yes," Jason said, joining Marty. The two men watched as an ambulance pulled away.

"They worked on the driver with a resuscitator and then covered him up. Big fat guy."

"Too bad. I was going to hire my investigator to tail him. Now we may never learn for whom he was working. Keep your eyes peeled for his replacement."

Marty left the window and sat on the couch. "Jason, doesn't it strike you as odd that rich people are perfectly willing to spend money to hire private investigators to watch other private investigators?"

"Now that you mention it."

6

THE FLUORESCENT LIGHT escaping from Brodsky's kitchen window danced with Daly City's evening fog. Inside, Brodsky circled his prize on the table like a lion examining its kill. He needed a break and today he got it.

In spades.

This morning he scouted the intersection where Dubichek had been dropped off. His plan was to stake it out after work. As he was about to leave he heard frantic honking, so he went over to investigate, thinking perhaps that the derelict had escaped and was in the process of kidnapping someone else. But he was disappointed that it was only a fat man having a massive coronary.

Until he opened the victim's attaché case.

One look at the high-tech surveillance gadgets told Brodsky there was more to the story, and that the attaché and its contents would be his.

This was the first time Brodsky had removed property belonging to a victim. But the situation was extraordinary. He suspected the attaché held evidence incriminating his enemies, and in the interest of justice he couldn't allow it to fall into their hands. And later when he learned the victim was Raymond Gorney, "The Famous Shamus," Brodsky knew he had made the right choice.

Brodsky licked his lips as he unlatched the case and raised the lid. One by one, he removed the high-tech equipment. First he carefully checked both cameras.

No exposed pictures!

Frustrated, he played the microcassette recorder.

Only noise!

He slammed the lid in frustration and stared at the case. Taking a deep breath, he tried to puzzle it out. Maybe Gorney had just started his surveillance. Still, there must be some clue here, something that would reveal what the investigator was doing on that particular street, something that might tie Gorney's assignment to the derelict. Brodsky lifted the lid again and removed the remaining contents—camera accessories, a penlight, extra batteries, unopened film—setting each item carefully on the table. In a side pocket he found a notepad containing the words:

GOLDEN FLEECE
RAPPAPORT
CROSSFIRE

Brodsky had been holding his breath. He now exhaled slowly. Was GOLDEN FLEECE a code name for Dubichek? He didn't know. Although the name RAPPAPORT seemed vaguely familiar, he couldn't quite place it at the moment. But the word CROSSFIRE sent chills down his spine.

When the chills subsided, Brodsky was left with an incredible insight: If Gorney had been tailing Dubichek, it might mean that Babcock's opponents were on to the mayor's plot to hide the vagrant. Brodsky allowed his mind to follow that train. If he could topple the mayor by proving conspiracy and obstruction of justice, he would most certainly be a hero in the next administration. His reward would be a high-level appointment, even chief of police wasn't out of the question now . . . .

Brodsky caught himself. First he must be certain that Gorney *was* watching Dubichek. The rich were always hiring investigators, and possibly Gorney was working on an unrelated matter.

Brodsky lingered over the name RAPPAPORT. His instincts told him it was somehow connected with the Howell case, and a search of CAL-NET might reveal the link. For the first time since his transfer, he was eager to return to work.

As Brodsky rotated the empty attaché case to admire its workmanship, something shifted inside. He set it down and pulled on a fabric tab in one corner, uncovering a compartment that hid a beautiful, pearl-handled 9-mm Walther P-38. Brodsky smiled broadly as he nestled the gun against his chest. "Thank you, Ray Gorney, thank you," he said.

7

SITTING IN JASON'S home theater, Marty watched news footage of government soldiers executing a rag-tag group of rebels. The voiceover described how the civil war in this tiny African nation had driven tens of thousands of civilians into crowded, fly-infested refugee camps.

Jason walked in and sat on the couch next to Marty. The announcer went on to say that the United States was airlifting emergency food and medical supplies to the refugees.

Marty clicked off the television. "In comparison with those poor folks, the homeless in America are on a picnic.

It's no wonder politicians are hardened to their plight. They act as if something will magically happen and the problem will go away. There's no concerted effort, like that airlift."

"I was just reading the papers I retrieved from the Net," Jason replied. "It's obvious that our leaders never considered what would happen to American workers when the country shifted from a manufacturing-based economy to a service economy. Instead of a transitioning plan to cushion the affect of massive layoffs, the Feds threw money at the problem, and created a welfare monster in the process."

"And now they get to slay it," Marty said.

"Well at least there's something I can do to get *you* off the dole. It's time you stopped hanging around here and watching TV all day."

"Ha!" Marty said.

"So what would you like to do at Cytex?"

"Play football. I used to play fullback and coach."

"What's your second choice?"

"Anything that earns me a decent living."

"I have something in mind. But first let me tell you about my company. We make electronic boxes called C-REAL."

Marty looked puzzled. "You make electronic cereal boxes?"

Jason sighed. "No. C and R - E - A - L spells *C-REAL*. It's a device that turns a personal computer into a powerful virtual reality machine."

Marty blinked.

"Think of it as a new kind of training tool. The user wears a visor over his eyes that seals off the real world. The software in the computer determines what he sees."

"Like a simulator?"

"Exactly. Except our product makes the experience so real users can forget it's a computer simulation."

"For example?"

"Let's say a psychologist has a patient with a fear of heights. For treatment the patient could confront his phobia by being placed on the roof of a fifty-story building. He would even hear the wind howling."

"Can he walk up to the edge?"

"Yes."

"What happens if he gets dizzy and falls?"

"That depends on the software. We could easily arrange a computerized demise."

"I get it."

"Here's an another example you'll relate to: C-REAL would allow a quarterback to read the defense, adjust his offensive line, and attempt to audible a play over the crowd noise."

"Would he see pass rushers in his face?"

"Absolutely. And if he were wearing a pressure suit, he would feel a terrific hit."

Marty's face lit up. "Cool!"

"That's just the tip of the iceberg," Jason said, briefly describing other applications in medicine, architecture, and aviation.

"But I don't have any technical training," Marty said. "Might you need a bouncer to keep the NFL owners from mobbing Cytex?"

"I think we can do better than that. You said you took computer classes?"

"Yeah, I'm a regular mouse potato. And when they installed an Internet terminal at the library, I taught myself how to surf. You'd be surprised how many homeless hackers spend all day in front of public terminals."

"Your computer experience will come in handy for the job I have in mind. In a few months we'll be receiving shipments of C-REAL from an overseas subcontractor. Each unit has to be inspected and tested before it's packaged and sent to customers. How would you like to work in our quality control group?"

Marty massaged his chin. "Doing what?"

"Sitting at a terminal and testing C-REAL. It's primarily a monitoring job since the test process will be highly automated. But if C-REAL takes off as I expect it will, the opportunity for advancement is excellent. You'll receive stock options."

"What about salary?"

"Twenty-four thousand a year."

Marty grinned. "When do I start?"

"I'm due back on Monday. We can commute to Cytex together until you get your own place."

"You've sealed the deal."

"I'll get the champagne," Jason said.

The intercom buzzed and Marty went to answer it while Jason went into the kitchen. He was opening the champagne when Liz walked in with Marty.

"The two of you look none the worse for wear," she said smiling. "I'm dying to hear all about your experiences."

"Okay," Jason said, pouring three glasses, "but first I'd like to propose a toast: To Marty, my newest friend and Cytex's newest employee."

Marty beamed. "Two of the nicest things anyone has ever said to me."

Jason and Marty settled into the living room couch while Liz took the armchair.

"What will Marty be doing at Cytex?" she asked Jason.

"Working on C-REAL."

"That's wonderful," she said, "imagine being able to change one's reality."

"Imagine," Jason echoed, holding her eyes.

"I could've used it about five years ago," Marty said.

"I want to try it soon," Liz said. "I *need* to try it soon. But right now tell me all about your adventures on the street. Leave nothing out."

Liz's eyes widened at Jason's story of the foul-smelling doorway and their visit to the Monday Night Club. She giggled when Marty recounted how Stan induced Jason to drink from the jug, and then how Jason unintentionally evened the score by showering Stan with baked beans at the men's shelter. But it was the image of Jason panhandling a quarter from a kindly old woman that brought tears of laughter to her eyes.

Jason pulled the coin out of his pocket and held it up. "I'm going to have it framed."

"What a riot," Liz said, dabbing at her eyes with a napkin. "I'll bet it was the toughest money you've ever made."

"Indeed," Jason smiled, reaching for the champagne bottle. But it was now empty.

"I'll get some more," Marty offered, "and some food, too. I'm starved."

"Chinese okay?" Jason suggested. "Ever try it with champagne? It's great, really."

"Count me in," Liz said.

After Marty left, Liz moved to the couch to sit by Jason. Still smiling, she turned to face him. "I can't remember the last time I laughed so hard. It felt good. Thanks."

"Any time you need a good chuckle at my expense, let me know."

Suddenly the smile drained from Liz's face. "It's over between me and Anton."

Jason felt like a train commuter who is engrossed in a newspaper when the engineer slams on the brakes. "What did you say?"

"I've made an appointment with a divorce lawyer."

Jason took a deep breath, trying to switch gears. "I'm sorry, Liz . . . does Anton know?"

She shook her head no. "And he's going to be mad as hell when he finds outs."

Jason took her hand. "Liz, more bad news is the last thing he needs right now. Are you sure you want to do this?"

"I have to. I can't live with someone who's simmering, always on the edge." Liz blinked away a tear. "Our marriage was over when he broke my music box, although I didn't realize it at the time. That box symbolized our love . . . he gave it to me shortly after we got engaged. But any illusions I had about repairing our marriage were shattered with that box."

Jason gently squeezed her hand. "Stay here. Take my bedroom. I'll sleep on the couch."

"No, Jason. If I'm staying here when I tell Anton our marriage is over, it's not *me* I'll have to worry about. Look, I'll be fine at the Penniston," she said, patting his hand. "Really."

"When are you planning to tell him?"

She closed her eyes. Jason detected movement behind her lids as if she were watching a scene unfolding.

Jason squeezed her hand again. "Liz . . . ?"

Her eyes opened and she stared at him. "As soon as I get the nerve."

EIGHTEEN
Thursday, January 26

1

SHORTLY AFTER 3:00 P.M. the door flew open and Mayor Babcock stormed into Conti's office. His neck was taut, his face red, his mood black. Conti was behind his polished oak desk with his eyes closed and his hands clasped over his stomach. The mayor's unannounced visit was just about to interrupt the chief's afternoon nap.

Conti's eyes snapped open. "Walt . . . ?"

The mayor shook a pudgy forefinger and glared. "Just one question, Rudy," he began in measured tones, "would I get the death penalty, or the Medal of Honor, if I killed Brodsky with my bare hands?"

Conti placed his palms on his desk to steady himself as if an earthquake had rumbled through the room. "Ah . . . what did he do now?"

"The crazy bastard sexually assaulted poor Jeanette, IN MY OWN GODDAMN OFFICE!"

Conti pulled himself to his feet, walked around his desk and closed the door. "God, no . . . when?"

"Tuesday morning, before the office opened. Brodsky threatened to have her fired if she talked, so she's been at her wit's end deciding whether to report the attack. Thank goodness her priest advised her to come directly to me. She told me a man claiming to be a homicide inspector bullied his way in and rubbed his body against hers. Poor Jeanette's terrified he'll return, and she's been unable to function. The homeless you banished from the plaza are camping in my reception area and the coffee tastes like shit!"

"Are you certain it was Brodsky?"

The mayor pressed on his sinuses. "Of course," he replied irritably. "I had Jeanette look at a file photo, and she immediately identified him. She said she would never forget 'those beady animal eyes.'"

"What was he doing there?"

"Trying to locate Dubichek."

Conti sighed. "Is she going to press charges?"

"I've talked her out of it. She's willing to drop the matter based on my assurance that he'll never bother her again. Fire his ass!"

The chief began to pace. "It's not that simple, Walt. Brodsky will have the right to appeal his dismissal before the Civil Service Commission. Knowing him, he'll take his case to the media, and Jeanette's allegation of sexual harassment by a member of my department will be front page news. Guaranteed."

Babcock gnashed his teeth. "Do something, Rudy! Find some other reason to fire him and make it stick. I won't have that madman assaulting the women on my staff!"

The chief stopped pacing. "Give me a couple of days to think of something. In the meantime he'll be kept under constant surveillance."

The mayor, still pressing his sinuses, grabbed the door handle with his free hand. "You had better think of something soon," he growled, "otherwise you're *both* history!"

2

IT WAS EARLY EVENING when Liz delivered the *Crossfire* video to Jason's condo. She was wearing a green silk sheath cut two inches above her knees. The dress shimmered as she moved. She must have sensed Jason's stare because she turned and locked eyes with him.

"Would you like a glass of champagne? Some wine?" he offered.

"I'll have a gin martini, straight up, very tall and very dry." She sat down on his living room couch, crossed her legs, and tugged at her dress.

Jason froze. "You told Anton."

Liz nodded.

He mixed two tall martinis and sat next to her.

She turned toward him and lifted her glass. "To new beginnings," she said, her voice cracking at the edges.

Jason watched her as he sipped. Her green eyes appeared to shimmer, like her dress. No, that wasn't it . . . she was crying.

"To new beginnings," he repeated.

"Which reminds me," Liz said, setting her drink down and reaching into her bag, "here's the *Crossfire* tape. Would you like to watch it now?" A tear squeezed out and rolled down her cheek.

Jason took the videotape and placed it on the coffee table. "No, let's wait for Marty. He's buying a wardrobe for his new job. And he finally decided to get a proper haircut." Jason ran his hands through his longish hair. "I guess I could use one too . . . and a shave."

Liz cocked her head, forcing a weak smile. "Don't be too hasty. Your beard sets off those beautiful blue eyes of yours. But best of all, you no longer resemble your older brother."

Jason set his glass down and took her hand. "Would you like to talk?"

Suddenly Liz's eyes overflowed. Jason slid closer and held her. Sobbing, she rested her head on his shoulder and wrapped her arms around him. He gently stroked her hair.

After a while her breathing steadied but her arms told him not to let go. He inched closer. Firm breasts rose and fell against his chest. He shut his eyes and inhaled deeply, allowing her fragrance to envelop him. He shifted his hand from her hair to the nape of her neck, marveling how her skin felt just like the silk of her dress.

Liz abruptly pulled away. "Late this afternoon I called Anton and told him it was over. I didn't have the courage to do it in person, but that will have to happen soon. I know him; he'll have to see the determination in my face."

"What did he say?" Jason asked.

"Nothing at first. Finally he said, 'We'll see, Liz,' and hung up. Afterward I became depressed. I felt as if I had just pulled a chain, and everything that once gave meaning to my life—my marriage, my job, my future—had been flushed down the toilet."

Jason picked up his martini. "Everything?"

"Well . . . no. Seeing you and Marty tonight was the one thing I still looked forward to. And although you may think it's shallow, I forced myself to shed my business suit and put on a new dress . . . off with the old and on with the new. But damn it," she said through fresh tears, "now I'm making a mess of myself." She reached in her bag, took out a compact, and dabbed at her eyes with a handkerchief.

Jason sipped and watched her.

Liz put her compact away, picked up her drink, took several sips, and sagged into the couch. After a long moment, she met his eyes and tilted her head back invitingly.

Jason leaned in, toward her mouth, but she turned her face away. Committed, he kissed her on the cheek. He was about to retreat when he felt her face turn slightly toward him. He closed his eyes and held his breath. She found his lips and engaged him in a deep, passionate kiss. He put his arms around her and she reciprocated, holding him tightly.

A voice in his head whispered: *Stop! She's your sister-in-law.*

He broke the kiss and listened.

She'll go back to him, warned the voice.

Jason blinked and looked at Liz. He now saw eyes filled with desire. Suddenly she reclined and pulled him on top of her. The voice was now lost in the loud thud-thud of his heart.

For a full minute he had neglected to breathe. He took several quick breaths, sweeping in Liz's fragrance and that only heightened the intoxicating affect of the gin. He closed his eyes and explored her neck with his lips, running his hand over the soft curve of her hip. Liz's body arched and she moaned. She took his head in both hands and hungrily found his mouth. She was maneuvering her body under his, and as they kissed he became aware that the hem of her dress had inched toward her waist.

She moaned again, her legs spreading, chest heaving, fingernails digging in his back . . . his muscles tightening, toes curling, loins aching with desire. As his hand moved upward on the inside of her thigh he felt her tugging at his shirttail, undoing his belt buckle—

The sound of the front door opening.

The rustling of packages.

Liz abruptly sat up and Jason tumbled onto the floor. She quickly straightened her dress, opened her handbag, and ran a brush through her hair. Jason pulled himself off the floor and tucked in his shirt. Lipstick was smeared around his mouth and beads of sweat dotted his forehead. He plopped on the couch.

"I feel like a teenager again," Liz giggled.

"I wouldn't know," he said, gulping air, "I skipped that part of my life and went straight to adulthood."

Marty entered the room whistling, looking dapper in a white shirt, gray slacks, and a blue blazer. His hair was neatly trimmed and combed back, and he was carrying a shopping bag in each hand. He stared for a long moment at the couple. "Uh . . . hi."

"Marty, you look great," Liz said, shaking out her hair.

"That's more than I can say for the two of you."

"Can I give you a hand?" Jason offered.

"No thanks, everything's under control."

"Not everything," Liz said, eyeing the bulge in Jason's lap. Smiling, she excused herself to powder her nose.

Marty also excused himself and went to his room to put his purchases away.

Jason picked up a cocktail napkin and wiped his face. Then he drew a deep sip from his martini and sank into the couch. Liz and her fragrance lingered. He felt as though he had been rudely awakened from an incredibly erotic dream.

After a few minutes Marty returned and eased into an armchair.

"Did you get everything you wanted?" Jason asked.

"Pretty much. How about you?"

Jason sighed and downed the rest of his martini.

"I went to that Huge 'N Tall place you told me about," Marty added. "The sizes started at XL and went all the way to KK."

"What's KK?"

"King Kong, my size."

"Well, you look like a million bucks."

"That's about what I spent. It wasn't easy to part with so much money. I'd forgotten how expensive regular clothes are . . ." A small plastic cube on the coffee table was distracting Marty. It had wires fanning out in all directions. He picked it up. "What's this? It looks like some kind of bug."

"That's exactly what it is. After they took the fat man away I asked my investigator, Tim Riley, to sweep the apartment. At first he found nothing. Then he called my number on his cell phone and sure enough that device you're holding began transmitting. It was hidden in my answering machine. Riley said it looked like the work of a pro by the name of Ray Gorney. I mentioned the Fairlane, and that confirmed it."

"Any clue who this Gorney fellow was working for?"

"No. Riley's going to try and find out, but he's not too optimistic. Gorney was a master at covering his tracks."

"Do you still suspect the mayor?"

"It's possible. Election year makes people do strange things. But if Babcock was watching us, by now he knows we're harmless and he'll leave us alone. On the other hand, if the surveillance persists, then Riley thinks we may have a Cytex competitor engaged in your run-of-the-mill industrial espionage. The morning of my accident I gave a lecture and mentioned that Cytex had developed a blockbuster product. Someone in the audience could be curious. Welcome back to the real world."

"I forgot how much fun it was."

Liz returned fresh-faced and smiling. "Well, boys, are you ready for some educational television?"

"Let's do it," Jason said. They moved into his home theater and Jason inserted the *Crossfire* tape into his VCR.

3

"HOMELESSNESS IS ONE of society's problems that just refuses to go away," said the female voiceover as video clips showed scenes of men and women sprawled on the sidewalk and sleeping on park benches. "During the last two decades we have seen more panhandlers in American cities, more drunks in doorways, more people pushing their possessions in shopping carts, and more men and women scavenging through the trash for food. And with welfare reform, the problem is worsening in many parts of the country. What, if anything, can be done?"

The studio camera cut to a close-up of an attractive and neatly-coifed woman. The text at the bottom of the screen identified her as "Cynthia Markum, senior editor for *Newsweek.*"

"To address this difficult question," Cynthia continued, "we have for the left, Dr. Simon Schultz, the founder of Outreach America, a national nonprofit organization that has sheltered, fed, and counseled thousands of homeless people."

Dr. Schultz, a lanky man with long hair, flashed a toothy grin.

"And for the right is Dr. Dillon Cromwell, a senior fellow of the Dimension Institute. His writings on modern social problems are often quoted by policymakers."

The diminutive Dr. Cromwell, nodded and adjusted his bow tie.

"Before we get into specifics," Cynthia said, "we need some foundational information. Dr. Schultz, let's start with you. Why do people become homeless?"

"Lack of affordable housing," Schultz said. "We can't pay people slave wages, charge them exorbitant rents, take away food stamps and subsidies, and force them to choose between paying the rent and eating. Of course people will become homeless."

Cynthia turned to Dr. Cromwell. "Do you agree that lack of affordable housing is the primary cause of homelessness, Doctor?"

"No, I do not," Cromwell said flatly. "Homelessness is rooted in the breakdown of the nuclear family. When an individual chooses alcohol and drugs over family values, he cannot maintain a roof over his head, regardless of the cost of housing. There are numerous instances in the history of this great nation when individuals faced hardship and adversity. Families pulled together, neighbors helped one another, and people managed without becoming homeless. Perhaps modern life is too comfortable."

Schultz came alive. "Too comfortable! Tell that to the unemployed building contractor enduring a frigid Chicago winter, sleeping on a steam grate to keep warm!"

Cromwell turned to Schultz. "That was his choice."

"Let's move on to the size of the homeless problem," Cynthia said, changing the subject. "Dr. Schultz, your estimate please."

"That's a difficult question because the homeless are never included in the census. But most experts believe that the problem afflicts about one percent of the general population. In other words, three to four million Americans are chronically homeless."

"Nonsense," Cromwell huffed. "During the last two decades, the homeless population never exceeded three to four hundred thousand. Tops."

"Who are you counting, Cromwell, just the panhandlers in New York City?"

"And who are *you* counting, Schultz? People doubling up and sharing rent?"

"No, and you're lucky I'm not. Twenty million working-age adults are forced to live in someone else's home.

Eventually Cromwell, many of these precariously housed individuals will find themselves on the street, replacing the homeless who are carried away every day and buried in Potter's Field.

"On top of that," Schultz bristled, "there are millions of single adults living alone, many of whom lack savings to cushion them from downsizing. Watch out, Cromwell, you might find yourself stepping over their bodies just to get to your country club!"

Cromwell aimed a forefinger at Schultz. "You and your liberal cohorts intentionally inflate the homeless population to fund your ill-conceived and ineffectual social programs."

"That's bull and you know it! We're in the business of saving lives. YOU and your conservative cronies deliberately understate the problem because you're afraid the government will eliminate the mortgage deduction subsidizing your vacation homes."

Cromwell narrowed his eyes. "Look Schultz, even if you count all of the people who die on the street plus all of the 'precariously housed' who *might* become homeless, you will not come anywhere near your fabricated figures."

"Okay, okay, gentlemen," Cynthia said, trying to regain control, "let's agree that no one has a precise count of the homeless population. Perhaps the figure depends on how homelessness is defined. Dr. Cromwell, let's hear from you."

"It is quite simple, Cynthia. A homeless person is an individual who routinely sleeps in an emergency shelter or in a public place."

"Wr-o-o-ng!" Schultz hooted, slapping his knee with his hand. "What about all those folks who sleep in cars and vans, in detox centers, in jails, in hospitals, in welfare hotels, under freeway overpasses, in abandoned buildings, in camps, in railroad cars, or in tunnels?" His voice was rising. "Speaking of tunnels, did you know the New York Transit Authority found six thousand poor souls living in decrepit nineteenth century tunnels under the city. They included kids FOR GOD'S SAKE!

"Gentlemen," Cynthia said, "we're not getting anywhere. Perhaps I can offer a simple definition with which we all can agree: A homeless person is one who can't afford a private place of his own."

"Too liberal," Cromwell said. "Your definition includes grown-up children living with their parents."

"Too conservative," Schultz said. "Your definition excludes individuals who live from day-to-day in rat-infested roach motels."

"My definition is the only one that is rational," Cromwell insisted. "We must use our limited resources for the people who sleep in public places and shelters, those who are of the most concern to society. Making wild guesses about the number of individuals who might be living in cars or sleeping in the bushes is patently absurd."

"What's absurd," Schultz sputtered, "is denying people housing while continuing to spend billions on useless weapons systems."

"It is far better to spend money on defense and create jobs than to give handouts to the idle so they can destroy themselves on drugs and alcohol."

Cynthia sighed. "This line isn't working either. Let's turn to demographics. Dr. Cromwell, how would you characterize the current homeless population in terms of the substance abusers, the mentally ill, and those still capable of working?"

Cromwell inspected his fingernails. "The largest segment of the homeless population consists of single males. About one-quarter suffers from mental illness, and most of the rest need treatment for substance abuse and disease. Few are homeless merely because they are between jobs."

"Well," Schultz said, cracking a smile, "if you're talking about the visible homeless, Doctor, I actually concur with your mental illness figures. But with regard to drugs, you're quite high."

"Very funny, Schultz. But the fact remains that the majority of the single homeless need treatment of one kind or another. Face it, these people are using their public assistance and panhandling monies to get stoned . . . ."

4

AT HIS STATION at the front desk in the Hall of Justice, Brodsky chewed on his fingernails, watching the time edge toward the dinner hour. He was anxious to run the name RAPPAPORT on CAL-NET. But he knew he had to be more careful this time. The activity level at the Bureau of Criminal Investigations would be greater this evening than it had been last Sunday when he learned that the chief had washed Dubichek's fingerprint file.

Deep down though, Brodsky knew he wouldn't be caught this time either. Things had been going extremely well for him, and he was beginning to feel invincible. For one thing, he had inherited an impressive array of high-tech surveillance equipment from Ray Gorney, as well as a classic 9 mm handgun. For another—and he recalled this with particular pleasure—he had boldly penetrated enemy territory and learned where the limo had taken Dubichek. It was a masterful move that gave his confidence a tremendous boost. And it wasn't lost on him that the dark-eyed piece of ass in the mayor's office had the hots for him. After he completed his mission he would take her to a cheap motel and give her a nice bang as a reward.

Brodsky snapped out of his reverie to find a citizen standing before him. The man mumbled something about being mugged. His face was disfigured, his head was bandaged and swollen, and his right arm was in a cast. The man's condition reminded Brodsky he needed to focus on finding Dubichek and torturing the truth out of him. A glance at his watch confirmed it was time to act. Brodsky left the man in the middle of a sentence and took the elevator up to BCI.

It brought a smile to his face when he saw that the room was completely empty. Yes, he was on a roll. He went over to the same terminal he used the other day and accessed the database. He typed in a date range followed by the word RAPPAPORT. The computer returned:

26 FILES FOUND.
ENTER ANOTHER KEYWORD.

Brodsky gnawed on his knuckles. There wasn't time to check twenty-six files. He was looking for a connection with Dubichek so he added the vagrant's name to the search criteria. He drummed his fingers and waited. The hourglass on the screen seemed to flicker for an interminable period.

Finally the monitor displayed:

NO MATCH.

"Shit!" escaped loudly from Brodsky's lips. Catching himself, he stood and peeked over the partition. Several clerks had just entered the room. They weren't looking his way, but he didn't want to tempt fate. This would have to be his last try. He deleted DUBICHEK and typed HOWELL.

Several uniforms were filtering in with food trays. "Hurry, you bitch," he said, slapping the monitor with his palm. He held his breath.

The screen displayed:

1 MATCH.

"Yes!" he exhaled, hitting a function key. The screen filled with data, listing the stats of the Howell Kidnapping Case. The last sentence was highlighted:

RAPPAPORT — ALIAS USED TO REGISTER JASON HOWELL AT CITY GENERAL HOSPITAL.

That's it! Gorney *was* tracking Dubichek! Shaking, he cleared the screen. Chills coursed through his body, making him quiver. He hunched his shoulders, waiting for the feeling to pass. The chills subsided and were replaced by a firm finger poking him in the small of his back.

He turned his head and looked up sheepishly.

His lieutenant was looming over him, glaring menacingly. "In my office, Brodsky, NOW!"

5

"OKAY, OKAY," Cynthia shouted, raising both arms in an attempt to allay the bickering. "God help us, but it's time to turn to the most difficult question of all. What does each of you think can be done to solve the homeless problem?"

"I'd like to comment first," Schultz said, raising his hand.

Cromwell shrugged and reached for his glass of water.

"As I said earlier, the answer lies in housing."

Cromwell rolled his eyes.

"If people are securely housed," Schultz continued unfazed, "everything is possible. All of our social programs—job training, detoxification, rehabilitation—can be effective. But if we continue to allow folks to live on the street, little can be done. Not only will they remain a financial burden on society, but we're condemning fellow human beings to death."

"I will agree with your concept of getting the homeless off our streets," Cromwell said. "That is a fine idea—"

"—you're twisting my words."

"Let me make my point, *please,*" Dr. Cromwell insisted. "Even if we found the money to house the entire homeless population, such a step would backfire since the very people we want off the street would not wind up housed."

"Why not?" Cynthia asked.

"Let us use Dr. Schultz's own reasoning. Earlier he told us that there are millions of adults who are doubling up or otherwise 'precariously housed.' These people will get themselves evicted just to qualify for Schultz's subsidized condos."

"Now let me make *my* point, Cromwell!" Schultz protested. "READ MY LIPS! If you expect the homeless to have any chance of attending a retraining program and getting a job, they'll need an address, access to a phone, and some privacy. I'm not talking about luxury condos. I'm talking about tiny cubicles with the barest of necessities, minuscule rooms that can be rented at fifty to sixty dollars a week.

"*No one* who is presently living alone or under someone else's roof would want to inhabit such a space. But a hell of a lot of people now sleeping in doorways would consider it Paradise."

Cromwell looked at Schultz. "Are you proposing that we return to the single room occupancy concept that failed in the Sixties?"

"Precisely. Except this time the states would build the SRO's using block grants, and run them under federal guidelines that specify minimum construction and health standards. That way we avoid the slumlords and decay that caused the downfall of the old SRO's. And as a pre-requisite for getting general assistance to pay the rent and buy food, the inhabitants would be required to attend job training and placement programs."

"If you brought back the SRO's, would you make sleeping in public against the law?" Cromwell asked.

"Absolutely not. Cyclical economic downturns could temporarily increase housing demand beyond supply. Therefore we must *never* outlaw reliever situations—whether it's a car, a tent, a park bench. People have to sleep somewhere.

"But during times when sufficient housing is available, anti-vagrancy laws would be superfluous. Why would someone choose to sleep out in the cold when they can be in a warm bed behind a locked door?"

"Well, Doctor, I think you have offered us an interesting idea," Cromwell said. "Unfortunately, it falls way short of the mark."

"And why pray tell is that?"

"Because your plan ignores society's fundamental problem with homelessness."

Schultz tugged at his lobes. "I'm all ears, Cromwell."

"As I have stated, substance abusers make up a large percentage of the homeless population. These people care more about drugs and alcohol than where they live. And as they do now, they will take their rent and food money, and stick it up their nose, into their arms, and down their gullet. That is why they are homeless in the first place."

"Your assumption of rampant substance abuse among the homeless is both baseless and cynical."

Cromwell smiled. "All right, my dear fellow, let us assume we suddenly find ourselves in Utopia, and the cubicle communities are magically drug-free. Still, because the inhabitants' discretionary income is so minuscule, those that have panhandled before will continue to beg in order to buy things that were impractical while living on the street—a television, a VCR, a cappuccino maker, perhaps.

"Face it, Schultz, you have not solved the problem bothering Americans the most: panhandling. Decent hardworking people want to enjoy their shopping districts, parks, and streets without being harassed by miserable miscreants."

Schultz crossed his arms over his chest. "I'm dying to hear what you would do."

"I am happy to tell you. But first, Doctor, I would suggest the reason that you and your liberal kind will never solve homelessness is that you are addressing the wrong problem."

"Oh what a dummy I am!" Schultz said, hitting his forehead with his palm. "I've wasted my life!"

"What you fail to understand is that the homeless problem is one of health and not of housing. The majority of the homeless suffer from disease, addiction, mental illness, or a combination of all three. And whether these people are on the streets or in cubicles, they will continue to use drugs and alcohol, and spread disease. They must be quarantined so they can be properly treated. You cannot shift their environment slightly and expect addictive behavior patterns to change and diseases to disappear."

"What are you proposing Cromwell? Shall we give them one-way tickets to France?" Schultz winked at Cynthia.

Cromwell ignored the remark and turned toward the moderator. "Cynthia, I would start by making it illegal to live on the streets. But instead of jail time, the homeless would be committed to a treatment program at one of our vacant military bases."

"A-HA! Concentration camps!" Schultz barked.

"Sanctuaries," Cromwell said softly to Cynthia. "Unused military bases offer a turnkey operation complete with barracks, mess halls, medical facilities, and classrooms. Of course, a security system would have to be in place to prevent people from wandering off."

"Electrified fences!" Schultz shouted.

"What would happen at these sanctuaries?" Cynthia asked.

"Upon arrival, individuals would undergo a seventy-two-hour evaluation to determine the appropriate treatment program. If the person had a drug or alcohol problem—as most will—they would go through detox for two months. Afterward they would attend classes and learn new skills. High school equivalency degrees and college credits would be given. At the end of a year they will graduate, receive a certificate, and be part of a formal job placement program. Employers would be encouraged to hire graduates using state and federal jobs credits. If, however, in spite of everything, an individual returns to his old ways, he would be recycled through the sanctuary."

Schultz began waving his arms. "Cromwell, you're perpetrating a fraud! All you're doing is warehousing people in army barracks under the guise of a treatment program. Warehousing has been tried everywhere! And guess what? It doesn't work! Why do you think big city shelters are empty on freezing nights? Because folks are attacked and killed in those shelters, that's why! Do you *really* think if you put street people in army barracks, the dangerous individuals among them will suddenly become Boy Scouts?"

"As I said," Cromwell explained to Cynthia, "the sanctuaries will have the necessary security."

"Give me a break!" Schultz shouted. "The big-city shelters have metal detectors and police guards, and folks still get stabbed and raped. What are you going to do to prevent that, Cromwell? Would your initial screening reveal the sex offenders so you could lop off their nuts?"

Cynthia held her hand over her mouth.

Schultz was hot. "And why only arrest street people?" he asked, throwing his head back, his hair flying. "What about the hidden homeless, the men, women and children living in horrendous conditions. What about unemployed aerospace workers who are innocent victims of downsizing? Are you going to hunt them down with police dogs so you can imprison them too?

"We have to start somewhere," Cromwell said, turning a smidgen toward Schultz. "*Your* plan is too soft. Solving homelessness requires tough love."

"Bull, Cromwell! You're sweeping the problem under the rug so citizens won't be reminded that you and your cronies in the government have allowed the homeless problem to get completely out of control! I can see it now," Schultz said, cupping his hand over his eyes. "As soon as some poor beggar emerges from a subway station, blinking in the bright daylight, the *Gestapo* will be lying in wait and it's off to the concentration camp! Am I right?"

"That is unfair, Schultz; there is due process."

"Sure, if he has blond hair and blue eyes . . . ."

6

JASON OPENED THE BAR in his home theatre and poured Cognac. He passed out the snifters and sat next to Liz.

They sipped in silence.

Finally Jason said, "If those experts truly represent the establishment's thinking, the homeless are in big trouble." Then he looked at Marty. "What do you think? You're the best expert we've got."

Marty took a sip and smacked his lips. "Great brandy; now I'm permanently ruined for rotgut."

"Be serious."

"Okay, you asked for it. First of all, those experts were fixing the blame and not the problem."

"That's true," Jason said, "Schultz blamed the conservatives and Cromwell blamed the homeless."

Marty nodded. "Secondarily, both of them used generalities and statistics, glossing over the fact that there are real people out on the street, people like Stan, Willie, and Doc, people who could get back on their feet if they had regular jobs."

"Are you saying the answer lies in jobs?"

"Yup. Providing decent jobs for people willing and able to work is the best way to reduce homelessness. Give Stan, Willie, and Sanchez jobs, and you not only get people off the dole, you get consumers and taxpayers in the bargain."

"What drop in homelessness would we see?"

Marty looked up at the ceiling. "God, I don't know— maybe one third, maybe more. Someone who's sleeping on a bench might not look like they're employable, but time and again I've seen those folks go into an experimental program and before you know it they're wearing three-piece suits."

":But what did you think of the experts' solutions?" Liz asked. "Weren't both saying that some type of stable living environment must come first?"

Marty shook his head. "Maybe for the homeless at the end of the line, like the plaza people. But if you take able-bodied individuals and isolate them in Dr. Schultz's cubicles, they'd slowly go mad. Or if they were forced to live in Dr. Cromwell's barracks with the sick, the criminal, and the crazy, they'd *quickly* go mad. Take your choice.

"I'm saying there's no need to fool around with elaborate and costly schemes when you have people who want to work. Give them jobs and they'll take care of themselves. Period."

"Are you talking about having the government create jobs like FDR did during the Great Depression?" Jason asked.

Marty took another sip. "Nope, that'll never happen. Not in today's world."

"Why not?" Jason asked.

Marty looked at Jason. "First let me ask you something: In the articles you fished from the net at the library, do you remember seeing any mention—from *anyone* in government—about creating jobs for the homeless?"

"No, now that you mention it."

"You won't, either."

"Go on."

"A certain amount of unemployment is considered healthy in our society. When I say 'unemployment' I'm talking about the newly unemployed, those people with the skills society values. If the size of this fresh labor pool drops too low, companies have to raise salaries to keep the workers they've got. Also they can't expand. Prices get driven up and—BOOM—we've got inflation.

"On the other hand, if unemployment goes too high, the government has to support additional people who aren't working, the tax base erodes, and the economy slows down. Consumers fret about their jobs and defer purchases. Companies react by laying more people off, making the situation even worse. Now we've got a recession." Marty winked at Liz. "I'll bet you didn't know I could talk dirty."

"Indeed," Liz said, winking back and smiling.

"I see what you're getting at," Jason said. "Since the government can't discriminate, the recently unemployed will have first crack at a jobs program. When that happens, unemployment goes down, the Federal Reserve Board raises interest rates, and the markets go south. It's suicide for the political party in power. Meanwhile the homeless are left out in the cold."

Marty nodded. "You got it. Picture the homeless at the end of a real long unemployment line. The politicians are only concerned with keeping the front secured; the back end just sways in the breeze."

"I see you've put your time at the library to good use," Jason said.

"Yup."

Liz was staring at Marty. "I find it hard to believe someone with your intelligence remained homeless for so long."

"Believe it. There are lots of educated people on the street—even physicists, doctors, stockbrokers. But without an address and a phone number, no one will give them the time of day, much less a job."

"I guess that's right," Liz said.

"The real unemployment level," Marty added, "is much higher then the government says because folks who have run out of benefits aren't even counted—that's several million people no one ever talks about."

"The discarded workers?" Liz asked.

"The very same. The longer they remain unemployed, the greater the risk they'll become burdens on society."

Jason got up from the couch to pace. He was beginning to feel another headache coming on. "Damn it, if the government can't or won't do anything, then industry should take responsibility for your discarded workers."

"*Our* discarded workers," Marty corrected.

"Okay, right. But without generous tax incentives or a drastic change in American labor costs, there isn't a single company out there who's going to pay the long-term unemployed a living wage when they can hire highly-skilled Third World workers for peanuts."

"Like Cytex is planning to do," Marty said.

Jason massaged his temple. "I'm afraid so. But maybe it doesn't have to be that way. Something you said earlier intrigues me—about giving jobs to people like Stan and Willie. They get off the dole *and* become taxpayers in the bargain. That's two-way leverage. In business, leverage equals opportunity. Maybe private industry can take advantage of it."

"How?" Liz asked.

Jason continued to pace. "I'm not sure; I'm thinking out loud now. Assume for the moment the government made its obsolete military bases available, like Cromwell was talking about. But instead of 'sanctuaries,' suppose they were converted into privately-run manufacturing enterprises. And with inexpensive housing on the base, the workers would have the stable living environment Schultz insisted was necessary. If the economics came together—and that's a big if—perhaps we can remove some of the incentive private industry now has to export jobs."

Marty downed his cognac and looked at Jason. "I don't think anyone is going to convince the government to turn its bases over to private industry so they can hire the homeless. Talk about paralysis through analysis."

Jason knew Marty was right. Discouraged, he sagged into the couch.

Liz patted the seat cushion next to her. He slid closer and she took his hand. "Why don't you try it yourself?"

"What do you mean?"

"Get a facility and hire Stan, Willie, and the others to manufacture C-REAL. Prove the concept. And even if it doesn't go any further, you'll have helped Marty's friends."

"Nice thought, Liz, but I doubt a private program can work on a such small scale. Even if I can get the blessing of Cytex's board, there's still the issue of finding and out-fitting a factory, training people, and cranking up C-REAL production in a couple of months. No, it's impossible."

"Think about it," she said, looking into his eyes. "You'll feel better if you can convince yourself one way or the other."

"Okay," Jason sighed, massaging his temple. "I'll run the numbers."

Liz squeezed his hand and smiled. Then she glanced at her watch. "How did it get so late? I have to go."

Marty stood and stretched. "I'll say goodnight, too. Heavy thinking tuckers me out."

Jason retrieved Liz's coat, and walked with her into the hallway. When they reached the elevator, he kissed her. "Stay here tonight," he urged.

"No, Jason," she replied softly. "Suddenly we both have a lot on our minds. Let's not complicate things any more right now." She pecked him on the cheek. "And it's obvious you're having a bad headache. Take two Tylenol and call me in the morning." With that, Liz stepped into the elevator, the doors closed, and she was gone.

NINETEEN
Friday, January 27

1

J ASON UNDRESSED, took his Tylenol, and went to bed. Although his headache eventually subsided, the ache in his loins had not. Liz was the most exciting woman he had ever met. He tried to imagine making love to her. The lights would be low, and the music soft and romantic. She would be wearing a clingy black dress. He would take her in his arms and dance slowly, waiting for the rhythm of her body to tell him she was ready. Then he would look at her, asking permission with his eyes. She would answer "yes" with a long and sensuous kiss. Slowly, he would undress her, caressing her body with his eyes, his hands, his lips. Then he would lead her to his bedroom and . . .

No, it wasn't working. There was nothing in his past experience to prepare him for a woman like Liz. Although he couldn't stop fantasizing about her, he knew any of the images he conjured up would fall short of reality. But one thing was certain: for the first time in his life he was deeply and hopelessly in love.

His thoughts turned to Anton. His brother would soon learn of Jason's betrayal, blame him for ruining his marriage, and seek revenge. Jason wondered what form the retribution would take. He agonized over his deep feelings for Liz, not because he feared Anton, but because he had truly wanted to reconcile with his brother. Now, of course, that was out of the question.

Sleep was also out of the question.

Jason got up, made a pot of coffee, and took a cup into his office. He switched on his computer and accessed a strategic planning program. Without expecting to accomplish much, he labeled fields, keyed in numbers, and built an economic model for manufacturing C-REAL in the United States. He assumed cheap housing would be available, and assemblers would be paid minimum wage. Although he had serious doubts, he also assumed that homeless Americans, although unskilled in high-tech manufacturing, could somehow match the efficiency of skilled overseas workers.

When he finished, with every number shaved and every assumption stretched, it didn't surprise him that the cost of manufacturing C-REAL in the United States would be more than double that of sending it overseas. There was nothing more to do. Without large subsidies from the government, there would be no way to pull it off.

At 4:00 a.m. he switched off the computer and stared at the blank screen.

Suddenly out of nowhere, the solution came to him! It had been there all along, literally staring him in the face. Stunned, he sat motionless, allowing the details to unfold in his mind. Then he turned the computer on and began modifying the model.

Just before dawn he collapsed into bed and slept for a few hours. Then he showered and made a fresh pot of coffee. It was now 9:30 a.m. On the refrigerator, Marty had left a note saying he went to the library to "bone up" on virtual reality. With a coffee cup in one hand, Jason picked up the kitchen phone and called Sam at her office. He briefed her about his research into homelessness.

"Did you get the feeling that the problem had no practical solution?" she asked.

"I did at first. But after working on it all night, I had a remarkable insight. That's why I'm calling to set up a meeting. I'm looking at a risky proposition and I'd like you to play devil's advocate."

"That happens to be my favorite role; when would you like to meet?"

"What's your schedule like today?"

"Jammed, but . . . let's see . . . lunch is free. Can you meet me at noon at the Bio-Burger, around the corner from my office?"

"I'll be there. But before you go, if my plan makes sense on paper, I'll want to test it on a small scale. That means I'll need a factory with cheap housing for one hundred workers. The whole project must be in full operation in eight weeks. I know that's a tall order, but the plan will live and die on the availability of such an integrated facility. If you have any ideas, bring them with you."

"I'll think about it, but it sounds like you need a real estate broker. Why don't you call Henderson's company?"

"I'll do that," Jason said. He hung up and was about to dial when the phone rang..

"How are you?" a deep voice asked. "We haven't talked in a while."

"Hello, Anton," Jason said, pulling up a chair. "I'm fine. I've been walking a lot, and my limp is nearly gone."

"Good. There's an extremely serious matter we need to talk about. Tonight, say six o'clock?"

Jason closed his eyes. "Where?"

"The Polo Lounge at my wife's hotel."

2

IN THE GRAY DRIZZLE of late morning, the Lincoln Town Car's wipers swished intermittently as the limo inched along Stockton Street toward Union Square. Although San Francisco's commute had long ended, the downtown area remained jammed with traffic. But unlike the harried drivers around him, Mayor Babcock was delighted. He was delighted because the streets were full of shoppers.

The mayor was on a scouting expedition, checking the effectiveness of the police and the Recreation and Park Department's coordinated effort to keep the area vagrant-free.

The car phone rang, and the mayor absently reached for the handset as he scanned for panhandlers. Not one in sight. "YES!" he effused, acknowledging this happy fact and the caller at the same time.

"Walt, it's Rudy," the chief said. "I badly need to talk to you."

The mayor's mood blackened. "What do you want? I am having such a wonderful time watching my happy-faced constituents shopping freely, unimpeded by beggars. And now you want to ruin it with your inevitable bad news. Call me some other—"

"Wait! Don't hang up!" Chief Conti urged. "This time I have *good* news."

Mayor Babcock sighed. "What is it?"

"Brodsky's resigned."

The mayor perked up. "Talk to me."

"Brodsky himself gets all the credit. His lieutenant caught him at BCI using CAL-NET without authorization. The system tagged him digging into the Howell file. And that happens to be a criminal offense."

"I thought police hacking was one violation you winked at," the mayor said.

"We enforce it when it serves our purposes."

The mayor switched the telephone handset to his other ear. "Continue."

"In return for dropping the charges, we offered a 'quiet-of-the-night-deal' to Brodsky."

"Meaning?"

"It's a deal we sometimes make with bad cops. If they go quietly, the charges are dismissed and we avoid an Internal Affairs investigation, an appeal before the Civil Service Commission, a criminal prosecution, and the inevitable negative publicity. Brodsky gets to keep the retirement he has vested, about 40 percent of an inspector's salary."

"Sounds pretty goddamn generous."

"Not when you consider how little we pay our inspectors. He'll be living right at the poverty level."

"But do you think he'll finally stop snooping around?" the mayor asked.

"Without a badge, a gun, and access to CAL-NET," the chief replied confidently, "we've neutered the son-of-a-bitch."

3

"BIO-BURGER," said the sign in front of the retro-seventies restaurant. The accompanying logo was a cornucopia of miscolored fruits and vegetables—the tomatoes were chartreuse, the bananas sienna, the onions mauve. Jason decided it looked like the horn of plenty on a bad trip. He paused to study the menu, trying to imagine what the food might taste like. He didn't have a clue.

Sam was sitting in a booth, reading a legal newspaper and sipping a purplish liquid that had black grains floating in suspension. "Hi, Jason," she said, putting down her paper and giving him a purple-toothed smile.

"What in God's name are you drinking?"

"It's a fruit smoothie," she said, licking purple from her teeth. "The color comes from boysenberries, raspberries, strawberries, among other things. It's refreshing. Want one?"

"No thanks," Jason said, pulling up a chair. "I've been up all night drinking coffee and crunching numbers. I hate to think what a sudden slug of fruit purée would do to my stomach. They would have to evacuate the restaurant. I'll stick with coffee."

Sam shook her head. "Sorry."

"Coke?"

"No."

"Bottled water?"

Sam shrugged. "The Bio-Burger chain subscribes to the latest dietary theories. Bottled water isn't *in* anymore." Sam patted his wrist. "But you'll be okay. There are a variety of veggie burgers to choose from. Twelve different colors."

The waitress arrived and enumerated today's specials. Jason was still clueless and passed. Sam ordered the seaweed burger, medium-rare.

After the waitress left, Jason took out his notes. "Thanks for meeting with me on short notice. As I mentioned on the phone, I want your opinion of a plan to buy a manufacturing facility. I intend to employ homeless people, namely Marty's friends and acquaintances, men and women who have lost their jobs and their unemployment benefits, but not their desire to work. They'll manufacture C-REAL for Cytex."

"Go on."

"If the experiment succeeds it will become a model for the private sector. Unused federal facilities could be converted into manufacturing enterprises competitive with skilled foreign contractors. The idea is to stem the flow of American jobs being sent out of the country."

Sam narrowed her eyes and tried to sip some smoothie, but the straw was now clotted with fiber. She pulled back from the straw and looked at Jason. "Did you happen to hear a sucking sound just now?"

Jason ignored the remark. "It's the nationwide plan I want to go over with you," he continued. "There's no point in embarking on a small-scale experiment if the broader concept is a pipe dream."

Sam stared disconcertingly at the viscous liquid and idly swished it with her straw. "In what instances will these enterprises be competitive with foreign labor?"

"In the assembly of labor-intensive products that require technical expertise: wiring of control panels, printed circuit board integration, fabrication of cables, manufacturing semi-precision mechanical devices—that sort of thing. Laser-based devices and other optical equipment are also candidates."

"Why not start with something simpler?"

Jason shook his head. "There's no future for low-tech jobs in America. And with our high standard of living, there's no way to compete with countries like China where laborers get two dollars a *day* to manufacture plastic towel holders and stuffed animals. My plan targets manufacturing situations where skilled foreign workers are paid $10 or $15 a day to assemble relatively complex products. Many of our Third World trading partners are in that category. These wages are still incredibly low by our standards, but they're unburdened, meaning they exclude overhead, profit, shipping charges, liaison costs, and so on. As a result, the advantage of foreign labor is not as much as one might think."

"What is their advantage?"

"No more than four to one."

Sam flinched.

"But that ratio is based on the average pay scale for skilled American assemblers," Jason explained. "If we can use unskilled labor and pay minimum wage, then the ratio is closer to two to one."

"Really? Only two to one? What a relief," Sam said, giving Jason a sideways glance.

"Assume I can live with that."

"Are you counting on government job credits?"

"No. I've deliberately excluded such credits from my model since they can disappear at the whim of the politicians. But if they're offered, we'll certainly take them."

Sam leaned forward. "Okay, turning to devil's advocacy, why should the government support your program?"

"Good question. As you'll see, my plan compliments the government's goals regarding our labor base."

"Go on."

Jason explained how a massive government jobs program would upset the unemployment rate, cause inflation, and not help the homeless in the bargain. "By contrast," he said, "the dislocated workers I intend to hire aren't in the unemployment statistics, so my program won't negatively impact the structural labor force and the economy.

"If my plan succeeds," he continued, "the government will have more resources to assist those who can't work, those with special needs. To me, that's the most sensible way to get the unemployable segment of the homeless population off the street and into social programs."

"So you're proposing to help the employable among the homeless with less government. Why does that sound like an oxymoron?"

"Call me a Republicrat. In my view, private industry should take some responsibility for training and hiring the Americans they've dislocated. But such responsibility can't be forced; it must make economic sense."

The waitress placed Sam's seaweed burger, open-faced, on the table. From Jason's angle the patty cast an iridescent green hue. Accompanying the dish were white serrated vegetables, vaguely resembling French fries. At Sam's urging Jason tried one, wondering as he chewed if the Styrofoam packaging that came with the restaurant's juicer had somehow ended up on her plate.

Meanwhile, with a knife, Sam swept the bean sprouts off the seven-grain bun. She doused the burger with a pale yellow liquid, took a bite, and looked at Jason.

Jason winced as he watched her chew.

"Let's get to the nitty-gritty," Sam said, liberating the straw from the smoothie and taking a straight purple gulp to wash down the burger. "Who'll own these facilities?"

"The government. It'll lease them for a dollar a year under a five-year term—ample time to learn if an enterprise is feasible. If it is, the lease is renewed; otherwise, the government gets the facility back."

"And who will provide capital improvements?" Sam asked.

"The government."

Sam lowered her burger and looked incredulous. "Without receiving rent?"

Jason smiled. "The taxes the enterprises will pay are the rent. Do you know how much the government collects from foreign companies and their workers when we manufacture our products overseas?"

"Zero?" Sam said through a mouthful of burger.

"Correct. And do you know how much the government collects in taxes from idle military bases?"

"Zero?"

"Right again." Jason was having as much difficulty *watching* her swallow as she was having in swallowing. He couldn't imagine what her food was like, but the taste of iron filings came to mind.

"What about working capital and equipment?" Sam asked, quickly gulping more smoothie.

"The Small Business Administration would grant loans secured by the equipment and accounts receivable. The enterprise would have to make regular loan payments, just like any other business."

"And who'll own these businesses?"

"Another good question. Because of the low wage scale, the rational answer is that the employees would be the owners; otherwise the scheme smacks of exploitation."

"Bold idea," Sam said, giving up on her half-eaten burger and pushing it aside. "Employee ownership should increase the probability of success. Am I correct then in assuming these enterprises will take the corporate form, and therefore the employees will be shareholders?" She dabbed at her mouth with a recycled paper napkin.

"Yes. When employees are hired, they'll get stock. Every year they remain with the enterprise, they'll get additional shares. At each shareholders' meeting, the employees will vote on issues like the election of officers and directors. Profits can be reinvested or distributed as decided by the employee-shareholders. Those who leave will have to return their shares to the corporate treasury. But it'll take a vote of two-thirds of all outstanding stock to terminate anyone. That'll give people a chance to resolve problems without fear of being fired arbitrarily."

"Makes sense. And now for the $64,000 question: How are you going to train people from diverse backgrounds, people who haven't worked in months or years, people who have been through God-knows-what kind of nightmare, to manufacture high-tech products more cheaply than skilled foreign workers?"

Jason leaned back. "Sam, of all the obstacles, that's the one which *appears* to be the most difficult. But before I reveal my insight, first assume that the workers are screened and given training in assembly techniques."

"Okay."

"The screening and training will be straightforward, and can be administered by the staff from the enterprises. Those who successfully complete the program will get job offers, starting with the individuals at the top of the class. That's one reason why private industry should run these enterprises. The government wouldn't get away with such a rigorous screening program."

"All right, the best students are hired. Then what?"

"Initially, I had no idea how I would get the necessary level of efficiency out of the workers. Then it came to me: C-REAL itself could be modified to accelerate the manufacturing process. That's the insight."

"What do you mean?"

"C-REAL makes virtual reality inexpensive and practical. In a normal VR application, a visor completely blocks out the real world so the user sees 3-D images projected by a computer. But what if the visor were *transparent* so an assembler could see the product he or she was working on? And what if illustrated, step-by-step assembly instructions were projected directly onto the product?"

"You tell me."

"For example, if the next manufacturing step were the connection of a wire to a certain point on a circuit board, a computer-generated image of that wire would appear, showing the assembler where it goes. A digitized voice instruction would accompany the image. There would be no time wasted referring to assembly manuals, schematics, or models."

"What happens if the assembler moves his or her head?"

"Sensors in the visor tell the computer to instantly reposition the image so it remains fixed in space relative to the product."

"Pretty slick," Sam said. "But is it feasible?"

"Absolutely. Neurosurgeons currently superimpose diagnostic images on the top of patients' skulls to precisely locate a tumor as they operate. And technicians at commercial aircraft companies use a similar system to overhaul complex jet turbine assemblies without having to stop and refer to drawings."

"What's the technique called?"

"Enhanced reality."

"What about foreign competition?"

"Good point. Fortunately, enhanced reality requires sophisticated hardware and software—an area of proprietary technology where Cytex has an enormous lead. Yes, the technique will eventually be copied. But by the time it spreads into the Third World, hundreds of thousands of homeless Americans will have return to the mainstream, ready, willing, and able to move up the job ladder. "

Sam swallowed the last of her smoothie. "Well, Jason, by throwing in a generous dose of good ol' American ingenuity, you've taken your idea from the impossible dream to merely the unlikely dream."

"Thanks for the vote of confidence."

"Don't mention it. What's next?"

The waitress approached with a cart.

"Dessert, I think," Jason said, scanning the array of multicolored dishes.

Sam and Jason declined, and the cart disappeared.

"So in order to prove the concept," he continued, "I'll need a small factory to manufacture C-REAL, staffed by workers who are sincerely interested in a fresh start."

Sam leaned back. "Hmmm, using C-REAL to assemble C-REAL . . . very clever."

"The only question remaining—and it's a biggie—is where to locate the plant. As I mentioned on the phone there isn't much time. We've committed to our Swiss buyer that C-REAL shipments would begin by May 1. To meet that deadline, the production line *must* be running in eight weeks."

Sam picked up the legal newspaper she had been reading earlier. She wet the tip of a finger and starting turning pages. "I assume you'll want a location where you won't stir up the neighbors, a place where the taxes are low and the local officials are permissive, yet a place that's not too far away?"

"Yes," Jason replied cautiously.

"And you said you wanted a facility that has space for manufacturing and living quarters?" Sam's head had disappeared behind the paper as she continued her search.

"Sure . . . ideally."

"And you're looking for a deal?"

Jason felt his excitement growing. "Of course."

Sam lowered the paper and snapped it with the back of her hand. "Here it is," she announced proudly. "This article concerns a gambling resort in a remote section of the Nevada desert. The backers in Tokyo were forced to abandon it when the Japanese economy dive-bombed. The casino and one of two hotel towers were finished when construction came to a grinding halt. It's about fifty miles southeast of Las Vegas, along the Colorado River on the eastern Nevada border. The idea was to provide hedonism and high rolling to wealthy Asian businessmen bored with Vegas' focus on family fun. There's a landing strip next to the facility and a dirt road connecting the resort to the highway going to Vegas.

"For the last couple of years," she explained, "the project has been in bankruptcy and embroiled in litigation. I've been following the case for one of my clients, a subcontractor. As it turns out, he won't see a penny.

"According to this article, the major players—the Tokyo investment group, the lending institution, and the bankruptcy court—have recently agreed to cut the property loose. Next Thursday the court is holding an auction. The opening bid is 25 percent of the secured liens."

"What are we talking about?"

"Five million dollars."

Jason ran his fingers through his hair. "That's half of my net worth."

Sam went on. "If there's a buyer, the court will grant a motion to approve the sale, subject to an overbid by other parties. But this news article anticipates no one will be crazy enough to bid on the albatross. In that event the court will order the hotel and its high-tech systems dismantled and sold for scrap." She pushed the paper toward him.

Jason's excitement drained from his face. "Jesus," he said, pushing the paper back. "You've got to be kidding, Sam. If I bought a gambling resort and the press found out, I'll be laughed out of The City. I can just see the headlines now: 'Howell Sends Homeless to High-Roller Hotel.' Give me a break!"

"It won't kill you to at least check it out."

Jason's shoulders slumped. His sporadic sleep during the last week had caught up with him. "Sam," he said dejectedly, "even if I love it, even if I'm willing to gamble half of my estate, there's no way to take title in time. They ought to paint turtle shells on the roofs of courthouses to warn everyone how long it takes to get anything through the legal system. Remember, C-REAL production must begin in two months." He sagged into his chair.

Sam looked sternly at Jason. "Listen to me for a second. Because the hotel is in bankruptcy, it can be acquired more quickly than any other property. The bankruptcy court has the power to transfer title free of liens. That means no title search, no title insurance, and no escrow. When the gavel comes down, the property goes to the highest bidder. Immediately. You said you're in a hurry."

"Okay, okay," Jason said, rubbing his eyes. "What's this godforsaken place called?"

"Last Chance."

Part IV

LAST CHANCE

TWENTY
Friday, January 27
Early Evening

1

FORMER HOMICIDE INSPECTOR James Brodsky
sat hunched on a bar stool, well into his third bourbon, wondering when the alcohol would finally kick
in; wondering when he would no longer cringe from the
odor of sweat, stale beer and peanuts; wondering when the
loud rap music would no longer crash through his head;
wondering when he would no longer feel like ending his
wretched existence.

He knew he couldn't go home. He knew he couldn't
face his gloomy apartment at the *Casa del Sol* with its yel-
lowing walls, dirty drapes, and green shag rug. He knew
if he went home he would go directly to his gun cabinet,
load his beloved Python .357 Magnum, and blow his
brains out.

An hour ago, not knowing what else to do, he rented a
room at a third-rate hotel on Market Street. His baggage
was a hastily packed cardboard box containing the rem-
nants of his fifteen years on the force. But he found the
hotel room even darker and more depressing than his

apartment. So he tossed the box on the bed, went back to the street, and slipped into this crummy topless bar where he now sat. The place was so vile and disgusting that Brodsky was certain he wouldn't run into even the most depraved among his former co-workers.

He looked dully at his watch. About now the bastards would be spilling out of the Hall of Justice, heading for happy hour at The City's fine watering holes. There they would socialize until the Friday evening commute became manageable.

"Did you hear about Brodsky getting axed?" someone would ask. At first they would simply gossip about him. Then the jokes would start, and everyone would laugh.

Brodsky bristled at the thought, gritting his teeth and clenching his fists. His eyes filled and tears ran down his cheeks.

He swallowed the remainder of his bourbon, slammed his glass down, and ordered another, having to shout over the rap music. Although Brodsky couldn't decipher the lyrics, it seemed as though the taunting message was aimed directly at him. In self-defense he placed his elbows on the bar and his fingers in his ears.

Suddenly, on the circular stage behind the bar, a topless dancer slithered into view. She gyrated directly in front of him, the tassels of her G-string jerking to the beat of the music. Brodsky snapped his eyes shut.

For a time he sat with his fingers in his ears and his eyes closed. He turned inward, searching for a bright spot, something positive to ease the pain. All he could think of was his severance check: $6,600 for his unused vacation time and sick leave, plus $5,000 as a special bonus. His lieutenant said the bonus came out of an emergency fund used to keep ex-cops afloat until they found jobs, and cautioned him to keep his mouth shut since the chief would be incensed if he learned of this act of generosity. So as soon as Brodsky left the Hall of Justice, he cashed both checks, paranoid that payment would be stopped.

Suddenly, from his right, Brodsky became aware of perfume mingling with the other odors of the bar. He slowly opened his eyes and turned to see a blonde sitting next to him. She was talking. Brodsky pulled his fingers out of his ears.

"This one's on me, honey," the woman said, indicating the fresh drink in front of Brodsky. "You look like you've had a rough day."

"I jusht losht my job," Brodsky admitted, surprised to hear his voice slurring. "Fifteen years on the force . . . I was the lasht honest cop."

The blonde nodded, raising her gin and tonic. "To the last honest cop."

Brodsky clinked glasses with her. The blonde took a sip and lit a cigarette.

"You know ish illegal to shmoke in here," he said, staring at her.

The blonde smiled disarmingly. "But you can't arrest me now, can you?"

Brodsky shook his head no. "So, what's your shtory?"

The blonde dragged deeply. "I lost my job too. You could say I was the last honest hooker. We're quite a pair, aren't we?"

Brodsky edged closer and regarded her through lidded eyes. "What happened?"

"I'm not into the kinky stuff," she said, facing him. "But that's where the money is these days. And most of the other girls do drugs. Not me. The Man said I wasn't hungry enough. So he fired my sorry ass."

"Too bad."

The blonde shrugged and took another drag.

Damn, this woman's attractive. She reminded him of someone good, someone from his past, someone who made him feel secure. But the connection eluded him so he thought about her perfume and how it overcame the foul odors, creating a more pleasing atmosphere for him. Even the discordant music no longer seemed so loud.

Brodsky downed his drink quickly. "Now ish my turn," he said, inhaling her fragrance. He waved his bulging wallet at the bartender. "Another round."

2

OUTSIDE THE POLO LOUNGE, Jason was debating whether to call Liz on the hotel's courtesy phone. But his instincts told him to wait until after he met with Anton.

The lounge was filled with well-heeled professionals talking quietly, using happy hour to wash away a week of wear and tear. The exception was a table of suited men with loosened ties who were drinking heavily and laughing raucously as they joked about a colleague who had just been fired.

Jason approached the bar, an ornate structure of polished paldao from the Philippines. As a centerpiece it had a large rectangular painting depicting horsemen in English riding outfits in pursuit of a fox. Jason hooked his wolfcane on the edge of the bar and climbed onto a stool.

"What'll you have?" the bartender asked, setting a cocktail napkin in front of him. The napkin was imprinted with a woodcut drawing of the same hunting scene.

Jason thought for a moment. "Club soda with a twist."

"Hold on!" boomed a deep voice. "Give him a double-Scotch-rocks. Same for me."

Jason felt a strong hand on his shoulder. He turned his head. "Hello, Anton."

"Hello, little brother," Anton said, squeezing Jason's shoulder. "I almost didn't recognize you with that long hair and beard. Still avoiding the press?"

"I'm not supposed to be in San Francisco."

"I'll get us a table," Anton said. He grabbed a handful of mixed nuts from a bowl and headed for an empty corner of the room, leaving Jason waiting for the drinks.

Jason tucked his cane under an arm and picked up two glasses brimming with Scotch, carefully balancing them as he maneuvered to the table. He handed one to Anton and took a seat.

"Here's to our Scottish ancestors," his brother toasted loudly, taking a deep sip. Then he set his glass down, leaned forward and locked eyes with Jason. "Are you fucking my wife?" His tone was matter-of-fact, as if he were talking about the weather.

Jason held his brother's stare. "No."

Anton watched Jason.

"But I do know that you and Liz are having difficulties," Jason said finally. "Do you want to talk about it?"

Anton downed the remainder of his drink in a large gulp and rapped the table with his glass. A waitress nodded and walked toward the bar. Then Anton leaned forward and locked eyes again. "There's nothing to talk about. She'll be back."

In his peripheral vision, Jason noticed that his brother's hand had slipped inside his jacket. He couldn't tell if Anton was reaching for a weapon or a wallet.

It was neither. An envelope appeared, and the older brother tossed it in front of Jason.

"What's that?"

"A partnership agreement."

Jason was stunned. A partnership was not in any of the scenarios he envisioned for this meeting.

Anton leaned back in his chair. "Liz mentioned that Cytex will be your last turnaround project. I'm offering you an extraordinarily profitable way to invest some of your net worth." Anton then summarized the offer. In return for cosigning on a three-million dollar note, Jason would receive a 40 percent interest in the assets of the Howell Development Corporation. Even if the commercial real estate market grew modestly over the next five years his investment would triple.

Jason opened the envelope and read the documents. The offer was genuine. Jason's mind raced. Why was his brother being so generous?

"Together," Anton went on, "we'll ensure that the Howell Development Corporation fulfills its promise of great wealth. But we have to act now. If I don't make good on my older notes soon, the banks will foreclose and force HDC into bankruptcy."

Jason took a sip of Scotch and thought quickly. What was going on? One thing was certain: A partnership with his brother would preclude Jason from having a relationship with Liz. And with Anton's troubles behind him, she would probably reconcile with her husband.

What if he turned his brother down? No, that would only send a clear signal that he wanted Anton ruined, and Liz would no longer see any difference between Jason and his brother. She would most likely throw up her hands and walk away from both of them.

Jason's heart sank. Whether he accepted or rejected the deal, he would lose Liz. Jason had been maneuvered into a classic lose-lose situation. He had no choice but to take the partnership offer as the lesser of two evils. In a single bold stroke, his brother had salvaged his company and, quite probably, his marriage in the bargain. It was brilliant.

During the minute Jason was silent, a grin had formed on Anton's face. "Ah, my brother, the consummate businessman. He knows never to accept the first offer, even from his own flesh and blood." Anton lifted his glass. "It's going to be a pleasure working with you. Okay, I'm prepared to offer you 49 percent."

Jason realized his shoulders had been sagging and he now sat straight, determined not to reveal the enormous weight of his loss. "Anton, your original offer is fair and I'm inclined to accept it." He was thinking that a partnership with his brother would at least keep Liz in the periphery of his life. It would have to be enough.

"I just need some time before I can give you a definitive answer," Jason continued. "I'm in the middle of investigating another investment opportunity, but there shouldn't be any conflict."

The waitress brought Anton his second drink. He took a sip and set his glass down too hard, splashing Scotch on the table. "When will you know?" he asked, ignoring the spill. "I can't hold the banks off much longer."

"How about meeting me here next Friday? Same time. Are you okay with that?"

"Sure, okay, little brother," Anton said, lifting his glass. "To us Howells—you, me, and Liz. One big happy family."

TWENTY-ONE
Saturday, January 28

1

MARTY WATCHED Jason pace back and forth in the General Aviation Terminal at San Francisco International Airport. "Please sit, Jason. Now you're making *me* nervous about flying. Where's your cane?"

"I forgot it," Jason said dourly. His emotions had reached a new low after yesterday's meeting with Anton. Last night he had tossed and turned in bed. Just before dawn, sleep finally came and he dreamt he was clinging to the leading edge of a wing of a small plane. The slip-stream was tearing at his grip and he knew he wouldn't be able to hold on much longer. He managed to bring his leg over and he kicked wildly at the cockpit door. The pilot turned and grinned diabolically. It was Anton. Then the wings started rocking, and Jason lost his grip. As the ground rocketed toward him, he jerked awake, his heart pounding and his body drenched in sweat.

"Why do we have to fly?" Marty asked as Jason's pacing took him near the big man. "Why don't we drive? It's only 8:00 a.m."

"No," Jason replied. "The roundtrip to Last Chance would take all weekend. Anyway, sooner or later, I'll have to fly again and I might as well get it over with." Jason excused himself to get a sip at the water fountain. His mouth was very dry.

When he returned, he found a tall man in a blue uniform standing in front of Marty. "Are you Happy?" the man was saying. Marty looked perplexed.

"Behind you," Jason announced. He had forgotten to tell Marty that Sam Paxton had chartered the flight to Last Chance under Jason's alias.

The tall man turned. He had a handsome face, an aquiline nose, and prematurely graying hair. His brown eyes twinkled as he talked. "Captain Vincent Delacorte, at your service," he said, firmly shaking hands. "Call me Vinnie."

"And I'm Happy," Jason replied in a monotone.

Marty stood and offered his hand. "I'm Woody Wilson," he said, picking up on the name game. "Say, Captain Vinnie, I was wondering if I could have a word with you."

"You betcha."

Marty shifted his weight. "Well, I've never been in a small plane before and I'm kinda nervous."

Vinnie considered the big man. "You're kidding."

"I just want to know what to expect." Marty glanced at Jason to make sure his companion was listening.

The twinkle in the pilot's eyes mushroomed. "Woody, my good man, there's nothing to be nervous about. In the three days since I got my license, I haven't lost a single airplane . . . . well, maybe I've misplaced a few passengers. But as we speak the guys in the front office are searching the mountains for them, and they have every confidence that their bodies will turn up soon."

Marty's eyes widened and he glanced again at Jason.

"Jus' kidding, boys. Actually I've been flying for nearly two decades, and my company has a perfect safety record. Our ride today is a Piper Aerostar 602P. She's a fast, pressurized twin that can land at tiny airstrips like the one we're going to attempt this morning."

"Ah . . . how's the weather?" Jason asked.

"Above the overcast it's CAVU—clear and visibility unlimited," the pilot said. "We'll be cruising at 19,000 feet, and the trip will take just over two hours." Vinnie abruptly turned and headed for the ramp.

Jason recognized the control technique. It was the same one car salesmen use on prospective buyers—they turn and walk toward the lot in the middle of a conversation. If the customer follows, the salesman has just sold a car.

Jason and Marty picked up their bags and followed.

Vinnie stopped at a sleek tan and beige twin and opened the baggage door. "What's in those duffels, boys?"

"Parachutes," Marty quipped.

Vinnie put his hands on his hips. *'I don' theenk so.* Now seriously, fellas, I gotta make sure you're not carrying any contraband. Whatcha got?"

"Underwear and sandwiches," Marty explained. "Wanna see?" He began to open his duffel bag.

Vinnie stopped him, shrugged, and chucked both bags into a rear compartment. Then he walked around the Aerostar's wing to the cockpit door. Again, Jason and Marty followed. "So which one of you boys wants to sit up front with ol' Capt'n Vinnie and keep him company?"

Jason took a deep breath. "Ah . . . I will," he said, climbing in and taking the copilot's seat.

Marty entered next, bending over in order to avoid hitting his head on the low roof of the cockpit. "You're awfully brave," he remarked as he passed Jason's ear.

"Not really. In the back I'll just worry about what's happening up front. Here, I'll know immediately when it's time to panic."

In preparation for boarding, Vinnie kicked the tires and kissed the nose of the airplane. Then he closed the cockpit door and plopped into the left seat. From his flight case he pulled out a chart and flipped it to Jason. "Happy, old boy, you're my navigator. See that pencil line running due east? That's our flight path. Once we're out of the Bay Area, we'll leave the overcast behind, and you'll be able follow the landmarks. Wake me if things don't seem right." Vinnie stretched, his eyes squeezed shut by a cavernous yawn.

Jason stared numbly at the pilot.

Vinnie shook himself and started the Aerostar's engines. "Smokin'," he announced, flashing white teeth at Jason as each engine belched a white cloud and roared to life. Vinnie then said something into the microphone. In response, Jason heard ground control clear the Aerostar to taxi behind a line of wide-body jets creeping along the taxiway.

Finally, after a seemingly endless stop-and-go crawl, the Aerostar turned onto the runway and was cleared to take off. Vinnie pushed the throttles forward. As the airplane accelerated, Jason tensed, steeling himself for the moment they would rise from the earth.

Almost immediately, before Jason was ready, the plane was climbing steeply. Suddenly the cockpit darkened. Droplets formed on the Plexiglas windshield and raced backwards. Jason felt like the events of three weeks ago were playing back—only in reverse. But in less than a minute they broke out into bright sunshine, the two engines resonating strongly, and the nose angled sharply toward a vast expanse of blue sky. Below them, falling away, was a cottony world with only the tops of the coastal mountains poking through. The transition from murky gray to bright sunshine had been so abrupt that Jason hadn't noticed that a sizable segment of his fear had been left behind. He exhaled slowly and began to relax.

After leveling off at 19,000 feet, Vinnie started a running commentary. Marty left his seat in the rear cabin and stuck his head inside the cockpit to listen.

"There's Fresno in the distance," Vinnie pointed. "The fields around the city will be full of grapes this summer. You say you haven't had any wine from Fresno lately? That's because they don't make wine in Fresno; you're looking at the 'Raisin Capital of the World.'"

Vinnie had the habit of asking and answering his own questions. Jason surmised that the pilot must spend a lot of time alone in the cockpit.

"And those mountains beyond Fresno?" Vinnie went on. "Why, they're the High Sierras. See that peak? That's Mt. Whitney, the tallest mountain in the Lower Forty-Eight. How high? Why, it's 14,500 feet."

Jason watched the snow-covered mountains rapidly approach. Soon the peaks were gliding by, their size and ruggedness greatly exaggerated by the long shadows of early morning. The mountains abruptly receded, and they were crossing a long and narrow rift in the land.

"Now we're over the Owens Valley," Vinnie answered, although no one had asked.

During the next fifteen minutes the terrain became increasingly desolate. The outside air was warming up and thermals began jostling the plane, and Marty returned to his seat and fastened his belt. But Jason, struck by the raw beauty of the lunar-like landscape, didn't mind the bumps.

"Happy, that's Death Valley you're looking at," Vinnie offered. "It's 280 feet *below* sea level. Imagine, within sixty miles of each other, you have the lowest and the highest points in the contiguous United States." The pilot's constant commentary and the dramatic scenery continued to have a soothing effect on Jason.

Just north of Las Vegas the air smoothed out, and Marty's head was back inside the cockpit. "Look, there's the Hoover Dam!" he exclaimed, pointing left. "Who built it? Why, the Public Works Administration. It got thousands of workers off the dole during the Depression."

"Hmmm," Vinnie said absently, scanning the horizon in front of them.

At first, Jason thought the pilot was only interested in his own questions and answers. But then the pitch of the engines changed and the Aerostar began descending. Jason now realized that the pilot was preoccupied with locating the tiny airstrip at Last Chance.

"Our destination should be about fifty miles in front of us," Vinnie said, "on the Nevada side of the Colorado river. We should see it shortly." With a pen he poked at the map Jason was holding. "About here, just east of the Dead Mountains, where the river widens."

Minutes passed and the Aerostar continued descending, drawing closer to the river, an aquamarine snake writhing through a beige and barren terrain.

Jason kept comparing the spot on the map with the landscape in front of them. "I think I see it," he said. "About eleven-thirty, there are a couple of buildings."

Vinnie grinned. "Good job, Happy. And Woody, old boy, if you'll take your seat . . . ."

A small paved airport came into view. To Jason's eye it looked too narrow and too short. Vinnie extended the Aerostar's gear and flaps, and made a low pass to inspect the runway. Then he banked and flew along the river, giving Jason an overview of the property. The airstrip was nestled against a broad arc in the river, adjacent to a dock. A dirt road seemed to come from nowhere and terminate at the airstrip. On the far side of the runway, on a plateau a few hundred yards away, was a twin tower complex. One tower was completed; the other was a skeleton of rust-red girders.

During the final approach, it dawned on Jason that no boats were tied to the dock, no planes sat on the airstrip, and no cars were on the road. Other than a few shrubs planted around the hotel and sporadic greenery along the river's edge, the place seemed devoid of life.

The Aerostar used most of the runway to land and braked hard. Then Vinnie taxied back to a parking area and shut down the engines. The three men climbed out into the bright sunshine and looked around. After two hours of engine noise, the sudden silence was unnerving.

"Hey, there's no *there* here," Vinnie remarked. "Are you sure you boys are gonna be able to pull yourself away when I return tomorrow?"

"It's going to be tough," Marty said, shielding his eyes.

"So what brings you two to the gambling hotel from hell?" Vinnie asked.

"The world's biggest crapshoot," Marty answered.

2

THE PHONE RANG and pulled Liz away from her computer screen. She hoped it was Jason calling. She had expected to hear from him yesterday, and once or twice she almost called him. But she thought better of it, not wanting to distract him from his project. Perhaps he was now calling with some good news. Eagerly, she reached for the phone.

"I'm downstairs in the Garden Room," said a tired and scratchy voice. "Can I buy you a cup of coffee?"

Liz closed her eyes and took a deep breath. "All right, Anton," she said, replacing the handset, steeling herself for the moment she had been dreading, the moment she had played out in her mind numerous times. Their conversation would start in polite and controlled tones. In short order it would deteriorate into accusations and profanities. And if he had been drinking, there was the real possibility of violence. In the aftermath, in one way or another, she knew she would come away scarred.

Much of the strength she needed to face her husband was coming from her feelings for Jason. But why hadn't he called? Was he having second thoughts? His silence undermined what she was about to do.

And something else was amiss: Anton's voice. He sounded defeated, conciliatory. What was he up to?

Liz paused to retrieve a framed eight-by-ten from a desk drawer. It showed her and Anton skiing in Banff on their honeymoon. They were rosy-faced, smiling, full of optimism, on top of the world. It was the precursor to their first few years of marriage. Although he was involved in building his real estate business, he remained good-natured and attentive, always making an effort to ensure their time together was special. There was even talk about children. Then his business crumbled, taking their plans and their marriage with it.

She replaced the photo and took out her compact to inspect her makeup. Tilting the mirror upward, she examined the fine lines around her eyes. They seemed deeper today. With a sigh, she put her compact away, picked up her purse, and walked out of the office.

Anton was sipping coffee at a table. A plate of poached eggs, hardly touched, sat in front of him. His suit was wrinkled, his white shirt open wide at the neck, his tie stuffed into his breast pocket. An air of stale whiskey floated about him. When he lowered his cup and looked at her, she saw a sallow face with bloodshot eyes peering out of dark circles. My God, she thought, how can a person change so much in just one week?

"Thanks for coming, Liz. It's good to see you. It's been hell without you."

"You *do* look like hell," she said, taking a chair across the table from him.

Anton rubbed the stubble on his cheek. "I woke up this morning not knowing where I was. That was a first."

"Where were you?"

"Here . . . at the Penniston. The last thing I remember was having drinks with Jason. I was planning to call you afterward, but unconsciousness intervened."

The waitress came over with a fresh pot of coffee. Liz declined while Anton held out his cup. His hand was shaking.

"Jason got you a room?"

"Yeah, my little brother took care of me . . . imagine. When we were kids, it was always the other way around."

Liz took a deep breath. *It was time.* "Anton, we have to talk—"

"Come home, Liz," Anton implored.

Liz took a deep breath. "No, Anton. We both need to get on with our lives."

Anton closed his eyes for a moment and rubbed his forehead. Finally he said, "Last night I asked Jason to become my partner."

"What?" Liz said, stiffening. She felt as though she had just received a hammer blow on the back of her head.

"I made him an offer he can't refuse, and I'm certain he won't refuse it. Jason said as much. "His financial resources and business acumen are just what HDC needs. It took me far too long to realize I needed help, that I can't do it alone. I need him . . . I need you."

Liz stared at her husband.

"Okay, I'll admit I've been horrible to you. But I want you to know I'm truly sorry for allowing my business to affect our relationship. I had no right to take my problems out on you. But with my brother's help—and with you at my side—I can put it all back together. And knowing Jason, he'll carry part of the load and I'll be home more often. Now we can have those kids I promised. As many as you'd like."

Liz watched Anton's eyes as he talked. They lacked luster. Instead, she saw a curious blend of hope and defeat. Last week, when she finally accepted the idea that the man she once loved was gone, she felt sadder than she thought possible. But this look in his eyes was raising her sorrow to new heights. Was it pity? No. It was something else, something more complex, something in her heart that the events of recent years had suppressed, but not erased. And as those feelings spread throughout her body, they welled in her eyes and choked off her voice. In self-defense, she picked up her purse and stood to leave.

"Just think about it," Anton said softly. "That's all I ask."

Liz nodded and hurriedly walked away.

3

A WARM GUST tossed a tumbleweed across the runway as Jason and Marty watched the Aerostar shrink to a speck and disappear.

With his sleeve, Marty wiped a bead of sweat from his forehead. "Feels like summer."

"It's at least eighty," Jason said, squinting. "Around here, you don't want to be outside during the real summer, when it's one hundred and fifteen in the shade."

Marty arched his eyebrows.

"By contrast," Jason continued, "the winter nights can be cold this time of year. Let's find the caretaker; we're going to need to sleep inside."

Marty cupped his hand over his eyes and turned in a circle. "Strange, I don't see him at the moment."

"He was supposed to meet us. Sam arranged a pre-auction tour, along with any other buyers that might show up to inspect the property."

"Well, that explains it!" Marty said, slapping his thigh. "The caretaker must be hosting a cocktail party in the ball-room. We better hurry or we'll miss out."

Jason unfolded a map of the property. "Maybe he's in the shack by the river. Let's check it out."

"Why do you think they put up a shack so far from the hotel?"

"Right now it's a storage shed," Jason said, glancing at the map. "But it looks like the Japanese were planning to expand it into a gas station, general store, and marina. Bait and beer, that sort of thing."

"More like *sushi* and *sake*," Marty quipped, padding behind Jason.

Jason turned his head. "C'mon, be serious. You're not going to think this place is so funny when a rattlesnake crawls up your pants leg."

"Oh, no, don't say that!" Marty shuddered. "I hate snakes more than anything."

At the shack, Jason took the palm of his hand and wiped a circle into the thick coating on the window. Inside, the room was empty except for several crumpled beer cans on the floor, and a few sacks of concrete piled in a corner. A ladder ran horizontally along a wall.

Meanwhile, Marty stood to one side and looked across the Colorado River toward Arizona. "You know, this place is kind of picturesque—in a weird sort of way."

"Maybe the Japanese weren't so crazy after all," Jason said, joining him.

Marty suddenly perked up. "An engine . . ."

They turned as a red pickup drove up to the shack and skidded to a halt, kicking up a cloud of dust. The driver opened a creaky door and hopped out. He wore ragged cut-off jeans, a tie-dyed T-shirt, and a blue bandanna around his head. "I'm Ike Abrams, the caretaker here," he said. "I was hunting in the mountains when I saw your plane land."

"Can you show us around?" Jason asked.

"Sure. You thinking of buying the place?"

"Could be."

"Vegas started small too."

"We're not interested in gaming; we're looking for a manufacturing facility."

"Novel idea," Ike said, wiping the back of his neck with a handkerchief. "You know, this place is not as isolated as it seems. It's only a short drive to the highway system interconnecting Nevada, Arizona, and California. And the Mexican border isn't far away, so inexpensive labor is plentiful."

Marty stepped forward. "We happen to have our own source of cheap labor: homeless Americans."

"Another novel idea," Ike grinned. "Hell, it makes no difference to me; I'll be out of a job when this place is sold . . . unless you happen to need a recovering alcoholic with a law degree."

Jason liked the man's directness, and he saw intelligence and humor in his eyes. "You never know."

They squeezed into the pickup, and the caretaker drove them around the hotel grounds. Between the fin-

ished and unfinished towers was a swimming pool, empty
except for a layer of sand and debris at the bottom. Raw
building materials were stacked neatly around the site as if
the construction crew had left for lunch one day and simply neglected to return.

Ike unlocked the front door of the completed building.
"This is the West Tower. The resort was only a few weeks
away from the delivery of gaming equipment and room
furnishings when the men-with-the-yen pulled the plug."

"What's the status of the building's systems?" Jason
asked.

"They're ultrahigh-tech and everything works," Ike
replied proudly. "My job has been to keep it all functioning: the elevator, the heating and air-conditioning system,
the fire monitoring and water systems, among other things.
They're all computer-controlled and have been maintained
according to a strict schedule. During the past three years
I've gotten to know everything inside and out. Aside from
hunting and fishing, there's not much else to do."

Ike led his guests through the main door. He showed
them the central gaming area, the cabaret, the Keno
lounge, the poker room, and the sports betting bar. At one
point Ike stopped. In a near-whisper he said, "On those
days when the wind comes out of the east and blows sand
against the windows, you can close your eyes and it almost
sounds as if there are people talking and laughing, and
hundreds of slot machines are in operation."

"You don't get a lot of company do you?" Marty said.

"You're my first visitors in a year."

The two men followed the caretaker to the rear of the
casino where the restaurant and kitchen were located. Adjacent was the health club, complete with saunas, Japanese
baths and massage rooms. Ike showed them the infirmary
and explained that it was fully stocked since the nearest
medical facilities were in Las Vegas.

Next Ike took his guests to the hotel lobby and invited them into a mirrored elevator, trimmed in polished brass. He pushed twelve, the top floor. "How many rooms?" Jason asked as they rapidly accelerated upward.

"Six hundred in each tower. Of course the unfinished East Tower lacks certain amenities like walls and floors, but the room rates have been discounted accordingly." The elevator decelerated smoothly, the doors parted, and they stepped into a hallway with gray rugs and burgundy walls, gently illuminated by silver sconces. Ike waved a key card near a proximity sensor on the wall and a door swung open. "This is a standard-sized room, and one of two models that are furnished; the other's a two-room suite."

Marty peered inside. "How come it's so small?"

"By Japanese standards this room is large. However," Ike said, eyeing Marty's huge frame, "you look like you might need a room for each leg. Anyway it's the extras that count: silk walls, a deep-pile rug, a wet bar, a tele-computer with a built-in DVD player, electronic controls for everything. There's even a small Jacuzzi in the bath-room."

Ike walked over to the nightstand and touched the screen of a sleek-looking clock radio. The drapes silently motored aside to reveal a windowed wall. "But if you feel closed in, all you have to do open the drapes."

"Whoa!" Marty exhaled as he cautiously stepped up to the picture window. Jason joined him. The view was to-ward the west, away from the river. Spread before them was an expansive plateau gently sloping toward the Dead Mountains, a broad, barren range whose tops were capped with snow. The mountains stood in bold relief against an impossibly blue sky. They looked too rugged, too stark, and too desolate to be real.

"It's like we're on another planet," Jason said in a hushed voice.

"You got that right," Ike agreed. "Those mountains are truly unspoiled. There are no billboards, no paved roads, and no telephone poles. The idea behind Last Chance was to offer a place far away from civilization while still offering all of the creature comforts."

Ike touched the control screen again and the drapes closed. "Speaking of creature comforts, my stomach says it's lunchtime. Meet me in my apartment in the staff annex at the rear of the building. It's unit number seven. Give me a half hour to fix us something. In the meantime, feel free to wander around."

Back on the ground floor Jason and Marty strolled around the property, inspecting the building's high-tech systems. Everything seemed to be in working order, just as Ike had represented. Jason took notes and made a few sketches. When it was time for lunch, they went to the annex and found Ike's apartment. He greeted them at the door, sat them at small kitchen table, and ladled out some stew.

"Different . . . but delicious," Marty said, slurping and chewing heartily. "I didn't realize how hungry I was."

"Mmmm, this is great," Jason added.

"Thanks," Ike said. "It's my own recipe. All local ingredients, mostly from hunting in the Dead Mountains. In spite of the name, the mountains are teeming with animals and plants, if you know where to look."

"So what are we eating?" Jason asked. "Some kind of game? Is it jackrabbit? Prairie chicken, perhaps?"

Ike stood and reached into the sink behind him. "Guess again," he grinned, shaking the dismembered tail of a diamondback snake.

TWENTY-TWO
Sunday, January 29

1

ALTHOUGH THE MORNING dawned chilly, the desert sun carried the promise of warmth later on. An exaggerated shadow followed Jason down the path from the tower complex to the river as he searched for Marty. Last night he had the big man sleep in the two-room suite while Jason took the smaller room. But this morning, when he knocked on Marty's door, there was no answer.

He must be down by the dock, Jason reasoned. Sure enough, at the end of the pier, Marty's clothes were in a pile. Jason cupped his hand over his eyes and scanned the expanse of swiftly-flowing water.

Nothing.

He checked the riverbank.

Still nothing.

Now beginning to worry, Jason sat on the end of the dock, looking down. Water splashed over boulders and foamed around the algae-covered pillars of the pier. He shivered at the thought of someone taking a swim in a river fed by melting snow.

What could have possessed the man? The icy water and its rapid movement were a deadly combination. Was Marty being self-destructive again? Although the big man became unglued during yesterday's lunch of rattler stew, he seemed fine at dinner when they ate their sandwiches and talked about Last Chance.

Suddenly something powerful gripped Jason's ankle. "What the . . . !" he recoiled, reflexively grabbing the edge of the dock, fighting to keep from being pulled into the river.

Marty's head emerged in a splash. "Good morning," he smiled, holding on to Jason's leg, using it to steady himself against the current.

"I've been looking all over for you," Jason said, trying to shake Marty's grip. B-R-R-R! That water is freezing!"

"Refreshing," Marty corrected, releasing Jason's leg and simultaneously grabbing the edge of the dock and hoisting himself up. Water droplets glistened as they traced the muscles of his body. "I was just taking my morning bath. But that current forced me to hang on to the slimy pillars under the dock. Your leg was a better choice."

"Not in my opinion," Jason said, wringing out his pants leg. "But I'll admit you're a brave soul. I cleaned up the wuzzy way, using the Jacuzzi in my room. It has a dial-up temperature control."

Marty hastily dried himself with a towel and climbed into his clothes. "My suite has the super-deluxe model," he explained, shivering. "It has so many buttons, I couldn't figure how to get any water into the tub. One button I pushed showed a Japanese porno movie on a TV set built into the bathroom wall. I was tempted to watch it, but the tub was too small for me and I'd have to sit with my knees in my face."

Jason laughed at the image. "Maybe you can view it later. Right now, we have to meet Ike for breakfast."

"No thanks."

"He'll be serving pancakes, French toast, and hot coffee. Everything comes from the store—you have my word."

"Well, then, let's not keep the man waiting!" Marty said, breaking into a jog.

At the breakfast table, Jason asked Ike about his plans if the property is sold.

"I'm afraid I don't have any," Ike answered. "I guess I'll look for another caretaker job. I could go back to the practice of law, but I don't think I'm quite ready to slay that dragon."

"Would you consider staying on as facilities manager if I buy Last Chance? The factory will need someone who can keep the machinery humming. The salary won't be much."

Ike grinned. "Count me in."

They finished eating and Ike drove Jason and Marty down to the runway to meet Vinnie. After saying goodbye, the caretaker continued on the dirt road for more hunting in the Dead Mountains. Jason and Marty sat on their duffel bags, watching the truck kick up a cloud of brown dust as it headed west.

"What do you think about this place?" Jason finally said.

Marty casually tossed a rock across the runway. "I think Ike should keep shooting and eating rattlers until there are no more left."

"You know what I mean."

Marty scanned the sky. "You're going to buy Last Chance, aren't you?"

Jason nodded. "Sam's instincts were right. It's perfect. We can use the casino area for assembly, and the smaller gaming rooms can be modified for product test, inventory, and quality control. The saunas can be converted into burn-in racks. Who would have thought a gambling resort would make a great factory? None of my companies ever had a pool."

"I'll bet they didn't have porno movies in the bathroom, either," Marty added, still searching the sky.

"Not that I was aware of. But the red velvet walls, the gold chandeliers, and those gaudy curtains in the casino have all got to go. It looks like a brothel."

"I think you should keep it just like it is," Marty said, standing as he spotted a plane approaching from the northwest.

"Why?"

"Because it's going to be awfully damn easy for street folks to leave the past behind and adjust to vastly improved surroundings. I speak from recent personal experience. The gambling decor will be a constant reminder that your scheme really is a giant crapshoot and that everyone could easily wind up on the street again."

Jason watched the Aerostar turn from base to final and line up with the runway. "What about the name 'Last Chance?' For a gambling resort right on the border of Nevada, it's appropriate. But for a factory, don't you think it sounds too negative?"

Marty picked up his duffel bag as the aircraft touched down. "Actually, I don't. For the people who'll be working here, that's exactly what it is."

2

SOMEONE WAS DRIVING a railroad spike into Brodsky's brain, and each thud ignited a phosphene fireworks display on the screen behind his eyelids. The pain caused him to sit up suddenly, which in turn forced him to grab the top of his skull to keep it from flying off. The abrupt movement stirred the air and filled his nostrils with cheap perfume, making him sneeze in rapid succession, detonating additional violent explosions inside his head.

When the sneezing subsided, he was left with a horrible realization: someone was in bed with him! His eyes were crusted shut, so all he could do was reach out blindly until he touched a soft, curvy thigh. He jerked his hand away and shivered.

He tried to piece it together. Late Friday afternoon he remembered slipping into a bar. Then his memory blurred into vague images of a blonde and perfume and a dark and musty hotel room. But was that yesterday . . . or the day before?

Brodsky rotated his body and planted his feet on the floor. With a thumb and a forefinger he pried open an eye, grimacing at the stabbing pain in his pupil as it recoiled from the daylight flooding the room. But he needed to know where he was, so he forced the eye to remain open, blinking repeatedly until it focused on an empty bottle of cheap bourbon lying on a green shag rug.

His rug.

The blonde must have driven him back to his apartment and stayed over. Finding himself at home made him feel a bit better. Brodsky unstuck his other eye and slowly rotated his head. The woman was sleeping with her lips parted, snoring softly. She was pretty, but considerably older than he remembered . . . .

Wait a minute!

Now, in the harsh light of day, Brodsky realized why the woman had seemed so familiar in the bar. She looked exactly like his mother! Acts of intimacy flashed by, taunting him, and he recoiled in disgust. Brodsky knew it was only his horrendous hangover that kept him from strangling the slut. Instead, he leaned over and shook her shoulder.

"Ummm, not again, Jimmy-boy," she murmured. "It's too early. Lemme sleep." The blonde pulled the blanket over her shoulders.

Brodsky gnashed his teeth. "Jimmy-boy" was his mother's pet name for him. In a moment of weakness he must have told the woman about his childhood. "Get the fuck out of here," he hissed, shaking her harder. "BITCH!" he added.

The blonde's eyes popped wide and she sat up, holding the covers around herself. "My, my, Jimmy-boy, aren't we cranky this morning."

Brodsky yanked the covers away. "NOW!"

"Okay, okay, take it easy!" she said, flashing angry eyes. She gathered her clothes and hurriedly left the room.

Brodsky's body bolted when the bathroom door slammed, shaking the walls. For some minutes he held his head in his hands and sat rocking on the edge of the bed. To distract himself from thoughts of the blonde and his mother, he focused on his wretched future. He knew that with his puny pension he couldn't even stay in this crummy apartment without finding some type of job. His dream of spending his retirement years spying on employees as the security chief for a large corporation had suddenly evaporated. And with the stigma of being discharged from the force, he would be lucky to find work as a night watchman at a Laundromat. Great. He could supplement his pension just enough to live in abject squalor.

Brodsky's eyes filled with tears as he thought about how quickly the years had slipped by, how he had no savings other than his severance money, how he had always thought of the SFPD as his family, how they would reward him for being a loyal son and take care of him when he was too old to work. Instead they conspired against him and then fired his ass. Brodsky's body shook as he sobbed.

Out in the hallway the blonde yelled, "So long, you motherfucker!" Then the front door slammed.

"Good, the whore-bitch is gone," he sniffled, wiping his eyes with the back of his hand. Her departure actually gave his spirits a tiny boost. He would take a long shower, eat a decent meal, and begin making plans. Maybe things weren't that bleak after all. At least his severance money would pay the rent until he found Dubichek, tortured a confession out of him, and blackmailed the mayor and the chief.

Brodsky tried to stand, but the room reeled and he had to use his nightstand for support. Then, leaning on his walls, he staggered down the hallway.

The blonde had left the bathroom door closed. When he opened it, a cloud of cheap perfume steamrolled over him, nearly driving him to his knees. He shouted profanities, bristling at the thought of the bitch saturating *his* air and making *his* bathroom uninhabitable. He fanned the door and turned on the ceiling vent, even though the noisy fan grated at raw nerve endings.

When he was finally able to enter the room, he plodded toward the shower, head hanging low, breathing shallowly through his mouth. Out of the corner of his eye he glimpsed something at the bottom of his grungy toilet bowl.

His wallet!

Contorting his face in disgust, he reached in and fished it out.

It was empty!

He gasped. His severance pay, his credit cards, his driver's license—all gone! The only item remaining was an old photo of his mother. She was smiling at him from the other side of a damp plastic window.

Brodsky screamed, and the wallet slipped out of his hands and splashed back into the bowl.

3

"HOW DID YOU ENJOY the return flight to San Francisco?" Marty asked.

Jason was bent over his computer, holding his chin in his hand, staring intently at the screen. "Ummm . . . what flight?"

"I'm glad to see you're completely over your fear of flying."

Jason turned. "Oh, I'm sorry, Marty, but I was engrossed in this cash flow analysis. I began developing it on the Aerostar, and the trip flew by—literally. So how did you like sitting up front with ol' Capt'n Vinnie?"

"It was great," Marty said excitedly. "He gave me the controls. It was me yankin' and bankin' us back to Frisco. It's easy. All you gotta know is right from left, and up from down." Marty extended his arms and tugged at an imaginary control wheel.

Jason stiffened.

"But Vinnie landed," Marty quickly added. "You know, I'm seriously considering saving part of each Cytex paycheck for flying lessons this summer."

Jason swiveled around to face Marty.

"And you know what else?" Marty continued. "I'm *really* looking forward to my job at Cytex. When I was at the library last Friday, I read all this cool stuff you can do with virtual reality. Did you know that a director can walk around the movie set even before it's built? And get this: soon the visors will be obsolete. They'll surgically implant a socket into your head and you'll connect the computer directly to your brains. It's called 'jacking in.'"

Jason took a deep breath. "Marty, we have to talk about your job at Cytex."

"What about it?"

"The factory at Last Chance will succeed only if it runs at an incredibly high level of efficiency. That means the workers must give it everything they've got. There's no margin for error. None."

Marty fidgeted. "So . . . what's that got to do with me?"

"You're needed at Last Chance."

Marty's face turned red. "Wait a damn minute, Jason! I said I'd help you check out Last Chance and that's what I did. You *never* asked me and I *never* said I'd participate in your social experiment for society's outcasts who've got no other choice! I've got a great future at Cytex! I've got stock options!" Marty was pleading and shouting at the same time.

Jason stood and approached the big man. "You misunderstand me."

Marty retreated and waved his finger at Jason. "You promised! I'm not going to sit on an assembly line wearing a high-tech headdress in the middle of goddamn NOWHERE! Forget it, man!"

Jason shook his head. "Simmer down; I'm asking you to be president."

Marty looked stunned. "Did you say . . . president?"

"Yes."

"The head honcho?"

"You bet. The enterprise needs a strong leader, someone who can command respect from the employees."

"But I'm not a professional manager."

"That's in your favor. Let's face it, living and working in Last Chance will be as different from shelter life as it can get. People will have a tough time adjusting. If I brought in a professional who didn't understand the special needs of the workers, they would mutiny in no time. We need someone who can foster teamwork. Like you, Coach Dubichek."

Marty began pacing. "From hobo to honcho in the span of a week. I don't know." Marty stopped and faced Jason. "Can I work at Cytex until the factory's ready? Jesus, it's been years since I held a regular job."

"Tomorrow you can go to Cytex for a briefing. But one day is all you can spare because it's going to be *your* job to bring the factory on line."

Marty stared at his shoes.

"You can do it. I'm notoriously good at spotting talent. I'll teach you everything you need to know. Here's your first lesson: Go to work with a list of all the things you want to accomplish. Then immediately stash the list in a desk drawer while you spend the day running around the factory, putting out fires and resolving employee disputes. Meet with your management team at the end of the day when they're too tired to argue. Finally, after everyone has gone to bed, take out the list and work on it."

Marty ran a hand through his hair. "How long do I have to get the factory on line?"

"C-REAL production must begin on Monday, April 3. The Cytex contract will be awarded in three weeks. It'll specify the delivery of four thousand reality engines a month beginning May 1 and continuing at that rate until

October 1. Therefore you have two months to get the plant ready and recruit one hundred people. That's it."

"Seems impossible."

"It probably is."

"But you don't even own the property yet."

"I'll take title later this week. Then you'll go to the bank and get a line of credit for construction materials, capital equipment, and furnishings. I'll personally guarantee the note." Jason picked up a page from the top of his laser printer and handed it to Marty. "This is a PERT chart. It explains everything you need to do between now and April 3, Mr. President."

"What's a PERT chart?"

"PERT is an acronym for Project Evaluation Reporting and Tracking."

Marty stared at a jumble of interconnected rectangles. "It makes no sense."

"You're holding it upside down."

Marty righted it. "It still makes no sense."

"Sit, and I'll give you lesson number two."

Marty sat.

"This chart shows the sequence of events that make up a project."

"Uh-huh."

"For example, if we were constructing a building, one of the rectangles might say 'Install Plumbing.' The next one in sequence would say 'Put Up Dry Wall.' You wouldn't want to reverse those tasks."

"I get it," Marty said, studying the chart. "Let's see, it says I need to recruit an initial construction crew of twenty to convert the hotel."

"Right. And you'll have to transport the crew this Friday. I suggest that you get a sleeper bus and transport them at night."

"Why at night?"

"There's no point in wasting daylight hours. To meet the schedule, the crew must start converting the property first thing on Saturday. The clock is ticking."

Marty kept staring at the chart. "Hmmm, I'll need tradespeople to construct walls, run additional electricity into the production area, add lighting, and install the equipment and furnishings as they're delivered."

"That's right," Jason said. "But make certain the people you choose can be trusted to keep quiet about the project. If the tabloids find out what we're doing they'll turn Last Chance into a freak show. The bank will get cold feet, there'll be no credit line, and no C-REAL contract. Secrecy is another reason for transporting people at night."

Marty looked dubious. "I don't see how you can keep this project under wraps forever."

"We don't have to. That brings us to lesson number three: In business, timing is everything. Americans love stories about people who work hard to turn their lives around. If we can keep the project quiet until Last Chance has had the opportunity to prove herself—after the first deliveries are made in May—then a well-timed news release will create positive publicity and more new business than you can handle."

"Okay, I probably know twenty people who can keep their mouths shut. But what about the rest of the workers?" Marty looked at the chart again. "Eighty additional people hired and trained by April 3? Even if I could recruit that many able-bodied homeless in such a short time, how are we going to keep them from spilling the beans?"

"By not telling them exactly what we're doing, nor the location of the factory, until they're on the bus." Jason pointed to the PERT chart. "During March, there'll be four one-week training classes on assembly techniques here in San Francisco. Sixty students will be recruited for each class, two hundred and forty in all. Classes will be held during the day, and students will be paid minimum wage for attending. The course will cover soldering, wiring harnesses, mechanical assembly, handling of printed circuit boards, and so on.

"At the end of the month, the best students will be offered jobs and shares in Last Chance Corporation. All they'll be told is that the plant is in Nevada. Don't forget that the property isn't on any road map, so I doubt it'll mean much to anyone even if the name 'Last Chance' slips out.

"The first eighty graduates who accept the deal will be bussed to the factory on Friday evening, March 31. They'll have a weekend for orientation and hands-on training with C-REAL." Jason pointed to the last rectangle. "On Monday, April 3, production must begin."

"But who are you going to get to teach the classes?"

"No, Marty, who are *you* going to get? It has to be someone from your world because he or she will also be production manager, the supervisor who'll have the most direct and continuous contact with the workers. Choose wisely since he or she can make or break the project."

Marty groaned. "There are plenty of tradespeople, assemblers—even computer nerds—on the street. But how the hell am I going to find someone who has experience both as a production manager and an instructor?"

"I don't know, just do it. Any other questions?"

"Yeah, one more: What about rules?"

"Rules?"

"You know, like shelter rules. Don't you think Last Chance should have strict rules like St. Andrews, so people don't screw up?"

"I think whatever rules Last Chance adopts should be decided on by its owners—you and the others. But I'll offer this advice: If you want Last Chance to be a normal, hardworking American community, you'll have to treat her that. way from the start. And just like any community, you're going to have problems. People will let you down, that's guaranteed. In fact, there'll come a time when just about everything goes wrong, and you'll wish you were never born. But you fight like hell and work through it. That's lesson number four."

"Sounds like great fun."

"If you want fun, wait for the next life. But I promise you, if Last Chance is successful, Coach, you'll feel like you've won the Super Bowl."

"Oh my God!" Marty shouted, dropping the PERT chart and dashing toward Jason's home theater.

"What's wrong?"

"It's Super Bowl Sunday! I completely forgot!"

Jason sighed. "This is *not* going to be easy."

4

WEARING HIS FAVORITE hunting jacket and hat, Brodsky sat in his Pontiac Trans Am, sipping coffee, idly listening to the Super Bowl and watching the amber street-lights flicker on. In comparison with his earlier mental state—hung over and robbed by the blonde—Brodsky was feeling a great deal better. For one thing, his headache was almost gone. For another, the parking space previously occupied by Gorney's Fairlane was waiting when he arrived in Pacific Heights. A particularly good omen, he thought.

Brodsky sensed Dubichek's presence nearby, and he knew it was only a matter of time before the derelict showed himself. Then, after torturing a confession out of him, he would hunt down the whore-bitch and make her pay.

Brodsky had Gorney's attaché case on the passenger's seat next to him. He opened it and removed the night-vision binoculars, which he placed around his neck, and the Walther P-38, which he placed in his lap. For practice he picked up the pistol and aimed it at a woman walking her dog. "Bang!" he said to himself.

Brodsky set his coffee cup down and stretched. He was ravenously hungry, but there was no way he would leave his station and miss spotting Dubichek. Besides, he had no money for food. To stave off the pangs of hunger, he poured himself another cup of coffee from a thermos and reached for one of the Snapper Bars he had bought with the coins he found buried deep in his sofa. He liberated the candy with his teeth and casually tossed the wrapper behind him.

TWENTY-THREE
Monday, January 30

1

A FTER MARTY TOURED Cytex, Jason left him in the company of Greg Thompson for a demonstration of C-REAL. With Marty occupied, Jason went to his office and called Sam, authorizing her to submit a bid of five million dollars for Last Chance on behalf of Crossfire Holdings, a company that would be organized under the laws of the State of California. The holding company would give Jason a measure of personal protection in the event of litigation, while providing him with a degree of anonymity.

For the enterprise itself, he asked her to form Last Chance Corporation under the laws of the State of Nevada. Finally, he requested that she prepare a contract, lease, a guarantee, and all other necessary agreements between the two companies to enable Martin Dubichek, as president of Last Chance Corporation, to secure a line of credit.

After he hung up, Jason was reaching for the stack of paperwork that had accumulated during his absence when Greg Thompson came to see him.

"How's Mr. Dubichek doing?" Jason asked.

"He's thoroughly immersed in C-REAL so I thought I'd break away to talk to you about production costs."

"Go ahead."

Greg pulled up a chair. "They're extremely tight. Only one of the overseas subcontractors came in with a bid low enough to meet the price point I-Cubed is demanding: a small outfit in Korea. But they're qualified to do the work and hungry for our business."

Jason looked at Greg. "What would you say if I told you we don't have to produce C-REAL overseas?"

"I'd say you needed some more time off," Greg said, grinning as though his boss were pulling his leg.

"It can be done."

Greg's grin evaporated. "Pardon me, but I don't see how. All costs have been shaved to the nubs. There's absolutely no way C-REAL can be made in America."

"It can be done," Jason repeated.

"I'm listening."

Jason told Greg about Last Chance and how an enhanced reality version of C-REAL would be used to accelerate the assembly process. Greg looked intrigued and troubled at the same time.

"What's wrong?" Jason asked.

Greg shifted uncomfortably. "Old man Simpson . . . he's comfortable with the overseas plan. How will he react when he learns you're awarding the contract to a bunch of . . . I mean an unproven manufacturing operation?"

"Don't worry. I'll meet with Simpson. When I'm finished with him," Jason said, holding Greg's eyes, "the only concern he'll have is whether your engineering team can develop the applications software in time."

Greg relaxed at his boss' familiar show of confidence. "Tell him we can do it."

2

BRODSKY WAS GLOATING.   Fate had finally dealt
him a winning hand.   Several hours ago—in spite of the
enormous volume of coffee he had consumed, and in spite
of pinching himself until he was black and blue—he had
succumbed to sleep.   Although that lapse could have been
costly, an overpowering urge to urinate had awakened him
just in time to see a Mercedes nosing out of the garage of
the building across the street.   He fumbled for his binoculars and zoomed in on the big man in the passenger seat.
   Dubichek!
   Adrenaline shot through Brodsky's body, causing him
to release his bladder.   To stem the flow he squeezed himself between his legs, using his other hand to train the binoculars on the driver.   The man had longish brown hair, a
scruffy beard, and wore dark sunglasses.   It suddenly
dawned on Brodsky that the chief would use a narc to
guard Dubichek.   That way the big vagrant could be kept
docile by feeding him illicit drugs.   Yes, his enemies were
pretty clever.
   Still squeezing himself, Brodsky used his free hand to
steer and shift as he expertly tailed the Mercedes across
town.   After the car turned into an office complex in China
Basin, he stationed himself at the rear of the parking lot
and watched the narc escort Dubichek into the building.
   That was an hour and forty-five minutes ago.   Since
then, Brodsky diligently kept the main entrance under surveillance, remaining stoic in spite of the pain mounting in
his groin.
   Although he had hoped to hold out until Dubichek
emerged, it now felt as if someone were twisting a rusty
knife in his abdomen.   Groaning, Brodsky doubled over
his steering wheel and snapped his eyes wide.   Through
the windshield he saw a sign on the wall of the building:

CYTEX CORPORATION

Brodsky's jaw dropped and he felt his lap get significantly wetter, forcing him to use both hands to stop the
flow.   Sucking air through clenched teeth, he knew he
must take action immediately.

He stole a glance around the parking lot.   There was
not a single soul outside.   So he pulled the brim of his
hunting cap low over his face, quickly exited his Trans
Am, hopped into the shrubbery, and fumbled with his fly.
But it caught on a thread and would only come down
halfway.   Cursing, he unbuckled his belt and wriggled out
of his pants until they were around his ankles.

Brodsky stood doubled over with his eyes squeezed
shut.   *Soon,* he told himself, *soon the pain would cease,
soon.*   But his muscles had been cramped so tightly and for
so long they refused to cooperate.   As a result, he stood in
the shrubs for an inordinately long time, moaning, bent
over, his torso swaying, desperately trying to coax a pa-
thetic dribble into a powerful stream.

"C'mon!" he urged.   "C'mon!"

It was only through a superhuman effort that Brodsky
was able to relax his muscles.   Cooing softly, he emptied
his bladder in a great spray over Cytex's shrubs.

When he finished, he sighed contentedly, and pulled
his pants up.   But his zipper, now ruined, remained open,
forcing him to cinch his belt to keep his pants up.   Brodsky
didn't care.   He felt like a new man, and it was far more
important he could now concentrate.   Whistling, he returned to the Trans Am, picked up his P-38 and checked
the magazine to make sure he had a bullet up the snout.

"All right," he said to himself, "now why would the
narc take the derelict to Howell's company?"   Then
Brodsky remembered this was the day Howell was scheduled to return from vacation.   Was the mayor showing off

to prove to Howell that his kidnapper was safely in custody and under complete control? Was this a way of getting Howell's cooperation with the mayor's scheme to
shelve the investigation until just before the election?

Brodsky put the gun in his lap, started the Trans Am,
and drove to an empty space several rows back from the
Mercedes so he would be ready when Dubichek and the
narc came out. He picked up the gun and released the
safety, knowing that his timing was critical. The narc
would unlock the doors with a key transmitter. After
Dubichek was in the car and the narc behind the wheel,
Brodsky would have only a few seconds to jump in the
back before the doors automatically locked and they drove
off. Once inside it was a simple matter of coldcocking the
narc and—

Wait a minute! That Mercedes seems familiar. He
rolled down his window and leaned out until he had the
binoculars focused on a small sign painted on the wall. It
said:

RESERVED
J. Howell, President

Brodsky stared numbly at the sign while mentally su-
perimposing the features of the bearded diver with those
of Howell.

The driver was Howell!

Brodsky's head spun while he desperately tried to
comprehend this new information. Had Howell been in on
a phony kidnapping plot from the beginning? Were Dubichek and Howell both working for the mayor? Had Brodsky been set up? He began to hyperventilate, and damn it
if he didn't have to pee again!

Just then, a black and white SFPD patrol car pulled up
behind him.

Brodsky was blocked!

He lifted his rear end off the driver's seat and quickly stuffed the P-38 into a crack in the old vinyl upholstery. He eased down and folded his hands in his lap in a futile attempt to cover his open fly.

In the rearview mirror, Brodsky watched a lowly patrolman climb out of the cruiser. It had a lightening bolt insignia on the door. A second cop was talking on the radio. The first officer sauntered over to the Trans Am. "Put your hands on the wheel," he ordered. "Real slow."

Brodsky, seething, complied.

The cop looked inside the car. His neutral expression rapidly transformed to disgust as he took in Brodsky's wet lap, his fly at half-mast, and the binoculars around his neck. "What in hell are you doing here?" the officer demanded, contempt dripping in his voice.

Brodsky stared straight ahead, breathing through clenched teeth. Now he was sorry he was sitting squarely on his gun. He briefly considered going for it, but with the safety off and a bullet up the snout, he risked shooting himself in the ass.

"Your ID," the cop ordered. "Use one hand and no sudden movements."

Snarling, Brodsky pulled his wallet out of his hunting jacket. Unable to face the cop, he snapped it open and held it up, forgetting for the moment that the wallet was empty except for a soggy photo of his mother.

The cop glanced at the wallet, then shoved it away with his elbow. "Mister, you're under arrest," he said, putting on white rubber gloves. "We can make this easy or we can make it hard. Now *slowly* step out of the car. Keep your hands in full view."

Brodsky turned to face the cop and summoned his last vestige of self-control. "What's the charge?" he growled, scorn narrowing his beady eyes to slits.

"For starters, you're trespassing on private property," the cop said while pulling up the rubber gloves. He moved closer to Brodsky's face. "The PEOPLE in that building saw you PISS in PUBLIC." With each "P" sound, Brodsky felt puffs of the officer's breath on his face.

Anger roiled inside of Brodsky, twisting his intestines into a tight coil. He abruptly turned from the patrolman and hunched over the steering wheel.

The cop leaned in. "Then they saw you PEEPING in the PARKING lot. Now out of the PONTIAC you PERVERT!" Each "P" sound drove spittle into Brodsky's ear.

Brodsky released his bladder again but he didn't care. He was now in a dark place where his vision had tunneled down to the image of Dubichek taunting him, as the vagrant had done in Petaluma. He abruptly turned and reached out, grabbing his enemy's warm neck, squeezing it as hard as he could.

Behind him he heard the passenger door open and someone yelling. But that was a million miles away . . . .

3

UNAWARE OF THE POLICE action in the parking lot, Jason sat with Marty in the company's lunchroom. The big man's face was tinged green and he gagged as Jason began eating a sandwich.

"Sure you don't want one of these?"

"Not hungry," Marty said, swallowing hard.

"You visited the virtual stomach?"

"Big mistake."

"You could try a different body part this afternoon."

"Not interested."

"Well, you have to admit C-REAL is pretty amazing."

"I'll admit that food will never pass these lips again. I'm ruined for life."

Jason ate heartily while Marty stared at the ceiling. Finally, Jason stopped chewing and said, "This afternoon will be better. You'll meet with our Production VP, Howard Armstrong, and he'll go over C-REAL's assembly and test procedures. He and Greg Johnson were going overseas to support our Korean subcontractor. But they're family men and don't want to live away from home. They'll be highly motivated to help make Last Chance successful."

"And after I meet with Armstrong?"

"You hit the streets and begin recruiting."

4

IN THE EBBING LIGHT of early evening, Marty climbed the embankment to the Monday Night Club. He stood at the entrance and peered inside. Because the hour was early and the weather mild, attendance was way down. But he was relieved to see the hard-core members at their stations: Stan was getting the fire started, Doc and Sanchez were setting up for cards, Willie was petting Shoo, and Annie was smoking a cigarette and gazing into space.

"Hey Marty, I didn't expect to see you again," Stan said, "especially by your own self."

"YO, MARTY!" the other men hailed in unison.

"How's the retard?" Stan asked.

"Happy? He's doing okay. How are things here?"

"Same ol' shit," Stan answered. "What's with you?"

Marty put his hands in his pockets. "Actually, my sponsor started a company and there are some job openings." He wasn't sure how his news would go over so he decided to take it slowly. Those in hearing range perked up. Only Annie remained disinterested.

"Whatcha got Marty?" Sanchez asked. "Another dangerous, low-wage job like Stan's always pushing?"

"Well, it doesn't pay much, but housing is included."

Doc stopped shuffling his cards. "You mean like working all day in a field and living in a rat-infested bunkhouse?" he asked.

"No," Marty said, shifting the dirt on the floor with his shoe. "It's more like a modern factory. You get your own room. They're kind of small . . . but the view's great."

Doc dealt a hand to Sanchez. "If it sounds too good to be true," he sighed, "it probably is."

"What's the catch?" Sanchez asked.

"The factory is in a remote part of the desert, but not too far from Las Vegas."

"That don't sound too bad," Stan said. "Never been to Vegas. So what do we gotta do? Make guns? Bombs?" Stan's eyes grew wide.

"Yeah," Sanchez chimed in, "is this some kinda secret government project that's too dangerous for regular people? They wanna inject us with some drug and see if our balls shrivel up and drop off?"

"Willie's got nothing to lose," Stan remarked.

Willie stopped petting Shoo and screwed his middle finger in the air.

The men laughed.

"It's not a government experiment," Marty explained. "This is the real deal. We'll run a private factory and make these high-tech virtual reality gadgets. Everyone will be trained and have the latest equipment."

"What's virtual reality?" Willie asked, idly scratching Shoo under his chin.

"I know," Doc jumped in, "it's a temporary condition caused by the absence of alcohol."

The men guffawed.

"Not quite," Marty replied. "You put on these big sunglasses and a computer takes you inside someone's stomach. It's like you're *really* there. You can see and hear what they had for breakfast. I tried it this morning."

Willie wrinkled his nose. "Yuk, it sounds disgusting."

"Yeah, it is," Marty acknowledged. "But people will pay big money to do it."

"Sounds pretty cool," Stan whistled, "I can think of some organs I'd like to inspect up close."

"Right," Willie remarked. "Now we can find out where Stan hides his brains."

More laughter.

"Whoever signs up will be an owner," Marty said, attempting to regain control of the conversation.

Doc rotated to face Marty. "Is this a gag?"

"It's no gag, Doc. I was at the site last weekend. It's on a scenic spot by a river. It's got a swimming pool and a health club." Marty turned to Stan. "You can even go hunting for snakes in the mountains."

"Why would anyone in their right mind want to hire *us*?" Doc asked.

"The sponsor thinks companies should keep manufacturing jobs here instead of sending them abroad. He wants to see if we can compete against foreign labor."

"So it *is* an experiment," Doc said.

"You could say that. And I'll tell you right up front it's not going to be easy. But if we succeed, we'll wind up with our own community."

"And if the experiment fails," Sanchez countered, "then we're stranded at some fuckin' hell hole in the desert."

Marty shook his head. "No. You can always bail."

"And go where?" Doc asked. "I'll lose my place at St. Andrews."

Marty shrugged. "Life is full of risks."

Stan raised his hand. "I'm in."

"JE-SUS, Stan, you're *always* in," Willie said, shaking his head. Then he turned to Marty and asked, "Can Shoo come? They won't let me keep him at St. Andrews."

"Sure."

"Okay, count me in, too." Then turning to the others Willie said, "If Marty says it's cool, then it's cool."

Doc and Sanchez weren't so sure. They continued to question Marty. But after he told them about getting stock, voting on profits, and making the rules, they agreed. Marty finished by explaining how the project would be ruined if outsiders got wind of it, and he swore everyone to secrecy.

The place buzzed, and only Annie remained quiet. She was sitting on a crate, holding her knees. "How about it, Annie?" Marty asked softly. "Want to come with us?"

Annie looked up at Marty. "My kids . . . can I bring them? I might get them back if I had a place of my own."

"I'm afraid not. The factory isn't set up for kids. Maybe someday."

"Then I'll pass," she said, turning away.

TWENTY-FOUR
Thursday, February 2

1

CHROME ELEVATOR DOORS parted and Jason stepped into an ultramodern reception area decorated in a Pacific Rim motif, a multiform mix of Oriental rugs, laminated plastics, and Australian primitive art. He walked over to an elegant African-American woman at the front desk and announced his appointment with Albert Simpson III. She smiled warmly and directed him to a softly-illuminated seating area decorated with rare paintings, urns, and figurines. Jason knew that each art piece represented a successful deal by Simpson's Pacific Investment Group. This was the way the chairman kept score, like the ace who paints a skull and crossbones on his plane after each kill.

Albert Simpson III believed that venture capital was the mother of business, birthing companies and giving life to commerce. He saw himself as the patriarch of the investment community, held in reverence by those who depended on him for their chance at the golden ring. His employees were bright and pedigreed, youthful and attractive, and immaculately dressed and coiffured. They were gracious in conversation, never raised their voices, and used a vocabulary liberally sprinkled with terms like "outsourcing," "re-engineering," and "restructuring." And most importantly, their focus never veered from the bottom line.

Plastic people, Jason thought.

Although it hadn't occurred to him before, it now seemed ironic that Simpson and his employees lacked passion, the one ingredient the chairman demanded of all the entrepreneurs who came before him to pitch their business plans.

Precisely at 9:00 a.m. the chairman appeared in the lobby. After smiling cordially and shaking hands, he escorted Jason into the conference room. They sat at a highly-polished teakwood conference table with Simpson at the head. The chairman cupped his hands, and politely asked Jason if he was rested after his vacation.

Jason pulled a file from his satchel. "To tell you the truth, Al, I spent my vacation time working on a new project."

"Why doesn't that surprise me?"

In keeping with the way the chairman preferred to conduct his meetings, Jason immediately opened his file and got to the point. "Shortly," he said, "I expect to own some property in the Nevada desert that will be converted into an extraordinarily efficient assembly facility. It will be capable of manufacturing C-REAL and other labor-intensive products at prices competitive with overseas subcontractors."

Simpson's eyes widened slightly. "Do you think that's feasible, Jason?"

"I do. Although there are risks, the benefits to Cytex make it worthwhile. We'll have simpler logistical support, rapid incorporation of design improvements, and quicker response to changing market conditions. As you know, flexibility is not a characteristic of overseas subcontractors. Once they begin turning the crank, it's difficult to get them to stop."

"Indeed."

"During the last two weeks, I've learned about a labor pool of unemployed Americans—people who have been terminated due to cutbacks and the exportation of manufacturing jobs, people who have not found other employment and have lost their homes. I personally know some of these dislocated workers and I'm convinced that they, and people like them, can be reintegrated into the work force."

Chairman Simpson's face was a blank slate as Jason talked. But his brow furrowed when he heard the level of efficiency required to make Howell's plan work. "Here's where you've lost me," he said. "I agree American workers can be remarkably productive when giving the right incentives. But I'm having trouble with the idea of taking untrained people off the street and making them twice as efficient as foreign assemblers."

Jason was ready. He opened his satchel, removed a digital video disk and inserted it into a player built into the conference table. Wall panels slid aside to reveal a large flat-panel television. The title "Just-In-Time-Assembly" appeared on the screen. The program showed a mock-up of an enhanced reality workstation, followed by a simulation of what an assembler would see through the visors.

When the show was over the chairman said, "That was quite interesting, Jason. You've created a labor corollary to 'Just-In-Time-Inventory,' the continuous parts flow process invented by the Japanese. I must admit I overlooked such a fundamental and potentially lucrative use of C-REAL."

"I did too," Jason admitted, "until I started analyzing ways to boost productivity."

"You might be on to something. The use of enhanced reality to increase manufacturing output is seductive. I can even see how your facility could switch to an entirely new product line with a minimum of downtime."

Jason nodded. It was time to go in for the kill. "The purpose of my desert project is to prove the concept's viability. Once the plant is operating smoothly, I'll publicize it as an example of how private industry, through innovation, can relieve a severe social problem. Public opinion will be on our side, and the government will be under full court press to make its vacant military facilities available for similar manufacturing enterprises."

Simpson rubbed his chin. "Hmmm, if the idea catches on, Cytex will be in a perfect position to supply all of the enhanced reality stations to those government bases. I can't imagine what that would do to our market projections."

Jason handed a printout to the chairman. "Our total available market will increase by a factor of ten."

Simpson scanned the page. "A successful outcome of your experiment, the resulting publicity, and even the *prospect* of the government turning surplus bases into manufacturing enterprises will significantly improve our negotiating stance with I-Cubed."

Jason nodded again.

"And I like the idea of making entrepreneurs out of dislocated workers, giving them a chance to re-employ themselves. There's a certain social symmetry to the idea."

Jason watched the chairman's face as he ran through the positives. The negatives would be next.

"On the other hand," Simpson said, his tone shifting on cue, "even if your experiment succeeds, the risk is considerable the Feds won't bite. Manufacturing products in America, using our own cheap labor, cuts against the grain of free trade agreements such as GATT and NAFTA. The White House sold these agreements to the public on the basis that they'll boost the buying power of the Third World and make it possible for foreign consumers to buy more of our products."

Jason squared his shoulders. "I'll agree that free trade is fine if we're talking about Third World countries consuming products manufactured in the United States. But if the citizens of Mexico, for example, are buying products we manufacture in Malaysia or Singapore, America's corporate coffers are fattened while doing little or nothing for millions of displaced factory workers. Then, one way or another, you and I have to support these people through social services. Perhaps we should export our welfare recipients along with their jobs."

"That would be a switch."

"Seriously," Jason said, "the continued outsourcing of manufacturing jobs will turn us into the world's managers. If it's in our national security interest to preserve what's left of our defense industry, then surely it's in our national economic interest to preserve what's left of our manufacturing capabilities. Otherwise we'll find ourselves sending in the troops when the men, women, and children in the Third World's sweat shops get tired of being exploited and go on strike."

Simpson eyed Jason. "That's an argument you should pocket for the future. We're a long way from becoming the world's managers. For that reason the government won't feel any urgency to act."

"We're not as far away as you might think. Ninety percent of all new jobs created in this country are in the service sector."

Simpson relented a bit. "I'll concede the government will be motivated by public opinion to take a hard look at your 'factory-sphere' in the desert. And I'll further concede that your plan appears sound. But I have one over-riding concern: What happens if your dislocated workers fail? In that event, you'll lose any hope of government support *and* blow the deal with I-Cubed."

"Those risks are worth the enormous return," Jason replied evenly. He was counting on Simpson jumping at the opportunity to bag another large trophy for his collection.

The chairman pressed his fingers together. He had a twinkle in his eyes. "Perhaps we can have it both ways. I'll support your idea to the extent of awarding half the contract to your desert factory, but the other half must go to the Korean supplier."

Jason shook his head. "It won't work. I ran that scenario through my computer model. The level of efficiency drops and the experiment collapses on itself. Besides, the factory is counting on a couple of my key men to provide on-site support: Greg Thompson in engineering and Howard Armstrong in production. Under a split contract, they must follow the portion going overseas."

The chairman wasn't buying. "Jason, there's no way I can endorse placing all of our eggs in one risky basket. However, I must say your passion for the project is refreshing. It gives me every confidence that you'll find a way to make it work."

Jason shook his head. "Last Chance is the mother of turnarounds; all of my other projects pale in comparison."

"I can't think of anyone better for the job."

"You're asking for the impossible."

Chairman Simpson looked at his watch and stood, signifying the meeting was over. "I always do."

2

BETWEEN THE MONDAY NIGHT CLUB and the St. Andrews shelter, Marty had signed up twelve men and four women. He figured he might find a few able bodies among the hackers at the library, but he had no leads for production manager. Out of desperation, he went to City General to talk with Crazy Eddie, the only person he knew who had managed a factory.

But Crazy Eddie wasn't to be found. He wasn't among the crowd in the waiting room. He wasn't standing by the vending machines. And he wasn't upstairs in the cafeteria. Marty even checked the bathrooms. Then he remembered he had given Crazy Eddie a hundred bucks. There was no telling where that money had taken the old man.

Marty was about to leave when someone tapped him on the shoulder.

"Guess who," Crazy Eddie announced merrily, dabbing at his forehead with a wad of toilet paper. "Been out jogging." Under his arm, angled back, was a metal crutch.

"I see you spent your money wisely," Marty said, nodding at the crutch. "Did you also get a room?"

"Nope. Changed my mind. Once you spend money on a room it's gone, and you've got nothing to show for it. I decided to stick around here and use the money for something that lasts."

"That crutch costs a hundred bucks?"

"Nah, only fifteen. I spent the rest on Christmas presents for my grandkids in Oakland. Better late than never. I piled packages of baby clothes on the doorway, rang the bell, and hid behind a bush. You should've seen the look on my daughter-in-law's face when she realized who 'Santa-Come-Lately' was."

"I'll bet," Marty said. He stared at Crazy Eddie for a moment and then made a decision. "I know it's early for lunch but how about a sandwich?"

Crazy Eddie grinned broadly. "I was hoping you'd ask."

The sunny weather inspired them to take their lunch outside. They chose a bench in park-like setting across from the psychiatric wing of the hospital. Marty was about broach the subject of a job when suddenly a patient on the sixth floor began ratcheting a metal cup against the bars while cursing and spitting out of the window.

Crazy Eddie looked up. "Sounds like he's yelling, 'I'm going to blow your fucking brains out!' Know him?"

Marty squinted into the sun. "I don't think so . . . but we've got to move; we can't talk over that racket."

The men gathered their lunch and found a bench around the corner. Eventually the screaming faded, and Marty explained to Crazy Eddie that he was looking to hire someone to teach assembly techniques in San Francisco, and then manage a factory in a remote part of the Nevada desert.

"Look no further," Crazy Eddie said, sticking a thumb into his chest. "I've got thirty years in an airplane factory. At one time I had two hundred and fifty people working for me. I know every manufacturing trick in the book. And I've taught assembly classes up the kazoo."

"Are you willing to live in the desert?"

"To work again? I'd go to the damn moon."

"What about your family in Oakland?"

"They'll be happy I got a job. I'll be able to call often and visit them from time to time, like a regular grandpa."

"The training classes start on March 1, less than a month away. Meanwhile, I'm putting a crew together to get the factory ready. Can you leave tomorrow night and spend the month helping us in Nevada?"

"Sure, but first I gotta pack," Crazy Eddie said, leaning over and picking up his new crutch. He positioned it under his arm as he stood. "Okay, I'm ready."

3

JASON WAS EATING lunch at his desk, trying to figure some way to squeeze more work out of fewer workers. How could he expect people who have spent years in slow motion suddenly switch gears and work at breakneck speed? Under a split contract, the success of Last Chance had shifted from the realm of the unlikely to the realm of the impossible.

The one good thing was the temporary nature of the situation. If the factory somehow met its first scheduled delivery in May, additional contracts from other companies would allow Last Chance to staff up to a more efficient size. But the larger question still remained: Could these people work eighteen-hour days without self-destructing?

The intercom buzzed. "Sam's holding," Sally announced. "She says it's urgent."

Jason picked up the phone and heard Sam take a deep breath. "I'm calling from bankruptcy court. I'm afraid we've run into a snag. A higher bid came in for Last Chance. Five point five million is now on the table."

"What? How could that be?" Jason rubbed his temple. "No other buyer has even inspected the property."

"Your competition, a Mr. Kenji Kobayashi, has already seen it. He was one of the original Japanese investors, and he believes the idea of an exclusive gambling resort south of Las Vegas is still viable—especially at fire sale prices. He's pulling the strings from Tokyo, relaying his bids through a local law firm. It looks like he has a strong yen for the property."

Jason sagged. "Sam, I'm not in the mood."

"It's now 12:30 p.m.," she continued. "The court has recessed for lunch. You have until 1:30 to raise your bid. But you should know that even if you decide to counter, it's not going to stop there. Kobayashi's attorney assured me his client is in this for the long run."

Jason closed his eyes. "Sam, I just came back from a meeting with Cytex's chairman of the board. At his insistence, we're splitting the contract between Last Chance and a Korean subcontractor. The chairman is staging a steeplechase between a three-legged nag and a thoroughbred." Jason massaged his temple. "Do you have any feel for how high the bidding will go?"

"No, except that it appears we've only had the opening volley. If you want to do battle, I'll need your authority to counter Kobayashi until we reach his threshold of pain. And because the court is handling other matters between bids, I expect the action to continue into tomorrow."

"Sam, my net worth is in the neighborhood of ten million. It sounds like it could go that high. Suddenly I'm getting major cold feet."

"Less than sixty minutes, Jason. Write this phone number down and call me before the afternoon session reconvenes. I'll be standing by. If I don't hear from you by 1:30, I'll have no choice but to tell the court we've folded our tent. Title will immediately go to Kobayashi."

Jason took the number and hung up. He badly needed to talk to Marty. The man never seemed all that keen on Last Chance. If Marty was having difficulty with his recruiting efforts, Jason would throw in the towel. Then Marty could work at Cytex, and Jason could help Anton save his business and his marriage.

In retrospect he knew he had been crazy to fall in love with Liz, crazy to interfere with his brother's marriage, and crazy to throw a way an opportunity to reconcile with Anton. What had gotten into him?

The one saving grace was that after his meeting with his brother last Friday, he had refrained from contacting Liz. And since seven days had gone by and she hadn't contacted him either, he was certain she was back with her husband.

Jason hurried to his car. He had no idea where Marty might be recruiting. He tried the bus station first. Then he checked the streets around the Civic Center Plaza. With ten minutes remaining Jason ran up the stairs to the library.

Marty was there!

He was huddled with two men and a woman around a terminal. Upon spotting Jason, Marty excused himself.

"There's not much time," Jason said, between breaths. "You only have a few minutes to make a decision that could affect you for the rest of your life."

"Calm down, what is it?"

Jason quickly explained that Last Chance was going to cost millions more while the initial C-REAL contract and the staffing level would be halved. The odds against success were skyrocketing. Jason didn't want to go forward unless Marty and his recruits were completely and utterly committed.

It was now 1:28 p.m.

Marty stared at his shoes. "That's a tough call. With those Net Geeks over there, the members of the Monday Night Club, and those I recruited from St. Andrews, I've got a crew of twenty ready to get on the bus tomorrow. That includes our production manager, Crazy Eddie. He's perfect. You should have seen his face . . . all of their faces. They're really counting on Last Chance." Marty paused for a second and looked at Jason. "Okay, I am too."

Jason took a deep breath and glanced at his watch.

One minute remained.

"Wait here," Jason said, dashing to a phone booth.

When he returned, his face was pallid. "I've authorized Sam to bet my entire net worth on Last Chance. I hope you didn't burn any bridges at your homeless shelter. I may need you to put in a good word for me."

TWENTY-FIVE
Friday, February 3

1

ANTON WAS NURSING a glass of club soda. "No Scotch this evening?" Jason asked as he pulled up a chair.

"No, little brother," Anton replied with a confident smile. He was looking handsome and fit, his face rosy, his eyes clear. "I'm on the wagon. Last week at this very table you saw me at the lowest point in my life. Thanks for taking care of me." Anton lifted his glass to Jason.

"That's what brothers are for."

"The one good thing about hitting rock bottom," Anton continued, "is the realization that things could only get better. Last Saturday morning I showed Liz a side she had never seen before. Then I asked her to come home."

"What did she say?"

"That we needed to get on with our lives. But when I told her about offering you a partnership in HDC, she softened. We've been talking by phone during the week and she now realizes I've come to my senses, and I can be a good husband to her. But before she'll come home she's wants to be sure our relationship won't continue to be burdened by financial problems. So it all comes down to you, little brother. You're holding both my wife and my business in your hands."

Jason took a deep breath. "Anton, I want to help you, but I can't right now. I just learned that a bid I placed on a piece of commercial property was accepted. The bidding ran to eight million dollars. I was forced to pledge my remaining assets to secure a bank line of credit for operating capital. One of the bank covenants says I can't further encumber my estate. I'm afraid all of my net worth is tied up."

Anton's body visibly tightened. "All of your net worth?"

"Yes. It came as a surprise. No other offers were expected, but a Japanese buyer showed up and started a bidding war. The selling price rose to a point where I don't have anything left for the Howell Development Corporation."

Anton was staring at Jason in wide-eyed disbelief. "What do need this property for?"

"For a manufacturing facility to produce C-REAL."

Anton relaxed. "Fine, little brother, that's great. As my partner, simply choose one of HDC's first class manufacturing facilities in Silicon Valley. If you don't like one of my vacant buildings, I'll be happy to evict someone." Anton was smiling. "And since the Japanese buyer wants this property so badly, let him have it. I'll personally handle the negotiations and get you out unscathed."

Jason shook his head. "I need this specific piece of real estate—the property is in the Nevada desert."

"Why the desert?" Anton asked, staring at Jason.

"Because the factory will employ the homeless . . . to prove that untrained workers can compete with overseas labor. The desert property was originally going to be a gambling resort. The workers will be housed in the hotel and the casino will be converted into a factory. The economics won't work locally."

Anton blinked. "You're going to send the homeless to a gambling resort?"

"Ah . . . yes."

Jason had been watching his brother's rosy glow deepen toward red. Anton rapped his fingers on the table. A long minute passed. Finally he said, "Is there any way I can talk you out of this?"

"I'm afraid not. I was committed to this project before your partnership offer. But if this experimental facility succeeds, it'll serve as the model for similar factories and the market for C-REAL will increase by a factor of ten. When Cytex is sold, as early as June, I'll be in an excellent position to—"

Anton abruptly stood. "That's too fucking late!" he glowered, turning and walking away.

2

AT THAT MOMENT, on the mezzanine level of the Penniston, Mayor Walter Babcock was in the Olympic Ballroom, standing at the podium, arms raised in acknowledgement of his audience's enthusiastic applause. A blue banner with gold letters was draped on the wall behind him. It said:

THE IMPERIAL MEN'S CLUB
OF
SAN FRANCISCO

Chief Conti, at the rear of the ballroom, watched as a sea of gray-haired executives laughed and clapped at Babcock's one-liners. It was the mayor's first major fundraiser of his re-election campaign, and it was going well. The chief had been around the political scene long enough to know that one could calibrate the laugh meter in dollars as well as decibels.

Mayor Babcock gave the victory sign and stepped down from the podium to thunderous applause. The chief made his way through the crowd and watched as the mayor, smiling broadly, received congratulations from the company heads clustered around him. It amazed the chief that the mayor knew all of his contributors by their first names and made specific inquiries about their wives and children.

After the crowd dissipated, Conti approached. "Congratulations, Walt, your decision to clean up the plaza appears to have worked. Your numbers in today's polls were terrific. And I would venture to guess that you just shook hands with a six-figure war chest."

Mayor Babcock's smile suddenly evaporated. His right eye twitched. He motioned for Conti's ear. "Rudy, the only thing I want to shake right now is my pecker. My prostate's acting up; I need to take a wicked whiz."

"Mind if I tag along? The men's room is actually an appropriate place to tell you the news."

The mayor bit his upper lip. "What news?" he asked suspiciously, shifting his weight from one leg to the other.

"About Brodsky."

Babcock flinched. He abruptly turned and walked away.

Conti trailed him by a few steps.

While the mayor stood at the urinal, Conti checked the stalls. After Babcock zipped up, he walked toward the sink and said to the chief, "All right, what about Brodsky?"

"This afternoon I got a call from the DA's office."

"Hmmm," the mayor said, washing his hands.

"Our boy has been arrested."

The mayor paused and looked at Conti in the mirror. "Arrested? For what?"

An unrestrained grin broke out on the chief's face. "Trespassing, peeping, indecent exposure, resisting arrest, *and* assaulting a Project Vector officer."

Babcock turned. "Indecent exposure? Peeping?"

"Can you believe it? A cruiser nabbed him in the parking lot of Howell's company. He was wearing binoculars. At one point he had his pants down, and was waving his thing around for the longest time, urinating all over the company's shrubs. He put on quite a show for the secretaries watching from the windows."

"What a pisser," the mayor whistled.

"You can say that again."

The mayor dried his hands and turned to face the chief. He had a glint in his eye. "Tell me more."

"Until yesterday, Brodsky was in the psych ward of City General on a seventy-two-hour hold. At the moment he's being detained in county jail, awaiting his appearance in muni court to formally enter a plea.

"At the arraignment he claimed he had been robbed by a prostitute and was completely broke, so the court appointed a public defender to represent him."

"He couldn't make bail?"

"Correct—he remains in custody."

The mayor looked pleased. "Go on."

"In fact they nearly kept him in the psych ward. Yesterday, as arrangements were being made to transfer him to county jail, he began banging a metal cup on his window bars and screaming profanities at people outside the building. The hospital was considering an intensive treatment program, but by the time the deputy sheriffs arrived to transport him, he had calmed down. I expect the hospital was anxious to get rid of him."

The mayor's face was beaming.

"When the DA's office learned that a former homicide inspector was in custody, they called my office. The DA is concerned that Brodsky will do hard time in state prison if he's convicted on the assault charge. It's a felony. The rest are misdemeanors. The DA knows that prison for an ex-homicide inspector is tantamount to a death sentence since Brodsky would be serving time with the perps he put away. They'll be drooling and sharpening their shivs when they learn about his incarceration."

The mayor started to say something but changed his mind. "The DA is suggesting a plea bargain?"

"Yes. Since it's Brodsky's first offense, he'll plead to trespassing, pay a fine, and he'll be sentenced to time served."

Mayor Babcock clasped his hands behind his back and began to pace in front of the sinks. "No, that's too lenient for the son-of-a-bitch. With state prison hanging over his head, we can do better. A lot better. Tell the DA that Brodsky must be charged with indecent exposure. I want him to cool his jets in jail for a couple of months—and not our new Glamour Slammer. I'm talking about the maximum security section in the old county jail, where we keep the pedophiles, the transvestites, and all of the other perverts."

"Walt, you do realize that with the indecent exposure conviction he'll have to register as a sex offender with the local police and the Feds for the rest of his life?"

The mayor stopped pacing and flashed a toothy grin. "Sounds good to me."

3

WHILE THE BUS DRIVER was loading the provisions of the initial crew of twenty departing for Last Chance, Marty walked down the aisle, greeting everyone. He was about to take his seat when the driver climbed aboard, holding up a jug of purple liquid. "Who belongs to this?" he asked. "It's not safe to stow an unprotected jar with the rest of the baggage."

"You can say that again," Doc remarked.

Marty put his hands on his hips. "What gives, Stan?"

Stan stood and took the jug. "I couldn't leave it behind, Marty. It brings me good luck. And you wouldn't want it to fall into enemy hands, would you?"

The men laughed.

"Just keep it under your seat," Marty ordered. "If we hit a bump and it blows, it's your ass."

"You mean it's his brains," Willie corrected.

The driver shook his head and settled behind the wheel. Soon they were off, winding through the Friday evening traffic toward the Freeway. The passengers were in a cheery mood, telling stories, cracking jokes, and singing songs.

When they were cruising on Interstate 5, Marty stood. "Can I have everyone's attention? We need to take care of some paperwork." Marty pulled out a stack of employment agreements and passed them around. "When you sign this paper, you become employees of a company called Last Chance. The agreement says you must keep our location in the desert confidential until management says it's okay to reveal it to outsiders."

"Who's management?" Doc wanted to know.

"Well, I'm president," Marty said. "Crazy Eddie, the man over there with the crutch, is in charge of training and production; Stan, the fellow with the jug, is construction foreman. Our facilities manager, Ike, is at the site. Other managers will be named as we go along."

"Marty, don't get me wrong," Doc said, "but who made you president?"

"Fair question. I was appointed by our sponsor, who wishes to keep his identity confidential. But I can tell you that neither the sponsor nor any outsider owns an interest in our company."

"You mean there ain't no regular people in this deal?" Sanchez asked.

"Nope, only us. As I've said before, we're the owners. In fact, after you sign the employment agreement, each of you will get an official stock certificate." Marty took out rectangular document with a fancy green border and held it up.

The passengers buzzed.

"Remember, you can bail at any time. But if you do, you'll have to return your shares to the company." Marty then explained the rest of the agreement, and after everyone had signed, he handed out the stock.

Willie stared at his certificate for a long time before setting it down on the empty seat next to him. Shoo, who had been dozing in Willie's lap, opened an eye and looked at the paper. He promptly got up and curled on the certificate, as if to stake his own claim to Last Chance.

TWENTY-SIX
Monday, February 6

1

THE STATIC CRESTED and then receded. Jason shouted into the phone, "SAY AGAIN, MARTY, YOU'RE BREAKING UP." He leaned his elbows on his desk and pressed the handset hard against his ear.

"I said I'm in the Dead Mountains so I could use this damn cell phone. I'm sitting on top of a damn boulder, trying to keep my damn ass from being bitten by the damn rattlesnakes. How come Ike's telephone doesn't work?"

"It was cut it off after the property was transferred on Friday. I'm doing everything I can to get it turned back on. How are things going?"

"Pretty good, actually. We finished the general cleanup by late Sunday afternoon. The hotel and grounds are gleaming. Everyone's been hauling. There were a couple of minor cuts and scrapes, and a few pulled muscles. Doc fixed them up. The infirmary's stocked with first class supplies.

"Last night we celebrated with a barbecue. Stan brought out the jug and tried to initiate the three Net Nerds I signed up at the library. But they already knew about the jug from a Chat Group and didn't get suckered. I told Stan he had to store it in the shack by the river. It's too danger-ous to keep at the hotel.

"When it got chilly, we watched a porno movie in my suite. You won't believe what you can do with sticky rice. First you wet it, and then you wrap it around—"

"Never mind that," Jason interrupted, worried he would lose the connection at any moment. "A convoy of six trucks will be arriving shortly with building materials and furnishings. You need to be back at the hotel to ac-cept delivery and help unload."

"Don't worry. I can see the road for miles from up here. Anyway," Marty continued, "starting this evening, and for the remainder of the month, the crew will be at-tending Crazy Eddie's assembly classes. It'll give him a chance to develop his course and wring out the bugs."

"Good move."

"One more thing: You should know that I've got a bunch of happy campers on my hands. Stan, I've never seen him so jazzed. He's even found a friend."

"Really? Who?"

"Ike. As we speak, the two of them are hunting to-night's dinner here in the mountains. They're firing rifles at anything that moves. If you hear a shot and the phone goes dead, get me an ambulance."

"Okay."

"Meanwhile, Doc and Sanchez are fishing in the river and playing cards. Some of the others are . . ."

Marty's voice faded and he was gone.

Jason replaced the receiver, feeling a bit optimistic for the first time. Last Chance appeared to be off to a good start. Although he still had serious doubts, it was begin-ning to look as if Marty and the others might just pull it off.

The intercom buzzed. "Mr. Howell, this is the receptionist. There's a man in the lobby who's been waiting for you to finish your call. He has a legal document for you."

Another agreement from Sam, Jason surmised. "Have him leave it with you."

"I'm sorry Mr. Howell, but he says he has to deliver it to you personally."

Jason sighed. "I'll be right out."

Standing in the lobby was a broad-shouldered man with a severe crewcut. He wore an old black leather jacket and a hoop earring. "Jason Howell?" he grunted.

"Yes."

The man shoved an envelope at Jason, then turned and walked out the door.

Jason went back to his office and opened the envelope. Inside was a document from Superior Court, County of San Francisco. At first he was stunned. Disbelief followed, and then outrage. The document said:

CITATION FOR CONSERVATORSHIP

To: Jason Howell

You are hereby cited and required to appear at a hearing in this court on February 21 at 9:00 a.m. to give any legal reason why, according to the verified petition filed with this court, you should not be found unable to manage your financial resources and by reason thereof, why the following person should not be appointed conservator of your estate:

Anton Howell.

"FUCK!" Jason screamed, crumpling the citation, squeezing it into a little ball as if he thought he could make it disappear.

Sally came running in. "Mr. Howell, are you okay?"

"NO!" he yelled, looking at the wad of paper slowly expanding in his hand. "Get Sam on the phone! Hurry!"

Sally hustled out of the office.

Jason sat transfixed, still staring at the crumpled paper.

The intercom came alive. "Sam's holding."

Jason picked up. "My goddamn brother is seeking a conservatorship on the twenty-first of this month. I can't believe he's doing this. He's retaliating because I turned down a partnership offer that would have kept him out of bankruptcy."

"Does he know about the Japanese buyer?"

"Yes."

"Then he wants to take control of Last Chance, sell it, and use the proceeds for his own benefit."

"He's always tried to control me, but this time he's gone too far. He must know he can't win."

"Maybe so. But this is an official legal action, and I must advise you to take it seriously."

"What are his chances of prevailing?"

"Admittedly, not good. It's difficult to get control of a relative's estate if it's contested and the relative appears reasonably competent. The burden is on your brother, and he must prove your incompetence by presenting clear and convincing evidence. He must show the court you are substantially unable to manage your estate. You'll have a choice of a judge or a jury, but I wouldn't roll the dice with a jury if I were you."

"No goddamn jury!" Jason seethed into the phone.

"Jason, simmer down and listen to me. For your part, you must *calmly* convince the court that your brother's petition is without merit and motivated by greed."

"That's for damn sure!"

"The court will want to do what's best to preserve your estate. We must emphasize that your investment in Last Chance is not a reckless gamble; rather it's a rational investment having the potential of a huge return as well as providing a valuable public service."

"Yeah, sure," Jason said, feeling another splitting headache coming on. He had been unconsciously grinding the phone against his left ear and it was making his temple throb even more. He shifted the receiver to his other ear. "What do we do?"

"Before the hearing, you'll be interviewed by a court-appointed investigator who'll report his findings to the judge. You must cooperate fully with the investigator. Then, at the hearing, we'll call everyone who has helped you with Last Chance. We'll tilt the scales of justice with the sheer weight of credible witnesses." Sam paused. "Okay, who can testify about the project?"

"Uh . . . Marty, Albert Simpson III, Greg Thompson, Liz, and you."

"Fine. I'll ask the witnesses to be at Superior Court on the twenty-first. I'll prepare each in person or by phone."

"No."

"What?"

"I said no. For starters, I'm not going to get Marty involved. He has an impossible task ahead of him and I don't want him distracted by this bullshit. I don't even want him to know. And I absolutely cannot have Simpson and Thompson dragged in. If my company finds out my competency is being challenged, the entire contract will go to the Koreans."

"And I suppose Liz is out of the question, too?"

"That's right. I doubt she'll testify against her husband. In any event, for personal reasons, I want her out of it. That leaves you, Sam."

"I'm afraid not. If I were to testify, we would waive the attorney-client privilege. All of our conversations and files become fair game. Anton's lawyer will pick and choose juicy tidbits to place you in the worst light possible. Most likely the mayor will get dragged in. And that'll attract the tabloids like vultures to road-kill. They'll have a field day picking over your respective carcasses, and you can kiss your merger goodbye."

"Then I'll go it alone. If I can persuade an ultra-conservative like Simpson about the viability of Last Chance, then I'm confident I can convince some judge. I can't see any way Anton can beat me."

Sam sighed. "Okay, it's your call."

2

IN A CRUEL TWIST of fate, Brodsky found himself back in the Hall of Justice. Only this time he was sitting on a bench in a holding cell on the second floor, awaiting his appearance at muni court next door. He looked around at the other defendants. Like him, they wore bright orange jail suits, and like him, their wrists and ankles were shackled. Bodies shifted nervously, and the sound of jingling chains filled the room.

He couldn't believe this was happening. Over the years, when he needed a break, Brodsky would come downstairs and peer into this very room, smirking at the shackled criminals, drawing strength from their misery. Then he would return to his desk, energized and ready to tackle an endless pile of paperwork.

Never, not even in his most bizarre nightmare, did he imagine himself in this room.

Wait! Maybe that's what this really is—a nightmare! He prayed silently for a minute and then tensed his wrists against his chains, grunting loudly, hoping the pain of the shackles biting into his flesh would awaken him. But the chains, the pain, and the nightmare persisted.

Two burly deputy sheriffs approached, and Brodsky stopped struggling. One unlocked him from the bench while the other stood by, grinning broadly. Then, with a deputy on each arm, Brodsky was escorted through a door and into the courtroom. The shackles on his legs restricted his motion to a jingling, duck-like waddle. The deputies guided him to the jury box where he sat alone and waited.

After a time, he heard the bailiff announce: "The People of the State of California versus James Brodsky." The deputies returned and led him to the defendant's table. Brodsky, vague and distant, looked at his hands while the public defender and the DA were at sidebar with the judge.

"And so, James Brodsky," the judge finally said, how do you plead to the reduced charge of indecent exposure?"

Brodsky looked up and blinked several times, trying to remember what he was supposed to do. The public defender came over and whispered, *'Nolo contendere*—no contest—remember?"

Brodsky lifted his arms and maneuvered the chain so he could hold the back of his head, which was still swollen from being whacked with a police baton. The dull ache made it difficult to think. He knew he had to say something, and he desperately wanted it to be: "Not guilty." But with the mayor and chief pulling the strings the alternative was five years in state prison, although, in reality, he knew it would be closer to five minutes.

"Mr. Brodsky," the judge repeated, "your plea?"

Strangely, dying in prison didn't bother Brodsky as much as knowing his demise would give his enemies ultimate victory. And there was no way he could let that happen. *'Nolo contendere,"* Brodsky mumbled.

"The court accepts your plea and hereby sentences you to sixty days in the county jail with credit for the seven days you have been in custody. Upon your release, you will be on formal probation for three years, during which time you will abstain from alcoholic beverages and illicit drugs. For the first six months of probation, you will attend weekly psychiatric counseling sessions at your own expense. You will pay a $500 fine plus $100 in court administrative expenses, and $75 for police costs.

"You will also make restitution to the arresting officer in the amount of $66.45 for tearing his uniform, and you will reimburse the officer's medical expenses once he is released from the hospital. I expect it will be a tidy sum.

"Finally, as a sex offender, you will register with the police in each community in which you reside, for as long as you shall live. Do you agree to abide by *all* of the terms and conditions of your probation?"

Brodsky became aware of people tittering around him. The deputies, the lawyers, the court staff, and all of the people in the gallery were chuckling. His vague and distant feelings quickly transformed into rage, causing his shoulders to hunch and his limbs to twitch against his shackles. Brodsky closed his eyes and shook until the giggling gallery was lost in the rattling of his chains.

"Mr. Brodsky," said the judge, impatiently raising his voice above the racket.

The chains continued to rattle.

"James Brodsky! Do you agree?"

Brodsky stopped shaking and looked dully at the judge. "Yes," he hissed.

Part V

NOTHING TO LOSE

TWENTY-SEVEN
Tuesday, February 21

1

"ALL RISE," the bailiff announced, "Superior Court for the Country of San Francisco is now in session, the Honorable Clayton Baxter, presiding."

Judge Baxter entered the courtroom from a side door. He was an elderly man, slight in build, wrapped in a large black robe that nearly swept the floor. His face was gaunt and weathered, his features prominent and angular, his demeanor crusty. Only a few wisps of gray hair remained, and those he plastered to his head.

Judge Baxter pulled out his chair and alighted. With a flourish of small hands, he signaled his courtroom to be seated. He deposited a pair of wire-framed spectacles on the tip of his nose as the clerk handed him a file.

Jason was watching the judge. "This old fellow looks conservative," he whispered to Sam. "Maybe I should have shaved my beard and trimmed my hair, but I don't want my brother to think he has any power over me. Once I start dancing to his tune, he's got me."

"Conservative is good for us," Sam whispered back. "He won't be inclined to upset the status quo. Anyway it's not your appearance that worries me," she said, looking beyond Jason at the silver-haired attorney sitting with Anton at the petitioner's table. Like his client, the lawyer was tall and handsome, an imposing figure in an expensive gray suit. "I'm more concerned with how the judge will react to your brother's attorney. He's one of San Francisco's slickest. Rumor has it that the governor is considering him for a seat on the state appellate court. The judge will take him seriously—"

Judge Baxter looked up from the file. "Are the parties ready to argue the conservatorship of Jason Howell?"

Anton's attorney stood. "Roger Newman, for the petitioner."

"Samantha Paxton, for the respondent."

Judge Baxter examined both attorneys over his spectacles. Then he pushed the sleeve of his robe back, exposed a gnarled finger, and waved it at Newman. "Begin."

Newman stood and smiled confidently. "Judge, I would like to introduce Anton Howell," he said in a sincere baritone, extending an arm toward his client. "This man is a highly-respected member of our community. Reluctantly, he has petitioned this court to appoint him as conservator over the estate of his younger brother, Jason Howell, who was a passenger in the small plane that crashed last January, killing the pilot. In that unfortunate accident, my client's brother fractured his skull, suffered amnesia, was partially paralyzed, and was held hostage by a band of street people.

"Since that time, Judge, the respondent Jason Howell has undergone drastic changes in appearance, personality, and behavior. To wit, in the span of the few short weeks since his accident, he has grossly mismanaged, and otherwise put at risk, an estate valued at ten million dollars."

Judge Baxter looked over his spectacles at Jason. Sam immediately stood. "Your Honor, the petitioner Anton Howell is not concerned with his brother's welfare; he is only concerned with seizing control of my client's estate for his own selfish purposes. It is Anton Howell who has 'grossly mismanaged and otherwise put at risk,' his own estate. As an exhibit to our papers contesting this petition we have included a partnership proposal to Jason Howell. The accompanying financials clearly show that Anton Howell has forsaken sound business practices in the pursuit of profits, and has brought his company to the brink of bankruptcy.

"If Anton Howell thought his brother Jason was exhibiting bizarre behavior," Sam continued, "he never would have offered him a partnership in a multimillion dollar real-estate business. Your Honor, this petition is a sham. It is simply a last-ditch effort by a greedy businessman to force Jason Howell to use his estate to bail out a sinking ship."

Judge Baxter, his face a blank slate, inspected Anton. Newman stood and walked around to the front of the petitioner's table and sat on a corner. "Judge," he said evenly, "what my colleague has conveniently omitted is the fact that my client invited his brother to become his partner under terms that are extraordinarily generous. Anton Howell made his proposal in good faith. My client merely wanted to involve his brother in a family business where he could be watched, cared for, and counseled. Anton Howell was merely trying to avoid the necessity of the legal action in which we now find ourselves embroiled.

"But, Judge," Newman went on, "my client's hand was forced when he learned that his brother, instead of investing a modest portion of his estate in prime Silicon Valley property, chose to commit *all* of it to a bizarre project involving the homeless and an incomplete and abandoned gambling resort in the Nevada desert. He encumbered ten million dollars for property that has lain fallow for years. My client petitioned for a conservatorship because, in all of God's Earth, there is but one other individual, a gentleman in Japan—Mr. Kobayashi—who wants the property as a private resort for his countrymen.

"Judge, as we speak, Mr. Kobayashi is in the market for another piece of property. If we do not act swiftly, the opportunity to undo Jason Howell's ill-advised purchase will be irretrievably lost."

Sam jumped up. "Your Honor, Jason Howell has a specific investment purpose in mind, and he expects a significant return from that desert property. He has a reputation as a talented visionary with an extraordinary record of business successes. Since these proceedings evidently hinge upon the wisdom of Jason Howell's investment, I ask—with the court's permission—that we now hear testimony from my client."

Judge Baxter looked at Newman, who shrugged. "Go ahead, Ms. Paxton," the judge said.

Jason was sworn in. He sat with his legs crossed and his body angled away from Anton so he wouldn't have to look at him. Under Sam's direct examination he described his company's enhanced reality product and how it would increase production efficiency using unskilled workers. He kept the technical jargon to a minimum and his answers concise, although irritation was evident in his voice.

"And who will this factory employ?" Sam asked.

"In order to compete with foreign labor the factory will hire the long-term unemployed, people who are willing to work at minimum wage."

"Will the factory have a contract?"

"Yes, from my company, Cytex. Once the workers demonstrate the feasibility of this state-of-the-art assembly technique, additional contracts from Cytex and other companies will ensue. If we remove the economic incentive to manufacture abroad, many American companies will choose to have their products built here to take advantage of improved logistics, flexibility, and faster turnaround."

"Now Jason, would you tell the court how you expect to multiply your investment in this assembly facility?"

Jason turned toward the judge. "The desert factory will serve as a proving ground for the conversion of unused military bases into private manufacturing enterprises. These enterprises will hire and house hundreds of thousands of displaced American workers. Each worker will need an enhanced reality workstation based on C-REAL, a proprietary product invented by my company. As a result of those sales, Cytex will have a market value in excess of two hundred million dollars. My current stock holdings will be worth at least fifty million dollars. Cytex already has a merger partner lined up."

Judge Baxter rested his chin on his hand and watched Jason.

Sam took a step closer to the witness stand. "Jason, besides multiplying the value of your estate, is there any other benefit your investment will have?"

Jason continued to address the judge. "Your Honor, a lot of our tax money is used to support displaced American workers whose jobs have been sent overseas. If we re-employ these people they will again contribute to society and become taxpayers themselves."

The judge pressed thin lips together and his head seemed to nod slightly.

"Nothing further, Your Honor," Sam said.

The judge turned to Roger Newman. "Cross?"

"Yes, Judge," Newman replied, striding over to the witness stand. "Jason . . . may I call you Jason?"

"Ah, yes."

Newman smiled. "Well, then, Jason, let me see if I understand this scheme of yours. You are going to take homeless people, transport them to a remote gambling resort, dress them in goggles, and expect them to beat the pants off our highly-skilled foreign trading partners?"

Sam stood. "Objection. He's misstating my client's testimony."

Judge Baxter was taking notes. "Overruled," he said without looking up. "If the witness' testimony has been misstated, then the witness is free to elaborate. Answer the question Mr. Howell."

Jason shifted in his seat and swallowed. He was feeling the onset of another bad headache. "Ah . . . we're not taking just anyone off the street. All applicants will be screened through detailed questionnaires and background checks to eliminate individuals who have behavioral problems, addictive disorders, or criminal records. Additionally, candidates must complete an intensive training class in assembly techniques. Only the top graduates will be hired."

"Nevertheless, you're hiring the homeless," Newman asserted, as he turned from Jason and faced the judge.

"Yes," Jason replied to Newman's back. "We need to demonstrate the viability of the concept under reasonably worst-case conditions. It's the only way the enterprise will receive the publicity it needs to generate follow-on contracts and get the government and private industry interested in the program. If the factory hires the readily employable, the project won't have proved anything. But the ultimate idea is to provide jobs for displaced workers regardless of whether or not they have homes in the conventional sense. This program is specifically designed to get the long-term unemployed back to work."

Newman was still looking at the judge. "Jason, you have a lot of experience as a manager, correct?"

"Fifteen years."

"What is your management involvement in your hotel-factory?"

Jason massaged his throbbing temple. "Planning and advisory only."

"So who will manage this alleged factory for you?"

"Management will come from the people who work there."

"The homeless?"

"Yes."

"And what might be your ownership interest in the manufacturing operation?"

"None. The employee-shareholders will be working long hours while paying themselves rock-bottom wages. If I were involved, it would appear predatory."

"So the homeless will own the business as well as manage it, is that not true?"

Jason's headache was worsening. "Yes."

"And so your primary role is landlord?"

"You could say that."

Newman turned to face the rear of the courtroom. "And as landlord, Jason, what rent might you be charging?" he asked, playing to an empty gallery.

"A dollar a year for five years. Then market rent."

"I see. What about operating capital? Where might the homeless be getting that?"

"From a bank line secured by the titles to Last Chance and other assets in my estate."

"Ah-ha!" Newman said, abruptly turning to face Jason. "Then would it not be fair to say you have structured this venture so that if your street people fail, your desert factory will collapse like a house of cards, and you will lose your entire estate, perhaps even becoming homeless yourself?"

"Perhaps, but I—"

"No further questions," Newman said.

Judge Baxter looked at Sam. "Redirect?"

"Not at this time, Your Honor. But I would like to reserve the right to recall this witness."

"All right, you may step down, Mr. Howell, but remember you're still under oath."

Jason slowly returned to the respondent's table. His face was flushed.

"You're having one of your bad headaches, aren't you?" Sam asked.

Jason nodded.

"I'm afraid Newman scored some direct hits. I've got to get you back on the stand for rebuttal. But I wanted to give you a break. I'll ask for a recess."

Jason shook his head. "No. I don't want to show any weakness . . . I'll be okay."

The judge looked at Newman. "Next witness."

"At this time, Judge," Newman said, "I would like to call Dr. John Sorensen."

Jason stared at his hands as his neurologist from the University Medical Center was sworn in. Newman's questions took the doctor through the diagnosis and treatment of his patient.

"Now, Doctor, let us talk about Jason Howell's prognosis. Will you tell the court about the latent effects of a head injury of the type and severity your patient had experienced?"

"The latent effects of a head trauma can vary considerably. They include headaches, dizziness, memory loss, and epilepsy."

"What about mental impairment?"

"Possibly."

Newman started pacing in front of the witness stand. "Is it not true, Doctor, the day Jason was placed under your care, Anton Howell met with you because he was concerned about his brother's welfare?"

Sam stood. "Objection, lacking in foundation. The petitioner's concern for his brother's welfare has not been established."

"Sustained," the judge grunted. "Rephrase your question, Counsel."

"Certainly, Judge," Newman said. He stopped pacing and stood by Sorensen. "Doctor, did my client inquire about his brother's condition?"

"Yes."

"And did you tell my client that a head injury of the nature sustained by his brother might alter his personality?"

"Yes."

"In fact, you did suggest that Jason Howell might become a 'zealot,' did you not?'"

"Yes. I said that. I've seen it happen, especially when a patient has a near-death experience."

"No further questions."

Judge Baxter removed his spectacles and rubbed his eyes. "Cross?"

Sam stood and approached the witness. "Dr. Sorensen, was there anything in Jason Howell's behavior while he was under your care that suggested he had become unstable or zealous about anything?"

"No."

"Is there any scientific way to predict such a personality change?"

"Not that I'm aware of. It's just that—"

"Do you have any formal training in psychoanalysis or any other psychiatric discipline?"

"No, but I've often observed—"

"So in fact, Doctor, the opinion you gave to Anton Howell a few hours after his brother's admission to the hospital was purely speculative, wasn't it?"

"Perhaps, but it's been my—"

"No further questions," Sam said, turning away from Sorensen and facing the judge. "Your Honor. I move that this witness' testimony regarding my client's personality changes be stricken from the record. By his own admission the doctor is not qualified to render such an opinion."

The judge looked at Newman. "I've heard enough. Despite the fact that I find the rationale behind the desert experiment risky and perhaps even a bit eccentric, the petitioner hasn't satisfied his burden to show that his brother is incompetent to manage his financial affairs." Judge Baxter held up a file. "The court investigator's report in here also corroborates this conclusion. And finally, Mr. Newman, I feel compelled to point out that your use of a treating neurologist to imply future psychological problems was overreaching to say the least."

Newman jumped up. "Judge, we are not representing to the court that Dr. Sorensen's testimony relates to Jason Howell's current state-of-mind; it is offered solely as the foundation for the state-of-mind of my client."

Judge Baxter removed his glasses and squinted at Newman. "What on God's Earth *are* you talking about?"

"I'll rephrase it, Judge. The good doctor's prognosis is foundational to Anton Howell's decision to gather compelling evidence of his brother's bizarre behavior, which goes directly to the issue of his competency."

Sam stood and sighed. "Objection Your Honor, Mr. Newman is burying us in a Byzantine morass of logic in a desperate attempt to prolong these proceedings. Whatever spin he's now placing on Dr. Sorensen's testimony, it's still irrelevant."

"Dr. Sorensen, you may step down," the judge directed. "I'll rule on Ms. Paxton's objection after I hear the petitioner's 'compelling evidence.' Proceed, Mr. Newman," Baxter said, waving a gnarled finger, "but I warn you, my patience is wearing thin."

Newman took a packet of twelve photographs from the table and casually handed them to the judge. Judge Baxter replaced his spectacles and examined the photographs one at a time. In short order, his eyebrows had arched.

Sam became alarmed. "Objection, Your Honor. Respondents haven't seen those photographs."

The judge ignored Sam and continued examining the prints. Finally, he put them in a stack and offered them to Sam. "You may see them now, Ms. Paxton." Then he turned to Newman. "I'll need an offer of proof."

Sam took the pictures back to her table and thumbed through them as Jason looked over her shoulder. The first photo showed him coming down the front steps of his building leaning on a cane. He was dressed in his navy pea coat and blue knit cap. In the next photo, he was walking with Marty on a littered street. Other pictures showed him sitting in a doorway with the big man, passing a bottle back and forth and high-fiving. By now Jason's headache had become debilitating, and he was dizzy and sick to his stomach. He turned away and closed his eyes.

Without waiting for Sam to finish her examination, Newman said, "Judge, here is my offer of proof: After Dr. Sorensen told Anton Howell that head trauma patients can become unstable, my client became concerned when Jason's appearance began to change. Fearing his younger brother had developed an abnormal attraction to the netherworld of the homeless, my client hired a private investigator to monitor Jason's activities.

"Unfortunately, the investigator, Mr. Raymond Gorney, had a massive coronary while monitoring the respondent. In the confusion surrounding his untimely death, a member of his staff misplaced the photographs now before the court. Only yesterday, the film was discovered, developed, and turned over to the petitioner."

Sam pulled herself together and stood, "Your Honor, without Mr. Gorney here to authenticate these photographs, they're utterly lacking in foundation. But unfortunately the court has already seen them, and we cannot unring the bell. And if Your Honor has any inclination to consider these misleading and highly prejudicial photographs, I would ask for a continuance in order to call the individual pictured with Jason Howell, as well as other witnesses who will testify that these photographs simply document my client in the act of researching the viability of his plan."

Newman stood. In a most sincere tone he said, "Judge, I must remind the court that time is of the essence. To grant a continuance in order to allow the respondent to find homeless witnesses to parade before us will not only waste our time, but will also eliminate any hope my client has to recover his brother's estate.

"Unhappily, Mr. Gorney cannot introduce these photographs. However, if the court insists on authentication, we are fortunate to have someone present who can accomplish that for us." Newman turned from the judge and winked at Sam. "At this time I would like to recall Mr. Jason Howell to testify on behalf of the petitioner, and note for the record that he is a hostile witness . . . ."

TWENTY-EIGHT
Wednesday, February 22

1

MARTY LEANED on his shovel, took out a hand-kerchief, and wiped the sweat from his brow. The desert mornings were appreciably warmer now, almost too warm to be trenching a sprinkling system. But Stan had begged Marty to go outside and quit pestering the crew with a million questions.

Marty had to admit that Stan and the others were doing a great job. They had been working long hours without complaint, and everybody now had their own quarters. Although furnishings were sparse and the rooms were a far cry from what the Japanese had envisioned, everyone was ecstatic just to have privacy. And work had already begun on the additional housing the factory would need for the next group of thirty workers scheduled to arrive in just over a month.

In the casino area, walls had been built, and in spite of the red velvet drapes and the crystal chandeliers, the place was beginning to look like a factory. The only hitch had been a friendly disagreement between the men and the women over the color of the new walls. The men wanted eggshell white while the women insisted on a shade of rose that would better complement the drapes. The women prevailed.

The week started with a milestone. On Monday, Last Chance received the Cytex production contract for ten thousand reality engines with deliveries to begin on May 1. Upon the arrival of the contract, Marty no longer felt as if he and the others were simply playacting at living and working like regular people. He proudly shared the news with the crew, and their excited reactions told him they felt the same way.

And just yesterday two prototype C-REAL systems arrived. Next week the software from Cytex was expected. Then, during March, the crew would use the prototypes to manufacture additional workstations. By the end of the month, the bugs would be worked out of the assembly process, and fifty C-REAL enhanced reality systems would be up and running. That was the plan. Marty knew a lot could go wrong, but in his heart he believed they would pull it off.

Marty resumed trenching. He was worrying out a large rock when Ike walked up. "Excuse me, Boss, but you're wanted on the telephone. Man says it's urgent."

Marty stuck the shovel into the ground and jogged over to Ike's apartment. Sweating, he sat at Ike's dinette table, dabbed at his face with his handkerchief, and picked up the phone. "This is Marty Dubichek."

"Mr. Dubichek, I'm Arnold Stratton, the assistant manager at the Golden State Bank of Commerce in San Francisco. I'm calling about your line of credit."

"Yes?"

"I regret to inform you it has been canceled."

"W-What did you say?"

"Your line of credit has been terminated. The bank will no longer honor checks written on your account."

"Hold on a damn minute, Stratton!" Marty yelled into the phone. "There must be some mistake! I've got mouths to feed! I've got components and equipment arriving! I've got accounts payable!"

"I can assure you there's no mistake. You'll have to take the matter up with your guarantor, Crossfire Holdings. They have withdrawn the guarantee. There's nothing I can do. I'm sorry."

Marty slammed the phone down and stared at it in disbelief. Then he picked it up and dialed Cytex. Sally told him Jason was out of the office on personal business. Marty tried Jason's home number without success. Then he dialed Jason's car phone and got a recording saying it was not in service. Marty began wringing his hands. The next number he dialed was Sam Paxton's.

"Didn't Jason call you with the news?" Sam asked.

"NO! What the hell's going on?"

"Look, I don't know how to break it to you . . . but yesterday the court took away Jason's estate and turned it over to his brother, Anton."

"What! You mean he's lost everything?"

"I'm afraid so. A couple of weeks ago Anton Howell filed a petition for a conservatorship. He didn't think his brother had any chance, so Jason didn't bother you with it. At the hearing, Anton's attorney, Roger Newman, had these surveillance photographs that had been taken by a private investigator before he died of a heart attack. He used Jason to authenticate them. The court permitted Newman to treat him as a hostile witness, which allows all kinds of leading questions. Jason became angry and lost it on the stand. He was having one of his bad headaches."

Marty slumped in his seat. "That Gorney fellow was working for Jason's brother?"

"Yes. Anton claimed he hired the investigator to watch Jason out of concern for his well-being. But Jason says it was really because his brother suspected him of having an affair with his wife."

Marty dropped his forehead in his hand. After a pause he asked, "Ah . . . how is Jason?"

"Not good. Toward the end of the hearing his neck and face turned red and I thought he was going to have a stroke. Afterwards his neurologist, Dr. Sorensen, who was there as a witness, prescribed some sedatives. I offered to fill you in, but Jason said it was his responsibility. I'm surprised he hasn't called; perhaps he's still sedated."

"What's going to happen to Last Chance?"

"Honestly, it doesn't look good. Anton Howell will cancel your line of credit—"

"HE JUST DID!" Marty screamed, pounding the table with his fist. "You don't know all the work we've put in!"

"I'm sorry, Marty. I really am."

"Can't you stop it? Isn't there some legal thing . . . ?"

"I truly wish there were. I'd work for free. But as far as the court is concerned, Anton now *stands* in Jason's shoes. Technically, Anton has become my client. If I tried to help you, his attorney would have me disqualified as having a conflict of interest."

"Wait a damn minute! Are you saying any legal action we take against Anton is really against Jason?" Marty's eyes were as big as saucers.

"I'm afraid so. That's the way a conservatorship works. But if you retained another lawyer, I would be willing to help on the side."

"Holy shit! Without that credit line, where are we going to get the money to hire another lawyer?" Marty was in shock. He had been shouldering a great deal of weight for the last few weeks, and suddenly it had become overwhelming, crushing his body into his chair, choking off his voice. The receiver fell out of his hand.

"Marty, are you all right? Marty . . . ?"

2

"MARTY, ARE YOU ALL RIGHT?" Ike said, shaking the big man's shoulders. He had returned to his apartment to find Marty at the dinette table with his head in his hands. The phone was dangling from its cord and making loud off-hook noises. "What's going on? Maybe I can help."

"We've lost our credit line . . . our sponsor . . . everything . . . ."

Ike replaced the receiver. "Did something happen to Jason Howell?"

Marty looked at Ike. "How did you know Howell was our sponsor? That's confidential."

"When the bankruptcy trustee told me Last Chance had been sold to Crossfire Holdings, I was curious. So I called the Corporations Commissioner in Sacramento and learned that Jason Howell was president. I *am* a lawyer, remember? Now calmly tell me what you know."

Marty filled Ike in.

"What do you have in writing?" Ike asked.

"Documents that say they've got to back our loan."

"Where are they?"

"In my room . . . . I'll get them."

Feeling a slight glimmer of hope, Marty rose and opened the door. About to knock was a man wearing cowboy boots and a ten-gallon hat.

"They said I could find Martin Dubichek here."

"That's me."

The stranger pushed an envelope into Marty's hands and walked away.

Ike came over. "Let me see that."

Marty gave it to him. "What is it?"

Ike rubbed his temple while he stared at the document. After a moment he said, "An eviction notice."

3

"PEOPLE, PEOPLE, can we please settle down?" Marty begged. "It's no good if everyone talks at once." He was standing behind a table in Last Chance's makeshift cafeteria trying to gain control of the meeting.

"We'll make a stand with Ike's rifles!" Stan yelled. "I'm not leaving without a goddamn fight! This is my home now. I've got this paper to prove it!" Stan stood on a chair, waved his stock certificate, and shouted, "WACO! WACO!"

"WACO! WACO!" the crew chanted, waving their certificates.

"They'll have to burn us out," Sanchez said defiantly. "There'll be nothin' fuckin' left."

Ike approached Marty. "You've crashed and burned without even leaving the ground. Do you mind if I give it a try?"

Marty shrugged and stepped aside.

Ike took off a boot and pounded it on the table. "Now let's have some order! Quiet down, GODDAMN-IT!"

The group hushed.

"We have rights," Ike began. "First of all, under Nevada law, we've got forty-five days—until April 7—before the sheriff comes to evict us. That buys us some time."

"How come you know so much?" Willie asked.

"Although I haven't practiced lately, I'm a lawyer."

"No shit," Willie whistled.

Doc jumped in. "Ike, even if you find some way to keep us from getting evicted, the whole point of being here is to make high-tech widgets. Without funds, how are we going to finish the factory and begin production?"

"And how are we going to eat?" Willie wanted to know.

"At least in San Francisco we had food!" a woman shouted.

"Okay, simmer down," Ike said. "I've studied the agreements behind our credit line and I believe they're legally binding. I might be able to convince a judge."

"C'mon, Ike, get real," Doc said. "We can't wait here without supplies until some judge gets around to deciding our fate. We'll be mummified by then."

"The law has provisions for emergencies. If I can get to San Francisco, I'll go to court and ask for a temporary restraining order. If it's granted, the money will flow again, allowing us to continue the factory conversion. Down the line, after a bunch of procedural stuff, the case will go to trial. In the meantime we'll do our best to deliver product to Cytex and prove ourselves. In that event I'm certain we'll never have to leave Last Chance."

"How'ya gonna get to San Francisco?" Sanchez asked.

"That's a good question," Ike said, shaking his head. "The bearings in my pickup are shot and—"

A set of car keys came flying through the air and landed on the table in front of Ike.

Everyone turned. They hadn't noticed a man with a cane slouching against the wall near the door.

"I'll be damned," Stan said, "if it ain't Happy."

TWENTY-NINE
Thursday, February 23

1

ÉJÀ VU, Marty thought as he stood at the entrance
to his suite, flashing back to his first day at the
Petaluma State Hospital. Only this time it was
Jason who would wake up disoriented, dehydrated, and
depressed; this time it was Jason who had lost everything.

Balancing a breakfast tray against his hip, Marty held
his key card against the wall sensor and the twin doors
swung open. He walked through the lavishly-furnished
model living room and rapped lightly on the bedroom
door. He waited a moment and entered the darkened
room. He found Jason in bed with his hands behind his
head, gazing at the ceiling. On the nightstand a prescrip-
tion bottle was on its side, with pills scattered about. His
cane was lying on the floor.

"How are we feeling today?" Marty asked, trying to
sound cheerful.

Jason slowly propped himself up and looked vaguely
at the big man.

Marty set the breakfast tray on the bed near Jason and touched the glowing screen of the control unit. The draperies drew aside and flooded the room with the bright rays of early morning. Marty stepped up to the window and looked at the Dead Mountains. At this hour only the top half of the mountains were illuminated. As he watched, the sunlit portion appeared to elongate, as if the Dead Mountains were alive and growing out of its own shadow.

After a long moment he turned from the window and approached the bed. "It's Thursday morning," he said, trying to anticipate what might be on his friend's mind. "You slept through Wednesday."

Jason remained motionless. In the morning light his eyes were flat, almost lifeless. Marty had seen that look on the street many times. It made him think of Annie.

Keep talking to him like George did in Petaluma, Marty told himself. He took a pillow and placed it behind Jason's back. "Go ahead, eat something," he urged. "I'll fill you in on your lost day. Come to think of it, that seems to be a recurring role for me."

Jason looked impassively at Marty and slowly reached for the orange juice.

Marty sat on the bed. "After I tucked you in here, I went back to the meeting. I told Ike to use your condo when he got to San Francisco. I hope you don't mind, but our travel and entertainment budget is pretty slim at the moment."

Jason took a bite of English muffin, chewing without enthusiasm. "You'll have to ask the condo's owner for permission."

"Last night Ike called when he arrived in San Francisco. He'll be meeting with your attorney this morning to map out a strategy to get your brother to honor the contract."

Jason stopped chewing for a moment. Marty thought he detected a tiny spark in his friend's eyes.

"While Ike was enroute," Marty continued, "I told the crew that you—Happy—had driven all night and were exhausted. After you rested, I'd find out what you were doing here. I stalled because I couldn't reveal you're our sponsor."

"I'm not your sponsor," Jason muttered. "The game is over. Tell them the truth. Tell them I've lost everything. Tell them the reason I came here was to join you and the rest of the world's losers."

"I wouldn't be so sure about that," Marty said.

Jason sipped coffee and gazed absently at the Dead Mountains.

"When the bank cut us loose," Marty went on, "I became more depressed than I've ever been. Even more than Petaluma, if you can believe that. But I quickly got over it. You know why? Because this time I don't have to face things alone. This time I've got Ike and a bunch of other people who'll stand with me to fight for what's rightfully ours. That's what you've got, too."

Jason pushed his tray away.

Marty picked up the remaining half of Jason's English muffin and took a bite. "Then I ended the meeting by telling the crew to press forward with the factory conversion. Precious hours have been lost."

"What's the food and supplies situation?"

"Frankly, it's critical. But if Ike's successful, we can still make our deadline and then we'll be a nice, peaceful factory. Otherwise, your brother is going to face a gang of armed and desperate people who have nowhere to go and nothing to lose."

2

IKE NERVOUSLY INSPECTED himself in an antique mirror hanging on the wall in the reception area. Staring back was someone slimmer, tanner, and healthier looking than the alcoholic who escaped the legal profession three years ago. He was dressed in one of Jason's expensive suits, and his hair was neatly combed and trimmed. The man in the mirror looked as though he could slay dragons. That made Ike even more nervous; he knew Jason's attorney would expect a lot from him.

He was adjusting his tie when an attractive woman approached. "You must be Ike Abrams," she said, smiling warmly and firmly shaking hands. "I'm Sam. Tell me how Jason's doing. I had no idea he went to Last Chance. He was supposed to call Marty and go to bed."

Ike was staring wide-eyed at this classy woman. In the excitement of yesterday, no one had told him that "Sam" was a female. Caught off guard, it took a moment for his brain to order his mouth to speak. "Uh . . . Jason's not doing too well," Ike managed. "When I called Last Chance this morning, I learned he had been sleeping for the last twenty-four hours."

Sam's expression turned somber. "I advised him not to go into his hearing without corroborating witnesses, so I shouldn't feel responsible for what happened, but I do. I'd like to do something to cheer him up."

"Do you have something in mind?"

"As a matter-of-fact I do," she said with a distant look in her eyes. "I'm working on it . . . but let's not get sidetracked; we need to focus on today's motion."

Ike followed Sam into her office. "Before we get started, I have a confession to make," he said. "I haven't been before a judge in over three years. And the flask of vodka I kept in my briefcase was the last thing I remember about practicing law. I don't know if I can argue effectively anymore."

"Don't worry, Mr. Abrams."

"Call me Ike."

"Okay, Ike. The practice of law is something an attorney never forgets . . . like riding a bicycle."

"Or, in my case, falling off one."

Sam smiled. Then she retrieved a folder from her desk. "With regard to being forgetful, I must ask you to forget where you learned the information I'm about to share with you. As you know, I technically represent Anton's interests, and that makes us adversaries." She began to open the file.

Ike placed his hand on hers. "Seeing your file won't be necessary. I've reviewed Marty's copies of the contracts, and perhaps all I'll need is some informal advice between friendly adversaries." Ike removed his hand and noticed Sam's ring finger was bare. He took a breath. "In return for your help, please have dinner with me. Naturally, you'll have to pay."

"It's a date," Sam said, smiling again. "Now if you use that charm on the judge, you'll do just fine."

3

HIS SPIRITS LIFTED, Ike drove to the underground parking garage at the Civic Center. He crossed the street and walked by the flashing martini sign of the Jury Room. It was late in the afternoon and the bar was brimming with trial lawyers, drinking and talking loudly.

For the first time since law school, Ike had no desire to join them. Instead he went directly to the county clerk's office at City Hall where he was assigned Superior Court Judge Morton Harbold. Ike recalled appearing before the judge in the past and his recollection was that Harbold was both smart and fair.

Ike paced in the hallway outside the judge's chambers, waiting for Harbold to complete his calendar. He clutched a leather satchel he had borrowed from Sam.

At 4:45 p.m. a door opened and the court clerk motioned him inside. Ike found himself facing a luxuriant mane of white hair. The judge was at his desk, head down, engrossed in a legal brief. He was in his shirt sleeves with his tie hanging loosely around his neck. His black robe and a tweed jacket with leather elbow patches hung on a coat rack in a corner of the room. File folders, paperwork, and legal newspapers were piled haphazardly everywhere.

Ike cleared his throat. "Pardon me, Your Honor, my name is Ike Abrams."

Judge Harbold looked up and recognition filled his eyes. "Yes, Ike, how are you?" he asked sincerely. "I haven't seen you in quite some time." The judge stood and shook hands. "You're looking fit."

"I've been on . . . an extended sabbatical."

"Did you a world of good. Could use one myself. Have a seat. What can I do for you?"

Ike removed a stack of files from a chair and sat down. "I'm here on behalf of my client, Last Chance Corporation," he said, nervously pulling papers from his satchel. "Earlier this month they entered into a contract with another company, Crossfire Holdings. As part of the agreement, Crossfire secured a bank line for the benefit of my client." Ike handed the judge a copy of the contract with the relevant paragraphs highlighted in yellow.

Judge Harbold read in silence.

When the judge looked up, Ike said, "Relying on this contract, my client hired a crew, gave each of them an ownership position in the corporation, and transported them to a partially-completed resort in the Nevada desert. They have been converting the resort into a high-tech factory with integrated living quarters.

"For the last three weeks both Last Chance Corporation and Crossfire Holdings have honored their commitments. But just yesterday"—Ike paused to take a breath— "my client was notified by its bank that Crossfire had terminated the credit line."

Judge Harbold glanced at the signature page and set the contract down.

Ike placed another document in front of the judge. "Your Honor, this is a proposed temporary restraining order that will force Crossfire to abide by its contract until we can get the matter straightened out."

Judge Harbold ignored the order and looked at Ike. "Counsel, you're here *ex parte* to seek a TRO to enforce an agreement. This is a highly unusual request, and one that is rarely granted. Tell me why you can't simply litigate the matter and go after contract damages?"

"Because there's an immediate public safety issue involved. The employees of Last Chance Corporation are former homeless people who have a unique opportunity to prove they can assemble sophisticated products in competition with overseas labor." Ike handed the judge a copy of the Cytex contract. "The workers are in a run-off competition with a Korean manufacturer. If my clients prevail—as I'm convinced they will—additional assembly contracts will follow to make the enterprise both enduring and successful. A large number of government-sponsored ventures are expected to spring from this model."

Judge Harbold scanned the production contract.

Ike waited a moment and said, "In order to win the competition, the initial crew, twenty men and women, must get the facility ready to accommodate thirty additional workers by the beginning of April. But even if we put aside the urgency created by the production contract, and even if the current crew had transportation to return them to San Francisco—which they do not—they have no money, no place to go, and they're running low on food."

Judge Harbold looked at Ike. "You're aware of the requirement to give the other party reasonable notice before coming here. Did you do that?"

"No, Your Honor. I was at Last Chance yesterday when the bank called. Then I spent the rest of the day driving here. I didn't learn the identity of Crossfire's counsel until a short time ago."

"And who might that be?"

"Roger Newman."

Judge Harbold eyebrows arched. He leaned his elbows on his desk and cupped his hands. "Ike, it has been my experience contracts are broken for a reason. What reason would opposing counsel give if he were here?"

Ike explained that the president of Crossfire Holdings, Jason Howell, lost his estate to his brother. "I expect the conservator would claim fiduciary duty."

"I appreciate your candor, Ike. Now tell me if the workers at the desert factory have enough food to get through the weekend."

"Yes, Your Honor . . . barely."

"All right then, because of the unusual nature of this case and the complex issues involved, I am going to give the other side a chance to present their position. Therefore, I'm going to deny your *ex parte* motion."

"But—"

Judge Harbold held up his hand while looking at his calendar. "However, I invite you to resubmit your motion, and I'll hear it at four o'clock on Monday afternoon." The judge looked at Ike. "And this time you'll provide proper notice to Mr. Newman, won't you?"

"Yes, Your Honor."

.

4

WHILE THEY WAITED for dinner, Stan was being tutored by Crazy Eddie. For the first two weeks of night school, Stan had been preoccupied with his construction responsibilities and wasn't absorbing his lessons on electrical assembly techniques. But under Crazy Eddie's private tutelage, Stan was coming up to speed.

Marty entered the cafeteria with Jason in tow and sat him next to Stan. Then Marty went to the front of the room and rapped a spoon loudly against a water glass, causing heads to lift and conversations to cease.

"I just spoke to Ike," he announced to the crew. "He met with a judge who's sympathetic to our situation. There'll be a hearing on Monday afternoon. Ike's optimistic we're going to get our money released."

A murmur broke out in the room followed by restrained applause.

"Ike's also consulting with the attorney who wrote the contracts. She's helping us on the side. In fact, she's sending a plane to take me to San Francisco on Saturday so Ike can prepare me to testify. Crazy Eddie is going along to make preparations for his assembly classes in San Francisco. I've already talked to St. Andrews and arranged for him to discuss the rental of the central hall during the day."

Crazy Eddie stood and bowed.

The room buzzed.

"In the meantime," Marty continued, "we'll have to ration our food. It'll be rice and beans again for dinner."

Everyone groaned.

Marty rejoined Stan's table and sat opposite Jason. Stan leaned toward Marty. "Rice and beans, eh? I hope Happy here ain't feeling spastic again tonight. I got on my best fatigues."

"Don't worry, Stan, Happy's motor functions are improving all the time."

Stan had a flurry of questions: "So what's he doing here? Was he also cut loose by the sponsor?"

"I guess you could say that," Marty replied.

Stan aimed a make-believe rifle. "If I ever set my sights on the bastard, whoever he is—"

"Happy's our sponsor," Marty interrupted.

"Former sponsor," Jason corrected, not looking up.

Stan's mouth dropped and he stared at Jason in wide-eyed disbelief. "He's our sponsor? He talks? What the fuck . . . ?"

Marty quickly explained that Happy was really Jason Howell, the president of Cytex, and how he and Pete found him in a doorway after his airplane crashed in Golden Gate Park. Happy injured his head and suffered from amnesia. After he became Jason Howell again he wanted to help the people who helped him, so he set up Last Chance.

Marty further explained that Jason's brother took control of the property after he tricked the court into thinking Jason had gone crazy. In deference to Jason's feelings, Marty didn't elaborate and wouldn't answer further questions. "I'll tell you the rest of the story some other time."

Stan's eyes were as big as saucers. "I'll be damned," he kept saying as he stared at Jason.

"Dinner's ready!" Doc announced, ringing a bell. He and Sanchez were on kitchen duty, and they had set out large bowls. Marty brought Jason's food back to the table while Stan and Crazy Eddie were still in line.

"Is it okay for me and Crazy Eddie to use your condo when we're in San Francisco?" Marty asked.

Jason shrugged. "If the lock hasn't been changed."

"So how did you like my announcement to the crew?"

Jason stared at his hands. "You put a hell of a positive spin on a completely fucked-up situation. You turned out to be a true manager. At least that was one thing I was right about."

"Well, I did choose my words carefully. It'll make it easier to get everyone through the weekend. Anyway, Ike did seem optimistic even though his first attempt to get the restraining order failed."

Jason looked up and stared coldly at Marty. "Just wait until you see Anton's attorney in action. My brother is right. I *must* be crazy to think that a bunch of bums could prevail against the pros in the real world."

THIRTY
Saturday, February 25

1

JASON SAT in Marty's suite, staring out of the picture window. The sun was dipping toward the Dead Mountains, blurring its ridges in the shadows of late afternoon. But Jason wasn't focused on the view. He was turned inward, his thoughts running in a narrow range between desperation and despair.

This morning Marty succeeded in getting him out of bed and into a T-shirt and slacks. But the big man had no luck in involving his friend in the work at Last Chance. All Jason wanted to do was sit on the living room couch and gaze at the Dead Mountains. At the moment he was reflecting on how Anton had finessed Liz, Last Chance, his condo—even his meadow. And he made it look so damn easy.

Behind him someone was rapping gently on the door.

"It's not locked," Jason said in a monotone.

"You chose a beautiful spot to watch the sunset," said a familiar voice.

Jason abruptly turned. Liz was standing in the doorway, dressed in jeans, a blue cotton blouse, and a brown suede jacket. She held a small overnight case in one hand.

"Liz . . . what are you doing here?"

"As a hotel professional, I couldn't pass an opportunity to visit such a fine resort. Nice suite. May I join you?"

"Y-yes, sure."

Liz set the suitcase down, took off her jacket, and sat on the couch next to Jason. She stared at the view while he stared at her. The sun had fallen behind the mountains, leaving the sky royal blue with a tinge of orange that bathed Liz in a golden light. Jason kept staring at her, alternating between inhaling her fragrance and pinching himself. "I didn't hear the airplane arrive," he finally said. "How was your flight?"

Liz smiled. "Just great. That Vinnie—what a character! I now know the history of every tree and rock between here and San Francisco. Have you ever heard of wine from Fresno?"

Jason grinned, and it suddenly dawned on him that the last time he had smiled was the last time he was with Liz, nearly a month ago. "How did you know I was here?"

"Sam called and told me. She said she was sending a plane to pick up Marty, and I jumped at the chance to visit you. She also filled me in on Anton's treachery. I'm truly sorry. She's trying to get you another hearing."

"That could take some time," Jason said. "It's only been four days since the last one. But it seems like an eternity."

Liz took Jason's hand and rotated to face him, her eyes filled with concern. "You're going through hell, aren't you?"

"If you define hell as being unable to live in your skin."

Liz nodded sympathetically.

"Just minutes ago I was sitting here, thinking about how stupid I was to believe that my time on the street, the Crossfire, and our conversations with Marty, gave me *any* idea of what it's really like to lose everything. But do you know what? I didn't have a clue, not an inkling. Nothing I've ever experienced prepared me for this. My entire world has been turned upside down."

"Then we'll have to right it, won't we?"

"What about Anton?"

"Fuck Anton—and not in the biblical sense, either."

Hatred flashed in Liz's eyes, and Jason now knew the high price his brother had paid.

She took his other hand and shifted so that their knees touched, and he felt a tingling sensation at the point of contact. She gazed into his eyes. "Jason, you need to know something. After Anton told me he had offered you a partnership, I seriously considered reconciling— especially when I hadn't heard from you. And had you accepted his offer, I would have gone back to him. Do you know why?"

Jason shook his head no.

"In order to be near you."

Tears suddenly welled up in Jason's eyes and streamed down his cheeks. As he embraced Liz, his tears trans-formed into laugher.

"What . . . ?" Liz said, startled by Jason's abrupt swing in emotions.

He broke the embrace, held her shoulders at arm's length and looked into her eyes. "*I* was planning to accept Anton's offer just to be near *you*. If Last Chance hadn't intervened, that's exactly what would have happened."

Liz took Jason's head in both hands and kissed him long and passionately. When they finally broke, she smiled enticingly.

Jason read it and said, "But I promised Marty I would sit here and not go back to bed. I gave him my word."

"Marty's on his way to San Francisco," she countered. "I won't tell."

Jason stood, took Liz's hand, and led her into the bedroom, stopping at the foot of the bed. The room was dark so he let go of her hand and went over to the control panel on the nightstand. As the drapes motored opened, he saw her reaching for the top button of her blouse. "No," he said softly. "Keep your hands at your sides. I've fantasized about this moment too many times."

Liz did as she was told. She stood with her back to the window, her hair aglow in the orange light of dusk.

He approached her and slowly unfastened her buttons, one by one. He separated the halves of the blouse and let the material slide to the floor. Then he unclasped her bra, pulling it away from her body. She stood there, her chest rising and falling, her head tilted slightly, looking at him expectantly, watching and waiting.

He took a step back and admired her firm breasts and the upward tilt of her nipples. His eyes returned to her face. Even in the golden light, she appeared to be blushing.

Jason pulled off his T-shirt and stepped closer, using his hands to gently brush her hair back from her face. He was admiring her high cheekbones, the flare of her nostrils, the slight dimple in her chin. She held his gaze. He took her by her waist and pulled her close to him, and she threw her head back and offered her neck. Their bare chests touched, sending heat to his loins. Taking a deep breath, he kissed her neck, tasted her perfumed earlobe, and advanced across her soft cheeks to her mouth.

While kissing Liz, Jason explored her breasts with his hands, gently holding them, memorizing their curves, marveling at their firmness and the electricity her nipples sent through his fingertips. He lowered his right hand to the snap on her jeans. He couldn't release the snap with one hand so he brought the other down to help. Suddenly her arms came alive and he felt her hands gripping his waist. She shoved firmly and he fell backwards onto the bed.

"What was that for?" he asked breathlessly, propping himself on his elbows.

"That's enough of your fantasy," she said, smiling impishly. "Now it's time for mine."

She bent over and unbuckled his belt. Jason became transfixed at the sight of her breasts jiggling over the bulge in his pants. She unzipped his fly and pulled his remaining clothes off, smoothly and efficiently. Then she stepped out of her platform shoes and wriggled out of her jeans. She stood there for him, red hair slightly disheveled, her body bare except for lace panties.

Liz held him with her eyes, watching Jason become more and more aroused. Then she slipped out of her panties and joined him in bed, kissing him all over his body. Jason's elbows jellied and he collapsed as her lips explored him.

In his fantasy, Jason had planned to do the same to her. But it was too late for that now; he was dangerously close to orgasm. Reaching down, he gently lifted her head. She understood and repositioned herself along side of him, bringing her face next to his.

He kissed her softly this time, stalling, trying to contain the volcano raging in his loins. But Liz wouldn't cooperate. She kissed him passionately on his face and neck, biting his lips and his ear lobes, wrapping her arms and legs around him, digging her nails into his back. She maneuvered him on top of her, and he could feel her moving rhythmically under him. Out of desperation he clenched his fists and curled his toes, searching for some vestige of self-control.

He could find none.

She spread her legs, rotated her hips, and drew him into a moist warm world, a place where every movement, every muscle contraction, every shudder, brought him closer to ecstasy.

"Wait . . . stop," he pleaded.

Liz, breathing heavily, didn't seem to hear. Moaning, she arched her torso, coaxing him deeper inside her.

Jason's heart was pounding so hard he was certain it was about to fail.

He didn't care.

In less than ten minutes, he had gone from despair to euphoria. His mind reeled, and he could no longer distinguish between pleasure and pain.

He didn't care.

Arching his back and tightening his buttocks, he probed deeper and faster. She, too, arched her body to receive his long stroking movements, squeezing him with her muscles to keep him inside her, holding him captive in a place unlike any he had experienced, a place of peak sensation, a place where the body had dominion over the mind, a place where souls entwined. By now, Jason's rational mind had become oblivious to everything but the awareness that Liz was in the midst of an intense climax. His last thought as he, too, swept over the summit, was that wherever he landed there would be no turning back.

THIRTY-ONE
Monday, February 27

1

MARTY AND IKE were the first to enter Judge Harbold's courtroom. Marty had never been in court before, and everything about the wood-paneled room made him nervous—the judge's bench, the jury box, the witness stand, the Great Seal of California hanging high on the far wall.

And it didn't help that the room was too warm.

Marty wanted to remove his blazer but he figured that would be inappropriate. He followed Ike to the plaintiffs' table and took a seat.

"I wish Sam could be here," Ike said, admitting to his own case of nerves. "I don't know why, but I have this gnawing feeling that the other side is going to drop a bomb on us."

Marty rubbed sweaty palms together. "Please, no bomb-talk. If the judge so much as looks at me cross-eyed, I'm going to soil myself."

The rear door opened slowly, and a metal crutch poked through. Crazy Eddie eased into the room in two large steps. Like Ike, he had borrowed his attire from Jason's wardrobe. But on Crazy Eddie, Jason's clothes were too large and he looked like he was wearing a zoot suit. He glanced around the room, and upon seeing his friends, tiptoed over. "I just came from St. Andrews," he whispered as if he were in church. "They'll rent us their central hall during March. It's perfecto," he said, making an "O" out of his thumb and forefinger. "Word is out and there's a whole bunch of street folks wanting to enroll."

"That's nice," Marty replied between calming breaths. "Now all we have to do is win."

Crazy Eddie's fingers changed to the thumbs up sign, and he turned to leave.

"You can sit here with us if you want," Ike offered. "You're a plaintiff, too, you know."

The old man did an abrupt about-face. He slid his crutch under the table, pushed his sleeves back so his hands poked through, lifted his coattail, and took a chair to the right of Marty.

The three men sat in silence.

Suddenly the rear door burst open and Crazy Eddie flinched. Anton and his attorney stormed in, marching down the aisle like military officers. They stopped at the defendant's table to banter and backslap, acting as if they were alone in the courtroom.

Ike tapped the point of his pencil on the table and stared straight ahead while Marty sized up their opponents. "Those slick fellows look like they came out of central casting," the big man commented under his breath.

Crazy Eddie squinted across the room at Anton. "That fella looks like a clean-shaven version of Happy—only bigger."

"And meaner," Ike added.

A few minutes passed and the court staff shuffled in from a side door and settled at their stations. The bailiff began his chant in a monotone: "All-rise-the-Superior-

Court-for-the-County-of-San-Francisco-is-now-in-session. Honorable-Morton-Harbold-presiding."

Judge Harbold walked in briskly from his chambers, his black robes flowing behind him. He paused to acknowledge the parties in the courtroom and then assumed his place at the bench. "Please be seated. Now in the matter of Last Chance Corporation versus Crossfire Holdings, will Counsel please identify themselves for the record?"

"Ike Abrams for the plaintiff, Your Honor."

"Roger Newman for the defendant."

The judge opened a file and read aloud, "Plaintiff Last Chance Corporation is seeking a temporary restraining order to cause defendant Crossfire Holdings to perform on a contract." Then he looked at Ike. "You're first, Mr. Abrams."

Ike stood and cleared his throat. "Yes, thank you, Your Honor. As I stated in my papers, the shareholders of Last Chance Corporation, twenty homeless men and women, left San Francisco and traveled to a remote location in the Nevada desert based on an employment agreement. Besides jobs, this agreement promised food and shelter, all of which were made possible by a credit line guaranteed by defendant Crossfire Holdings.

"Your Honor, Crossfire suddenly directed my client's bank to terminate that line of credit. It was done unilaterally, without notice, without just cause, and in clear violation of the terms of defendant's covenant with Last Chance." Ike's voice was cracking and he paused to take a sip of water.

Newman seized the moment. "Judge," he said, standing, "as I stated in *my* papers, the plaintiff has no right to this hearing. The California Code of Civil Procedure clearly bars a restraining order to enforce a contract. These . . . ah, homeless persons are wasting the court's time." Newman sat down.

"How do you propose to get around our Code of Civil Procedure, Mr. Abrams?" Judge Harbold asked.

"Your Honor, through an exception that allows the court latitude to grant a TRO if the defendant causes the plaintiff to breach a contract with a third party. In this case, the actions of Crossfire Holdings are preventing my client from performing on its production contract with Cytex, and from fulfilling its agreements with its employees. Furthermore, the proceeds from the production contract are necessary to repay my client's bank loan. Thus, defendant's actions have caused not one, but *three* third party breaches."

Newman stood. "Judge, there is no breach with the bank since they have a lien on the property, and they will be repaid when it is sold. My client has executed an agreement with a buyer, a Japanese businessman. Escrow will close when the squatters quit the property. This they can do voluntarily, or when the sheriff forcibly evicts them on April 7.

"Furthermore, there are no other contract breaches since there is no functioning factory. All we have is a band of derelicts in the desert, occupying an unfinished resort. At the moment the only thing these beggars are fabricating is an incredible cover story to allow them to bleed my client dry. They will never deliver anything to anybody."

Marty's face grew red. He clenched his fists, pushed his chair back, and started to stand. Crazy Eddie quickly grabbed the big man's shoulder and pulled him down.

"Objection!" Ike said. "I object to the slandering of my clients by calling them derelicts and beggars!"

Newman turned to face Ike. "I *beg* your pardon," he said smugly.

Judge Harbold looked annoyed. "Mr. Newman, please confine your argument to legal issues and refrain from negative characterizations. Your wit is not appreciated." Then he addressed Ike. "As for you, Mr. Abrams, you'll need to do better than the mere prospect of a third party breach."

"Yes, Your Honor," Ike replied as he referred to his notes. "This court can also grant a restraining order to avoid the sanctioning of a fraud. My clients have been seduced into the desert and then abandoned by the fraudulent acts of Crossfire Holdings."

Newman stood and sighed. "Look, Judge, when my client terminated the line of credit last week, he was simply fulfilling his obligation as a court-appointed conservator. In that capacity, he has the fiduciary responsibility to protect his brother's substantial estate. He was unaware that Jason Howell had sent the poor beg . . . ah, these naïve and unfortunate individuals . . . into the desert. As the court knows, there cannot be fraud without knowledge or intent."

"I disagree," Ike argued. "As conservator, Anton Howell now stands in his brother's shoes and is therefore accountable for all acts of Crossfire Holdings, past, present, and future. Furthermore, defendant's fraud will result in more than the loss of my clients' livelihood—without food, money, or transportation, they're facing the loss of their lives. The defendant won't have to evict them if he can kill them first."

Judge Harbold looked at Newman.

"Judge, in spite of what Counsel says, my client is not a heartless man. He is prepared to dispatch a bus loaded with food. A rolling soup kitchen, if you will. After these unwitting victims of his brother's ill-conceived scheme are fed, he will transport them back to San Francisco. That charitable act will remove any urgency there may be in this matter, while eliminating the need for a restraining order. The plaintiffs are then free to litigate and seek money damages, if they are foolish enough to attempt it."

Judge Harbold looked at Ike.

"Your Honor, as an officer of the court, I'll represent to you that these 'unwitting victims' will not voluntarily leave their homes and jobs. At this time, I request the court's permission to allow testimony from Martin Dubichek, president of Last Chance Corporation. He'll describe the status of the factory and explain why this matter cannot be resolved by the simple dispatch of a bus."

Judge Harbold nodded. "Proceed."

Marty stood. He flicked a bead of sweat from his temple and then nervously flexed his hands as if he were about to take a hand-off from a quarterback. Ike leaned over and whispered, "Just remember what we rehearsed."

Marty was sworn in and testified that the initial crew of twenty men and women had labored day and night to convert the unfinished resort at Last Chance into a state-of-the-art production facility. They were only one month away from completion. It would be tight, but they could still meet their contractual commitment to Cytex if their line of credit were restored immediately. Marty answered haltingly at first, but as time passed he became more relaxed. Crazy Eddie kept nodding and smiling his approval.

"And so, Mr. Dubichek," Ike said, "would you and your co-workers have a roof over your heads if you abandoned your homes at Last Chance and returned to San Francisco?"

"No. Most of us came from shelters. We'd have to reapply. Because of the enormous demand, it could take months, even years."

"In the meantime, where would you live?"

Marty turned and pointed at the window. "Across the street, in the plaza."

Ike moved closer to Marty. "Mr. Dubichek, are you and the other employee-shareholders of Last Chance going to give up your jobs and your homes in order to live in the Civic Center Plaza?"

Marty turned and looked squarely at Anton. "Over our dead bodies."

Crazy Eddie lightly clapped his hands together.

"No further questions," Ike said, returning to his seat.

"Cross, Mr. Newman?"

Newman whispered something to Anton. Then he looked up and said, "Not at this time."

This caught Ike off guard—something was going on.

Judge Harbold turned to Marty. "Mr. Dubichek, you may step down. But remember you're still under oath and subject to recall."

Marty nodded and joined Ike and Crazy Eddie.

Meanwhile Anton and Newman continued to whisper. Anton nodded and Newman stood. "Judge, I must confess that my client and I found Mr. Dubichek's testimony enlightening. Anton Howell now appreciates the unfortunate plight of these people whose hopes and expectations have been cruelly elevated by the well-intentioned, albeit misguided actions of his mentally incompetent brother. In spite of the fact that we have great difficulty swallowing the notion of street people turning a gambling resort into a high-tech factory, we had not realized how strongly they feel about their desert domicile. Therefore, before we consume any more of the court's valuable time, may I suggest that we take a short recess to have the parties meet and confer. Perhaps we can settle this matter amicably."

"What do you have in mind?" Judge Harbold inquired.

Ike leaned toward Marty and whispered, "Hold on to your wallet."

"Here comes the bomb," Marty whispered back.

"I smell it," Crazy Eddie said, holding his nose.

Newman approached the bench. In a most sincere voice he said, "Judge, upon close of escrow with our Japanese buyer, my client will pay a quarter of a million dollars directly to the men and women of Last Chance. This gesture will more than compensate them for their trouble and help them to get back on their feet."

All three jaws at the plaintiff's table dropped together.

Ike recovered first. "Holy shit," he whispered, "Anton's having Newman bias the judge against us while using Jason's own money to buy off the crew. It's the old 'divide and conquer' scheme. It's brilliant."

Judge Harbold stood and stretched. "Interesting proposition, Mr. Newman. Settlement is always a good idea. The court will take a thirty-minute recess while the parties confer."

"Thank you, Judge," Newman said, flashing a white-toothed smile.

2

STAN AND SANCHEZ were in the converted casino area, wrestling with one of the prototype systems Cytex had shipped. The men had placed the reality engine and the computer on a bench along with a keyboard and a color monitor. Everything had been interconnected according to the diagram Greg Thompson had sent, but nothing worked. They were worried because the production software would be arriving shortly, and they needed to load and test it in the real world of the factory—assuming they still had a factory after today's hearing in San Francisco.

Stan sat on a chair and fitted the visor. "I don't see nothing," he grumbled. "What's wrong? Do something, Sanchez."

Sanchez typed on the keyboard. "How 'bout now?"

"Nah, just blackness. You got it hooked up right?"

Sanchez shrugged. "Yeah, I think so . . . I doubled-checked everything three times."

"I wish Marty was here," Stan said. "He knows how to work this damn thing."

Someone approached from behind. "What are you guys up to?"

Stan pulled off the visor. "Well, if it ain't Happy. And you d-o-o-o look happy today."

"Can ya blame him?" Sanchez said. "I'd give my left nut for a weekend with Red."

"I only had to give up my estate," Jason said.

"So where's Red at?" Sanchez asked.

"Liz went exploring. She hasn't had a chance to look around. I've been monopolizing her."

"I'll bet," Sanchez said winking and poking Stan in the ribs with an elbow.

"Any word from court?" Jason asked.

"Nope," Stan replied. "But they only got going a little while ago. Doc is standing by the phone."

"Can you help us with this C-REAL engine?" Sanchez asked. "All Stan gets is *nada*."

"That's the story of my life."

Jason picked up the visor. "You had it upside down. These round buttons on the top are motion detectors. You have to keep them face up; otherwise the system won't work. It's a safety feature. You don't want to be immersed in a realistic virtual world with up and down, and left and right reversed. Trust me."

Stan sat in the chair and donned the visor properly.

"Now let's see what demo software is in here," Jason said, typing in a command. The monitor displayed:

DRAGONS & DINOSAURS, VERSION 3.0.

"Am I going into the stomach?" Stan asked.

Jason typed in another command. "No, I think you'll find this more to your liking."

Sanchez leaned in toward the monitor. "Does he see anything yet?"

Jason looked at message on the screen. "Yes."

Stan started squirming in his seat. Then he began ducking this way and that, flailing his arms and yelling. The commotion attracted several of the crew. Their faces quickly transformed from quizzical to amused. Soon they were doubled over laughing.

"What the fuck's he doing?" Sanchez asked Jason.

"Meeting his first dragon."

Stan suddenly froze with his knees up and his body curled into the fetal position. He was making mewing sounds. Jason pushed the spacebar key.

Stan pulled the visor off, unfolded his body and sat up. He was red-faced and sweating. "Holy shit," he exhaled.

Jason pulled a pistol-like device out of the shipping carton. It had a cable coming from the grip and he plugged it into a connector at the rear of the reality engine. He handed the gun to Stan. "This will level the playing field. But remember to watch the sky behind you. There's a hungry pterodactyl flying around."

Stan licked his lips and put the visor back on. This time he remained standing with his legs spread and arms extended, using both hands to steady the gun. "HIT IT!" he yelled.

Jason pushed the spacebar key and Stan's body bolted. By now, the entire crew had gathered around. Muffled explosions came out of the visor's headphones as Stan whipped his body to and fro, up and down, pulling the trigger. He threw off so much energy that people in the crowd reflexively ducked when he pointed the pistol in their direction. A huge grin formed on Stan's face.

After a few minutes, Jason pushed the spacebar key again and Stan lowered the pistol. He removed the visor and looked at Jason. "C-o-o-l," he said, exhaling and flopping into the chair.

"Uh . . . can I go next?" Sanchez asked, hesitantly.

"Then me," Willie chimed in.

Jason nodded. "Sure, everybody can have—"

Suddenly Doc came jogging over. "I have Marty on the phone," he said, pausing to catch his breath. "We don't have much time."

Stan jumped up. "Time for what?"

"Everyone gather around," Doc said, waving his arms. "Happy's brother wants to settle with us."

"What do you mean?" Willie asked.

"If we agree to leave, he'll send a bus and pay us a quarter of a million dollars."

"What!" Stan exclaimed, falling back into the chair.

"You're shitting me," Willie said. "What's the catch?"

Doc looked at his watch. "We have to let Marty know before he goes back into the courtroom. He's keeping the line open. We have twenty minutes left; after that the deal's off the table."

"What does Marty recommend?" Sanchez asked.

"He said we have to vote. If we decide to turn the deal down it should be unanimous."

"Why unanimous?" Willie asked.

"Because the only way Last Chance can succeed is if we're 110 percent committed—all of us."

Stan pulled himself back to his feet and looked around. "Hey, where'd Happy go?" Then he spotted Jason standing apart from the crowd. The group separated to allow Stan to approach Jason and then reformed around the two men. "Is this deal for real?" Stan asked.

"Yes," Jason said.

"What should we do?"

"Like the man says, take a vote."

Stan was biting his nails. "We sure could do a lot with two hundred and fifty grand."

"Indeed."

"But can we make more if we stay here?"

"Perhaps, but not without a great deal of work and risk. My brother is offering you a sure thing."

Sanchez was counting on his fingers. "That's . . . twelve thousand each, more than a year's wages."

"Yeah," Stan said, regaining his composure. "But once the money's gone, it's gone. A year from now—or sooner—most of our sorry asses will be back on the street."

"Fifteen minutes," Doc warned, staring at his watch.

"But if we don't take the deal and we get evicted," Willie argued, "then we'll either be dead or homeless again. Either way we'll have nothing to show for it. Still, something doesn't smell right."

"How do you mean?" Stan asked.

"Happy's brother reminds me of this slumlord who owned a rat-trap of an apartment building. One evening the place filled up with smoke. The slumlord ran around in a gas mask, knocking on doors, guiding everyone to safety. When the fire department showed, they closed the building even though all they found was a pile of oily rags smoldering in the basement.

"But there were other hazards in the building, so the fire department wouldn't let the residents return. The slumlord pulled out a big roll of bills and gave each family a couple of hundred bucks to hold them over while they found another place to stay. The newspapers—even most of the residents—called the man a hero. But my friend was suspicious."

"Wait a minute," Sanchez said, "are you saying the sonovabitch smoked his own damn place?"

"That's what my friend figured. Six months later he found a city parking garage where the building had been. Then he knew the slumlord had flushed the residents out of their homes so he could sell the property to the city. Why else would the slumlord just *happen* to have a gas mask and a wad of hundred dollar bills?"

"Hurry up, guys," Doc urged. "Only ten minutes left."

Stan turned to Jason. "C'mon, Happy, work with me. Marty said your brother's got some humongous financial problems. Where's he gonna get a quarter of a million bucks?"

"He controls Last Chance, and he has a buyer for it. But the property is in escrow and he can't get his hands on the money until you people leave. He needs the proceeds to keep his own company out of bankruptcy. Having control of my estate has bought him time, but his banks aren't going to wait much longer."

"So he'll be paying us off with *your* money?" Willie concluded.

Jason nodded. "It's the way business is done in the real world. My brother knows if the line of credit is reinstated, the continued factory conversion will burn up a couple of hundred thousand dollars until he gets you all evicted."

"Who's the buyer?" Willie asked.

"A Japanese businessman who wants Last Chance for a gambling resort. He'll have to undo everything you've accomplished here."

"But if we stay," Stan asked, "is it possible for you to get your money back from your brother?"

"Perhaps. My attorney is trying to arrange a new hearing."

"So if we leave willingly," Stan said, "then your brother can put *your* money into *his* deal before you have a chance to get your estate back."

"You have the picture."

"Five minutes," Doc announced.

"Well, then, that's it," Stan said, crossing his arms over his chest. "I ain't gonna be conned, especially when Happy put everything on the line for us. If we take this deal, he'll get squat. So *I* ain't leaving. Now let's take a vote: All ASSHOLES in favor of grabbing Happy's money and bailing say aye."

Dead silence.

All GOOD FOLKS opposed, say NAY."

"NAY!" everyone shouted.

3

MARTY PRESSED the receiver to his ear, shifting his weight nervously like a racehorse at the starting gate. The air in the phone booth was heavy, and Marty had trouble breathing. He looked at his watch: it was almost time to return to court. Then he heard someone fumbling with the receiver on the other end of the line.

"Tell Happy's brother to take a flying fuck!" Stan proclaimed.

"Are you sure?"

"Yeah, it was unanimous."

Marty hung up and rushed back into the courtroom. Crazy Eddie was sitting alone at the plaintiff's table. Marty turned his thumbs down. "No deal. Where's Ike?"

Crazy Eddie was fidgeting with his crutch, looking bewildered as he tried to assimilate the news. "Uh, he went to call Sam. Here he comes now."

Ike hurried over. Marty told him about the vote.

"It's for the best," Ike said, taking his seat. "I ran the deal by Sam, and she smelled a rat, too. So she made a phone call and learned something that drastically changes the equation. She figures the other side also knows it. We both wondered why Newman hadn't challenged the validity of the contracts since all he had to argue was that Jason was legally incompetent when he signed the agreements. Now the reason behind Newman's avoidance of the issue makes perfect sense."

"What is it?" Marty urged.

"Give," Crazy Eddie said.

The door flew open, and in walked Anton and Newman.

Ike put his forefinger to his lips.

Anton returned to his seat and Newman strode over to Ike, ignoring Marty and Crazy Eddie as if they were invisible. "What is your answer?" he asked impatiently, placing his hands on his hips. "Do we have a deal so we can put an end this nonsense and bus your beggars home?"

Marty stood. As tall as Newman was, Marty was half a head taller. And broader. "Our 'beggars' *are* home, you fuckhead," he growled, "and that's where they're staying."

Newman's face bloomed red. He did an abrupt one-eighty and sat next to Anton. Shortly, Judge Harbold entered the courtroom. Everyone but Newman stood for the judge.

"What is the status of settlement?" Harbold inquired.

Ike spoke up. "Your Honor, although plaintiff appreciates defendant's attempt to resolve this matter, their offer has been rejected by my clients. By unanimous vote of the shareholders, they wish to remain at Last Chance."

The judge sighed. "All right then. Let's proceed." He turned to Newman. "You're on, Counsel."

Newman stood rigidly, his face tense, his eyes glaring. "Judge, as the court bears witness, my client has bent over backwards to help these people. But evidently they are beyond help. We now ask the court to deny plaintiffs' motion for a temporary restraining order on the basis that the Crossfire agreements, executed by Jason Howell, became invalid when he was declared legally incompetent. This court cannot grant a restraining order to enforce contracts that do not exist. Period."

Ike winked at Marty and stood. "Your Honor, the validity of those agreements is not at issue before this court. As a matter-of-fact, during the recess I learned that Judge Baxter has agreed to hear a petition on Monday, April 3, to terminate Jason Howell's conservatorship. I respectfully suggest that the proper forum for the contract validity issue is in Judge Baxter's court."

Judge Harbold arched his eyebrows and began writing in his file. "I would agree with that, Mr. Abrams."

Marty nudged Crazy Eddie under the table, "Ike just lit our own damn fuse," he whispered.

"Judge, as I explained before the recess," Newman said, raising his voice, "my client has a fiduciary responsibility to protect the estate placed in his trust. If you order the restoration of the credit line, you will not only undermine my client's ability to fulfill his court-ordered responsibilities, but you will give the plaintiffs free reign to bleed the estate dry. This they will certainly do, knowing they will soon be evicted. They have made this fact abundantly clear when they turned down my client's generous settlement offer of a quarter of a million dollars. Thus, if the court accedes to the restoration of the credit line, you will be sanctioning fraud on the part of the plaintiffs!" Newman was hot.

"Your Honor," Ike retorted calmly, "in consideration of defendant's concerns, the plaintiff proposes the court issue an order directing the bank to limit the line of credit to $250,000, an amount I'll represent is sufficient to complete the factory conversion. Thus, the defendant will have no exposure other than the amount he was willing to spend a short time ago."

Judge Harbold was still writing.

"The fuse is getting shorter," Crazy Eddie whispered.

Judge Harbold looked up. "I've heard enough argument. The court is convinced that the people of Last Chance will stay at least until April 3, when Judge Baxter determines who shall control Jason Howell's estate. If Anton Howell remains as its conservator, then he shall be free to evict the tenants and sell the property. On the other hand, if the conservatorship is terminated, then Jason Howell shall be free to make it into a factory."

Crazy Eddie made a sizzling sound.

"Since the property is currently in escrow," Judge Harbold continued, "the court finds that a temporary restraining order will not prejudice either side, providing the credit line is limited to $250,000. With that restriction, the court orders the defendant to immediately contact the bank and reinstate the line of credit." Judge Harbold brought his gavel down.

"Ka-boom," Marty said.

THIRTY-TWO
Tuesday, February 28

1

IT WAS LATE MORNING when the Aerostar touched
down at Last Chance. Marty and Ike emerged from
the plane to a round of applause. The two men high-
fived everyone and thanked them for their solidarity. Ike
reported that a shipment of foodstuffs and building materials was on the way. Marty encouraged the crew to press
harder than ever because of the time lost and the enormous
amount of work remaining before the factory was ready.

After Marty and the others left for the tower complex,
Ike remained to brief Jason and Liz before the couple
boarded the plane and returned to San Francisco.

"Congratulations, Ike," Jason said. "My disastrous
experience in court last week had destroyed my faith in the
legal system. I didn't think there was any way to beat
Newman. I still can't believe you and Marty pulled it off."

"It *was* miraculous," Ike admitted. "Especially since
we were asking for a restraining order to enforce a contract—a remedy California law specifically disallows."

"What was your strategy?" Liz asked.

"Smoke and mirrors, mostly. Sam and I had concocted two abstract legal theories about breaching third
party contracts and the sanctioning of a fraud by the court.
Newman used them for target practice. By contrast, his
job was a lot easier. All he needed was a ruling that the
Crossfire's contracts were invalid by virtue of Baxter's ruling that Jason was incompetent. But Newman avoided
this simple argument, and it made me suspicious.

"So while Last Chance was debating Anton's offer I
called Sam. She was suspicious, too, and a light bulb went
off in her head. She immediately called Baxter's clerk and
learned that the judge had granted Jason's new hearing for
April 3. Until yesterday, the best date Sam could get was
months away. But she had kept the pressure on, and it
worked. Baxter relented when she argued that any hearing
date after April 3 would dump a bunch of angry homeless
people into the Civic Center Plaza, right outside of his
courtroom.

"With hindsight, we now know Newman learned of
the new hearing before coming to court. Only he couldn't
be sure if we also knew, so he played it close to the vest.
Then he and Anton were forced to throw money at the
crew when Marty's testimony convinced them it was going
to take more than a bus and a bowl of soup to dislodge
us."

Jason shook his head. "My brother was setting up a
classical win-win. He needed to get the crew out before
the new hearing so he could use the proceeds from Last
Chance to save his company. That way, even if I were to
prevail on April 3, Last Chance would be history and I
would be his partner whether I liked it or not. My brother
is an incorrigible bastard. He reminds me of me."

"But what they didn't count on," Ike went on, "was the
crew unanimously rejecting the $250,000 offer. Once that
happened, the momentum shifted to us because Harbold

would never piss on Baxter's turf, knowing his colleague would be resolving the entire matter in a short period of time."

"Great job," Jason said.

"I like Ike," Liz said, hugging him.

"Thanks. But we've only won a skirmish. The big battle lies ahead. Procedurally there's supposed to be a preliminary injunction hearing where Newman gets a shot at killing the restraining order. But Judge Harbold, in his wisdom, scheduled it for Friday, April 10. He knows as a practical matter, if Jason loses on the third and we get evicted on the seventh, it's all over but the shouting.

"So it's all coming down to your competency rehearing, Jason. Only this time the burden shifts to *you* to prove you're competent, and you deserve to get your estate back. And you can be sure Anton and Newman will not leave anything to chance. The next time they enter the courtroom they'll be armed to the teeth, and they're going to come out with both barrels blasting."

2

"HOW MANY DAYS did we lose, Stan?" Marty asked as he took a fresh shirt from his closet.

"A couple," Stan replied. "But don't worry. The crew's so jazzed we'll make it up."

Marty heard the roar of airplane engines and walked over to the bedroom window to watch the Aerostar depart with Liz and Jason. It made a low pass over the complex and rocked its wings. "That reminds me," Marty said, buttoning his shirt, "I need to call Crazy Eddie and tell him to get his *culo* out of the condo."

Stan stepped up and stood by Marty's side, and the two men followed the aircraft as it climbed steeply toward the northwest. "I already took care of it," Stan said. "I figured Happy and Red wouldn't appreciate Crazy Eddie poking his crutch where it don't belong. I told the old man to stay at the Duval Hotel, near St. Andrews."

"Good move. Did he mention how enrollment was going? He's supposed to start his first class tomorrow."

"Yeah, he's ready to roll. He's got twenty men from St. Andrews and ten women from Annie's shelter."

"Did Annie sign up?"

Stan shook his head no.

"Okay, let's haul."

Stan remained at the window, gazing at the Dead Mountains. "Marty, can say something?"

"What?"

"I just wanted to say thanks for including me in this deal. I finally feel like I belong somewhere. I know Pete hated my guts, and you weren't all that crazy about me neither. You could've left my ass in San Francisco."

Marty returned to the window and put his hand on Stan's shoulder. "Willie told me it was you who rallied the troops yesterday. You did good, Stan."

"You wanna know something else, Marty? I've been disappointed so many times that I tried real hard not to get attached to this place. I told myself we was all part of this crazy experiment to see what happened if you mixed people nobody wanted with property nobody wanted. I know Sanchez and some of the others felt the same way. But yesterday I realized I finally owned a piece of something valuable, something regular people wanted real bad." Stan's eyes glistened.

Marty stood by his side, silently staring at the view. Then he said, "This place is changing all of us, Stan. We're becoming like those mountains, tall and rugged."

"And maybe dead, too," Stan said, "if they try and make us leave."

3

"DIE DUBICHEK seventy-one . . . die Dubichek seventy-two," Brodsky exhaled breathlessly. His deltoids and pectorals were screaming from incessant push-ups. He gnashed his teeth and continued his set . . . up-down, up-down . . . imagining he was Dubichek and the severe burning in his chest came from being riddled with .357 Magnum bullets.

At the count of one hundred, Brodsky's arms collapsed and he lay panting on the cement floor of his cell. In his field of vision stood two pairs of legs on the other side of the bars. One pair wore the polished boots of a deputy sheriff, the other the open sandals of a prisoner. Brodsky looked up. The prisoner was Michael from two cells down. He was running his eyes over Brodsky's body.

Brodsky hissed, and the legs shuffled on. But his reaction was more out of habit than anger. In the past he would have kept a list, and planned horrible deaths for the homosexuals and child abusers who were incarcerated with him. But Brodsky was a changed man. His obsession with Dubichek was so encompassing, it left no room to hate anyone else, not even the mayor and the chief.

One more month to freedom.

Brodsky rose to his feet and began pacing. After deducting the space consumed by his metal cot and his combination sink and toilet, all that remained was a narrow aisle he could traverse in three small steps—an area proportionately smaller than that allocated to a zoo animal.

In the first few days of his incarceration, Brodsky examined every inch of his cell: the graffiti, the chunks missing from the walls, the permanent stains on the floor, and the wire-encased fluorescent ceiling lamp that threw a cold light on everything. In an odd way he took pride in having acclimated so quickly to this place and its utter lack of privacy. After the first week he no longer sat on the toilet with a towel over his lap. After the second week he no longer noticed Gerald, the prisoner occupying the cell across the narrow hallway. Gerald wore an oversized orange sweatshirt, pulled down to expose his dark, narrow shoulders. It was tied smartly above his flat stomach, exposing a bare, brown midriff. Gerald rarely moved. But when he did, it was gracefully, in flowing angles. He seemed content to lie on his cot, his chin in his hands, watching everything Brodsky did.

Brodsky no longer minded any of this because the sameness of each day blurred the beige walls, the steel bars, and even Gerald. The sameness of each day made his routine of push-ups, eating, sleeping, or sitting on the toilet, seem dreamlike, surreal.

Reality came only in the long, dark hours of night. He would lie in his cot, close his eyes, and instantly transport himself to the main entrance of Cytex where he would intercept Dubichek as the big man left the building. Brodsky would smile as he raised his Colt Python .357 Magnum to chest level. Then without saying a word, he would fire hollow-point rounds into the derelict at close range, the concussions reverberating through the walls of the building, bringing startled secretaries to the windows just in time to watch a pool of blood spread outward, draining life from the huge hulk, who would scream and writhe and beg for mercy on the pavement.

Brodsky never got much beyond this point in his vision. Sometimes he had thoughts of taking the secretaries hostage and having his way with them before engaging in a shoot-out with the SWAT team; other times he thought he would simply place the Python in his mouth and squeeze the trigger. It no longer mattered.

Yes, Brodsky was a changed man.

THIRTY-THREE
Friday, March 31

1

BRODSKY BOUNDED DOWN the front steps of the Hall of Justice as he had done so often over the last fifteen years. Only this time he had entered the building during late winter and was leaving in early spring—a fact driven home more by the warm weather than the actual passage of time. The hunting cap and jacket he wore when he was arrested were no longer appropriate. He removed the jacket, revealing a chest that strained at the buttons of his flannel shirt. Constant push-ups had overdeveloped his upper body, giving him a Bluto-like appearance.

A short time ago, at the property room in the basement, the deputy snickered when Brodsky claimed his binoculars and attaché case. The man's reaction told him that every employee in the Hall of Justice must know he had been jailed as a sex offender. He hissed at the deputy and walked away.

With his jacket slung over a shoulder, and the brim of his hunting cap pulled down to shade eyes unaccustomed to bright daylight, Brodsky strolled over to the bus station and boarded the local for Daly City.

It was early afternoon by the time he arrived at his apartment at the *Casa del Sol.* Unlike the sunny weather in San Francisco, the sky here was its usual shade of dark gray. But Brodsky didn't care. He was in a peaceful mood, focused only on changing into fresh hunting clothes and packing his gun collection, especially his beloved Colt Python.

Curiously, though, his key didn't fit. So he went to the manager's unit and rang the bell. After an inordinate delay, an obese woman in a faded floral muumuu opened the door. Even from two feet away, she reeked of cigarette smoke and cheap wine. A soap opera blared on the TV.

"I live in apartment three," Brodsky announced over the din. "I've been away and my key doesn't fit."

The woman transferred her cigarette from a yellow-stained hand to a yellow-stained mouth. She squinted through the smoke with rheumy eyes. "Oh, yeah, you're Brodsky. You ain't paid the rent, so you've been evicted."

Brodsky wasn't fazed. He wouldn't need his crummy apartment anyway. "Where's my stuff?"

The woman took a deep drag from her cigarette, narrowed her eyes, and plucked a key hanging from a nail in the wall next to the door. "This is for the storage room," she said, exhaling smoke in Brodsky's face. "Take what's left of your crap—not one thing more."

"What do you mean what's left?"

"I mean what I mean," she said impatiently. "You abandoned your apartment so some of your crap was sold. I sent you an eighteen-day notice as required by law."

"I said I was away. Where did you send this notice?"

"To your apartment, as required by law."

Brodsky turned abruptly and went to the storage room. Piled haphazardly in one corner were his dinette set, his couch, his bed, and a couple of end tables. Odd pieces of his wardrobe were stuffed into two green garbage bags. His gun collection and everything else of value were gone.

Brodsky picked up the garbage bags, went back to the manager's unit and pounded on the door. "You stole my guns!" he screamed when the door opened.

The woman took a drag on her cigarette, shrugged, and blew more smoke into Brodsky's face.

Brodsky set down his attaché case and garbage bags, and grabbed the woman's neck, squeezing it in his powerful hands, his fingers disappearing into her fleshy folds. Her cigarette fell from her mouth as she struggled desperately, grasping wildly at his huge forearms. She tried to scream, but only a puff of foul smoke and a thick, whitish tongue emerged. Brodsky took this as a taunt, and it incited him to squeeze harder and harder until purple veins bulged in her temples. Then, as if to have the last say, the woman loudly expelled a large quantity of gas.

Brodsky was now in a frenzy, squeezing the woman's neck until her entire face was purple and her eyes rolled back. Finally, long after she had stopped squirming, he let her body collapse heavily to the floor. She came to rest flat on her back, smoke trickling from her nose and mouth.

Ignoring the fallen cigarette smoldering in the rug, Brodsky closed the front door and found the woman's purse in the kitchen. Inside was a deposit envelope containing several rent checks and six hundred dollars in cash. He pocketed the cash, returned to the living room, and lifted the woman under her huge, flabby arms. He grunted loudly as he dragged her onto an old recliner in front of the TV. He turned down the volume and cocked his head to admire his work. Aside from the bluish cast, the blood vessels that had burst in her face, and her mouth frozen in a permanent scream, she looked as though she were sleeping peacefully while an afternoon soap droned on.

Brodsky picked up the telephone, called Cytex, and asked for Jason Howell's secretary. "After-r-noon, miss," he said a little breathlessly. "This is Father McCallister. I'm lookin' for Mar-r-rtin Dubichek. I believe he's an associate of Mister-r-r Howell's."

"I'm sorry, Father," Sally said, "I haven't seen Mr. Dubichek in weeks. But I believe Mr. Howell knows where he is. Shall I see if he's available to assist you?"

"No, miss, I wouldn't want to t-r-r-ouble the man," Brodsky said, hanging up. Next he called a taxi company and told the dispatcher to have the cab meet him on Serramonte Boulevard, a main thoroughfare several blocks south of the *Casa del Sol.*

Brodsky returned to the kitchen and rummaged through drawers until he found a can of lighter fluid. Back in the living room, he picked up the still-smoldering cigarette butt and placed it on the rug directly under the woman's dangling right arm. Then he poured lighter fluid around the cigarette butt and waited until a flame erupted. For good measure he splashed fluid on the recliner, all over the woman's body, and under the drapes.

As the flame ignited the woman's muumuu, Brodsky replaced the lighter fluid in the kitchen drawer and picked up his belongings. He pulled the brim of his hunting cap down, walked out of the manager's apartment and closed the door. Without glancing back he strolled over to Serramonte Boulevard.

The cab was pulling up as Brodsky arrived. He sat in the back seat with his attaché case and garbage bags and gave the driver the address of the police towing yard in San Francisco's Mission District. But the taxi had to remain parked at the curb to allow several fire engines to race by. They were heading north toward a giant column of black smoke spiraling into Daly City's gray sky.

2

BRODSKY PAID the cabby, gathered his belongings, and walked into the garage of the police towing yard. He inquired about his car and was directed to a man sitting in a small cubicle. The supervisor massaged his chin with a grimy hand and motioned Brodsky to follow him to the rear lot. Parked in the furthest possible corner was his Trans Am, covered by a layer of caked dirt.

"You're lucky," the supervisor said.

"Why's that?"

"That old muscle car's a classic. Could've brought a grand at auction—easy." He snapped his fingers. "But it reeks from piss smell and nobody wanted it. We tried keeping the windows down to air it out. But the more it sat, the riper it got. Every damn cat in the neighborhood was attracted to it and went inside to do its business. A few dogs, too. So we had to close the sucker back up.

"Lately, it's been baking in the sun pretty good. If it was up to me, I'd give it back to you for free just to get rid of the stinking pile of shit. But I gotta charge you for storage. It's the law."

"How much?"

The supervisor took out a grimy calculator from his overalls. "Lemme see . . . $88.25 per day for sixty days. That's $5,295."

"I'll give you $500—take it or leave it."

The supervisor glanced at the car and massaged his chin again. "Deal."

Brodsky paid the man, got the keys, and brought his belongings over to the car. Even through the grit, Brodsky could tell the windows were steamed on the inside. When he opened the driver's door, it released an ammonia smell so foul and so putrid that he nearly lost his breakfast. Gagging, he quickly backed away from the car, dragging his garbage bags and the attaché case with him. At a safe distance, he rummaged through his clothing until he found a red bandanna. He folded it diagonally and tied it tightly over his mouth and nose.

Returning to his car, he tossed the garbage bags in the back along with his hunting jacket. Then he placed the attaché case in its proper position on the front passenger seat. Brodsky glanced around to assure himself no one was watching, and then reached into the torn upholstery of the driver's seat, carefully feeling for the P-38.

The gun was still there!

Behind his bandanna, for the first time in months, Brodsky smiled. He retrieved the pistol, engaged the safety, and placed it in the glove compartment. Then he climbed behind the wheel and put the key in the ignition. But the starter only made clicking noises.

Brodsky got out and trudged back to the man in the cubicle. In a muffled voice behind the bandanna he said, "I need a jump."

"That'll cost you twenty-five bucks," the supervisor said, eyeing the masked man. "I could charge you more under the circumstances."

Brodsky counted out the money. After paying the cab fare and the storage charges for his car, all he had left was $50 in bills and a few coins.

While a tow truck driver hooked up jumper cables, Brodsky worked a large grimy circle into the windshield with the sleeve of his flannel shirt. Then he got behind the wheel. The truck driver, pinching his nostrils, nodded he was ready. The motor cranked for a while and finally fired. Soon, in a cloud of black smoke, Brodsky, wearing his hunting cap and bandanna, drove off. Although the fetid odor still penetrated his mask, he found it tolerable as long as he kept the windows down, the vents open, and the Trans Am moving quickly.

3

IT WAS 3:00 P.M. when Brodsky arrived at Cytex. This time, leaving nothing to chance, he remained on the street and kept the engine idling to charge the battery. Through the black exhaust wafting around his car, he easily spotted Howell's Mercedes parked in its reserved spot. *Patience, patience*, he told himself. Sooner or later Howell would emerge and lead him to Dubichek.

Meanwhile, he listened to the radio, perking up at a news story about a four-alarm fire that had gutted the *Casa del Sol* apartment complex in Daly City, killing the manager. "After a preliminary investigation," the announcer said, "the authorities believe the fire started when the 55-year-old woman fell asleep while smoking a cigarette."

Brodsky grinned.

The announcer moved on to another story. "An hour ago, a swarthy man and a middle-aged blond woman robbed a liquor store on Market Street. In their haste to flee, the man's credit card was left behind. It belongs to James Brodsky, a former homicide inspector who police say was just today released from jail after serving time for sex crimes. A warrant has been issued for his arrest."

Brodsky angrily snapped the radio off and slouched in his seat. "Bitch," he hissed.

After another forty-five minutes, Howell came out of the building and drove away. Brodsky, still slouching in his seat, tailed him to a church complex several blocks south of the Civic Center. Howell parked, took a camcorder out of his trunk, and entered a sandstone building next to the church. The sign above the entrance read: "St. Andrews Shelter for Men."

Brodsky drove past the shelter and parked around the corner. Still wearing his bandanna, he leaned out of the window and checked the street. The only person in the immediate vicinity was a vagrant pushing a shopping cart. Brodsky retrieved the P-38 from his glove compartment and jumped out of the car. "Gimme the shopping cart!" he demanded from behind his mask.

The vagrant looked at the masked man in total disbelief and simply said, "Fuck you." Then shaking his head, he continued on his way.

Brodsky rushed up behind the vagrant. Using the butt of his gun he gave the man a good whack at the base of his skull. The man groaned and crumpled to the sidewalk.

Brodsky stuffed the gun into his waistband and pulled his red bandanna down around his neck. Stealing a glance around the street to confirm there were no witnesses, he dragged the body into a doorway, removed the man's tattered windbreaker, and put it on. Pleased with his new disguise, he walked around the corner toward St. Andrews, pushing the shopping cart before him.

For the better part of an hour he stood in front of the church adjacent to the shelter, one hand on his gun, the other holding a Styrofoam cup he had found in the cart. Even though he aggressively shoved the cup at people as they walked by, it remained empty except for the change he had placed there himself.

At approximately 5:00 p.m. Howell emerged from St. Andrews, put the camcorder back in his trunk, and drove away. Shortly thereafter, a group of men and women, laughing and talking excitedly, filtered out of the building. Brodsky fingered his gun and wet his lips. But after several minutes no one else emerged, and only a couple of men lingered on the street. They were joking and patting each other on the back.

Brodsky noticed that each man carried a rolled-up document. He edged closer. They were chatting excitedly about some graduation ceremony. Brodsky tossed out some bait. "Are those diplomas you fellows are holding?" he inquired, keeping his windbreaker closed over the P-38.

"Yeah, brother," one of the men said proudly, unrolling his certificate and holding it up.

Brodsky stepped closer and leaned in. The signature line at the bottom of the document contained the name "Martin Dubichek." Brodsky shook himself and looked again.

Dubichek!

He couldn't believe it!

The man beamed. "About 120 of us went to school at St. Andrews. We learned how to assemble stuff. But only thirty of us are going to this secret factory in the desert. We leave on a chartered bus from the Greyhound Terminal tonight at seven."

"How do I sign up?" Brodsky said, trying not to sound too interested.

The graduate rolled up his certificate. "Sorry, there aren't any more classes. Everybody on the street knew about this deal—say, where've you been?"

"In jail."

Just then the wind shifted, and the two men caught a whiff of Brodsky. "Sh-e-e-s-h!" they winced in unison, holding their noses and backing away.

THIRTY-FOUR
Saturday, April 1

1

THE COLD NIGHT AIR whipped through the Trans Am as Brodsky tailed the bus south and then east across California. For protection against the stench he kept his red bandanna over his mouth and nose; for warmth he wore his hunting jacket and his cap. Although he had been traveling for ten hours, he wasn't worried about falling asleep since plenty of ammonia odor penetrated the bandanna, having exactly the same effect as smelling salts.

Now, in the first light of dawn, the bus was silhouetted against the orange glow of the sky. He had used his last $50 for two tanks of gas: the first before he left San Francisco, and the second at a rest stop near Bakersfield. But now, with his fuel gage nearing empty, he cursed the people who had walked by the church yesterday. If they had only seen fit to put money into his cup he would have been able to refuel when the bus stopped in Barstow.

The cheap fucks.

It was appreciably lighter now as he drove deep into the Nevada desert on Highway 164. After a few miles, the bus climbed a hill and disappeared over the other side. When Brodsky reached the crest, the bus was no longer on the main highway. He quickly scanned the desert. There it was to his right, heading south on a two-lane blacktop.

As Brodsky approached the turnoff, he slowed to allow the bus to pull ahead. He assumed there would be little traffic on the blacktop, and he didn't want to arouse suspicion by following too closely. He waited until the bus shrank to a speck before edging back to sixty-five.

Brodsky glanced at his fuel gage: the needle was now solidly pegged on "E." He sat tensed, hunched over the wheel, waiting for the engine to quit.

After a short distance the bus turned east again. From the dust it kicked up Brodsky surmised it was traveling on a dirt road, and that probably meant it was nearing its destination. His spirits lifted, Brodsky momentarily took his hands off the steering wheel and rubbed them together.

A mile later the Trans Am's engine began to miss and surge. Then it coughed and died, and Brodsky swerved into the desert, bringing the car to a skidding stop behind a rocky outcropping.

He opened the attaché case, removed the binoculars, and placed them around his neck. Using the hood and roof of the Trans Am as a stepladder, he mounted the outcropping and scrabbled to the top. He felt a soft breeze and pulled off his bandanna to suck in some fresh air. But after hours of inhaling the foul stench, his lungs weren't working properly and he could no longer take a deep breath. He shrugged and trained the binoculars on the dwindling dust cloud. The bus was heading toward a twin-tower building complex several miles away.

Brodsky climbed down the rocks and removed the P-38 from the glove compartment. He shoved it into a jacket pocket, picked up his attaché case, and began the long trek down the dirt road and toward his destiny.

2

STAN WOKE EARLY, showered, and dressed in his best fatigues. Then he took the elevator down to the assembly area and, with his hands clasped behind his back, strolled along the rows of workstations like a drill sergeant inspecting his troops. All fifty stations were illuminated by a screensaver that started as a pattern of dots, rapidly coalescing into the words LAST CHANCE. The letters grew until they pressed against the sides of the screen, squeezing together until they exploded into a dazzling light show.

To maximize assembly space, Stan had the crew mount the monitors on swivel stands attached to the rear wall of the benches. Visors hung on hooks, keyboards sat on sliding trays, and PC's and reality engines occupied lower bays. All in all, an impressive sight.

Stan stopped at one of the stations, tapped a touchpad on the bench and the screensaver was replaced by a menu. He highlighted the words POWER SUPPLY MODULE and tapped the pad again. Then he took out a blank printed circuit board from a bin, placed it in a holder, and donned a visor. The view of the bench was unobstructed except for a white rectangle that was floating in space in front of him. It had registration crosses in each corner. He moved his head until the crosses were aligned with identical marks on the printed circuit board. With his foot, he pressed a button on a floor pedal that locked the image in the visor to the circuit board. He pressed the button again and a 3-D picture of an inductor appeared in space, suspended just above the board. Green arrows showed him where the component belonged. Stan moved his head left and right, and up and down, but the image remained fixed in space relative to the board. Then he pressed a second button on the foot pedal and listened. The audio message said, "Take an inductor from bin number one and insert it into the board as shown."

Satisfied that everything was working, Stan was about to exit the program when a bright light flashed in his face. His first thought was that the workstation had short-circuited and his heart sank. He ripped off his visor to find a digital camera pointing at him.

"Smile," Ike said as the flash went off again.

"You scared the shit out of me!" Stan protested, blinking at the white dots in front of his eyes.

Ike looked through the camera. "I was just checking the lighting in here. I need pictures of the assemblers at their stations for Happy's hearing on Monday. What's the schedule for Crazy Eddie and his graduates?"

Stan looked at his watch. "Their bus should be here any minute. Then they go to their rooms and have an hour to unpack and clean up. After breakfast, they get a quick tour of the grounds. They'll be back here for training at 9:00 a.m., and you can take your damn photos then."

"That'll work. In the meantime I'll take a few shots outside. The morning light makes this place sparkle." Ike smiled and turned to leave.

"Wait, Ike. Before you go . . . how do things look with the new hearing and all? Everyone's shitting bricks."

"Yesterday I spoke with Sam, Happy's attorney, and she tells me he is in a great frame of mind. In fact, she suggested he come down here to relax and see for himself how well we're doing. He's on the bus, too."

Stan got excited. "Really? Is he gonna bring Red?"

"No, Happy is only staying overnight. Tomorrow the Aerostar will fly him and Marty to San Francisco. They'll all meet in Sam's office Sunday night for one last run-through before Monday's hearing. Then it's up to the judge."

Stan rubbed his neck. "That's what worries me."

Ike smiled reassuringly. "Say, you know what we both need? A little diversion. After I get my pictures, let's head for the mountains for some hunting. In honor of the new crew, let's prepare the house specialty for dinner."

Stan made a rattling sound. "Good idea. It'll probably be our last outing. I'll ask Happy and Marty to join us. Doc too. The more guns the better. We're going to have a lot of hungry mouths to feed."

3

ALTHOUGH BRODSKY had walked for the better part of an hour, he was still a considerable distance from the tower complex. He scanned the grounds with his binoculars. None of the beggars seemed to be outside. During his dusty trek the sun had climbed higher, sending strong rays directly into his face, forcing him to shed his hunting jacket.

After another hour Brodsky's face was red, his lips parched and cracked, his mouth dry, his stomach growling, and his energy sapped. But he had made it. He was at the southern boundary of a small airstrip that ran parallel to a wide river. Midway along the runway was a shack. Brodsky trained his binoculars on its dirty windows. It looked abandoned. Still, to be on the safe side, Brodsky stayed close to the river. He cautiously approached the back of the shack and knelt, watching the rear entrance for a few minutes. Other than the water foaming around the pylons of a jetty, there was no sound and no movement.

Brodsky took out the P-38 and tied his hunting jacket around his waist. Crouching low, his gun ready, he stealthily approached the rear door. The upper half was glass. He rubbed at the dirt with his shirt sleeve and peered into the room. It was empty except for a pile of cement bags and a ladder resting horizontally against a wall. After he verified that the door jamb wasn't wired, he turned the knob. It was unlocked.

Once inside, Brodsky looked around for a sink. He was badly dehydrated, but the shack lacked plumbing. He was about to go outside and drink from the river when he noticed the neck of a jug poking out of the cement bags. He grunted as he shoved the bags aside and pulled out a gallon bottle that sloshed with purple liquid. Brodsky conjectured that the jug belonged to one of the winos working at the factory. He stuffed the P-38 into his waistband, unscrewed the cap, and sniffed the liquid. It smelled like stale urine, which told him nothing since everything for the past eighteen hours had smelled like that. Gingerly, he took a sip and licked around his lips. It had an oily consistency and burned his throat going down. "Beggars can't be choosers," he quipped, taking several large gulps.

In surprisingly short order, Brodsky felt energized, even a little giddy. Grinning and whistling, he took the ladder outside and used it to climb onto the roof where he established his observation post. He took his hunting jacket, his attaché case, and the jug with him. He reclined on the eastern slope of the roof, on the river side, and inched upward until he could peek over the ridge. He trained his binoculars on the parking lot. Only the bus, now empty, and an old red pickup, occupied the lot.

Although it was still early in the morning, the sun was relentless, causing the air around Brodsky to ripple in waves. He was forced to use his hunting jacket to insulate himself from the roof's scorching black asphalt shingles. He kept the jug braced against a nearby vent, sipped from it occasionally, and it seemed to quench both his thirst and his appetite. But it was difficult to drink while prone, and some of the purple liquid dribbled under the bandanna around his neck and ran inside his flannel shirt, burning his chest and making him itch.

Since it was quiet at the complex, Brodsky decided to leave his post and take a dip in the river. He was about to climb down the ladder when he spotted an eighteen-wheeler kicking up a cloud of dust as it headed toward the complex. Lifting his binoculars, he tracked the van until it stopped at the completed West Tower. But Brodsky wondered why the image of the truck jittered and went in and out of focus. Then he realized his hands were trembling and his vision was badly blurred.

Brodsky cursed the rotgut. With great difficulty, he watched the area around the truck. A handful of men and women came out of the building and began unloading large crates. Meanwhile another group emerged and walked briskly down the road, heading directly toward Brodsky. The man in the lead carried a crutch and was using it as a pointer. Although the image in the binoculars was blurry, Brodsky easily identified the big man bringing up the rear.

Dubichek!

Brodsky pulled his gun out of his waistband and tried to train it on Dubichek, who would be in range in another minute. But even using two hands and his arms braced on the roof, the gun kept bobbing. Cursing profusely, he hastily climbed down from his post. And although the world was now reeling, he managed to slide the ladder back into the shack, close the door, stagger a short distance along the river embankment, and fall into the reeds.

It was only through sheer force of will that Brodsky got the spinning world to stop. He parted the reeds and watched the group gather on the dock. He prayed that the wino wouldn't steal away for a quick sip from the jug, notice it was missing, and discover Brodsky's observation post.

His prayers were answered. The crowd remained on the jetty for only a minute as they listened to the man in front say something while pointing his crutch across the river. Then the group turned and marched back toward the tower complex, with Dubichek still bringing up the rear.

Brodsky waited a few minutes and then dragged his body into the river, scooped some cold water, and drank it voraciously. Then he splashed it on his face and neck and down the front of his shirt. Although he itched badly and his head throbbed, the water helped. A bit steadier, he retrieved the ladder and returned to his post. He lifted his binoculars in time to watch the group file one-by-one into the West Tower.

Brodsky wiped his neck with his bandanna and patted his gun. Although he missed an opportunity to pop the derelict, he felt better just knowing that his prey was here.

It wouldn't be long now.

4

AFTER THE GROUP TOUR, Marty, Stan, and Crazy Eddie settled the new crew into their workstations so Ike could take his pictures. Then Marty joined Jason, who was eating breakfast alone in the cafeteria.

Marty poured himself a cup of coffee and pulled up a chair. "How was the bus trip?"

"Fine," Jason replied. "The new employees were so excited they didn't calm down until we reached the vineyards of Fresno. Then everyone slept until dawn."

Marty sipped some coffee. "By the way, thanks for attending the graduation at St. Andrews. I wish I could've been there."

Jason reached into a satchel and handed Marty a videotape of the ceremony. "Here's the next best thing, although it won't be as interesting as your Japanese porno movies."

"Don't bet on it," Marty smiled. "So what's on the agenda while you're here?"

"Nothing special. I'm just going to walk around, admire what you and the crew have accomplished. After that, I've agreed to go hunting with Ike, Stan, and Doc—on condition that they first give me some target practice. Believe it or not, I've never fired a gun. Will you be joining us?"

Marty shook his head no. "Even if I didn't mind being surrounded by rattlers, I need the time to review the exhibits I'll be introducing in court."

"How's it going?"

"Pretty good. Besides Ike's photos, we have some elaborate poster boards showing our business plan and profit projections. I plan to know them backwards and forwards."

"You'll be a great star witness."

Marty stared into his coffee cup. "I hope so. But I'm worried about Newman. This time he's going to attack my credibility, and there's a lot in my background I'm not particularly proud of. When will I prepare for his cross-examination?"

"Tomorrow evening in Sam's office. She'll pretend she's Newman and grill you with every nasty question he might ask. Don't worry, by Monday morning you'll be ready."

Marty sipped coffee. "I guess. But what about you? Are you going to testify?"

"No. The judge has heard what I've had to say and ruled against me. But tomorrow morning, before court, I'm going to shave this beard, get a haircut, and wear my best suit. I'm not taking any chances this time."

"Will Liz testify?"

"No."

"Why not?"

"Because she's served Anton with divorce papers and is now living with me. Newman would rip her to shreds."

"And Ike? Is he going to help Sam?"

"I know he wants to, but I'm afraid he can't."

"Why not?"

"He has to preserve the lawsuit against Crossfire Holdings in the event I lose. But if all goes well on Monday, I'll get everything back and Ike will drop the suit. Besides, if he were a member of my legal team, Newman would surely rant and rave about the conflict of interest."

Marty shook his head and sighed. "And I thought football strategy was complicated."

"It's probably okay if Ike watches from the visitor's gallery," Jason added.

"No. If he can't help you, I can't spare him. The minute you win, we'll need every oar in the water for our race against the Koreans. On the other hand, Stan says we could be ready to crank up the line as soon as Sunday evening. I'll spare Ike if we can get a head—"

Jason cut Marty off. "No, you can't begin production early. If I lose, those crates of components that were just delivered must go to Korea. I gave Simpson my word when I briefed him on my situation with Anton. Of course, he gave me this I-told-you-so look about the wisdom of splitting the contract. Actually, he was right. That split contract saved our bacon; otherwise, there would be no way the old man would wait until Monday's hearing before pulling the plug on Last Chance."

5

BRODSKY BROILED in the midafternoon sun. He was not only hot, but ravenously hungry, mentally and physically exhausted, and severely hungover. But in spite of these problems, his spirits were lifted when the bus drove away without any passengers. That meant only the red pickup remained as the derelict's means of escape. After nightfall, Brodsky would sabotage it, and Dubichek would be trapped.

Brodsky closed his eyes and began making plans. Later this evening, he would use his binoculars to verify that the vagrants hadn't posted a guard. He doubted they would because they were inherently lazy and careless, and they would believe their isolation provided security. He even bet himself that like the shack, the West Tower's doors would be unlocked.

Then after everyone was asleep, he would go inside the building and set it on fire, sending everyone scurrying outside. Naturally, Brodsky would be hidden in the shadows with his gun, waiting for Dubichek to emerge . . . .

Suddenly he heard loud voices and laughter, and Brodsky jerked his eyes open. Had he dozed off? Three men were approaching the runway carrying high-powered rifles! Brodsky flattened himself on the hot roof and tracked them with his P-38. Adrenaline raced through his bloodstream. He would have to open fire if they got any closer, but he was still shaky and he doubted he could take out three heavily-armed men.

But before they reached the runway they stopped, and Brodsky breathed a sigh of relief. He lifted his binoculars and studied their faces.

He recognized all of them!

The first man was Howell. The second man, in fatigues, was the smirking degenerate Brodsky had befriended when he was disguised as Father McCallister. The third man was the deranged old coot who had chattered incessantly about commies and homeless vets taking over the government.

The ponytailed vagrant removed several tin cans from a plastic garbage bag and set them on a cactus. For the next ten minutes they took turns firing until the red pickup arrived. Then they climbed into the bed of the truck and headed toward the mountains.

Brodsky rubbed his forehead. What was Howell doing here with those vagrants? Why were they taking target practice? His headache made it impossible to concentrate. It had been a day and a half since he had any real sleep, and his lids were unbearably heavy. Perhaps he could think better if he closed his eyes for a few minutes and . . .

THIRTY-FIVE
Sunday, April 2

1

. . . DARKNESS CREPT into the Civic Center, stealing the warmth from the air. Father McCallister shivered as he stood near the main entrance of City Hall, cursing himself for not wearing an overcoat. Near him, on the front steps, a homeless man in army fatigues was sitting on a rolled-up sleeping bag, looking around as though he were waiting for someone to come or something to happen. Father McCallister clasped his hands together and walked over. The vagrant reached down to tie his boot laces. A cigarette hung loosely from his mouth.

"Bless you, my son," Father McCallister muttered.

The man looked up with cold, wary eyes. His face was leathery, his hair receding and streaked with gray.

"I'm looking for Mar-r-rtin Dubichek. Do you know where I might find him?"

The man took the cigarette out of his mouth. "You better get the fuck out of here, Father," he said, glancing in the direction of the plaza. "Hell's a coming."

Father McCallister turned. The plaza was full of vagrants dressed in fatigues and sitting in rows, alert as if waiting in a staging area.

Father McCallister shivered again.

When he turned back to the man to ask what was happening, he saw the muzzle of an M-1 rifle protruding from the sleeping bag. He quickly backed away and ran south on Polk Street, looking for a public phone. At the corner of Polk and Hayes, he spotted a white, unmarked van with a satellite dish on the roof. He recognized it as the mobile command post for the SWAT team. Relieved, he rushed over and knocked on the side door. It cracked opened. A cold, blue eyeball appeared, looked him over, and the door slid aside. It was Chief Conti. "Ah, Father, what a pleasant surprise! Come in, come in. You must be freezing dressed like that."

Father McCallister climbed in, breathless and shivering. Several men were busy at computer screens, wearing headsets and talking into microphones.

"Chief, there's something going on in the plaza, some kind of homeless military action!"

"Yes, Father, we know," Chief Conti smiled, patting him on the back. "But if you'd like, you can give a statement to my assistant. He's right behind you."

Father McCallister turned to find the barrel of a Colt Python an inch from his forehead.

His Python!

"We meet again, you PUSSY!" Dubichek said as he squeezed the trigger . . .

"NO!" Brodsky shouted, his scream permeating the night air. His body bolted, which caused him to slide down the side of the roof. As he went over the edge he threw his arms out and grabbed a vent. Although he was able to halt his slide, his flailing arms had knocked the jug loose, causing it to tumble and crash onto a cement walk-way. A bright flash and an explosion ensued, engulfing him in a black mushroom cloud.

Brodsky dangled in a black pungent cloud, half on and half off the roof, sweating and shivering at the same time. Flames licked at the bottom of his shoes and his pants began to smoke. It was nearly impossible to breathe.

A long moment passed. Aside from the crackle of the fire, the desert had become eerily quiet. Then slowly, the cicadas along the riverbank, temporarily silenced by the explosion, resumed their raucous song. As the mushroom cloud dissipated, Brodsky became enveloped in a cacoph-ony of river sounds. Deep within the discordant chorus, he heard a breathless voice whispering the words, *"Cross-fire . . . Crossfire."*

Brodsky shook himself, causing his grip to loosen. He was about to fall into the fire, but he managed to grab the rain gutter with his free hand. With his last ounce of strength, he swung himself onto the roof and collapsed face down. He was still shivering so he crawled up to his jacket and hat and put them on. He hugged himself as he squinted in the direction of the building complex to see if anyone had heard the explosion. But all of the rooms re-mained dark. He located his attaché case, and was thank-ful it had not fallen into the fire. He took out the binocu-lars and checked the grounds. No one appeared to be outside.

For a while he sat huddled, listening to the cicadas, listening for the voice. But it was impossible to concen-trate with his teeth chattering, his neck and chest itching, the hair on his legs singed, and the sunburn on his face. Worst of all, he was completely drained, and an awful gnawing in the pit of his stomach told him he had better eat . . . and soon.

By now the fire had burned itself out, so Brodsky transferred his P-38 from his waistband to his jacket pocket, reached for his attaché case, and slowly climbed down the ladder. Every muscle movement was agony. Fighting dizziness, shivering, and knocking knees, he dragged the ladder back into the shack and hid the attaché case among the cement bags. Then hugging himself again, he shuffled somnolently toward the tower complex.

At the parking lot, he stopped at the pickup. The hood creaked as he raised it, and he paused to make sure the noise hadn't given him away. Again, no lights came on. Bracing the hood with one hand, he reached into the engine compartment and yanked off the spark plug wires, stuffing them into his coat pocket. His hand was full of engine grease, and he idly wiped it on his pants before closing the hood.

A solitary floodlight illuminated the walkway along rear of the West Tower, and he instinctively headed for it like a moth toward a flame. On the way, he came across a Dumpster. He stared at it for a moment, and then lifted the lid and quietly propped it against the wall of the building. He reached inside and poked around, pulling out several plastic trash bags, ripping them open and spilling the contents on the ground. Among paper plates, crumpled napkins and rotting fruit, he found small chunks of whitish meat. He picked up a piece, rubbed it on his pants, and then inspected it in the dim light. Although he couldn't identify the meat, he had no choice but to consume it. The meat was cold and rubbery, and that forced him to chew slowly. He closed his eyes and tried not to gag as he swallowed. But it seemed edible, so he selected more pieces from the garbage and ate heartily.

After he had his fill of meat, he again rummaged through the garbage until he found a few soggy pieces of bread coated with coffee grounds. He sat with his back against the Dumpster and ate greedily, coffee grounds and all. Although he was still weak, the nourishment was beginning to make him feel better. In fact he was warming up, so he opened his hunting jacket, placed his hands on his belly, and belched contentedly.

Suddenly, an animal, its sharp claws extended, jumped onto Brodsky's chest. The creature had yellow eyes, and it hissed loudly as it flashed its fangs. Brodsky yelped and lurched backwards against the Dumpster. The lid crashed down heavily, and Brodsky screamed as the creature's claws dug deeply into his chest before it leaped off and scampered away.

Lights came on.

Brodsky collected himself. Crawling on all fours, he slipped behind the Dumpster.

There were footsteps on the walkway. A flashlight played over the area and a man's voice exclaimed, "What the hell!?" The man lifted the Dumpster's lid and scooped up the trash. After a while he padded away, continuing to shine his flashlight over the area.

Brodsky waited several minutes before crawling out from his hiding place. He remained on all fours until he was well away from the building. Then he stood and plodded back to the river shack.

2

JASON WAS HAVING BREAKFAST with Stan and Crazy Eddie when Marty joined them. "How did the orientation go yesterday?" the big man asked.

"Great," Stan replied. "The new crew flipped over their workstations. One more run-through and they'll be ready." Then Stan lowered his voice. "Later on, as an initiation ceremony, I'm gonna load *Dragons & Dino-*

saurs. Just wait until the new crew finds out what their workstations can *really* do."

"Thirty freakin' freaks," Crazy Eddie said. "This I gotta see."

Ike entered the cafeteria, looked around, and hurriedly walked over to Marty. "Someone or something raided the Dumpster last night," he announced.

Marty looked incredulous. "Sure, sure."

Crazy Eddie squinted at Ike. "I hate it when that happens."

"Hey, I'm not kidding, guys. About 2:00 a.m. I hear this crashing noise followed by an unearthly scream. I went outside with a flashlight and found garbage strewn around the Dumpster. As near as I can tell, whatever it was went after leftover chunks of you-know-what."

"Somebody didn't eat the house special," Stan said, pointing an accusing finger.

"Guilty," Marty volunteered, raising his hand.

"Me too," Crazy Eddie admitted.

"Me three," Jason echoed.

"Shoo was out there," Ike continued. "He was standing in the shadows, his hackles up, meowing. He was really agitated. After checking around the grounds, I picked him up and took him inside my apartment to calm him down."

"Are there raccoons around here?" Jason asked.

Stan shook his head. "I don't think so. Anyways, ain't no raccoon I ever heard of can lift the lid of a Dumpster."

"You got that right," Ike said. "When I stooped down to clean the mess up, there were large footprints in the sand and this god-awful piss-smell." Ike wrinkled his nose.

"Oh, no!" Stan exclaimed, wide-eyed and holding hands-to-cheeks in mock alarm. "We're being attacked by the Abominable Pissman!"

The men laughed.

"Quit pulling our legs, Ike," Crazy Eddie said, his eyes twinkling. "April Fool's was yesterday."

"It's no joke," Ike said. "We may have a rotten apple in the barrel."

"Are you saying one of the recruits rummaged through our garbage?" Marty asked, giving Ike a sideways glance.

"Old habits die hard," Crazy Eddie said.

The men laughed again.

Ike rubbed his chin. "I don't have any other explanation. Maybe a psycho fell through the screening. It could happen."

Stan turned to Crazy Eddie. "Hey, did'ya here about the humming hobo who escaped from the Psych Ward? H-M-M-M?"

More laughter.

"Okay, okay, Ike," Marty said. "If it'll make you feel better we'll put up more floodlights and post a guard."

A thundering sound interrupted the conversation. Dishes and silverware vibrated on the table.

"Hey, that must be Vinnie," Marty said, looking at his watch. "But he's early. And why's he showing off?"

Jason hurriedly stood. "I think I know."

3

INSIDE THE RIVER SHACK, Brodsky lay curled under a tarp. He had been in a peaceful, dreamless sleep until an airplane roared overhead and rudely awakened him. He quickly stood and looked outside. The airplane was circling to land. Judging from the angle of the sun it was early morning. Although he had slept longer than he had planned, he was thankful he decided to spend the night inside the shack. If he had remained on the roof, he surely would have been detected by the airplane.

As the plane landed, Brodsky took the P-38 out of his jacket pocket and released the safety. Then he exited through the rear of the shack and peered around the corner, watching the aircraft taxi to the parking ramp. A man jogged up to the plane as its engines shut down. It was Howell.

The airstair descended and the pilot, a tall man wearing a dark blue uniform and aviator's sunglasses, emerged. He stood attentively as a red-haired woman appeared at the door. The two men fussed over who would help her down the stairs. The pilot won. But when she was on the tarmac, she hurried over to Howell and they kissed.

Brodsky hissed and trained his gun on the couple. It would be so easy to squeeze the trigger and end their happiness. But he stifled the impulse, knowing that he must save all his bullets for Dubichek.

After the trio left for the tower complex, Brodsky walked a hundred yards south along the river until he found a small alcove where he could sip water and sit out of the view of prying eyes. It was a serene setting, and only the gurgling of the river and the chirping of birds broke the silence. Brodsky put on his hat to keep his blistered face out of the sun. Then he spread his jacket out on the ground. There was a bulge in one of his pockets, and he remembered the spark plug cables. He yanked them out and tossed them into the river. The action caused a flattened Snapper Bar to drop into the sand. He picked it up and looked at it longingly. Seeing no way to separate the wrapper from the candy, he consumed it all.

Brodsky sat on the bank for a time, skimming rocks, watching how they zigged and zagged, skipping faster and faster before sinking into the river. Eventually, he tired of the game and reclined on the bank, waiting and listening.

As the sun lowered in the western sky, the cicadas returned. The words came softly at first, almost indistinguishable from the soft sounds of the river. Brodsky sat up and cocked an ear. The words were becoming clearer.

Soon Brodsky began to nod. "Yes, Ray Gorney," he said, "I understand, I understand."

4

"DAMN IT!" Ike cursed, pumping the accelerator of the pickup as the starter chugged ineffectually. The odor of raw fuel told him the engine was flooded. Ike checked his watch. It was nearing 5:30 p.m., and the sun was already behind the Dead Mountains. Over Vinnie's objections, Ike had delayed the Aerostar's scheduled departure because of last-minute changes he wanted to make in one of the exhibits. And now, without the pickup to haul the exhibits and the baggage down to the Aerostar, the aircraft's departure would be further delayed. Vinnie had made it clear that the lack of runway lights at Last Chance made it impossible to take off after sunset.

Ike needed help and he needed it now. He looked around and spotted Crazy Eddie and Willie coming toward him. Willie wore a sweatband and Crazy Eddie had his crutch tucked under his arm as they jogged along the road. Shoo playfully darted in and out of their feet.

"Hey guys!" Ike shouted. "I need a hand."

Crazy Eddie and Willie skidded to a halt. They looked at each other and gave Ike a big round of applause.

Ike jumped out of the truck. "C'mon fellas, the damn pickup won't start and I've got to load the plane A-S-A-P. It's got to take off before dark."

"Righto," Crazy Eddie said as he tossed his crutch into the truck bed. There were a dozen poster board exhibits grouped into two sets, each neatly wrapped in brown pa-per. Crazy Eddie took one set while Willie took the other, and Ike grabbed Jason and Marty's suitcases.

With Shoo bobbing alongside, the three men brought the cargo to the Aerostar. After everything was stowed, Ike and Crazy Eddie jogged back to the complex to notify Vinnie. Meanwhile Willie went to fetch Shoo who had disappeared around the back of the shack. He was meow-ing loudly.

5

JASON WALKED with his wolf-cane as he and Marty followed the path toward the runway. Vinnie and Liz trailed a few steps behind, engaged in conversation about the ancient Snake Indians who had inhabited this part of the desert.

At the Aerostar, Liz whispered something in Vinnie's ear. He nodded and went into the cockpit while she walked over to Jason and took his hand. "I have a surprise for you, darling," she said. "It's a good luck present."

Vinnie emerged with a small box wrapped in silver paper and tied with a red ribbon.

A knowing smile crossed Jason's face. "Floppy disks! Liz, you shouldn't have. I hope they're formatted."

"Of course they are, silly."

Jason tucked the cane under his arm and pulled off the wrapping. Inside was a lacquered box. The cover had a painting of an angel playing an ancient string instrument.

"It's a Botticelli," Liz explained.

"I knew that."

"Sure you did. Lift the lid."

The crystalline tones of the old Dick Haymes' tune, "You'll Never Know," filled the air.

Jason set the box on the Aerostar's wing, handed Marty the cane, and took Liz in his arms. They danced slowly, gazing into each other's eyes.

Vinnie glanced at his watch. "Uh, excuse me, folks. If we're not out of here in a few minutes—"

A loud caterwauling from the direction of the shack caused everyone to freeze. They looked across the runway. A body was lying on the ground in front of the shack.

They rushed over.

It was Willie. He was on his back, his chest rising and falling slowly, the right side of his sweatband soaked red. Shoo was several feet away, meowing and hissing. A foul ammonia-like odor permeated the air.

Marty dropped Jason's wolf-cane, knelt, and listened to Willie's chest. "His heart sounds strong."

Jason bent closer to examine Willie's injury. "What could have happened to him?"

Suddenly the front door of the shack flew open and an horrendous-looking creature stepped out, waving a pistol. "*I* happened to him," he announced arrogantly, striding behind an oversized chest. "Do as I say or *I'll* happen to you, too." His voice was raspy and alien, his shirt stained purple. He wore a dirty red bandanna around his neck and a hunting cap on his head. His pants were charred, his lips cracked, and his face badly blistered. His odor reminded Jason of that abandoned doorway where he and Marty had shared brandy—only much worse.

The creature circled away from the shack, positioning himself beyond the group. "Move away from the nigger and stand spread-eagled with your hands against the shack. MOVE!"

They did as they were told. One-by-one the creature pressed the gun barrel against the back of their heads, patting them down. When he got to Liz, he lingered over her

breasts and thighs. She shuddered at his touch, his smell,
his foul breath. Jason watched in revulsion out of the corner of his eye. He dug his nails into the wall and bit his lip
to restrain himself. This man was insane, and Jason knew
if he tried to help Liz, she would be killed instantly.

At last the man-thing backed away and pointed the
pistol at Vinnie. "YOU! Pilot-asshole! Go inside and
bring the ladder out. Lean it against the roof. Try any he-
roics and the bitch dies." The creature grabbed Liz's hair,
pulled her head back, and forced the barrel into her mouth.

Vinnie hurriedly dragged the ladder out and propped it
against the shack.

"Now I want you and the bitch on the roof. Nice and
easy. Cooperate and you'll live. I'll even allow the bitch
to live, too, so she can give me a nice blow job when you
fly me out of here." The madman laughed maniacally.
But as quickly as the outburst began, it stopped. He released Liz and took a step toward Willie. "But if anybody
tries anything," he said evenly, "everyone dies, like the
nigger here." With that, the creature leaned over and
pumped a shell into Willie's chest, causing his body to jerk
and his eyes to snap open. Shoo, who had been hanging
back a few feet, shrieked and scampered toward the river.
Jason winced and swallowed hard. His sense was that the
gunshot brought Willie around just in time to realize he
had been murdered.

Willie's chest heaved once and then was still, his face
frozen in wide-eyed surprise. Liz screamed. Marty
started for the madman but Jason grabbed him. The creature whipped around with both arms extended and trained
the gun on Marty's face. "Don't worry, you'll get yours,
you big PUSSY. But first we're going to have a nice
chat." The madman took a couple of steps back and
pointed the pistol at Liz and Vinnie. "Up the fucking ladder! NOW!"

Vinnie and Liz scrambled up the ladder.

The creature kicked the ladder away. Then he forced Jason and Marty to sit on the ground with Willie between them, as if to remind them of their fate. He stood a few feet away, facing them, waving the pistol back and forth. The entire front of Willie's shirt was red. Marty felt his friend's neck and then closed Willie's eyes. A tear ran down the big man's cheek.

The madman was watching. "So who's the big PUSSY now?"

Jason's mind was racing. At first he thought the creature might be a disgruntled homeless person who had flunked out of Crazy Eddie's class. But his "pussy" remarks triggered something Marty had once told him.

"We finally meet, Inspector," Jason said.

"Hello, Howell," Brodsky rasped.

Jason's mind continued to race. The only weapon he had was his skill as a negotiator. He would have to learn what was driving Brodsky. Once inside his mind, Jason would try to expose the man's ego and stroke it. At that point the man would be most vulnerable, and Jason might be able to disarm him. But he was aware that if he failed, it could cost him and the others their lives. He would have to get it right the first time.

"What brings you here, Inspector?"

Brodsky pointed the pistol at Marty's head. His eyes were filled with hate.

The cop is obsessed with Marty.

It meant his friend must refrain from talking or doing anything that might set off the madman. "You must be hungry," Jason said gently, recalling Ike's story about the Dumpster. "The night will get cold soon, so why don't we all go over to the main building where we can have a nice dinner and talk privately?" Jason then shifted his eyes to

Marty. "Just the two of us, Inspector, without anyone in-
terfering with our private conversation."

Marty nodded slightly.

"We'll chat right here," Brodsky hissed.

"Okay, fine, if that's what you want."

Temporarily silenced by the gunfire, the cicadas were
now at full volume and Brodsky cocked his ear. A minute
passed. "I know about Operation Crossfire."

"That's incredible. How did you find out?" Jason
asked, feigning surprise.

"Ray Gorney told me."

Jason nodded. "Of course."

"You're code name is Rappaport. I learned that myself."

"Good work, Inspector."

"And the big PUSSY . . . he's the Golden Fleece?"

"Right again."

Brodsky chuckled. "Was Ray Gorney working for the
mayor's opposition?"

Jason wasn't sure how to answer. "Yes," he chanced.

Brodsky's chapped lips twisted into a smile. "And the
mayor ordered him killed because he was getting too close
to learning about your scheme?"

Jason thought he had better play this one close to the
vest. "You know I can't talk about that."

"Why have you been recruiting bums?"

"You already know, Inspector; please tell me."

Keep him talking.

Brodsky stood with his hand outstretched and his gun
pointed at Marty's temple. "This is a paramilitary camp,"
he said, shifting his weight. "You've just received a truck-
load of M-1 rifles and you're training vagrant vets for a
terrorist attack on San Francisco. I learned that last night,
too. You're telling your wino recruits that this is their
chance to get revenge for Project Vector. You're telling

them the attack will embarrass the mayor, and he won't be re-elected in November. Then the vagrants can reclaim the Civic Center Plaza, Union Square, Golden Gate Park, and the rest of The City.

"What they don't know is that they're being double-crossed, and that you and the big PUSSY are secretly working for Babcock. Just before the election, when you send your vagrant vets into the Civic Center, Chief Conti will have the SWAT team and dozens of police units surrounding the plaza, and the mayor will kill hundreds of homeless scum. He'll win the election because the citizens will be too frightened by the attack to vote for anyone else. It's a brilliant scheme," Brodsky said, throwing his head back and laughing maniacally again. Then his red eyes grew wide. "The mistake you all made was to keep me out of it. *I* could have made Operation Crossfire a success." Brodsky waved his gun in a circle at Marty's head and raised his voice. "But instead you put this big PUSSY in charge, and that's why it'll fail!"

"That's absolutely brilliant detective work, Inspector," Jason replied, shaking his head in amazement. "Operation Crossfire had the strictest secrecy at all levels. I'm *astounded* you know so much. Tell me more."

Brodsky stared at Jason. "Besides being the money man, Howell, you were helping with the recruiting. That's what you were doing when your plane accidentally crashed and almost blew the scheme wide open."

"Go on."

"That crash was the only missing piece and it came to me today, by the river. I now know there were really three people on your plane—the pilot, you, and Sergeant Sykes, a psychopathic vet you recruited out of Petaluma. The pilot and Sykes were both badly injured in the crash, and *you* torched the whole thing to hide the evidence." Brodsky had a self-satisfied look on his face. He paused to listen to the cicadas, squeezing his eyes shut for a moment. Then he squatted, scratching his chest with his free hand.

Jason watched the madman settle in. He was becoming vulnerable, and the time to act was fast approaching. His wolf-cane was lying in the shadows next to Willie's body where Marty had dropped it. Jason's hand inched toward it.

"To distract the media, the mayor and the chief conspired to have you disappear under the cover of a phony kidnapping," Brodsky continued. "But because of Operation Crossfire's critical timing, you couldn't stay underground for long. So you turn up at the hospital a couple of days later pretending to have amnesia, to avoid being questioned by the media. Meanwhile your so-called kidnappers conveniently disappear and the investigation is suspended." Brodsky turned toward Marty. "But *I* was coming for you, you big PUSSY."

With Brodsky's attention on Marty, Jason inched closer to his cane.

"You, Dubichek, pretended to have a breakdown at the Civic Center as an excuse to go undercover as well. But instead of being sent to that awful psyche ward at City General where they held me, the chief booked you into a suite at Petaluma so you could spend your time recruiting more vets.

"But when you tried to get a message to Howell, his secretary inadvertently informed me about your call."

Jason's hand was now touching the cane.

"In spite of Conti washing your fingerprint files to throw me off," Brodsky continued, staring into space with watery eyes, "*I* was on to them. They should have trusted me . . . let me work on the project . . . instead of trying to destroy me . . . with that blond bitch . . . the trumped-up sex charge . . . the liquor store theft." Brodsky's voice broke and his eyes now filled with tears.

Jason was nodding sympathetically. His fingers were around the bottom of the cane. "If only we had known how brilliant you are, Inspector," he said soothingly. "Look, I'll be happy to tell Mayor Babcock about your incredible police work. I'll see to it you're put in charge of Operation Crossfire." Then Jason lowered his voice as if he were in a church, forcing Brodsky to lean in. "But there's something extremely important you need to know. The mayor is planning to dump Conti, and as we speak he's looking for a new chief to run things. Under the circumstances, the job is yours."

Brodsky's eyes were distant and he had his head cocked toward the sounds of the river.

"But it's getting dark and this airport has no lights," Jason continued softly, tightening his grip on the cane. "We have to take off immediately if we're going to get to San Francisco and make it all happen. I know where the mayor is having dinner and we can meet him there."

'Les Moules,'" Brodsky sniffled, his head still cocked toward the river.

"That's right," Jason said, tensing his muscles, getting ready. "You're amazing, Inspector."

Brodsky was nodding agreeably. "Okay, Howell. It's a deal. But first the big PUSSY dies." Still squatting, Brodsky pressed the pistol against Marty's temple. Marty closed his eyes. At that moment Shoo, with his claws extended and fangs flashing, leaped onto Brodsky's chest. Brodsky yelped and fell backwards, firing just over Marty's head. A flash came out of the barrel. The bullet hit the shack immediately below Liz and Vinnie, and they flattened themselves.

Shoo scampered away.

Marty jumped Brodsky, fighting for control of the gun. Jason was on his feet with his cane angled back. Marty and Brodsky were struggling mightily. Jason was trying to get a bead on Brodsky's head, but the two men were rolling around on the ground. It was obvious that Marty, although bigger, was having difficulty overcoming the crazed man's immense upper body strength.

Another shot rang out.

Jason flinched.

Brodsky was yelling incoherently.

Marty continued struggling for control but he was losing. Brodsky maneuvered himself on top with the gun in Marty's face. The big man's eyes were glazed, the color draining from his face. Jason, with his cane still angled back, swung it like a golf club, bringing the heavy ivory wolf-handle down in a blurring arc.

THUNK!

Brodsky's head jerked sideways, the gun went flying, and he crumpled onto the ground. Grunting, Marty tried to stand, but fell backward. His chest was heaving. A red circle was spreading rapidly on the right side of his shirt.

From the roof Liz screamed, "MARTY, NO!"

Jason dropped to his knees and held his friend's head. "Take it easy buddy, you'll be okay."

Marty was sweating, trying to catch his breath. Even in the fading light, Jason saw that his friend's face had turned ashen.

"Now . . . I know . . . how Pete felt," Marty gasped. "Can't . . . seem . . . to . . . breathe."

"Hang on, buddy, we'll get help."

Jason stood and hurriedly righted the ladder for Vinnie and Liz. "Get Doc!" Jason ordered. Vinnie scrambled down the ladder and ran at full speed toward the complex.

Marty was shivering. "You're going . . . to get me . . . a horse doctor?"

Liz came down the ladder and knelt by Marty. "Don't talk," she said, taking his hand. "Focus on breathing." She turned to Jason. Worry filled her eyes. "He's cold."

Jason found a tarp in the shack and covered Marty. Liz continued to hold his hand while Jason located Brodsky's gun.

Stan came running, armed with a rifle. "I was outside when I heard shots. Vinnie said there's a lunatic—"

Jason pointed the P-38 toward Brodsky. "Cover him. I whacked him pretty good but he might come around. He's raving."

With his rifle in Brodsky's face, Stan bent over for a closer look. He recoiled when he caught a whiff of the man. "Hey, it's that cretin cop who interrogated me," he said, wrinkling his nose and backing away. "I'll never forget that single thick eyebrow—" Stan paused when he spotted another body lying on the ground. "What's with Willie?"

Jason shook his head. "He's gone."

"NO!" Stan cried, his face contorted. He turned back to Brodsky, took a wide stance, leaned over, and pressed the rifle barrel against his head. "SONOVABITCH!"

"Don't shoot!" Jason ordered. "We've got enough trouble. Marty's down, too." Jason pointed at the tarp.

Stan backed away from Brodsky and knelt by Marty, giving Jason a questioning look.

"He saved us. He took one in the chest trying to wrestle the gun away. He'll be okay," Jason said, his voice lacking conviction. "Here comes Doc."

The old man, accompanied by Ike and Vinnie, hurried over. Ike carried a first aid kit and Vinnie had a stretcher. Liz pulled the tarp back and Doc knelt, checking the big man's pulse. He unlatched the kit and removed a small flashlight, examining Marty's face and checking his pupils. Then he took out a stethoscope and listened to his chest.

Jason and Liz watched anxiously.

Marty was barely breathing and he had slipped into unconsciousness. His face now had a bluish cast.

Everyone knew Marty was dying.

Jason moved closer to the old man. "What is it, Doc? Do something!"

Doc held his hands together as if in prayer. He was shaking his head. "We're losing him . . . I'm only a washed-up veterinarian . . . I can't . . ."

Jason grabbed the front of Doc's shirt. "He's not breathing! DO SOMETHING GODDAMN-IT!"

Doc snapped out of it and started talking to himself. "His chest cavity is pressurized. His right lung's collapsed. I think his mediastinum is pressing against his heart. I need a pocket knife. HURRY!"

Stan took a Swiss Army knife out of his fatigues and tossed it over. Doc extended the blade. Holding the knife with both hands, the old man positioned it over the wound in Marty's chest. Doc's hands were shaking.

Liz covered her eyes.

Ike turned away.

"What are you doing!" Jason yelled.

"Shut the fuck up!" Doc shouted as he plunged the knife into Marty's chest, releasing a whoosh of air.

Marty's body jerked, but his eyes remained closed. Only a slight rising motion of the protruding knife handle gave any indication the big man was still alive.

Doc eased the knife out and used it to cut a short length of plastic tubing from the first aid kit. He took out a rubber glove, sliced off the thumb, and secured it around the end of the tube with adhesive tape. Then he cut a small slit in the tip of the rubber thumb and worked the open end of the tube into the knife hole in Marty's chest.

Several long seconds passed.

Marty's chest began rising and falling rhythmically. Doc held the penlight up to Marty's face. "His color's returning."

Jason pointed at the contraption sticking out of Marty's chest. "What's that?"

"A Heimlich Valve. It's standard first aid for a *tension pneumo-thorax*. The bullet wound allowed air into his chest cavity, pressurizing it and preventing his lungs from inflating. I once used the procedure to save a client's dog who had been shot by an angry neighbor."

Marty's eyelids fluttered. "I . . . heard . . . that."

Doc stood and took Jason aside. "We've got to get him to the hospital immediately. The bullet is still lodged in his chest. I can't do any more for him. He's in grave danger."

Marty was muttering. "I dreamt about . . . the Monday Night Club . . . the fire was going . . . it was warm . . . I wanted to stay . . . but Pete and Willie said . . . 'Go back'."

Liz was sobbing. She squeezed Marty's hand.

Jason turned to Vinnie. "Can you fly him to Vegas?"

"No way. The airstrip is too narrow and there isn't enough light. If a tire wanders into the sand the Aerostar will wheelbarrow and I'll be eating a cactus sandwich."

Jason turned to Doc. "Can he make it in the pickup?"

Doc shrugged. "I don't know."

Ike stepped up. "That's not an option anyway. The madman must have sabotaged the engine. The ignition wires are missing."

"Then it's *got* to be the Aerostar," Jason said. He thought for a moment. "Vinnie, if the crew held candles along both sides of the runway, can you get Marty out?"

Vinnie took a deep breath. "Maybe. But until I see what it looks like from the departure end of the runway, I won't know if I've got the balls to try it."

6

STAN SECURED Brodsky's hands and legs using the Aerostar's tie-down ropes and then wrapped him in the tarp to contain his smell. Meanwhile Ike and Crazy Eddie rounded up the crew. Candles were distributed, and everyone was positioned at 100-foot intervals along both sides of the runway. Marty, on a stretcher, was taken aboard the Aerostar. Brodsky, still unconscious, was strapped into a rear seat. Only his swollen head protruded from the tarp.

Although nervous about taking off by candlelight, Doc volunteered to ride along to administer to Marty. Jason handed him the P-38 and told the old man to shoot Brodsky if he somehow got loose. Standing at the top of the airstair, Doc said goodbye as if he didn't expect to see any of his friends again. Stan offered to take his place, but Doc insisted on going with his patient.

Jason quickly away walked from the aircraft and took his position near the middle of the airstrip. Liz was directly across from him. To his left, at the departure end of the runway, Jason saw the Aerostar's red and green navigation lights turn on. He knew these were the only lights the pilot dared to use because the glare from the instrument panel and the reflections from the landing lights would overwhelm the minuscule glow of the candles. So without the benefit of instruments, Vinnie would have to make a dangerous takeoff by sound and feel alone.

Jason lit his candle and that signaled everyone else to light their candles as well. Then he watched the Aerostar's navigation lights for any sign of movement. But nothing happened. Several long moments passed, and Jason began to think that Vinnie wasn't going to attempt it. Suddenly the aircraft's engines revved and Jason's heart began to pound. Sweat beaded on his forehead in spite of the cool evening temperature.

Jason looked at the twin rows of flickering candles. Many of the crew held their heads down in prayer.

The Aerostar's engines were roaring now and the airplane began to accelerate. Jason was also praying. He prayed that Vinnie could keep the Aerostar heading straight and true. If it veered off the narrow runway and caught a tire in the sand it would cartwheel and crash. In the process people would be killed. The Aerostar's engines hung low, and its propellers were perfectly positioned to decapitate anyone in its path.

The Aerostar's progress was dramatized by candles blowing out by the propwash as the airplane raced down the runway. Suddenly Jason felt an enormous blast of cold air and his candle was out, too. The Aerostar continued to accelerate and appeared to be going straight . . . so far.

Jason now prayed that the people standing along the remaining portion of the runway would hold their positions. If some of them reflexively moved back, Vinnie would track their candles with disastrous results. But in spite of the aircraft's long wings passing a few feet in front of their faces, everyone held their ground.

A scant dozen yards before the end of the runway the Aerostar rose sharply and retracted its gear. With its strobe lights now flashing it turned steeply toward Las Vegas.

Everyone cheered.

When the sound of the Aerostar faded, Jason had the crew gather around him. He briefed them about the intruder and the battle at the river shack. While Jason was talking and answering questions, Stan got a stretcher for Willie and covered his body with a blanket. Then everyone re-lit their candles. Ike, Crazy Eddie, Stan, and Sanchez were pallbearers, and they led the crew back to the twin tower complex in a long candlelight procession. Shoo stayed close to the stretcher. Jason and Liz, walking

immediately behind Willie, held hands. A man with a
deep and powerful voice started singing *Amazing Grace,*
and everyone joined in:

> *Amazing grace, how sweet the sound*
> *That saved a wretch like me.*
> *I once was lost, but now I'm found,*
> *Was blind, but now I see . . . .*

7

WHILE MARTY WAS EN ROUTE to the hospital, Ike
went to his apartment to call Sam. Jason and Liz joined
him at his kitchen table as Ike filled her in.

"How awful," Sam said. "My thoughts and prayers
are with Marty . . . but now we'll have to ask Judge Baxter
to continue the hearing; Marty's testimony is essential if
we're going to convince the judge to reverse himself."
Sam's voice sounded weary.

Ike frowned. "But that'll mean a delay of weeks, even
months before we're back on his calendar."

"I'm afraid so."

Jason took the phone. "Sam, we *have* to go forward.
If we don't, there'll be no Last Chance. We've got to try;
we have nothing to lose."

"Here we go again," Sam said, sighing heavily, "walking blindfolded into the lion's den with our hands tied behind our backs. Remember Jason, the burden of proof has
shifted to you. Our job is considerably more difficult this
time."

There was a long moment of silence on the line.

"All right," Sam relented, "is there someone else who
can testify for Marty? It must be a former homeless person who knows the operation of the factory and can intro-

duce the exhibits and photos. One of the company's managers?"

Jason ran a hand through his hair. "Perhaps Crazy Eddie can do it. Although he doesn't know the business plan, he knows the factory. He might be able to learn Ike's exhibits by tomorrow morning. But he can't testify about what I was doing in Gorney's photos."

"I can," Liz said.

"No, Liz," Jason said. "You only have indirect knowledge. Newman will assassinate you."

"Jason, if you want to go forward," Sam interjected, "I'll have no choice but to put Liz and this Crazy Eddie person on the stand. But I must warn you: the chance that Baxter will reverse his order is rapidly changing from slim to none."

"I know, Sam," Jason said, "I know." Then he terminated the conversation to keep the line open for word on Marty.

The three of them waited in silence, lost in thought.

The phone rang and snapped everyone back. Jason picked up. It was Doc.

"I'm in the emergency room. Marty's vitals are good," Doc said. "He's going to be recuperating for a while, but he'll make it."

Jason broke into a big grin and high-fived with Liz and Ike. They cheered and hooted. Then Jason asked, "What about Brodsky?"

"We radioed ahead. The police have him in custody."

"Good. Is Vinnie there?"

"Just a minute."

Vinnie picked up.

"Can you return for me, Liz, and Crazy Eddie, and fly us to San Francisco?" Jason asked.

"Sorry, that's not an option. The Nevada State Police wants to interview me and Doc."

"Have them talk to Doc first. He can tell them all about the Cabal, and how they're plotting to overthrow the government. That should give you plenty of time to get us to San Francisco. When you return to Las Vegas they'll be ready to interview you."

"That's what I'm afraid of. Anyway there's another slight problem. As romantic as it might seem, I'm not going to land by candlelight. As it is, you need to buy me a new pair of shorts." Vinnie paused for a moment. "But I'll tell you what—I'll give you an hour to set up two solid rows of bonfires."

THIRTY-SIX
Monday, April 3

1

JUDGE BAXTER PEERED impatiently over his spectacles. "Ms. Paxton," he grunted, "I have rearranged, against my better judgment, an extremely full calendar and granted this rehearing based upon your representation of new and compelling evidence. Shall we get on with it?"

Sam glanced at Jason, sitting at her right. Clean-shaven and wearing his most expensive business suit, he looked like his former, well-turned-out self, except for the bags under his eyes and the worry lines furrowed in his brow. Sam took a deep breath. "Ah, I regret to inform the court that Martin Dubichek, the president of Last Chance Corporation and my key witness, cannot introduce that evidence. He was gravely injured in a gun battle yesterday and is recuperating at a hospital in Las Vegas."

The judge sighed and rapped his fingers.

Newman whispered something in Anton's ear, and the two men broke out in twin grins.

"However," Sam added, "the petitioner is prepared to proceed with two alternates. For my first witness I would like to call Ms. Liz Howell."

Avoiding her husband's eyes, Liz walked quickly to the witness stand. She was dressed in a navy blue suit with pearl buttons. As she took the stand she turned and acknowledged Judge Baxter with a nod and a polite smile.

Sam was greatly relieved that Liz had pulled herself together. Out in the hallway, she had been pacing, wringing her hands, and acting uncharacteristically short-tempered. Sam knew she had a major credibility problem with Liz, and she worried the judge might equate nervousness with untruthfulness.

After Liz was sworn in, Sam established that the witness was married to the conservator, Anton Howell, and that she was seeking a divorce.

Judge Baxter squinted at Liz and scribbled a note.

Next, Sam retrieved Gorney's pictures from the court clerk and handed them to Liz. "Ms. Howell, as you review these photos, I will represent to you that Mr. Newman has established that they were taken surreptitiously by your husband's agent, a Mr. Raymond Gorney, between Saturday, January 21, and Monday, January 23, of this year. Were you acquainted with Jason Howell at that time?"

"Yes."

"Did you have an occasion to meet with Jason Howell and the other man depicted in these photos?"

"Yes, I met with Jason Howell and Martin Dubichek for several hours on Sunday, January 22. "

"Did you observe anything unusual about Jason Howell's behavior?"

"No."

Sam stood in front of Liz. "What did you discuss?"

"Martin Dubichek's background and the homeless problem in general."

Newman stood. "Objection. Hearsay, Judge."

Sam quickly turned to face Judge Baxter. "Your Honor, I can show that Jason Howell's subsequent actions, which were based on these conversations, are relevant to these proceedings."

Judge Baxter glanced at Newman. "Overruled."

Sam turned back to Liz. "Now, Ms. Howell, did Jason reach any conclusion about the homeless problem?"

"Only that it was very complex and he wanted to learn more."

"Is that what he was doing in these photographs?"

"Yes."

"How do you know?"

"Because on Wednesday, January 25, when Jason returned from the street, he and Mr. Dubichek described their experiences to me in detail. The photos document those experiences."

"Thank you. Now, returning to the prior Sunday meeting, what else did Jason Howell decide to do in order to better understand the homeless problem?"

Newman raised his hand. "Objection. Rank hearsay."

Sam shook her head. "Your Honor, again it's not hearsay since this line of questioning goes to Jason Howell's state-of-mind." Then she abruptly turned to Newman. "And isn't that why we're all here, Counselor?"

"I'll allow it," Judge Baxter said. "But it had better be good, Ms. Paxton."

Sam returned to the witness. Under direct examination, Liz testified how Jason asked her to get a videotape of a recent CNN program on homelessness. She watched the tape with Jason and Marty on the following Thursday night. Sam put the tape into evidence and played the portion where the experts described their conflicting solutions to homelessness.

"What happened after the three of you watched this tape?" Sam asked.

"We discussed it for a while . . . about how the problem seemed intractable. Jason felt private industry should attempt a solution by converting military bases into factories with integrated housing. As you just saw from the video, these are elements taken from each experts' ideas. But in order to prove the feasibility of his solution, Jason decided to try it on a small scale."

"Who suggested the idea?"

"Actually, I did."

Sam paused and looked at Liz. "And as a result of your suggestion, did Jason eventually purchase the desert property known as Last Chance."

"Yes."

Newman jumped up. "Objection! Speculation, hearsay, and completely lacking in foundation."

Judge Baxter nodded. "Sustained."

Sam knew this was as far as she could go with this witness. Liz could not be used to establish a connection between the idea behind Last Chance and its viability. That would be Crazy Eddie's job. She turned and headed for her seat. "No further questions."

Judge Baxter wrote something in his file and looked at Newman.

Newman strolled over to Liz, placed his hands on the witness stand, and leaned toward her. She leaned back, but held eye contact.

"It is nice to see you, Liz," Newman said smiling.

Liz nodded stiffly.

"And you look ravishing, as usual."

"Thank you," Liz replied, without returning the smile.

"Objection," Sam said, her voice brimming with anger. "Your Honor, this isn't the proper time and place for idle chitchat. And please instruct Counsel to stand back from the witness and address her properly."

Judge Baxter sighed. "Back off, Mr. Newman. Do you have a question?"

"Yes, sorry, Judge," Newman said, retreating a couple of steps. "All right, Mrs. Howell, let us pick up where you and Ms. Paxton left off. How *did* you learn about the purchase of the desert property?"

"Ah, Sam Paxton."

"And who arranged the purchase?"

"Same answer."

Judge Baxter glanced at Sam and took more notes.

Newman smirked. "I see. Now Liz . . . ah, Mrs. Howell, you began your testimony with Sunday, the twenty-second of January. But let us go back to the prior Friday afternoon, shall we?" Newman turned and winked at Anton.

Sam jumped up. "Objection! What happened on Friday the twentieth is completely beyond the scope of cross-examination."

Newman rolled his eyes. "Judge, what happened on that Friday is an integral part of subsequent events and therefore foundational."

"I'll allow it."

Newman turned back to Liz. "On that Friday, is it not true that you and Jason, masquerading as a fictional couple, 'The Rappaports,' went to the state mental hospital in Petaluma to visit Martin Dubichek, our mystery witness for today."

"Objection, Your Honor," Sam said.

Judge Baxter peered at Newman. "Please refrain from editorializing, Counselor."

"Yes, Judge," Newman said insincerely. "Now, Mrs. Howell, were you aware at the time of your visit to Petaluma that Mr. Dubichek had been involuntarily committed for psychiatric treatment by the police after he went berserk and stormed City Hall."

"Y-yes."

"And were you aware he was suicidal?"

Liz looked at Sam and Sam looked at Jason. This caught them all by surprise. Somehow Newman managed to see Marty's medical records.

"Yes, Jason and I suspected it," Liz answered cautiously.

"And is it not true that later in the day, after you told your husband, Anton Howell, about the incident, he became alarmed, expressing extreme displeasure about your behavior?"

"Yes."

"And your husband advised you to stay away from his brother and refrain from engaging in his obsession with the homeless?"

"Y-yes."

"And that precipitated an argument, wherein you stormed out and never returned?"

Sam stood. "Objection! Counsel's questions have drifted far afield from the legitimate scope of cross-examination."

"Judge," Newman countered, "I would like some latitude here. These questions go to the veracity of the witness and her motivation for testifying against her husband."

Judge Baxter took off his spectacles and rubbed his eyes. "I'll allow it, but make it short. Answer the question, Mrs. Howell."

Liz shifted in the witness chair. "That argument was one of several between me and Anton. We were having problems in our marriage for some time."

Newman approached Liz from the side. "Are you currently having sexual intercourse with your brother-in-law?" he asked in soft, measured tones.

Sam put her head in her hands.

Liz set her jaw and looked toward Jason. "Yes . . . I love him."

Judge Baxter squinted at Liz and Jason in turn, shook his head, and took more notes.

"Sure you do," Newman said. "Are you planning to marry him?"

"He hasn't asked me."

"Would you if he did?"

Liz looked at Jason.

Jason nodded strongly in the affirmative.

"Yes," she replied to Jason, accepting his marriage proposal and answering the question at the same time.

Newman leaned toward Liz, forcing her to return her attention to him. "Well, well, how romantic," he said sarcastically. Then he abruptly raised his voice. "And convenient, too. By hopping between brothers, you will not have to change the name on your credit cards!"

Liz blinked back tears.

Sam stood. "Objection! He's badgering the witness."

"Sustained. Get to the point or sit, Mr. Newman."

Newman backed off. "My sincere apologies, Judge. Now, Mrs. Howell, is it not true that if your brother-in-law and lover regains control of his estate and you marry him, you will share in that estate?"

"I assume so," Liz said, "but that's not why—"

"On the other hand, if Anton Howell remains as conservator, you will have no legal right to a penny of that estate?"

"I suppose . . ."

"Therefore, Liz, would it not be financially in your best interest to testify on behalf of the brother of your current affection?"

"Objection!"

"No further questions."

Judge Baxter scribbled more notes. "Redirect, Ms. Paxton?"

Sam glanced at Jason. He was vehemently shaking his head no. She stifled her frustration. "Your Honor, may we take a brief recess?"

Judge Baxter glanced at the clock on the wall. It was almost ten-thirty. "Fifteen minutes," he grunted.

2

CRAZY EDDIE was pacing in front of Ike's poster boards, which leaned haphazardly against the wall of the jury room. Photos of Last Chance were scattered all over the conference table. Earlier, with the permission of the bailiff, Sam had arranged to have Crazy Eddie use the jury room so he could continue to study the exhibits until he was called to testify.

Crazy Eddie flinched when Sam, followed by Jason and Liz, stormed into the room. Sam was hot, Jason was grim-faced, and Liz was making a courageous effort to hold back tears.

"Are you ready to testify?" Sam asked Crazy Eddie impatiently.

Crazy Eddie scratched his head. "I dunno . . . I'm kinda nervous. I left my lucky crutch on the airplane." He looked numbly at the exhibits.

Sam gripped him by the arm and led him to the door. "Why don't you get yourself some coffee? I need to talk to Jason and Liz in private."

"Can I have a sandwich?"

Sam put her hands on her hips. "GO!"

Crazy Eddie wandered off, muttering.

Sam, red-faced, turned to Jason. Her nostrils were flaring. "Are you crazy! I've *got* to put Liz back on the stand to rehabilitate her. We're going down in flames. Again!"

Jason stood firm. "No, Sam. I'm not going to give that bastard Newman another shot at her. It's abundantly clear my brother has pulled out all the stops; he no longer gives a damn about Liz. He's told Newman to destroy her, but I won't allow it. Let him have my fucking estate." He pulled his bride-to-be closer. "I've got the better part of the bargain."

Liz looked tenderly at Jason. "Darling, I appreciate your concern for me, but we have Marty and the rest of the people at Last Chance to think about. I hate the idea of Willie dying and Marty being shot for no reason. I want to testify . . . for them."

Jason shook his head. "Liz, I feel the same way, but can't you see it's hopeless. Crazy Eddie is spacey; he can't even remember his own name. He's shark bait." Jason turned to Sam. "Let's call it quits while we all still have a modicum of self-respect."

Sam sighed. "It's your call."

Suddenly there was a knock on the door and Crazy Eddie hopped in. His demeanor had changed, his eyes sparkled, and he was grinning from ear-to-ear. "I found my lucky crutch!" he announced, pointing behind him.

Jason started to say something when Marty limped in, leaning on Crazy Eddie's crutch. "Sorry I'm late," he said. He grimaced as he eased himself into a chair.

Everyone sat in stunned silence as Marty explained what had happened. This morning, when he awoke at the hospital, his doctor told him he hadn't lost much blood and didn't require a transfusion. X-rays had revealed that the 9-mm slug was lodged in a location which wasn't worrisome, and there were no immediate plans to remove it. Although weak and sore, he found he could stand. He took the antibiotics they gave him, but not the painkillers since he wanted to remain clearheaded. "Actually, my football injuries were a lot worse," he explained.

When Doc and Vinnie came to the hospital to check on him and deliver his suitcase, Marty made a decision. He dressed in his good clothes and checked out of the hospital in Vinnie's care. While Doc was driving back to Last Chance with an investigating unit from the Nevada State Police, Vinnie flew Marty to San Francisco.

After Vinnie landed, Marty took a cab to Superior Court. It was fortuitous that Crazy Eddie had left his crutch on the plane because it made it that much easier for Marty to get around. Inside the courthouse, Crazy Eddie was wandering around looking for the cafeteria when Marty bumped into him.

The big man then addressed Sam. "I called your office from the airport in Vegas while Vinnie was refueling, but you'd already left for court. I was hoping for some last-minute help with Newman's cross-examination. Frankly, I'm worried."

Sam was grinning from ear-to-ear. "My dear, Marty, there's nothing to be concerned about. Newman's questions will only require simple answers. Just don't elaborate. And whatever you do, don't let him goad you. Most of all—and this is critical—don't try to justify your past. Act proud, smile a lot, and you'll do fine."

3

IT WAS TIME for court to reconvene, and Sam and Jason assisted Marty to the witness stand. Judge Baxter seemed impressed that Marty had left a hospital bed in order to testify.

Sam established that Marty was the president of Last Chance Corporation, and had him introduce the poster board exhibits. Marty calmly answered Sam's questions about profit projections, manpower loading, sales and marketing strategies, and expansion plans.

Judge Baxter listened intently.

Next, Marty introduced the photos showing the company's high-tech facility. Judge Baxter studied the pictures, and appeared fascinated by the visors worn by the workers. He personally questioned Marty about the workstations, and Marty explained how Cytex's engines "drove" the visors and greatly accelerated the assembly process.

Finally, Sam had Marty confirm Liz's testimony about what he and Jason were doing in Ray Gorney's photos.

"Your witness," she said to Newman, smiling at Jason as she took her seat next to him.

Newman got up and stood in front of the witness chair, pressing his fingers together and glaring at Marty.

Marty wasn't fazed. His energy level was low, and he was trying not to yawn.

"Do you have a question for this witness, Mr. Newman?" Judge Baxter asked.

"I was just wondering why Ms. Paxton deliberately avoided asking this man about his background, about what he had been doing before he suddenly found himself as the alleged president of an alleged multimillion dollar corporation that will end homelessness, once and for all."

Judge Baxter was tapping a gnarled finger on his desk. "Use your own time for contemplation, Counsel. My calendar is full and the clock is ticking. If you have a question, ask it; otherwise I'm going to rule and call my next case."

"Yes, Judge," Newman said, taking a step toward Marty. "Mr. Dubichek, when did you first meet Jason Howell?"

"Last January, on the ninth."

"And what was Jason Howell doing when you encountered him?"

"Sitting in a doorway."

"And where were you living at the time?"

"At the St. Andrews Shelter for Men."

"Is that a homeless shelter?"

"Yes, sir," Marty smiled. "A fine one."

"How long were you homeless?"

"Three years."

"And during those three years, did you also live on the street?"

"Yes, sir."

"Were you a drunk on the street?"

"Yes, I was."

"And after you met Jason Howell, did you spend time in a mental institution?"

"Mental health hospital," Marty corrected.

"Were you planning to commit suicide?"

"Yes, sir, I was."

"And what stopped you?"

"A visit by Jason and Liz. They gave me hope."

Newman continued probing into Marty's background. Although much of it was objectionable, Sam made no attempt at containment. She allowed Newman to badger Marty about losing his job, his home, his family, and about waking up in cardboard boxes.

It finally dawned on Marty that Sam was allowing Newman to hang himself with his own rope. The more Newman attacked Marty and his history of failure and homelessness, the better the factory at Last Chance would look to the judge. Marty recalled Jason's lesson about the importance of timing. At the original competency hearing, Jason's idea must have sounded flaky. But now, Marty thought, Ike's photos of the converted casino and the fancy poster boards clearly showed that the factory at Last Chance was for real.

The judge interrupted Newman. "What *is* your point, Counselor?"

During his cross-examination, Newman's voice had become shrill. He went over to Anton, whispered something, and then glared at the Judge. He was running out of time and he knew it. Anton began sketching something on a poster board. Marty figured Anton and Newman were going to make a final stab at salvaging the situation.

"My point, Judge," Newman said, wetting his lips, "is that the petitioner is trying to perpetrate a fraud on this court. During the five weeks between the last hearing and this one, they have concocted a clever act. This witness is a suicidal mental patient and a drunk. Clearly, he is incapable of running a high-tech factory. So he has carefully been coached to mindlessly spout complex business concepts in an attempt to validate Jason Howell's demented scheme. They have turned this courtroom into a three-ring circus!"

Marty toyed with Crazy Eddie's crutch and stared impassively at Newman.

"Judge, I would like to show the witness one of *my* client's exhibits," Newman raved, "one used extensively in business. Let us see if he really knows what he is talking about or if we are merely being entertained by a trained monkey act!" Newman's face was red, and the veins in his temples stood out.

Judge Baxter looked dourly at Newman, glanced at the clock on the wall, and then turned to Sam. "Any objections?"

"No, Your Honor."

Anton finished sketching and handed the poster board to Newman who shoved it in Marty's face. It contained a series of interconnected rectangles. "What is this, Dubichek?" Newman demanded, holding the exhibit at arm's length while watching the judge.

Marty yawned and covered his mouth. "Sorry." Then he cocked his head. "You're holding it upside down."

Newman righted it. "I ask you again, what is this!"

"It's a PERT chart," Marty said. "P-E-R-T."

"And what does 'PERT' stand for?"

"Project Evaluation Reporting and Tracking."

Newman bit his lip. "And its purpose?" he asked, his voice beginning to fade.

"It's a planning tool that spells out the sequence of events for a project—a construction project in this case. The chart includes dependency links, milestones, and status. At Last Chance, we use such planning aids all the time. As a matter-of-fact, that's how we converted the casino into a factory in such a short period of time."

The exhibit sagged and fell to the floor. There was dead silence in the courtroom.

Anton stared at his hands.

Sam, Jason, Liz, and Crazy Eddie were all grinning.

Marty yawned again.

"I've heard enough," Judge Baxter announced. "I'm going to rule." Newman picked up the exhibit, returned to his table, and slumped in his seat. Sam pulled out a yellow legal pad and sat erect with her pen poised.

"The court finds it erred on February 21 when it granted Anton Howell's petition for a conservatorship. Although Jason Howell's experimental idea of creating jobs for the homeless in a desert factory seemed highly unusual at the time, the court realizes that extraordinary problems require extraordinary solutions. The new evidence brought before the court today is clear and convincing, indicating that Jason Howell knew *exactly* what he was doing. Therefore, the petition to terminate the conservatorship of Jason Howell is granted." Judge Baxter's gavel came down.

"YES!" Crazy Eddie shouted from the gallery.

Anton and Newman slithered out of the courtroom. Sam thanked the judge while Jason and Liz helped Marty to a pay phone in the hallway. Marty called Ike at Last Chance.

"Is everyone at their stations?" Marty asked. "Are all the computers and reality engines ready to go?"

"You bet," Ike replied.

"Put me on the loudspeaker."

Marty turned to Jason, covering the mouthpiece with his hand. "While flying back from Vegas, I was thinking about what I would announce to the crew in the event we won."

Jason, still grinning, patted Marty on the back.

"Then it came to me; it's something I've always wanted to say."

"You're on," Ike said.

"LADIES AND GENTS OF LAST CHANCE," Marty announced, his voice booming throughout the factory, "YOU MAY START YOUR ENGINES!"

THE END

462   Ira Harris Spector

Epilogue
Tuesday, January 9
The Following Year

HIGH OVERHEAD, white contrails bisected the blue sky. Lying in a hammock strung between twin oaks on his meadow, Jason watched the jet speed north. A Dalmatian puppy, a wedding gift from Liz, dozed in the shade of the hammock.

It was the one-year anniversary of his first visit to the meadow, and Jason was thinking about the plane crash and the monster storm that had swept down from Alaska, forcing him to seek shelter in a doorway. And if it hadn't been for Marty and Pete, his story might have ended right there on the street.

Alaska.

Jason wondered if the airliner was headed there. It was a place he had wanted to visit ever since he was a small child and his father had showed him a picture book on the northern lights. Next month, Jason thought, when the contractors were finally out of the house, he and Liz planned to get away for a week and visit Anchorage and Fairbanks. And when they weren't being entertained by the aurora borealis, they could spend the long nights entertaining each other. It would be a good place to start a family.

He turned his head so he could see Liz through the kitchen window of their Spanish-style house. She appeared to be hacking at something with a knife.

"I'm starting to get the hang of cooking, really," Liz had assured him earlier, when she hustled him out the door. "Now go and relax while I mangle some meat for dinner."

"Okay, but scream if you need help," Jason chided, remembering one of her comments from last year.

Jason continued to reminisce until he was interrupted by the sound of a car crunching the gravel on the unfinished circular driveway in front of the house. The puppy stood, excitedly wagging its tail in anticipation of a visitor. It playfully nipped at Jason's feet as he walked around the house to see who had taken the trouble to drive up the long and winding dirt road.

A big man got out of a car. He had a large orange tabby draped over his shoulder.

"Marty! And Shoo! What a surprise!" Jason said. "It's great to see both of you!"

"I was in the neighborhood and all that," Marty replied, releasing Shoo. Once on the ground, the big cat sniffed around while the puppy hunkered down and placed its muzzle between its front paws, not knowing what to make of this strange orange creature who acted like he owned the place.

"Willie," Jason said to the Dalmatian, "meet Shoo."

On cue, the puppy tucked its tail in and crawled submissively over to the cat, greeting Shoo by touching noses. Shoo arched his back momentarily, but then relaxed, giving Willie permission to stay. With that, the puppy sprang to his feet, his tail wagging wildly as he sniffed around the cat's huge body. Then using a silent language only animals share, he and Shoo agreed to explore the meadow. In a flash they were gone.

"Let me show you around as well," Jason offered.

"Okay, but where's Liz?" Marty asked.

"She's inside, trying to coerce something into dinner. But don't worry, in deference to your shaky stomach we'll give the kitchen a wide berth."

"Some things never change."

"I'll let you in on a secret," Jason said, lowering his voice. "My brother was right. Liz is the only cook in the world who can burn water."

Liz approached from behind, wiping her hands on an apron and feigning anger. "Tsk, tsk, is number two brother casting aspersions on my culinary disability?" She hugged Marty and thanked him for accepting her invitation to surprise Jason. "I'll get some refreshments."

Jason took Marty for a tour of the meadow, showed him the valley view, and then invited his friend to sit in a deck chair by the barbecue.

"You were right about this place," Marty said. "It *is* beautiful, and I should've visited sooner. Actually, I was fairly close about a year ago," he commented, pointing to a sprawling hospital complex on the valley floor.

"You've been busy."

"You can say that again. I almost wish our project hadn't made such a big splash. It caused me to miss your wedding last month. I'm sorry. But as you know I was hosting a Congressional delegation at the time. One minute I'm a tour guide, traipsing around Last Chance with reporters from *Time, Newsweek* and *People,* the next minute I'm hosting a bunch of dignitaries."

"Soon you'll be doing the talk show circuit," Jason remarked.

"No way, Renée."

"It's only a matter of time."

"Look, it's bad enough I have to stay up all night answering inquiries and bidding jobs. I was even tempted to turn down that invitation from the White House."

"The signing of the Military Base Conversion Bill was our *raison d'être*. We both had to go to that one."

Liz came out with two glasses of champagne from a local winery. She waited until the two men sipped and nodded their approval. Shortly after she left, Shoo meandered back and jumped into Jason's lap and began to purr. The Dalmatian puppy also returned, sniffed Marty's shoes, and plopped across the big man's right foot.

"What brings you to Northern California?" Jason asked, absently stroking Shoo.

"I never thought I'd say this . . . ol' Mayor Babcock. Yesterday I attended his swearing-in ceremony, which was followed by an inaugural ball in the Great Rotunda at City Hall. I declined at first, but the mayor kept bugging me. He said he'd make it worth my while. It turns out he wanted to show me off to The City's mucky-mucks and take the credit for sending San Francisco's homeless to Nevada."

"You'll have to admit he played a major role in all of this."

"I'll say."

Shoo stretched and shifted, and Jason took the opportunity to sip some champagne. "Actually, Liz and I were invited as well. But she was too busy harassing our contractors, and I had my monthly meeting with Anton. And then there was my Monday night racquetball game with old man Simpson. My reflexes aren't as sharp as they were before the accident, and I think Al lets me win some of—"

"Wait!" Marty interrupted. "Did you say you're meeting with Anton?"

"Don't be so shocked. After we thoroughly kicked his butt in court last April, he called to apologize. Your testimony and the evidence we presented finally convinced him Last Chance was the real deal. Until that point, Anton truly believed I had gone mad. Trust me, before my accident, I'd have thought the same of him if the situation were reversed."

Marty ran his hand through his hair. "You've reconciled with him?"

"Not at all. But since the merger of Cytex last summer, I've been making investments using the proceeds. One of them was the Howell Development Corporation, which I took out of bankruptcy. I needed someone to run it. Anton, having lost his business and his home, was available. It occurred to me that if I didn't offer the position to him, he might wind up in a doorway. It was not something I would wish on my worst enemy—much less my own flesh and blood."

Marty was staring at Jason.

"So I made him managing partner. Of course, we don't socialize, and we probably never will, but we do talk business on the phone and meet monthly in San Francisco. Let's face it, even though he lost his wife, he ultimately wound up with what he really wanted: an incredibly efficient money-making machine."

"It's amazing how quickly things can change," Marty said, sipping champagne.

Jason also sipped. "You're right. Just before you arrived I was thinking about the events of the past year and how I've changed. Before my accident, I saw everything in black and white: A deal was worth doing or it wasn't; an employee was worth keeping or he wasn't. There were no shades of gray. I now realize that this way of thinking had limited my success."

"In what way?" Marty asked.

"Suppose when I took over Cytex my assignment was to find a way to make the company profitable without massive layoffs? With that mind-set I might have conceived the enhanced reality application of C-REAL from the start, and included it in the company's strategic plan as a simpler and more marketable first step on the path to full virtual reality. Thus, with a modicum of effort, I could have saved jobs while providing the investors with an early and sizable return-on-investment."

"It's too bad other managers haven't seen the light," Marty said. "People still get downsized in droves."

"I know. That's why I've been spending my time on this lofty perch writing articles and creating management seminars for groups like the Young Turks Organization. The country doesn't need any more discarded workers."

"I'll drink to that," Marty said, lifting his glass.

"Speaking of discarded workers," Jason said, "how did Last Chance end the year?"

"With a nice profit, thank you. At next week's shareholders' meeting I'm going to recommend we reinvest 50 percent, divide 25 percent among ourselves as a bonus, and give 25 percent to the shelters that screen recruits for us and administer our training programs." Marty paused to take a dollar bill out of his pocket. "By the way, here's the rent."

Jason accepted the bill. "Thanks. Now tell me about your current staffing situation?"

"We're up to two hundred and fifty employees. But at our phenomenal growth rate, we'll need the East Tower completed by this summer. We're working on it now.

"We've turned the Poker Bar into a Daycare Center for employees with families. I'm not just talking about new hires. Now that people have stability, relationships are forming fast and furious, and it seems like couples have been busing to Vegas and getting married like there's no tomorrow. Even Stan has a lady who shares his interest in snakes. If they decide to get married, I'm going to write to Iraq and ask them to send us a jug of SCUD fuel as a wedding present."

Jason smiled as he stroked Shoo, reflecting on Stan, the jug, the fire in the fifty-gallon drum, and the Monday Night Club. "What ever happened to Annie?" he asked.

"Since we now have childcare, she signed up and took the training program. And guess which newly-elected, top-ranking city official intervened with Social Services so she could get her kids back?"

"You learn fast," Jason said, lifting his glass.

"I had a good teacher."

"Have you had any problems at Last Chance? Has any one bailed?"

"Surprisingly few. Some don't want to work so hard; others take one look at the isolation, shake their heads, and return to The City. But so far, no one has rummaged through the trash. Mostly, people love the place. Did you know that Greg Thompson is joining the company next month?"

Jason looked at Marty. "Really?"

"Yup. I called him in Korea. I figured we need extra insurance that Cytex will award us all future production contracts. Naturally, the Koreans are pissed."

"That's business."

"Greg will head up our engineering department. One of his first assignments will be a live video link via the web so customers can visit our assembly line without leaving their desks. It'll give new clients a confidence boost."

"With that kind of innovation you'll soon have a small city on your hands. What are you doing about civic planning?"

"On January 1, we incorporated the community. We're officially known as the 'Town of Last Chance.' Accordingly, we're developing a General Plan."

"Are you the mayor?"

"No, I've got enough to do. Ike's mayor. He likes proposing ordinances and holding meetings—when he's not entertaining a certain visitor."

"Sam?"

"Yup. Anyway, we're currently expanding the river shack into a large town hall for Ike's meetings. Stan has already placed a plaque over the front door. It says: Dedicated to the memories of Sherwood 'Pete' Petersen and William Randolf Jefferson."

"To Pete and Willie," Jason toasted, clinking glasses. Upon hearing his name, the puppy looked up at Jason and wagged its tail.

The two men sipped in silence. Then Marty made a small gap with his thumb and forefinger. "A number of times both of us were *that* close to disaster," he said, shaking his head. "That tiny gap was the difference between being heroes or madmen in the eyes of the world."

"So true," Jason said.

"Speaking of madmen," Marty said, "what ever happened to the Abominable Pissman?"

"He was extradited to California and is currently under psychiatric care until he's deemed competent to stand trial. Among other crimes, he's suspected of killing his landlady and burning down his apartment complex." Jason turned and pointed at the valley floor. "He's our neighbor."

Marty followed Jason's hand. "He's at Petaluma?"

"Yes. They have him in the Forensic Care Unit under constant surveillance. Liz and I visited him over the Christmas holidays. They put him in a Plexiglas booth, and we talked by phone. He was wearing a straitjacket."

"Did he recognize you?"

"I'm not sure. In any event he seemed glad to have company. I think we were his first visitors. He did say he was planning to run for mayor of San Francisco when he gets out."

Marty grinned broadly. Then the grin evaporated and he touched his cheek with his hand. "I shudder to think what would have happened if Shoo hadn't jumped Brodsky when he did. Talk about saving face."

"What made him do that?" Jason asked, stroking the cat. Shoo lifted his head and urged Jason to scratch under his chin. Jason obliged and Shoo cranked up his motor a notch.

"I'm not sure. I would like to think he was aware of the danger and came to my rescue. But more likely, because of Brodsky's odor, Shoo may have considered him a competitor. He's never been neutered—Shoo, that is."

"Are you saying Shoo deliberately picked a territorial cat fight with Brodsky?"

"Hmmm, quite possibly," Marty said, taking a sip of champagne. "And if that was the case, then Shoo finally settled my long-standing argument with Brodsky."

"What argument?"

Marty's eyes twinkled. "Who was the bigger pussy in the end."

* * *

FOR COMMENTS, CORRESPONDENCE, OR TO
ORDER ADDITIONAL COPIES OF LAST CHANCE

Write:
Arius Publications
121 Edelen Avenue
Los Gatos, CA 95030
(408) 357-4852
ariuspub@hotmail.com

US $13.50 / $19.00 CAN

The author may be contacted through Arius Publications
or directly via e-mail at:
ira_spector@msn.com

ABOUT THE AUTHOR

Ira Harris Spector lives in Northern California with his wife
Barbara.   His stories have appeared in *Reader's Digest,
Popular Electronics, Chicken Soup for the Soul,* and other
major publications.

LAST CHANCE grew out of the author's concern for the
increasing number of homeless individuals and families in
America. "The homeless represent our country's crazy uncle
who lives in the attic. I wanted a vehicle to take the uncle
out of that attic and have people see the homeless as human
beings."